The Tessera Trilogy continues.

About the author Donald Rowe, writing under pen name DP Tolan, was born in coastal Maine. Don grew up loving books and adventure. Attending both parochial and public schools, he graduated from Scarborough High School in 1962 and the Naval Academy in 1966. His Fleet service was in the Pacific, including service in the Republic of Viet Nam as an advisor. Later, in one of his last tours, he was again an advisor in Saudi Arabia.

Why Written – *The Tessera Trilogy* was conceived when the author was serving in the Kingdom of Saudi Arabia as a military advisor. It is the hope of the author that the events depicted in the novel remain fictional, and do not occur.

Acknowledgements – I wish to acknowledge the help, insights, and encouragement contributed to this effort by Greg, Madalin, Jorge, Shelia, Maxine, Bronwen, John, Aaron, Harlem, Ann, June, Deborah, Alex, Dan, the other Dan, Dave, Rob, and a host of others – members of the Riverside Writers Group and the Books-A-Million critique group. Thanks also to the Central Rappahannock Regional Library (CRRL) for support.

Dedication – ***Kashan Kashmeeri*** is dedicated to Marguerite 'Ma' Leary.

Kashan Kashmeeri unfolds in a region of ancient wounds, struggles within and between families, amidst the spices, scents, and intrigue of Arabia. Its fictional characters, Tooley O'Toole, Amir Ubaidi, and Stefano Gaiuso struggle as they encounter the proximity of war and strange connections.

For readers of military- geopolitical struggles in a turbulent world, the novel is filled with excitement, tension, lovers embracing, missiles and bullets, and tanks. Against the backdrop only someone who lived there can depict with such insight, it will immerse you in the tension that is the Middle East today.

Read with awe as Iran and Iraq seem poised for another war, before intriguing changes force the region, and the world, to the brink. Follow the thrilling narrative, and its characters' words. All you expect from author DP Tolan, and more, you'll find the novel nuanced, clear ... specific yet vague, suggestive and scary to the last moment. It is a story that had to be told. To the last gesture, question and threat you'll be on the edge of your reading space, wondering if the Middle East, and the world, will descend into war, or rise to peace.

Don't put ***Kashan Kashmeeri*** down until you discover the answer.

Chapter - 1

Saving the life of that wounded American overwhelmed Anh. The joy of salvaging him as he hallucinated balanced with the terror of those moments. Michael O'Toole almost died, finally beginning to mumble, then spoke clearly in Vietnamese.

Anh had helped him, in fact she'd saved his life. Then he'd professed love. His eyes had spoken of a future with her. But there had been no calls, no letters, and no flowers in the weeks since. Had he been delirious when he spoke of his feelings?

Heart pounding, she tried without breathing to put the pieces of the story together. She recalled his look and eyes, the warmth of his words. Anh Nguyen's being ached to know. Her pulse spiked.

A tear ran down her cheek as her roommate Patty came through the front door. "Ann, you're crying again. What is the problem? Was it another Saudi asshole?"

"No, it wasn't that."

"What then?"

"It was that American patient I told you about. He was shot and almost died. An infection left him delirious and rambling in Vietnamese. They called me to interpret and I helped nurse him back to health. Michael recovered, and saw me as his savior."

"Well, many patients react that way." Patty offered.

Anh pulled back. "Well, yes, but he said he was in love with me. Turns out he'd married a relative who died in the war. But I haven't heard from him since. I'm afraid ...."

"Of what?"

Tears welled up and her voice quivered, "That he didn't mean what he said."

Patty pulled her close, "Ann, maybe that card is from him. Did you open it?"

Anh's voice quivered, "What card?"

Patty pointed to the table by the door of their room in the Female Nurses Residence Hall.

He had written a note on the invite. The words brought back memories of his recovery from the infection suspending him precariously close to death. He'd almost died, again, then met that nurse, an angel. *What do I know of her – saved my life, Vietnamese, related somehow to Tuyet. She's American and cute.* His mind returned to the thought of being saved. I need to thank her, and see if she heard what I said, see if it registered, meant something to her beyond the ramblings of a grateful patient.

Scurrying to the table where they kept their mail, Anh picked up the envelope. It was embossed with the official seal and address of the US Embassy in Riyadh. Her name was written boldly on the front. A smile crept across her face as she wiped away tears of anxiety. She opened it cautiously. Perhaps it was from Michael. He worked there.

Anh read the invite aloud, "I need to talk with you. Please come." It was signed Tooley. She sensed caution in the words, neither inspiring hope nor showing finality.

Patty put her arm around Anh, "Guys are all like that. They can't find the right words even if they have them printed in big block letters on 3X5 cards. Few guys are sensitive, or good in bed." She stared at Anh, "Which is he?"

"I don't know, but he seems sensitive. I'll tell you more about the other part after a few dates ... if he asks me out."

Their first date was awkward, Tooley fairly dripping with anxiety and hope. He met her at the embassy's entrance. "Anh, it's wonderful to see you again. This is the first Embassy Pool Party I've been to. It will let us get reacquainted. Did you bring a swimsuit?"

"Swimsuit! Always with the jokes."

"You don't like?"

"No, I do like jokes," a grin crept across her face, "even yours." Her look became serious, "Did you mean what you said?"

His experience told him to be passive, not show emotion, but anxiety spread across his face. Self control wasn't working. He could tell by her expression. Any positive expression would be fine, anything that said he had a chance. She was his savior. He sipped at his drink, then stared into her eyes, "What did I say?"

Cute! He told himself, a replica of his dead wife Tuyet, with glossy black hair, an almond shaped face, and a small figure filled with fire. Her dress was sensuous, but not overly inviting, California, but not Valley Girl. He saw a stir in her eyes.

Anh held out her hand, touching his wrist, whispering cautiously with obvious anxiety. "You said I saved you – and you were in love with me." Her statement begged for an answer, an affirmation of words uttered on a hospital bed from the edge of life. He looked at her.

"I know little about you, but you saved me. I think I could love you if you gave me a chance – *Nha Toi*." He used the intimate Vietnamese term meaning you are my house, my refuge in life. He put his cards on the table.

She squeezed his hand, "I want to give you that chance."

There was a smile, subtle but comforting. "Anh, every man likes to date a beautiful woman."

"Am I?"

"I think so! Tell me about yourself, your family."

"We came to California through Hong Kong in 1977, and settled in San Jose. The first years were rough, but my parents kept us together. I finished High School there. I made a big effort to fit in, to learn English."

"Your accent is perfect. Is everyone in your family so accomplished with English?"

"No, just me" she said confidently. "I had the best teacher in all of California, Marguerite Leary. 'Malaria' or 'Ma' was a presence; she didn't come into our classroom, she made an entrance, regally. She gave us huge tests, some with over a hundred questions. Every single question was 'critical' to her. If I didn't accomplish or perform to her expectations she would keep me after school. She called it inviting us for cookies. She made me pronounce every single word I had problems with until I got it just right."

"Wow, few teachers are that insistent."

"Yes, so I speak very well. My parents, however, struggle with English and the constantly California's changing idioms. They own a small restaurant in San Jose. My mom is an excellent cook, especially with French dishes. My sister Bai and brother Nham live at home.

Another brother, Duoc, died in a refugee camp." Her eyes teared, "His death inspired me to become a nurse."

Tooley reminisced about Tuyet, recalling his memories of her. His eyes moistened, "She was pregnant and died when artillery rounds hit her village. Many were killed in that barrage."

"Michael, your wife Tuyet was a cousin. My parents called her 'Auntie.' I'm sorry for your loss."

"Thank you. She was a wonderful person." He paused, softly squeezing her hand, "That seems so long ago, so remote now. I feel more hopeful now," his face softened, "Do you enjoy my jokes?"

"Yes. I even like some of the lame ones. I have a Black Belt, so don't make them all lame." Her eyes brightened and her cheeks flushed.

"Why did you get a Black Belt?"

"I had a boyfriend in High School, a star on the Varsity football team. He was very controlling. I finally had enough of his games and decided I needed to be able to kick his ass if he tried beating me again. It worked."

"So not a fox, but maybe a lioness?"

Anh grinned, baring her teeth, "Yes, but I only use my teeth when I get really mad."

"OK. ... Do you want another wine, or to search for prey? I vote for refills."

"A drink will do." She pointed across the pool to a man whose face looked familiar, "It's your cousin from the hospital. You'll have to reintroduce me."

They walked to the outside bar and got refills. He suggested, "Now let's go see Stefano" as they strolled past the end of the pool, "and here he is."

"Stefano, nice to see you could make it." The two men hugged briefly then Tooley gently moved to place Anh front and center. "This is Anh Nguyen, the nurse who saved me. Anh, this is my cousin Stefano Gaiuso. He's a CNN journalist."

"Stefano, that's an fascinating profession. What do you report on?"

"Wars and piracy, blood and DNA. Exciting stuff." He smiled, "I spy on the side; it helps pay the bills."

"Tell me," Anh asked both men without looking at either, "how you discovered your family connection."

Stefano raised his glass, "That would be my fault. I was researching a story on blood donations and DNA analysis at King Khalid. The hospital lab analyzed our blood and discovered we share a common ancestor from hundreds of years ago. We're eightieth cousins."

Eightieth cousins, wow, and the connection came from analyzing just two drops of blood. It's amazing what you can find out with big computers," Anh observed as his eight CD system added background sounds.

They danced until both were tired. It finally showed as he stepped on her toes - twice. Finally Anh had had enough, "I need some rest. Can you drive me home, some of us have to work for a living? I have to be back before midnight."

He bowed, theatrically swinging his hand regally toward the car. "Sure Cinderella, your horses and pumpkin carriage await."

Anh thought of the pair, Stefano and her Michael. They might be cousins, but they were so different. Stef, as she now called him, wanted to find *the* story no matter the risk, then tell it or sell it as widely and secretly as he could. He was a spy, and a journalist out to get a story. Michael obviously couldn't want that story told.

The story of the blood program, Stef had stumbled to it. DNA sequencing was not widely known of here in the Kingdom, but he found it. That story, and their new relationship, was worth every second of his efforts to find the story. Now he'd an in with his newfound cousin, a Saudi general, if he needed a Get Outa Jail card.

Anh gave him a hug, said good bye to Stef, then Michael drove them to her quarters. At the door their night ended with a kiss, which promised more.

OK Ann, how was the date?"

"I was afraid we'd encounter some random police checkpoint on the way home, but we lucked out. Oh," she paused, "you want to know about him. He's older, a little gray, but he's trim. He's always joking. And he's not bad as a dancer, until he gets tired." The edges of her mouth curved upwards, "He said he was hopeful about 'us' and meant what he'd said."

"That's cool. Does he mean it?"

"I think so. Michael asked me on another date, some camel race out in the desert next month."

"Cool! That race is a big deal for the natives. It's colorful, hot, and the King's there. There's poetry, the King's Band, all sorts of pomp and stuff. It'll be very hard on us women though, but I'm getting used to that. And there'll be lots of single expats."

"At least we don't have to worry about getting there. There's a hospital shuttle and Michael said he'll arrange seats in the diplomatic pavilion. He said to invite you. Do you want to go?"

"Really? I'd love to! It'll be a chance to meet some single embassy guys." Patty rolled her eyes, "They have nice parties, away from the religious police." Her eyes lit up with understanding, "Hey, I'll bet he said to ask me so you'll have a female friend along to keep assholes away. You going?"

"I wouldn't miss it."

Chapter - 2

Getting to the annual Camel Race took over an hour. After the drive north of the capital, the driver parked the van and the nurses walked a quarter mile to the pavilions. They had to sit on carpets or cushions brought from home. Woven fans at the pavilion by every cushion didn't help much. It was hot, much hotter than in the air conditioned bus which brought them.

Patty and Anh saw few other women aside from those in the diplomatic pavilion. Several hundred yards away dozens of camels milled around beyond the track railing, shuffling their feet. They were anxious to run their hearts out, about eighty registered to race, their necks marked with Arabic numerals. The riders began to mount from stools as the camels knelt, hobbles on their feet.

Soon each camel was topped by a kid who looked like a junior version of some international racing champion, but every bit as serious. Freed of the hobbles the animals twitched nervously, braying and spitting. It was a heavily wagered race. The winner would receive a huge Mercedes water truck from the King, valued at 100,000 USD.

The crowd exuded an excited rumble of Arabic encouragement, shrieking *Yella, Yella*. They gestured their picks and wagers, and constantly touched *thoubs* to adjust their crotches. The dry heat wasn't enough to dull all senses.

A cannon fired off to the left beyond the King's pavilion, jarring all from whatever they were doing. All eyes swept towards the track, camels accelerated to the first flags marking the circuit. White Toyota pickups and medics raced to keep up with the expanding mob of beasts as they circled the flat course's four loops around giant fixed track flags. Dust churned into the hot air, so dry it sucked the moisture from throats.

Riders struggled to hold the hump ahead of their flimsy saddle as they lurched back and forth with increasing frequency. Dromedaries and riders, eyes glazed from the jerky rhythm, rounded the course once, twice and yet again.

The camel in the lead appeared from the dust in a wide column of others. Head coverings wrapped across riders' faces as they rhythmically bounced with each step of the awkward gait. At the finish line soldiers crouched, mere yards from the shaded pavilions. They waited, then sprinted to the finalists with small batons signifying place.

Owners and friends raced to the finish line where the riders dismounted en masse, parched and glad it was all over. Each rider received water bottles, and the youngsters walked with grandfatherly owners to cool their prized ships of the sands. Early finishers, gleeful at the results, retraced the path back in front of the King's pavilion, where music emerged as the royal band marched and played in their resplendent lion skin capes. A bagpiper in kilts accented the kettle drummers and wind instruments.

The royal pavilion was elevated above all others, hung with Bedouin weavings to soften any sandstorm. The King, surrounded by concentric circles of guards, wore a traditional white robe accented with golden trim. Bedouin tribal flags fluttered in the breeze. At lower levels other tents held diplomats, military, Saudi citizens, and foreign guests.

This year King Badir bin Fahd as Saud waved regally to his subjects, then read in serious tones a proclamation in Arabic over the PA system, extolling an American's bravery. He sent a messenger to summon a Padrick Marcus Michael O'Toole from the diplomatic pavilion.

An English announcement followed that in Arabic; Anh heard both. Eyes within the pavilion focused on her Michael. She turned to him, "What was that about?"

Tooley held her hand, his face conflicted, serious but grinning, "It was nothing. I was just in the wrong spot at the wrong time; remember my wounds." He released her hand and rose, "I'll be back."

O'Toole accompanied Ambassador Lucardi to a position in front of and just below His Majesty, opposite the finish line. Tooley struggled to keep in step with the ambassador - left, right, left, right. *Dammit, keep in step. Wish he'd been in the military and knew how to keep up a regular pace. We need to send him to Boot Camp.*

His Majesty asked O'Toole to step forward. Polite, restrained applause rippled through the crowd. General Amir Bin Ubaidi stood three paces behind and to the King's left, reflecting on his luck that this friend was at Sooley Base when Israelis attacked. O'Toole had saved his life.

Tooley stepped toward the King, stopping two paces away.

"Mister O'Toole, we are very pleased to meet you at last. Thank you for saving my general; we have so few in my armies." The words made him wonder if HM was serious, until Tooley saw a smirk.

The King turned to an attendant carrying a large padded box and solemnly extracted a large gold medal with a green and gold sash. Tooley bowed his head as the Protocols Officer had briefed him.

Placing the medal over Tooley's head, King Badir reiterated the Arabia's thanks, then glanced to General Amir, "My thanks for your service in this instance" emphasized with eye contact. The King ceremoniously shook hands with the American, O'Toole's left hand fixed at his side per custom here. "Please come visit us in Riyadh. We are most pleased with your actions," using the imperial language anticipated.

O'Toole bowed slightly. *That sounded serious, like an order. That's what heads of state do, right?*

General Amir accompanied his friend back to the diplomatic pavilion, "Thanks again for saving my life. I owe you one."

"You're welcome, but it was too close for comfort this time," Tooley said with the hint of a smile, "just don't invite me to a base unless you're sure it's safe."

"I'll do that. But first, come to our house next month so we can meet your Anh." A smile crept across Amir's face as he clasped his friends' arm, "We have good news."

How was the second date?" Patty inquired.

Anh responded with a look, not of indecision, but reflecting uncertainty at what that date had meant, or not meant. "I'm not sure yet – You were there."

"Yeah I was, but I was preoccupied with other guys."

"It was hot, smelly, a different experience straight out of Arabian Nights. Seeing Michael get an award from a King, for getting shot, was bizarre. He has other wounds. I've seen them." Her face softened, "The King himself talked with him, just like a normal guy. Michael said he was very friendly. He even said ... 'Anything you want.' I would have asked for a big Mercedes."

Patty looked at Anh, "I would have asked for two cars, but hey! You seem hooked on him. I mean, not saying he'd pop the question, but if he did, would you say yes? I would?"

"That is a serious question. You're hot for anything in pants, and I've considered it. He probably won't ask, so I won't lose sleep over it. It's way too early to say. But it would be difficult to say no. He is a hunk, great job, exciting and has a gentle side. ... I've been thinking about him."

"How?" Patty asked, her face verifying fascination with all things male.

"Well, like does he sing in a shower, cook his own meals, or have flowers in his apartment? But now ... I get to find out this weekend."

"This weekend huh?" Patty smirked, "I hope you catch him showering."

"Yeah, that would be something to write home about. My mom would freak out if I told her. Better to just say his touch gave me goose bumps, but touching him now seems natural. Best not tell her that; it might freak her out more. I'll just tell her I feel relaxed with him; that says enough."

"That's a start." Patty twirled her hair and gave a subtle come hither look, "What does he want to be when he grows up, anything special?"

"He wants to get married, have kids, and then run a home

brewery."

"Gawd. I'll take him – if you don't want him." Patty gestured, "He is single, right?"

A determined look on Anh's face said 'he's taken.'

Anh went on, "Michael, *my* Michael, seems a good man, although a bit rough on the outside. I'll get him to feel comfortable with me. We have a date this weekend."

Patty frowned, stuck a finger in her mouth, and mimicked vomiting. Then she smirked. *Yeah – single, cute ... single, steady, mature ... single! Is there a theme here? Have to find out how her date goes.*

It was Thursday, the start of the Muslim weekend. Tooley picked Anh up and they had just parked his white Chevy Caprice by his villa, a concrete block one story stuccoed in white. Every other apartment was the same. They walked to the front where she saw heavy metal screening at the entry. *Is that to keep burglars out? I heard they don't have robberies here? Or they get their hands chopped off. Wonder what it will be like inside, probably drab and masculine.*

He opened the door and held it for her. They entered and the door closed, Anh scanning the place, "Show me around. I want to check out your place."

The first thing that caught her attention was his collection of stuff on the wall. It was an eclectic mix of photos, plaques, and nautical nicnacs.

He noticed her enquiring stare, "This is my 'I love me' wall. Most military retirees have them, mementoes of previous commands, souvenir weapons, and photos of buddies from special classes and promotion ceremonies. We call those 'wetting downs.' If you have questions ask away."

"OK matey. I see a plaque from *USS Constellation*; that's a carrier right?"

"You got it. Biggest damn thing afloat, other than those huge oil tankers; they're bigger. But *we* had better toys - planes and bombs."

"Planes and bombs ... guy stuff. *USS Liberty* ... what was that?"

"*Liberty* was a spy ship. We listened to military transmissions, the 'other guys.'"

"I see, listening in, radios and satellites; must've been boring?"

"Anything but boring. Well, most military duty is ninety nine percent boring, but that other one percent can be hell. We were attacked once, machine gunned, rocketed, napalmed. More than half of us were wounded ... dozens died. I shot down a plane which strafed us."

"Who attacked?"

"Our friends, the Israelis! Later they said it was a mistake, a spasm in the June 67 war."

"Wow, and you got shot by an Israeli at that base too. Hope it doesn't become a habit."

Anh saw an angry look inch across Michael's face and changed the subject, "These pictures are of Navy guys from a RAG something. What's a RAG, some crazy group of tailors?"

"RAG 40 was a River Assault Group. We escorted convoys of supply craft, small watercraft, hauling food, ammo, stuff of all sorts to wherever it was going in the Mekong Delta."

Anh slowly surveyed the stuff on his wall, touching several picture frames. *He has so many memories.* Then a photo whose appearance didn't fit in caught her attention, "Who is this," pointing to a photo of an Asian male.

"That's Hung Nguyen," he stuttered with emotion. "He was a brave soldier ... and your cousin. Hung, Tuyet's brother, we fought together. He saved me more than once. He was how I met her. Late in my tour an Army captain arranged to kill her with an artillery barrage after she turned down his attention."

Tooley's jaw tightened and tone deepened, "Hung and I killed him. That captain was one Ugly American. I'm glad that sonofabitch is dead. Tuyet was pregnant when she died." His jaw line tensed and he took a deep breath, "Years later Hung died in my arms."

His confession startled her. It was something from deep within. *He took a risk confiding it, something like that could ruin his career, his life if it saw the light of day.* She touched his arm, "Michael, thank you." She looked into his eyes, saw sorrow, but also a twinkle of hope. *Michael is a good man, one who cares deeply, passionately.*

He feigned a look of surprise, a healing from her eyes infected him. That expression verified to her that some intangible weight had just lifted from his heart. His gaze lingered on her face, then he pointed back to his 'wall', identifying framed photos of parents, a brother Evan and his wife.

Michael edged them towards the kitchen, holding her hand. The aroma of spices called, and his Blood Pressure accelerated.

As they walked into the family area she spotted a bookcase which held well used paperbacks. She bent over to check the titles. *Better check these out. Hmm, Clancy, Forsythe, Baldacci - all detective or military fiction. Could Michael be in a Clancy book?* He *would be a character of action, strong beliefs but no face! ... Take a* <u>*deep*</u> *breath.*

She continued, spotted one or two titles by Nicholas Sparks. *Good, he has a soft side.* A collection of National Geographic magazines rounded out his collected works. On the floor adjoining the bookcase, against an otherwise drab white wall were highly colored baskets, all woven in Arabia's southwest. There were others lining the entryway floor. None were exotic, just the touristy Bedouin sorts seen in Riyadh souqs.

"Sorry to be such a bad host. I haven't entertained, or dated in ages." His hands moved awkwardly to and fro grasping symbolically for the right words, "Care for a beer, wine, or a soda?"

She wafted air towards her nose, "What is that smell, it seems yummy?"

"It's a marinade I use with steaks. I make it from teriyaki sauce, garlic, mustard, and ginger. The steaks have been soaking in it for a day."

"Sounds great. And I'll take some wine, rosé if you have it."

"I stocked up. I have chilled Riesling and Lancers."

"I'll take Lancers. I've never had it, but heard it's good."

"It is." She followed him to the kitchen, her eyes taking in the sink, stove, and fridge. *Is he neat? Eww, dirty dishes in the sink. I'll bet his bathroom smells of Lysol. Few flowers, just a few wilted posies here and there, probably bought em at one of the expat compound fairs.*

Tooley's fingers drummed his lips, "Why did you come here?"

"It was an incredible job offer with great pay. And I <u>had</u> to get away; my parents were pressuring me to get married and settle in San Jose. I wasn't ready for that. I wanted to travel, experience life. Nursing in a foreign land will look great on my resume. I've made a few good friends along the way, like Angie Tamayo, Celia Washington, Dave Hill, Patty, and you."

"So I'm a good friend am I," his face tightened, then softened, "one of a few?"

She ran her hand flirtatiously across his chest, "For now. What about you?"

"I'd be overseas," he replied, "and see Amir again. We've been friends for years. I almost died saving him. I consider myself in very special company, as your 'good' friend."

"What kind of work do you do exactly, and how the hell did you get shot?"

"I can tell you," he accentuated his words, "but then I have to dump you out in the desert." Anh rolled her eyes.

"Since I like you I'll only say this," his eyes made a small circuit of the ceiling, looking for an exit strategy to change the subject, "my job ... is to serve eviction notices."

"Eviction notices?" *This story ought to be good.* "to whom?"

"*Bedus* north of Riyadh, they didn't pay parking tickets for their camels, and I confiscated their tents." There was just the slightest uptick at the corners of his mouth. She saw it.

Anh put her hand over her mouth, stifling a grin and trying not to laugh or choke, "Where do you store their tents? I'd like to see them - they're colorful." There was a long pause, and a look of interrupted skepticism, "Look, I read Clancy. I think you're a spy, but I won't tell."

"OK smarty pants, what tells you that?"

"Well, the Saudis let you visit a SECRET base, and see whatever was so damn important there. Then you got shot, and got a medal from a King!"

He knew she'd figured out more. "You're cute, and you did save my life, but I'd still have to bury you in the desert. Up to your neck so I can still watch your smile." He shuffled his feet slowly to and fro, then asked, "Did you like that camel race?"

She *wasn't* buying it. "I liked the camel race, but then again I'd like to see you try and bury me," she moved her hands to her waist, "I have a Black Belt."

He moved closer and whispered, "I have a Black Belt too." the hint of a grin crept up the edges of his mouth." They stared intently at each other, postured martial arts gestures, and then laughed.

"I don't know whether to believe you. You're either joking or you're dead serious." *I refuse to guess which.*

"I'm joking. I kissed the Blarney Stone. Hanging upside down and kissing a rock covered with germs rattles your brains. I've been a story teller ever since."

“I’d bet you were a story teller long before that, after you loosen up with people.” Her face tightened, the smile gone. “Does that mean you were just telling a fairy tale when you said you loved me?” Her pulse quickened.

“No. That was …” he touched her arm, the warmth bringing a smile and the answer.

“The steaks are from a Brit market on SANG Road. I have two bottles of Lancer’s Rose´, ‘chilled, not shaken or stirred’ he whispered in a perfect imitation of Sean Connery, Agent 007. “The steaks were marinated with my secret sauce. Say, can you help with the salad?”

“Sure. Are the spices you use CLASSIFIED?”

“No, and you’re cleared for spices. I don’t have any allergies in case you were going to ask.”

“I wasn’t, but I don’t have any.”

“None here either. I take my beer cold and wine poured.” They sipped Lancers as the charcoals seared the steaks and a salad took shape. Dinner materialized from the grille and a salad of leafy greens emerged, topped with chopped tomatoes, shredded carrots, cashew halves, and a vinaigrette dressing Anh concocted. They ate in a courtyard, casually on paver tiles atop a rug bordered with red, white and black bedu cushions.

Tooley puffed up his cushion, “Amir gave me these. They were woven by the *Shammar*, his tribe.”

“They’re colorful, and handy to lean on. I haven’t eaten a picnic on the floor in years. It’s nice. I’ll help clean up later, with the dishes,” she offered, “but only if you have a dish washer.” Her hands were now on her waist, “When do we eat?”

“I have a dish washer, and soon. Dessert is apple pie a la mode, with Baskin-Robbins vanilla ice cream. My car has a special option,” He grinned, “every time I drive past a Baskin-Robbins here the car turns in and shuts off until I buy ice cream.”

“I wish I had the chance to get ice cream, but I’m stuck back at the Nurses’ Residence Hall and can’t get out much.”

“We’ll have to change that … if you’d like” he offered with his eyes and lips.

“I’d like that.” Her warm touch on his arm made it official. “Would you like Irish coffee later? I make it with Bailey’s Irish Cream, or Irish whiskey, or brandy. Have you ever had it?”

“I’ve never tried it, but if you insist,” all forty four muscles at the corners of her mouth moved to form the universal response of delight, "You're not trying to lower my defenses are you?"

"The thought has crossed my mind," He pulled her close. They kissed, slowly. Pie and ice cream would wait, undisturbed for another time.

He drove her back Friday evening, with an obligatory stop for B&R ice cream. "You're good," she said rubbing his shoulder, his hand on her thigh as he drove.

"I know!"

"Be safe. I don't want you getting hurt on your trip. Where was it you're going?"

"Baghdad. Don't tell anyone."

"I won't."

Chapter – 3

Patty looked up at as Anh returned, a smile beaming on her face. Patty wanted to know the story that smile told. "Must have been a great weekend. Ann, tell me all about it."

"Well, he cooked steaks and I made salad. We were going to have apple pie and ice cream for dessert."

"You *were going to have* dessert, but ... *what*?" Patty's smirk emphasized her question, "Spill the beans! I know you weren't here last night. Does this mean you have a tooth brush at his place?"

"We ate, drank, talked for hours. I was sitting next to him and as he moved closer to wipe something off my chin, I pulled him closer and we kissed. Our kiss was long, very long. Then we had breakfast."

She smiled. "He made *huevos rancheros* and *gazpacho*. He can cook!"

Patty coughed and rolled her eyes, "He cooks. That's good, because you can't."

"And, no I don't have a tooth brush at his place!" She smiled, and then a puzzled look spread on her face. "Say, weren't you out with that embassy guy? Tony something?"

"Well, yes I was. But I didn't get lucky with Tommy!"

"I'm sure you will, and I told Michael if he wasn't good I was going to kick his ass."

"Whoa! What was his reaction?"

"He grinned, called me 'Babe,' and we made love. We cuddled after that. Then he said if he had been a good boy I had to kiss his ass. I almost gagged when he said that, but then I thought about it for a moment." There was a pause.

"No! ... I said I'd kick his ass, not kiss it." Anh paused, "We laughed and made love again, took care of pent up needs."

"So no kicking his ass, but kissing it maybe." Patty frowned, "Is he kinky?"

"No, but he enjoys sex." Her face lightened with satisfaction, "We spent the night loving, touching and kissing." A smirk extended over her face, "He's taller and has me by fifty pounds; it's not like I can kick his ass. Besides, his butt is very nice. Tight butts drive me nuts."

She turned to Patty, said "*Cinco*" and gestured for a High Five. They did a hand smack and laughed.

Patty cocked her head to the side. "You are like such a Valley Girl."

He drove the white Chevy Caprice into the visitor's lot, got out, and walked to Anh's door at the Nurse Residence Hall. It had been eight weeks and many dates since their first sleepover. Within moments they were headed north of the capitol to Amir and Munirah's home for a weekend.

Anh was tense. *This feels almost like meeting his parents, the checkout and scrutiny.*

Michael saw the look, brought her back to Planet Earth, "Buckle up Babe, we have a long trip, and the world's craziest drivers are ahead."

"How long?"

"Depends on traffic, but I guess about three to four hours ... at warp speed."

"Why warp speed?" a puzzled expression spread on her face as she tightened her seat belt.

"We have to keep up with the locals. Most Saudis drive 100 MPH on long highways. We'll just be keeping up with the flow of traffic."

"Are there any sights to see or do we just get to watch as the sands drift by" she asked with fears of hours of boredom ahead.

"Nothing to see but a few camel bridges and the occasional camel."

"What's a camel bridge?"

"Camels roam freely in the desert and if you drive into one its body comes through the window straight into your lap. It ruins your whole day. So they put up fences parallel to the highway to corral them to go up and over the bridges. It cuts down on highway fatalities."

"Is that one up ahead?"

"Yeah. Take a gander at that camel off to the right. By the way ... did you bring an overnight bag?"

"I brought a bag with all the necessities ... clothes, makeup, underwear, bra ... and skimpy nighties." She grinned and rubbed his leg.

"Babe, you can so read my mind."

"Mikey, what are the sleeping arrangements tonight?" She tugged his shirt, "Will they let us sleep together?"

"Normally they'd be cool with it, but their nine year old daughter Fadia will be at home, so sleeping together might create a problem for them to explain to her - the not married yet part. But we might get adjoining rooms with a connecting door."

"I'll keep my fingers crossed for connecting rooms. What's their home like?" Anh asked as more camels wandered beside the highway.

"It's quite a place. It won several international architectural awards. Amir and Munirah designed it. It's earth-sheltered; the whole place is underground. It has a garden where she grows herbs, and there is even a fountain in a courtyard. Oh, the place is solar powered – very, very expensive. I'd guess it set them back ten million dollars or more."

"Whoa, Saudi generals must get paid well."

"Not really, but Amir's also a business and financial genius, as is Munirah. She markets a line of clothing and fragrances. He's into recycling, plastics, construction, and anything electronic. He's very successful; he's my family here. I think he's worth close to fifty, a hundred million."

"Must be nice. Was their marriage arranged?"

"No. Quite the opposite, he met Munirah at her parents' shop in Lebanon, and fell hard. The rest is history and you'll have to ask her about it. We're about there, give or take a few more miles of sand."

"If their house is in the boonies and under the desert, where do we park?"

"Their 'garage' is more like an aircraft revetment, of concrete blocks serving as a wind and sand barrier."

"What's a revetment?"

"It's a series of sloped walls of earth, metal slats, or sand like here. They are placed around aircraft to deflect the exhaust of one plane from hitting another. They keeps planes separate during an attack, so blowing one up doesn't destroy others. It'll make more sense when you see them"

As he drove in and parked, Anh looked around and saw only brown gray sands in every direction beyond the block walls. Except for two personal vehicles and a Hummer with camouflaged military markings parked between the walls, there was no hint of a home.

They got out and moved to a smaller block enclosure housing the home's entrance. Descending the stairs Anh held the railing and squeezed Michael's hand. Sensing anxiety he assured her, "Don't be nervous; you'll love them. I guarantee it."

Anh heard a fountain bubbling in the underground courtyard, its soothing rippling noise bringing serenity as they reached the tiled floor. Between the fountain and the living area was a huge rug, its pattern identical to the rug at Michael's. Its Tree of Life design spoke of life, death, and rebirth, the complex story of earth, sky and waters woven in its colors.

Michael saw her stare. "The prayer rug is aligned to the east, to an 'older temple', not Mecca. Please don't mention that in front of them." *Hell, now I have another story to explain on the trip back.*

The couples greeted, and hugged. Amir gave Tooley a kiss on both cheeks and a small peck on Anh's forehead in the Arabic sign of respect.

Amir and Tooley walked into the living area talking excitedly about some technical matter.

Munirah stared, gently touched Anh's jet black hair, cut in a short bob with wisps of blond streaks. "How did you do that? I like it."

"My friend Patty cut and styled it; I added the streaks. I can provide you a bottle if you'd like."

Munirah's smile said yes. She was dressed in an almost sheer gown, set with bejeweled golden earrings, bracelets, and a necklace adding glitter to the eye. Anh wore small gold earrings with red Bedu beads in her ear lobes, the clip-on style. Her simple yellow dress had red stripes, matching her scarf, handbag, and belt.

Anh smelled Munirah's sandalwood perfume, "What is that scent? I love it."

"It is a fragrance I sell in this region, called 'Shezam.' I will send you a small bottle."Munirah's attention quickly shifted to Anh's left hand, where the younger woman fingered a diamond ring.

Anh smiled, "It's my engagement ring, a two carat Princess cut." She giggled, "Michael says it has deep internal brilliance, for a Princess, like me."

Fadia eyed the ring with curiosity, "Did he get on one knee to ask? I hear it is your custom."

"Yes. He asked me at a Baskin-Robbins in Riyadh. All the men cheered and hugged him when I said YES."

Munirah's face froze, "Was Baskin-Robbins romantic enough?"

"Yes. I will treasure that moment always. Now, tell me how you and Amir met."

Munirah's eyes lit up as she shared the story of romantic times with Amir.

Anh spotted Fadia hovering, listening intently and analyzing every word with the intensity of a TV Game Show host asking 'What is behind Curtain Two?' She glanced at the young girl, "Fadia, someday you'll meet your Prince."

"I will," responded, the girl grinning, "he'll be tall, dark, and drive a Bentley, or a camel." The women chuckled.

Seeing Anh's glances Munirah pointed to the walls and *Bedu* items, "Amir designed our home, with lots of my ideas. He would have built it like a cold, industrial block so I had to put my feet down ... Is that how you say it?"

"Yes that's correct. You put your foot down, you insisted." Anh scanned the walls. *Bedu* rugs, camel and tent paraphernalia hung discretely on the tan concrete walls, adding a distinctive character. "I love your style. You have a flair for color."

"Thank you. I wanted to include both Amir's *Bedouin* and my city roots. The house stays cool by cycling water from an aquifer. Our home under the sands is a refuge from the madness above."

Anh sniffed, "What is that wonderful scent?"

Munirah pointed to the smoke coming from a large censor standing nearby, coals burning inside. "It's incense, dried resin from special trees. The scent is from the time of the Romans."

Grayish incense fumes wafted upward through the open leaf design cut into burner's top. The censor's long copper feet held the bowl where Munirah dropped several nuggets of frankincense and myrrh, adding a call for calm.

Tooley came nearer, smelled the incense and shared a recollection of Easter services with a Bishop swinging a censor and adding bits of myrrh, "The sweetness of the fumes tingled my nose."

Amir told Anh, "It is a prayer to the good spirits, to ward off evil *jinn*."

"Can you help?" Munirah asked, grabbing Anh's arm and pulling her toward the kitchen. An eight burner high end gas grille was near a stainless hood extending up from the kitchen.

Anh looked up and pointed to a sky light, "I like that."

"It was my idea to bring in light but not heat." Munirah pointed at solar panels, "Those were his idea. We live miles from power lines so we adapted." She glowed, "One of Amir's companies now builds homes like this in other provinces."

"Where did you meet Michael?" Anh asked.

"We've known him for years, since study in Monterey. Your man is the bravest I know. It will grieve me if you hurt his heart."

"Don't worry; I want only to make Michael happy. Of course he is so clueless sometimes, and only wants to go out to hunt tigers, dodo birds, and wooly mammoths. Sometimes I think they're right about men being from another planet."

Munirah smiled, "I was sick this morning," and she gently rubbed her stomach.

"I was also." Anh's smile competed for first place.

Munirah gave an approving look, "That is wonderful. How far along are you?" Munirah's face turned serious as she took Anh's hands in hers, "Does Tooley know?"

"No, Michael doesn't know. I just missed this month."

Anh touched Munirah's hand gently, enhancing their new bond, "Let's tell him during dinner."

The two women chatted animatedly as they set the table with bowls of fruits. Fadia placed rosewater finger bowls to cleanse hands and spirits, the scent adding to the pleasures. The meal was *cous cous* with raisins, cardamom cloves, seasoned to an amber color with saffron, and topped with lamb morsels soon appeared. Salad rested in deeply carved bowls. Utensils of elegant bronze spoke of great antiquity.

Amir offered two carafes as they ate at a long rosewood table, "This is grape juice, vinegar you would say." He looked at Tooley and smiled.

Tooley covered his mouth and whispered to Anh, "Vinegar is code for wine, so we can deny he offered alcohol."

Both women refused the vinegar. Aware of his wife's pregnancy, Amir understood the clue. Everyone at the table turned and stared at Tooley. He looked at those around the table, his face slowly grasping the clues.

Dropping his fork, he rushed to Anh's side as she rose to hug him. "Oh my God, Babe. I'm so very, very happy." Tooley slurred his words, his vital signs off the charts, tiny bursts of light marching briefly across his pupils.

"Yeah," Anh blurted out, "I'll bet you tell all your fiancés that." The host and hostess gave puzzled looks until their daughter's laughter informed them of the joking reference.

"You're a fun couple. Please come back," nine year old Fadia pleaded.

"We will."

Patty, I had such a great experience at the Ubaidi's, like something out of Arabian Nights. I was segregated for a feast with six other women in a female only tent, the openings hung with dangling *bedu* fabrics which softened the breeze. Wives from Amir's tribe were all around, their hands and feet intricately hennaed. Rug patterns from the distant past were next to modern jeweled cell phones. I was under the microscope like bacteria in a petri dish, stunned by what I saw."

"Wish I had been there, Anh. I'm so jealous. Tell me about it. I'll never get to experience something like that."

"Munirah saw me staring at the hennaed hair, feet, and eye-lining which accented most eyes. She said the henna is enough to distinguish one woman from another. She can recognize friends by their feet, sandals or anklets. Several of the women I met were part of multi-wife families; two had the same husband. It seemed so strange, but they made little of it."

"It's hard to conceive sharing a husband. I guess if I were from Utah I could picture that arrangement. Amir has only one wife though, right?"

"Yes, only Munirah. She has such style and a sense of fashion. She wears delicate gold anklets, rather than using henna. *Bedouin* fashion ideas must be helpful in cities with all the women in veils." Munirah continued, "Out in the desert women are free to uncover, even drive."

Patty grimaced. "I sympathize with Saudi women. I feel like a nun here, having to wear an *abaya*."

"I was overwhelmed by all the faces, by Bedu women with golden daggers on their waists. I noticed Munirah's daughter staring at me with the look of someone dying to ask a serious question. Fadia then dropped a bombshell, bluntly asking, 'Before you go, tell me how much he paid for you.' I was so startled I stopped to consider what to say. I didn't want to insult Fadia or the women, who all stared at me for an answer as though *I* were from another planet."

"What did you say?"

"I told them 'we don't have dowries in our country, though the bride's family often pays for a wedding. They were surprised. One blurted out 'we make them pay here; they should.' Most nodded or gestured in agreement."

"Did that answer their curiosity?"

"No. Their eyes said they wanted more. So I told them, "if we did dowries I'd have asked my parents to demand bags of gold."

Anh smiled, "We ate a delicious meal on rugs and talked. The women examined the highlighting you did to my hair. It spurred a lot of excited comments in Arabic. Before we left they smiled and touched my engagement ring. Then they had a contest hugging me in what I took as approval. Munirah and I didn't let on about my being pregnant though."

"I think I'd have kept being pregnant to myself. So where were Michael and Amir?"

"The men were off in separate tents the whole time, eating a goat grab, as we expats say. It was lamb and vegetables on a bed of spiced cous-cous. Ours was delicious. You eat it rolled in a lump like finger food."

"The cousin bit was a big deal among the *bedus*. I know the women chatted about it, though I didn't understand a word they said.

Blood relationships are really important here."

"As we left we thanked Amir and Munirah profusely. I told Munirah, I would treasure the times we visited and stayed with them, especially with Michael and Amir being cousins."

It was the next Thursday morning, at the start of the Muslim weekend. Anh was at the hospital for blood tests required for pre-natal care, anxious to ensure all was well. "Your blood tests were fine Miss Gwinn ... but I was surprised by the data. There was something rather startling. Our DNA system searches for family connections, and it discovered you have relatives in the Kingdom."

Anh Nguyen's face tensed, "Are you sure?" Her face displayed skepticism, "Could there be a false positive, a false cousin? I have some I wouldn't want to admit even knowing."

"I ran the search routine four times; each run gave the same results. The data shows that about sixteen hundred years ago you had ancestors here. Your cousins are between seventy-fifth and eightieth degree" the tech explained, emphasizing the remoteness of the relation.

"OK. Tell me who these cousins are."

Seeing a look of disbelief he added, "I'm certain; one hundred percent. One is Stefano Gaiuso, an Italian; the second is American, Padrick O'Toole. Others are of the family of General Amir Ubaidi."

"Oh my gawd! I'm related to Michael? I can't wait to see his face when I tell him. His blood pressure will go off the chart, another seismic event before our wedding in Bahrain." *Wow! How could this be? Who were those ancestors? Ancestor zero had to have been one hell of a world traveler, probably a swabby.*

His fingers ran through salt and pepper hairs. *Gritty! Should have washed my hair this morning. It's going to be a long, boring day.* Tooley looked around, at the MODA hospital's blood donation center, to pay back for blood used when he got shot. No Saudis were in the center that afternoon. Few could, or did donate blood, except new drivers who had to donate to get their license. Saudi drivers were all males, with a frightening fatality rate. He wondered if they thought themselves immortal, somehow beyond crashes.

The tech broke the silence, "The Kingdom is very sensitive to 'improper' blood. Lots of blood products are purchased from abroad, or from expats who get wads of riyals for a pint. Blood from certain countries is excluded due to the potential of HIV/AIDS or hepatitis contamination. For safety I have to label all sample tubes in exacting detail to identify your blood." *Thank God for that, and that I got the right stuff when I needed it.*

The phlebotomist jabbed the end of the patient's little finger, and drops of Tooley's blood went into a small capillary tester. The blood's iron content was tested by the tech in an electronic scanner. He applied a small band-aid to Tooley's finger tip, "We appreciate your donation."

A green light lit, "Good. The results and your blood's iron levels are acceptable," the technician said. He then tightened a rubber band around O'Toole's upper arm, revealing prominent veins, "Lie still Mister O'Toole. I'll take care of everything." He patted the arm and grinned, "As soon as we have enough blood we'll send samples to the lab for testing."

Tooley looked to the side of the table he lay on. Blood surged through a plastic tube to a weighted pouch below. It soon filled and the balance beam tilted, signifying the required pint was in the container. The tech methodically applied a metallic clamp to interrupt the flow as he drew five tubes for analysis.

"You're done. After you leave drink plenty of water, avoid alcohol, no strenuous physical exercise, and have a nice day."

"Did you say drink alcohol and avoid water? I want to make sure I get that part straight. You are a doctor and are giving me a prescription. Correct?"

"Well yes ... and no. I'm not a doctor, and it wasn't a prescription." He motioned with his thumb through the window, "Watch what you do out there."

"I'll try. Now I need to see another doc, to see if this Tin Man really does have a heart, now that you've drained my blood."

"Good luck then; just remember, you're really not in Kansas."

Chapter - 4

The phone rang in Germany where Evan was stationed. Once, twice it rang, then Tooley heard the receiver lift, "Ev, it's happened again."

"Shit! You didn't get shot again did you, Squirt?"

"No ... fell in love. Her name is pronounced Ahh nn, like in aunt. We're getting married next month in Bahrain."

There was silence from the phone, then Tooley's older brother, the senior enlisted at the Army's European Command in Heidelberg, said, "So, Squirt, another Asian chick? What is it with you?"

"Ev, it's not because she is Asian, or beautiful, or even funny. She saved my life, and she's the one."

"Tell me more."

"She brings out the best in me."

"Well someone had to. Don't screw this up."

"No chance. She makes me laugh and you know how long it has been since I've felt like laughing. She turned me around, Bro, brought me back, smart, sensible and more handsome than ever." Tooley figured his remark would amuse Ev.

Evan said "Uh Huh." *What can I say without bringing back what must be terrible memories.* "Well, congratulations on finding someone. You were pretty glum all those years. I'm glad to hear you so happy, Bro."

"Yeah, and more full of Blarney."

"Don't forget, I'm still Mom's favorite."

"We both know that's not true. Well, now for the real news. We're expecting; you'll be an uncle. Maa and Daa don't know yet, so don't tell them. I plan to call in a moment."

"Great, Squirt! This will make up for those losers you dated back in the day. Like that goodie grabber Margaret. I'm so glad you got away from her. You fell for her hook, line and sinker, and she just wanted a sugar daddy. She left you a wreck."

He sighed, "I was."

"You're wiser now, Squirt. But then again you never had a clue when someone was shooting at you. You must have nine lives. Life chewed you up, but you survived ... several times."

"Sure was lucky, Ev. I want to be around to enjoy my

retirement with Anh. Listen, here are some planning dates." He went over the schedule and the rough list of expected guests, hoping for helpful suggestions.

"We'll pay for you and Kelsi to fly here if you can cover the hotel bill. ... Will you be my Best Man?"

"You bet I will."

They ate that evening they at a US military compound and Anh revealed her discovery, "Mikey, I need to find out more about this cousin thing."

"What cousin thing?"

"You, your Italian friend, Amir and me; we're cousins," Anh explained.

Tooley's chin fell to the floor. "I'll be damned! There's a really good story there - Stefano, Amir, and you! I don't understand how it could be. We'll have to figure it out, but I still want to marry you." They embraced.

"I'll tell Patty; she'll think it's cute being cousins. She is fun, but sometimes she can be a twit. She pulls shit at work. Instead of saying *Marhabaa*, that's Hello, she blurts out Mother Hubbard. She knows she's saying it wrong, but does it on purpose. I try to keep from exposing her to Saudi women. Those we treat seem to understand what she says and don't react, but I get embarrassed. Patty says men are emotionally challenged, and only talk about weather, gardens, sports, or their jobs. But she doesn't say that about you. She's jealous. But she said she'll be my Maid of Honor."

Chapter - 5

Months later Tooley and Anh had separate rooms to accommodate her mothers' sensitivities before their wedding. Tooley's Maa, Daa, older brother Evan and his wife were in Manama. Anh's father stayed in California to keep the business going, but her mother Bai made it. Many others were in Bahrain for the wedding. Most other attendees were Tooley's coworkers or longtime buddies from under every proverbial rock in the neighborhood.

"Ann, I'm Kelsi, Evan's wife. It's wonderful to finally meet you. Congratulations. Tooley told me wonderful things about you, and you've had such an exciting life."

"Thanks. I'm so happy, and lucky."

"Your English is so polished, better than mine. How did you pull that off, I mean, being an immigrant?"

Anh told Kelsi about Ma Leary, her favorite teacher. "She gave huge tests, a few with over a hundred questions. Every single question was 'critical' to her. If I didn't perform to her expectations she would keep me after school. I got to stay a lot. She taught me everything about grammar, spelling, punctuation, and speaking properly."

They chatted for hours, talking about morning sickness, men, and raising babies. Later, after hours of chatting, most of the group crashed to accommodate jet lag.

The next day, after they finished the morning buffet, Kelsi suggested an outing to Anh, Bai, Patty, Tooley's mother, and Munirah. "We girls need to get away from the guys."

Eager for a chance at the infrequent chance for western company, Munirah jumped in, "Sign me up."

There were signs of agreement all around. "Let's go souqing, have lunch there, and get to know each other. We can catch a cab I guess and leave ... about 10:00?" Kelsi suggested. Patty and Munirah voiced agreement and enthusiasm, while Bai and Tooley's mother seemed hesitant.

"Let's go to the fabric souq," Kelsi suggested, "it will be my only time in this part of the world and I've heard so many stories." She looked at Anh, "and I want to find some of the fabrics you wear."

Anh had on a coordinated outfit, touches of saffron and reds on her sneakers matching those on her scarf, skirt, and fingernail polish. "These were the national colors of my country," she explained to Munirah. "We'll see amazing fabrics in the souqs. The smells and colors of the spices alone will create visions of an international food court."

"You're a great salesman. Let's go," Patty whispered, "I want to buy some perfumes. I hear they're a real bargain."

"They are," Anh affirmed. There was agreeing nods; thumbs went up all around at the thought of heady scents on the cheap.

Two hours later they were at the hotel's entrance and ready for a souq run. "I'm ready, as long as we go to a Baskin-Robbins," Anh proposed.

"And they have pickle ice cream," Munirah added. The two pregnant women looked at each other and giggled. Snickers from the others filled the air as the group agreed to a fare with the cab driver, got in, and motored to the souqs.

Anh told Evan's wife her experiences dating in the Kingdom, "It was stressful sneaking around to see each other. Women can't go anywhere by themselves without fear of being arrested," Anh whined.

"What do you mean?"

"The religious police say Islam requires women to be with a man at their side to direct every move. It's dangerous for a woman to be seen alone, unless her father, brother, son or male relative is present. What single western woman has a brother around? Offenders are taken to their court system and jails. They only exist in Saudi Arabia. They take it upon themselves to close businesses during prayer call, and enforce their idea of medieval modesty."

Munirah chimed in, "It's really about power over women."

"The *Mutaawah*, that's the name for the religious police," Anh clarified for Bai, who looked puzzled. "They say they protect women, but I can defend myself. I have a Black Belt."

"Why," Kelsi asked, "did you get a Black Belt?"

"I had a boyfriend in High School. He thought he could tell me what to do, even who I could talk to. He became abusive, so I gave him a body throw which fractured his elbow. He couldn't play football that season. He was mad, but that asshole never bothered *me* again!"

Bai chimed in, "I never liked him."

Anh added, "Michael told me that it's OK to say anything about someone if you follow it with 'Bless his heart.' So I have to say that high school flame was an asshole, Bless his heart."

Kelsi and Patty laughed, tears forming. "An asshole huh?" Kelsi responded, then added, "So these religious police, did they interfere?"

"Michael and I could only get together safely at embassy gatherings or in western compounds. Later we met at his hooch."

"What's a hooch?"

"That's what Michael calls his villa in the compound. It is a term he picked up in Vietnam. Our moments were few and far between," Anh's face reddened, "as we discovered the attraction."

Anh and Evan's wife hugged, with Bai and Tooley's mother watching in puzzlement. Kelsi rubbed Anh's hands, "Tooley focused on work for long, lonely years; he lost countless opportunities for any relationship. He sponsored Hung, and they lived dangerously in strange places, doing crazy things. And now you – Anh. He is so happy."

"He has so many scars. I hope to heal them," Anh stated.

Kelsi smiled, "You seem to be doing it. I've never seen him so happy."

Munirah and Mrs. O'Toole grabbed each other's hands and chimed in, "Nor I." Patty gestured agreement.

"He's so tender," Anh smiled, "and a great cook. He even knows when to agree. I didn't even have to train him." The younger women smiled. Bai and Tooley's mother again showed uncertainty at the remarks' meaning.

Evan looked around at those attending his brothers' bachelor party. Military haircuts abounded. *Damn swabbies. Most of these geezers will be telling sea stories, making things up on the fly of days at sea, flying around in planes that are out of service, retelling lies until the cows come home.*

He must have looked alone and rejected to Tooley, who moved next to him. "Ev, we're all friends here, grunts, swabbies, and gyrenes," The groom-to-be paused, coughed and added, "and family."

Soon his brothers' buds from NAM were recalling and chanting old radio call signs, calling in and responding to helo and artillery support, fast mover jets, gunfire support from Navy ships offshore, or coordinating radar contacts held by someplace called Monkey Mountain. Moon River, Jolly Roger, and some crazy Falcon codes were references Evan didn't understand, but elicited laughter from the Vietnam vets. Evan saw he, his dad, and Amir were equally puzzled by this banter, but enjoyed the moment.

Tooley became the butt of numerous jokes and put downs, the centerpiece of a few because he was a Boat School or Naval Academy grad. "You had to be there to understand how nuts it was ... probably still is. The funniest thing I can remember of graduation week, besides my graduating, occurred during the Final Parade. The Brigade Commander, that's the senior student position, he called out just as the middies stepped off 'Brigade, Piss in your shoe' rather than the required 'Pass in review.' That classmate was replaced that afternoon, but every midshipman laughed like hell."

Laughter reverberated amidst clinking of beer bottles and drink glasses. Tooley interrupted, "Everyone should believe in something. I believe I'll have another beer."

The groom-to-be paused to swig at his beer, letting his dad thrill those in ear shot with WWII stories that awed all but Tooley and Evan, who'd heard them many times. The father of the groom reminisced of the wintery Battle of the Bulge, the Nazis' last gasp. Tooley's father continued, "Patton stormed to our rescue as we fought it out with German Tiger tanks in the town of *Arshlock*." The guys stared in awe until he finished.

"His story beat all others hands down," Amir offered. Stefano nodded agreement.

"Except those with bullet holes, you've got four that I know of," Tooley's former boss Frank noted, eyeing the subject of the party.

Tooley looked up at stares, "Five, but who's counting." "It wasn't something I planned, just happened to be in the wrong spots at the wrong times," he injected to minimize the scrutiny.

"You are one lucky SOB, O'Toole. Let's get fresh drinks before we all fall down. Bartender, another round for my friends ... and the groom." Amir then broke into a limerick chorus familiar to many of the vets. Most joined in, laughing. Stefano alone hadn't heard the song, but understood its sentiment.

Aye, aye, aye aye
In China they do it for chili
I'll sing you another verse
Worse than the other verse
So waltz me around again Willy.

Tooley reminisced about the song as three more verses followed Amir's chorus. Even Tooley's Dad joined in. Grabbing his brother's shoulder he said, "Ev, now that we've had a few I need to tell you something."

"You don't need to tell me; I know. You never could sing, Squirt."

"I can't, and *neither* can you. But here's the thing. We have special family here." He gave some background as Evan's face frowned.

"I understand about Anh; she saved your life and you're marrying her. And Amir, you've known him for years and just saved his life. What about Stefano; what makes him special?"

"You've probably seen the movie *Top Gun*, right?"

"Yeah."

"Let's just say I can tell you but then ... well, you know the rest. We ... ah ... collaborate. He is one hell of a photographer, journalist, and detective. He has worked as a source, and I prevented him from revealing some very sensitive stuff. But you don't need to know about it any of that. So he holds a special spot in my circle of friends." *I still worry if he'll spill the beans, or get drunk somewhere, sometime and start a war.*

Evan looked puzzled, "And we're related?"

"Yeah, very distant cousins. I figure our common ancestor traces from Roman times, and Stefano is way more Roman than the rest of us. You and I know lots of physical, real life cuzzes in Maine, and tons more we figured we had ... if we cared to find em. Cousins are just people connected by a name; most we probably wouldn't even like. These guys, they're more than blood; they're like Jedi who played a crucial part in my life."

The lobby of Bahrain's Gulf Hotel was almost empty. Few guests were up the next morning. Something was afoot, a Japanese tour group gone to take photos. Just a few early morning shoppers and breakfast types sat and ate the obligatory buffet. They were up to get a start at the souqs and the local treasure, essences that could be diluted to recreate very expensive European perfumes, or to consume alcohol forbidden in the Kingdom.

US Marines and a number of security guards in civvies stood watch anxiously outside the hotel's entrances during the rooftop wedding festivities. The large presence of the groom's friends, now senior US military officers and government types, made the venue a potential target for terrorists.

The guests sat as a gentle breeze ruffled bouquets of flowers by the couple. Anh wore short heels, but they still added several inches to her height. Her hair was rolled back in a bun, accented with slender red and saffron ribbons to match the bridal bouquet she carried to the altar.

"Who gives Miss Nguyen away?"

Anh's mother Bai spoke up, "My husband and I do."

As the afternoon sun descended, a breeze cooled the humid air on the rooftop and the raised platform where they stood surrounded by plants and ornately carved windscreens. Tooley and Anh recited vows they personally wrote, a mélange of Buddhist and Catholic verses and phrases of love and commitment. The clergy, a Catholic chaplain and a Buddhist monk from Singapore, wrapped a white silk band around their clasped hands, and together pronounced them married.

The clergy's "You may kiss your bride" echoed, and the couple exchanged a long passionate kiss and embraced to universal cheers. Tooley and Anh moved among family and friends, thanking all for coming. Tooley resurrected a juxtaposition of Vietnamese and English to express his feelings to Bai. He reverted to bits of Vietnamese he recalled, accentuated by holding up one finger. "So mot, number one" as he hugged Anh. His words worked with his mother-in-law, but Tooley's parents appeared puzzled as the families moved to the head table.

The meal was simple, featuring chicken, carved lamb and beef roasts, and an alluring array of visually colorful vegetables. Catered by the hotel, dinner was followed by a three layer cake adorned with ornate flower buds. Tooley cut the cake with his Navy sword. Anh and Tooley gently placed a sliver of cake in each others' mouths, then toasts followed from Evan and Patty.

The couple skipped the traditional garter, but a bridal bouquet was carefully thrown to Patty, and applause echoed across the rooftop. A DJ provided hours of music, the final set followed by a rooftop fireworks display, a gift from Munirah and Amir.

Patty set out to find a single guy and party all night.

Amir hugged Tooley, "My friend who saved my life. Munirah and I expect you to visit us in London soon." Munirah and Anh embraced, and then gently rubbed each other's stomachs.

Stefano added his invite, "Isabella and I want to see you all in Rome. Please come and stay" glancing at the O'Toole's and the

Ubaidi's. He handed them cards, "Here's our address."

"Will this be the last time we see you, Stef?" Anh asked.

"I think, for a while. I accepted a position with CNN, and I doubt you'll be going to Iraq's border with Iran. I fly home tomorrow, vacation with Sophia and our children, and fly to Baghdad in three weeks. Then I'll get to hunker down and count the bullets."

"Ask Sophia to come stay with us in Paris. I'll call and give her our address when we get settled. We're family." Then Tooley whispered to the Italian, "Keep your head down, and like I warned you before, don't start a war."

"I won't have to; I'll have a front row seat." Stefano looked at Tooley and Amir, "I'll be stuck between lots of very angry soldiers determined to kill everyone in the middle."

Chapter - 6

The newlyweds slipped away to honeymoon in the Emerald Isle the next morning. She stared at him, "How can you say you're Irish? You weren't born here, while I was born in Vietnam. You relish all things Irish, and not just on St. Patrick's Day. And that dark yukk, Guinness. ... Yukk! Oh, those Irish drinking songs you sing, they're all off key. But at least you know the words." Anh was on a roll, smiled, and tugged his shirt, "Kiss me, like you mean it ... Paddy."

"I do ... do, do, do."

O'Toole twitched awake, reminded anew of all the reasons for his happiness. He wanted to stay awake, savor her. He breathed in the scent of her hair. She was next to him, Anh Nguyen O'Toole, his better half. *Ah, that was why.*

She seemed but a wee fairy lying there, a pillow pulled up under her neck. He reached around her slender body, pulled her closer, and cupped his hand on her breast. *Heaven*! He pulled her closer still, moved his hand. *Hmm* ... he found them, lacey, slippery skivvies, so soft his hands slid off. They were meant to be touched, removed.

Anh lay there, asleep, snoring gently. *Do other women snore?* He whispered, "I'm so glad we found each other."

She rolled over, towards him, puffed up the pillow ... "Feeling frisky?"

He kissed her ear, ear lobe, ran tickling fingers across her stomach, "Uh huh."

Their honeymoon on the auld sod, so green, moist, so lush. Here it was cool at night, and a bit humid, not so dry your nose bled. They'd left the room's windows open; it was ... grand. The temperature of the air helped you sense the warmth of the body joined to yours.

'Himself,' he liked that quaintly Irish term. She was, by definition of the 'I dos,' the better half. He discovered she liked talking - more than he did. She seemed to talk incessantly, but he dare not make that observation aloud. She rambled about shoes, lipstick shades, clothes, kids in school, germs, places ... everything. He liked to ponder, about the same sorts of things, but analytically ... photos, movie clips, characters in books, all structured, precise in his mind. She said things in an odd way; he dissected them, but not thoroughly.

Anh rolled over; she had a long list of questions about why he chose this place for a honeymoon, and she intended to get answers. She looked at *himself*, ran a finger down his nose, then poked his gut, "Where do we go first, Mister Tour Guide?"

"Our first destination will be the capital and a double decker bus tour of Dublin. Then to see Guinness made, at the brewery itself. They let us taste it. This is all in Dublin, then a walk over the Liffey River, your first European capital.

She interrupted, "Yes ... Why are we here exactly? I hate this beer. It's dark," she wrinkled her nose, "gloomy, and bitter.

"But it's full of vitamins, more than fish oil pills."

"But it looks like tar, like they cooked something too much and it burned in the bottom of the pan, and I hate fish oil. It's probably why they drive on the wrong side of the road."

They bantered back and forth, blah, blah, blah at the Guinness brewery cafeteria ... "Later we'll drive north to see my ancestral lands, passing the Hill of Tara where tribes swore allegiance to Irish High Kings.

"More green mounds," Anh mocked, "rocks aligned to some passing comet, or the nearest pub,"

"No," he retorted, and rubbed her shoulder, "aligned to heavenly bodies, like yours."

"Doolin's Dew is nearby," he stated, "it's the center of social life here. It offers simple sandwiches, stews, stamps, and a selection of beverages," according to the Internet guides. That evening they walked to the only local pub, where locals were playing Celtic music.

Tooley whispered, "I'll sing, something bawdy, slowly like a poet, so they can't tell I'm off key." Across the pub a story teller sat on a stool by a low stage. He rambled on in random directions. He shared Irish legends and myths, ignoring details of each conquest, but not his pint of Guinness.

"These conquerors were a temporary thing," the singer smiled, "they were the reason we perfected whiskey. They came in waves and beat up our High Kings. Each battle was fought by the bravest of Celtic warriors, the strongest males, and the most beautiful of women – all with swords in hand." He looked around, they'd heard it before.

The lead strummed his guitar, then sipped from his glass. A set started, ended. "Soon the conquerors were gone. They left just crumbling ruins, and the memory of defeat. Their identity is not known ... nor cared about."

Anh smiled, "I love the music and the lilt of Gaelic. ... Irish this, Celtic that ... tra la, la la, la la la." All eyes now fixed on her. She taunted him, "Blah, blah, blah, blah, Guinness blah, blah, blah." She faked a Valley Girl accent, "Like totally."

Tooley looked around, noticed the stares and blurted, "I've never seen this woman before."

Anh smacked his leg, and gentle laughter rippled through the pub. She rubbed her stomach, "Yes he has."

After two minutes he stood, flapped his arms as if to fly away, "I lied; she's mine." He scanned the customers, met their eyes, "Hot huh?"

That night a peat fire glowed in the fireplace of a thatch roofed cottage where they spent several blissful nights. Two days later, as they drove west, on the wrong side of the road, Anh gripped the arm rest nervously. "So," she said, "these are the Emerald Isles? I want to see the emerald mines. Are the stones as green as the fields and mountains? I want a ring made from them."

She looked out the window, past branches arching above the rental on what seemed a one lane road, "Where are the emerald mines exactly? Why do they call this the Emerald Isle if there weren't lots of them around? Are they on today's' tour?"

Late afternoon, after the sun rested beyond, at the edge of the sea, past the glimmering Ring of Kerry, they checked in. That night they ventured to a medieval banquet at a medieval tourist castle. The tourist trap featured modern day stand-ins for Kings, Celtic warriors, serving wenches, primitive eating utensils, and delicious overcooked foods with simple spices. The meats were roasted over old spits at the end of a cavernous hall, next to pots hanging over a fire with firewood blazing.

Tooley grinned, "Remember to say 'what ho wench' to get something to drink. You have to follow the custom, although this place was probably named after some old fart," they laughed. "Goblets of wine, grape juice, mythic serpents and gods, and wenches -what could be better?"

She looked at him, eyes askance, "Take peat, water and a blender ... you get Guinness, right?"

I'll say that, 'what ho, wench,' when you cook. It might not happen often, because you almost never cook," he snickered, rubbing it in that he was the cook de jour. "I'd be amazed if you cooked. I'd write a note in the journal. Only once you'll have a few more recipes to use. Will the menu include peat from the bogs, with a special sauce?"

Great music, costumes, like a festival ... a special treat ... Medieval musicians strolled closer, serenaded them. Anh asked, "What are they singing about?"

"It's always about some struggle. It is a grand Irish song, it is. They sang of all things great, beautiful and brave. The tax man, British, Romans, Vikings, and now, tourists. And everything is low calorie and non-fattening."

"This was fun and so different," Anh whispered. They flirted like they had to win a joist to win the heart of each other, the fair damsel, and the noble knight, but without the goofy medieval clothes.

"Tomorrow it gets better," he smiled. "Tomorrow it's Blarney Castle and you get to kiss the stone, Babe." his eyes begged as he stared into her eyes. "Then you'll be able to spin your own yarns like I spin mine."

"You've got to be kidding me. You expect me to hang upside down, kiss an old rock with phlegm and drool all over it? No way."

"How can it hurt? Take the chance, kiss the Stone."

Anh counted on her fingers, touching each twice as she recited a list of bacteria, "and that doesn't even include the microbes in moss and mold."

"Hmm ... I'll take that as a no." He offered to patronize a small Vietnamese restaurant in Galway, if she kissed the famous stone. The offer didn't sway her.

"That's your comeback? Can't you do better, give me the speech?"

"What speech?"

"The one about Irish this, Irish that, some battle here, some feminine there, shamrocks, pots of gold, rainbows and leprechauns, et cetera, et cetera, et cetera?" They teased each other, threatening, verbally prodding, finding weaknesses and strengths, squirming from reactions no matter how slight or feigned ... finding the personality traits hidden back in the sandbox, where the normal actions and reactions of life were precluded, *harram* - forbidden in public.

"You can't sing," she grinned devilishly, "though you're kinda cute, with hairy, stinky arm pits. I like how the scars on your body tingle when I touch them."

They parried, ducked, weaved, sparring. He stared back after each verbal joust. He thought ... life was so wonderfully different with her in it ... scents, touches, showers, sex. Their lives had a different rhythm, more flowers now, a schedule for washing clothes, more people activities, most with couples. The marriage meant new friends, different ones with outlooks poles apart, and kids. Most of his friends were single, involved in parts of his business.

A er Lingus 747 flight took off from Shannon airport, and Tooley pointed down to the ruins of Clon MacNois aside the Shannon River below. "Anh, the Vikings came here, destroyed that and many other monasteries, until after years of pillaging they found this island better than their home and stayed. It's peaceful here."

"And so green. Glad we saw Ireland together, even if it was expensive to see the 'old sod.' The sod, though, was green on top. Did we eat some of it, the old sod? A pile of rocks, and gritty dark lager? Did we miss any of it?" she asked.

"Babe, I had to show you my roots," he smiled.

"I never knew you had root rot." She caressed his arm, looked out the window. "Off into the sunset. Bet it'll be warm there."

Seven hours later they were on the ground in hot, brown Saudi Arabia. "Babe, we're back in the sandbox." A sea of sands spread below as the plane banked to approach the runway ... heat rising from the roads from the airport. In the 13th century, here it was 100 degrees outside at midnight.

"Babe huh? I could get used to that." She hugged him, then spotted a Saudi man in the airport baggage claim area gawking. She showed her wedding ring, "We just got married."

'Mohammed', as Anh termed all Saudi males until corrected with a personal name, gave a thumbs up. He extended his hand and they shook hands. She smiled. *Wow, never thought that would happen. Females are prohibited from being with strange men, those not in your family. But, we are in an airport, and there are no religious police here.*

She nudged Michael, and he shook Mohammed's hand.

"That was a nice welcome" his better half said with a grin, holding his hand as they walked to their car, "We better get in any public display of affection before Riyadh closes in."

"I've got you until then," *himself* said.

She put her arm around his waist. Other Saudi males looked on, but their smiles seemed genuine. Mohammed glared. Anh noticed his stare, "Guess our honeymoon is over."

They motored back to home in the DQ, in a solemn silence, very much stifled by the searing brown which swept to the horizon. Reality, if only for a few brief weeks ... "It seemed like all the worlds green is in Ireland, sure isn't here," Anh whispered.

"Not enough Guinness," Tooley replied. "It was fun sharing, embellishing, and retelling old sea stories at the reception. I was surprised how old some buddies looked, with wavy gray hair and wrinkles. It seemed like Old Home week for spooks and gumshoes." Tooley saw her puzzled look and explained the common terms used to identify spies.

"Oh," Anh whispered hesitantly. "Does that mean I'll be followed?"

"Yes, some of the time, some places, and you have to promise you won't divulge to anyone what I do."

"What a bunch of hooey," she poked his stomach with a finger and snapped back, "I'll tell everybody."

Reality had crept in; they were back in the Land of the Prophet, if only for a short time. Anh had too much time on her hands and little to do. With a new American passport in her married name, she was stuck. US protocols prevented her from surrendering it for a work permit. Overcoming Saudi bureaucracy, to work a few weeks, was too formidable. "Our new assignment is weeks away. We're being transferred to greener pastures, wider boulevards," he boasted.

"I can't believe we're going to Paris," she exclaimed.

"Believe it. My embassy job will be challenging, but we'll get to travel," he looked at her baby bump, "with a big bag of diapers."

Jimmy Buffett's music was playing and Tooley started humming, "Babe, it's 5 PM somewhere. Let's go to the Camel's Breath Saloon for the sing-a-long." Soon lyrics emerged from what Anh described as Tooley's gravelly voice. His volume went up, a rendition of a ditty with the word 'tattoo' in it.

Anh grinned, it was party time, She looked at him, touched his cheek ..."Who would have thought, an Irishman who couldn't carry a tune in a wheel barrow. You can't sing. Try to keep it clean."

"No. I'll make it bawdy, sensuous," Tooley suggested, "They'll never see us again! ... or will forget."

"Not if we do it slow and sexy." She scanned his arms and neck, "Did you get a tattoo?"

"Sure did, in Paris when I was apartment hunting. It's a Celtic knot around your name. You're not keeping track, are you?" He rolled down a sock and pointed, "Now that I showed you mine you have to show me yours."

The implication was clear; it would be play time when they got home, searching for real or imaginary tattoos. "You're in a particularly good mood," Anh said as she finished blow drying her hair, "What's up?"

"Paris of course, and our new family," he touched her stomach, "It's our last night in the sand box. The workers pick up our household goods tomorrow. Think of it like we're traveling minstrels, flying away to a gig in a distant place?"

Anh hummed, "Not San Jose at all. Tell me again where we're going. I still can't believe it."

"We're going to Paree, the City of Light, but its karaoke time and the crew are waiting." His face softened with a big, toothy grin.

"*You* don't get a chance at the mike; it's Gals Night. Lets get down and dirty. These folks won't see us again."

"I'll bring my violin then," he jabbed. Neither had a violin, or talent with strings, brass, woodwinds, percussion, or keyboards.

"I'll sing; you provide accompaniment this time. That's OK, isn't it?" Anh knew her rhythm was better than his, though he knew the lyrics of every Irish drinking song.

He caved, "Deal. You sing, I'll mouth the words and try to stay synced with the rhythm. ... doo be doo, be doo."

Chapter - 7

Do you have anything to disclose?" the Air France attendant asked as she handed out blank forms, "if so please note it on your customs declaration."

Anh answered first, "I don't have anything."

Tooley looked at her and touched her hand, "I do, you Babe - you. And a great job coming up, not a shit job like Amir."

"What's he doing? They'll be in London, how bad can it be?" Amir and Munirah had moved there the previous week, Munirah also very pregnant.

"London, yes, but his job sucks. It involves tracking Saudi dissidents, and counseling royals who go astray of the law and get in the tabloids. He dislikes his job more than anything I've ever heard him talk of. Amir doesn't need more enemies, especially royals."

I thought British courts were tolerant of such indiscretions since they have their own royalty."

"Not really, British judges seem to be especially critical of Saudi royal family on drugs or who can't keep their wieners in their pants. It has to do with upholding the tradition of being 'to the manor born.'"

"I get it. How about Munirah? What will she be doing, besides watching Fadia and keeping French suitors at a distance?"

"I expect after the baby arrives she'll take up the reins in her fragrance company, maybe expand into cosmetics. I'm sure Fadia will find some nice guy."

"It could happen. I found one."

"I'm so jazzed. We're almost to Paris," she said excitedly, then hesitated and stared. "Munirah and family are in London, and Stef's wife and kids are in Rome, so how do we get together?"

Tooley raised his seat and looked at Anh, "What do you mean?"

"We'll all be in different parts of Europe, and Stefano's away in a war zone risking his life for a story."

"OK, after we get settled in, we call everyone and whip up a plan to meet."

Anh rubbed her stomach and whispered, "Any get together will be after we have our babies. Munirah's due in two weeks."

"It'll all work out, once the babies are big enough to travel." Tooley adjusted his seat belt, straining against his gut. *Too many sugared coffees, with cream. Too many of Anh's great meals. Daa always said 'People are starving in China.' I can't waste food.*

His face tensed, "I wish this flight would end. I want to get back on the ground."

"Look at you. You're such a baby, afraid of flying but not bullets." Anh jabbed his stomach, not wanting to miss a chance to poke fun, "Explain that to me."

His eyes scanned the passenger area, avoiding an answer to her question. *Comfortable, no threat. No one is strafing me with rockets or bullets like before, not in a plane flying straight from Riyadh.* Tooley looked out the window. White cumulus clouds were layered below, as their flight flew towards Charles DeGaulle airport.

Moisture droplets rolled back across the wing's upper surface as a cool air mass shed its moisture. *More engines mean a better chance of survival if one fails.* A refrain familiar to air travelers soon echoed from overhead speakers, "Please put your tray tables up! Follow along as I go over the seat pocket plane evacuation instructions ... 'yackety yack, yackety yack.' Turn off all electronic devices. If you don't know how, ask the teenager across the aisle."

The last announcement got everyone's smiles. All recognized the 'yackety yack, yackety yack.' Belts tightened, tray tables cleaned and elevated, trash was collected by flight attendants, and long lines formed to rest rooms, confirming that it had been a long flight. Soon the plane descended at a noticeable angle.

4

38 Rue de Champagne, Paris, Apt nr 5 - A three year tour lay ahead, but they were in Paris and after that they'd be off to somewhere else outside the US, for Tooley to manage a network of local sources. Just now he and Anh were having a frantic week, buying cleaning products, identifying food shops and bakeries, and acquiring venetian blinds and other necessities of life before their baby arrived.

Their top floor apartment, protected by the French Diplomatic Protective Service, came with a rooftop patio. Tooley looked out a window, across a wide boulevard to the park beyond, then scanned their two bedroom apartment. *I need to baby proof this place. Better pick up some ideas at the office.*

The phone rang in his embassy office. He stared out the window, across the Place De La Concorde and the Tuileries Gardens, past an ancient obelisk appropriated from Egypt. Two blocks from the River Seine the phone readout identified Tooley's caller as Amir Ubaidi, calling from London.

What can it be, trouble? No, can't be anything exciting, not from staid old England. Ah, good news ... the baby. Tooley lifted the handset, excitement on his face and in his voice, "Hey buddy. How are things?"

Amir's reply was excited, jubilant, "Munirah and our son Mahomet are both fine, very fine. He was born yesterday in the morning, very early. He is quiet now ... but soon he'll be a handful and a needed education for his older sister Fadia. He is dark haired like us, skinny. She'd done this before, so it went fast, and they'll be home in a day or two. Munirah said it was how you say, 'a breeze.'" The conversation continued and Tooley solicited advice on a nursery.

"I have a most interesting job. I was run off the road twice last week ... by the same prince. I wasn't hurt and put the fear of Allah in that bastard. He swore it wouldn't happen again and I told him it better not, or I'd ship his ass back to live in a desert tent."

"What the hell are you doing, Amir? I thought you had some cushy commercial job."

"No, my tour, and for four years, is to identify bad royals, talk with them, then counsel them to change their ways or suffer the consequences. One killed his girlfriend with an overdose. He says he has to convince them to enroll in substance abuse treatment or counseling, or they lose their stipends. A few are dangerous. Each visiting royal must see me to collect their passports and deal with the British authorities for all troubling legal matters. I later return their documents. A few are troubled souls. There is much drama with each."

"I could put out a contract on them if you'd like?"

"No. I could take care of them also, but keep that to yourself. How is Anh?"

"She is doing great. Our baby is due in three weeks."

Maternity ward, Paris hospital - Not quite a month later, following hours and hours of labor, Michael O'Toole was 'launched' as Tooley boasted. His displacement was eight pounds and two ounces and he came outfitted with all the proper male accessories, a warm, cuddly, eighteen inch long screaming bundle of energy.

The hospital gave the couple a new parent package of diapers, ointments, vitamins and folder on how to do all the things new parents do. There were no instructions on getting the baby to sleep through the night. The next two weeks dragged by slowly. They struggled nightly to balance changing diapers, poop parcels, and feedings. Traffic noise was drowned out by their baby's cries, and sleep deprivation blurred reality. It was a time of domestic stress, in a world at war.

The phone rang, rang again, and then a third time. Before the fourth ring Amir lifted the receiver, recognizing his friend on the line. Pleasantries filled the start of their conversation, interrupted by Tooley's announcement.

"Our trip is on hold again, we can't go anywhere for awhile, even across the channel to see you and Munirah. We're expecting again, and the doctor said not to travel for six weeks."

"Congratulations! That is such good news ... It's much better news than mine."

"Which is bad news I'll bet? What's up?"

Amir told him of being threatened by a Saud family member,

"He's a royal with drug problems, and I arranged his being barred from returning home. He is my private war."

"What did he do?"

"He is what you would say 'arrogant prick'. He physically abused his female servants. He threatened me, said he'd do more than run me off road next time. I'd like to cut off his balls."

"I know a course your driver should take. It goes over maneuvers to evade or even disable a pursuing vehicle." He heard an interested grumble, and asked, "Is your driver armed?"

"Yes, as am I. Why do you ask?" Amir's voice was confident but concerned.

"Because there are many things a crazy can do worse than running you off the road."

"I just took a marksmanship course. I'll check on that driving course"

"That sounds better, for the next time some Israeli commando wants to shoot you, and I happen to be in the way."

"Amen" Amir fingered prayer beads in his pocket, "My life seems a small war at times, and every village and hamlet here has monuments to battles and wars, especially in the park next door."

"What's next door?"

"Our home is next to Bletchley Park, where some Brits won WWII."

"I know the place, the home of the team that cracked Germany's wartime codes. Visiting there has been a lifelong goal."

"Munirah, Fadia, Mahomet and I live just a short drive from Bletchley. I want to visit the place."

"Me too buddy. I was a math whiz and dabbled with codes at one time, centuries ago."

"Arrange a tour for us; you have a better chance to arrange one up than I do. You can stay with us."

"I'll set up a trip to London. I need to see people there anyway. We can swap baby stories when we get together. I wish Stefano could come; he must have some wild stories from being under fire."

Tooley walked to the embassy that morning, figuring out how to arrange a *required* trip to England, and Bletchley Park. He and Anh had talked of family options. *Two children – that's what we want.*

These thoughts brought a smile and a nervous surge to his steps as he walked along the wide boulevard. His thoughts of diapers were interrupted by a French security guard outside the embassy.

"Bonjour, Monsieur. You have, what you say, a brave woman." It was said offhandedly, accompanied by a smirk that infused O'Toole with curiosity, "She is surprising for an American woman."

"What do you mean?"

"The guards speak of your woman. She was accosted by a pickpocket while walking baby in park, and reacted instinctively. The attacker ran away, his right arm broken I hear." The HIPS Sergeant, of France's competent diplomatic protective service, explained in greater detail.

I'll have to talk with Anh ASAP. God, I could have lost her. Whoever said Paris was the City of Light? At noon, after a hurried walk home, worrying with every step, he got to the apartment door. He unlocked the door and went in. Out of breath, he found Anh asleep on the couch.

He gently touched her arm, "Anh, I'm glad you're safe. Why didn't you tell me?"

"Oh, that thing in the park. I took care of him, kicked his gypsy butt. I told him off in angry French and threw him to the ground. It was no big deal, but he'll never mess with another woman walking a baby."

"The gendarme said you're a local celebrity - but I worried. Why did I have to hear of the attack from a French guard? Some of these toughs just look to score money for their next fix." He paused, "but I know you can defend yourself, after hearing what you did, I'm going to call <u>you</u> the next time someone shoots at me."

Anh touched his hand, concern blocking her normal smile, "Promise there won't be a next time, and that you'll be careful. It's hard Mikey, the baby, the diapers, staying at home. Then you, coming home from work frazzled and wrung out by God knows what."

"At least no one is shooting at me. It's civilized here, not like where Stef is." A smile spread across his face and he sat next to her on the couch. "Babe, there's a story here, a good one." His face flushed, he unbuttoned her blouse, and she his shirt. Temperature and heart rates increasing, they slipped out of their clothes. "I have an idea," Anh pulled him closer.

"I think I have the same idea."

Hours later the baby's cries woke Tooley. He rose quietly, and changed Michael's diapers while Anh slept on the rug. He fed the baby and rocked it gently to sleep, singing 'The wheels on the bus' over and over again. Tooley returned to her side on the rug with a quilt. They cuddled as he pulled the fabric over them. Her warmth was welcome; the apartment was cool. She woke and pulled him close and they snuggled and hummed.

"I need a shower, can we continue there? Life isn't all about an endless stream of dirty diapers."

"Yes." Soon luxurious French fragrances filled the shower as they applied soapy lubricants over every curve and crevice.

They woke late, dressed and checked on baby Michael, still asleep. Their passion lingered, and Anh tugged his arm. "Mikey, it was wonderful to spice things up before we're overcome by diapers. What was the best part for you?"

A grin spread on his face, "The low flow shower head."

She punched him lightly, "You are such a joker. I hope you won't repeat our shower story."

"I certainly will, and you're being pregnant and kicking a thief's butt is worth telling family. It's a better tale than Stefano would tell."

She gave his arm another jab, "The best part is you're not near any shooting. Tell me again why you got shot at so often?"

"It's not often, just bad luck. My profession has two halves, Ops and Intel, and I'm in the safe half. There's no shooting; at least that's what they promised. It's not like Stefano's situation, having to worry daily about snipers seeing and homing in on his satellite dish or driving over some IED along some dusty road."

Tooley frowned, "I wonder if he interviews them, the ones captured or blown almost to death, the wounded clinging to life in a hospital bed or a cell. He must be lonely as hell."

"Let's call and cheer him up."

"OK." Tooley lifted the phone, and punched in Stefano's number. Half a world away a phone rang in a CNN satellite van and the war correspondent answered, "How's it going, Cuz? Where the hell are you?"

"I can't disclose my location; the army would pull the plug." His voice seemed nervous.

"Are you safe?" Anh leaned over and asked. "What's up?

"Yes ... mostly. I can say only the men we capture on screen, soldiers with lives to live, seem lethargic, not committed to fighting."

Tooley was not surprised at the response, "Is their morale low?" His ears perked up. *A frontline observer ... wonder if he'll say anything of value. I'd better stick to good news.*

"No – no! I'm saying that the fighting was at times intense. I expected to see men fighting off human wave attacks by crazed teenagers, like when Iraq fought Iran before. It was madness then, madness now. All madness - these men know it. They know sunrise might not warm their bodies again. You feel that fear in their eyes." *And you're sitting back there, drinking cappuccinos while my ass in on the line.*

"Please be careful, stay safe for Sophia and your children. We want to get together sometime soon, after our baby is born and we can all travel. Maybe you can you come here before then?"

Stefano was embedded with US troops at an undisclosed location. "No, I do not think possible, if the *Jihadis* get better with IEDs I may end up in a hospital next time."

"Next time? Let's pray there isn't a next time. And, we've great news. Anh is expecting. She told Sophia she still hopes her nursing career can continue. For the next couple of months she has a temporary job at a clinic in an Asian district of Paris. She's relearning Vietnamese and a lot of French. It seems to be working out; she's happy."

Chapter – 8

Maternity ward, Paris – Months later, in September of 1992, Bai O'Toole was born. The specs as Tooley boasted at her 'launch' were eight pounds or 3.1 kilograms, and 18 inches or 45 centimeters. Bai came as another small energetic handful, no surprise after her brothers' first year.

Anh later told Munirah "It's better we not have any more. We both agree on that, especially not if they are like Bai. She runs me ragged. I love her, but if she had been born first, we'd have had only one child."

Munirah laughed. "I know the feeling. My parents said that

about my brother Ahmad. Our son Mahomet isn't like that; he's a pleasure, and it's good we have Fadia to help."

Anh called Sophia in Rome and gave a family update, then suggested another gathering. "It's been ages since we've seen each other and the kids, ours and Munirah's son, are finally able to travel. Our youngest, Bai, sleeps through the night now, though they both crawl to all parts of the apartment unless we lock doors. Bai tags along with Michael, because he knows where to find forbidden things. Tooley baby proofed everything below counter top level, but Michael tries to prove that wrong. I remember how nice it was when you, Marta, and Marcus flew to London in 1993, but after two long years it's our time to do the traveling. Can we get together again?"

"Where?" Sophia asked quietly.

Anh recognized hesitance in Sophia's voice, perhaps sorrow but repeated the suggestion. Anh perceived that Sophia hadn't volunteered as she had so often, forcefully as though visits to Italy were a redeeming Papal edict. "Our children are big enough to travel, as is Munirah's young son Mahomet. Can we come to see you this time?" *Hopefully all the 'kids' can get along.*

Sophia agreed ... slowly. "It will be good to have you come, perhaps Florence, our home there. I will write with directions. I must call now Stefano to ..." Her voice grew quiet and the connection was gone.

Sophia had written both families describing how to get to their home. She suggested a time 'after Marta's engagement in two months.' She offered an idea, "Drive from Rome on Italy's high speed motorway system to near Florence. You can drive Autostrade at speed, then slow in curve through hills. The scene at road edge most beauty, and the canyons below. Drive here. It easy, fast roads."

A reunion was agreed after more telephone calls between Paris and London. The three families, Ubaidis, O'Tooles, and Gaiusos, were to gather in Tuscany, hosted by Stefano and Sophia. At the last reunion Sophia, Marcus and Marta Gaiuso had flown to the UK, Stefano still away reporting on the end of the war. Now he was home, safe. Marcus was in his teens, and Marta would by then be engaged, the siblings a welcome pair for teen Fadia to hang out with, away from her young brother.

Amir, to speed up the gathering, proposed a last minute change, to travel in his personal jet. There were no objections and the Ubaidi's and O'Tooles were now airborne enroute Florence. At the controls was Amir's corporate pilot, an Air Force vet. The Gulf Stream's twin turbines hum was mind dulling for Tooley, who glanced across the aisle to see Fadia grinning, her head phones off momentarily, blaring with music, oblivious to her brother in Mom's lap. Even his second glass of wine failed to materially reduce O'Toole's in-flight anxiety. Friend's plane or not, his blood pressure went up on every flight. *All the same, this flight is luxurious. It's nice to have a wealthy Saudi General as family. It's even better he's a friend, even if occasionally a target.* He noticed the plane's descent. *Oh good, Mother Earth.*

The families settled in smaller seats for the trip into Tuscany's foothills, luggage jammed in the trunk. Tooley glanced at the body guard as the man drove the gleaming black limo along, then turned off the national highway and crept onto twisting local roads. He saw the guards' eyes sweep the road's borders. No guardrails were along the thoroughfare, only rows of trees painted a mute white to designate the line beyond which drivers must not go. O'Toole saw the driver's intensity, knuckles whitened while maneuvering switch backs, his tension mirrored by parents as they gawked ominously into canyons dotted with gray green trees and bright flowers.

A roadside marker finally appeared by the curb ahead, its welcome arrow and blue shape and white letters announcing their destination to Tooley and a now relaxed driver. The town of Rufina was but 4 KM ahead. *That road sign bordered by flowers, hopefully they're for some local memory and not an accident. Thank God he's a cautious pilot and driver.*

The sign's visual welcome built anticipation in the limo. Munirah, Anh and Fadia chatted in the back, buckled into supple leather seats as they neared Sophia's country home in Tuscany, in the hills beyond Firenze. Vineyard followed vineyard, row after row of grape vines climbed to cables supported by old stone posts, each bordered by adjacent family olive groves as the limo ascended towards Rufina.

Anh smiled and pointed out the window as the car circled the driveway. An ancient stone fountain stood before the imposing Gaiuso home. The structure's yellow brown stucco was accented by cobbled stonework over and around windows. Ivy climbed to the roof at each corner, absent mindedly around lower windows. She marveled aloud at the flowers festively drooping over the edges of planters, "They're wonderful, their color warms the exterior."

The eyes of both families scanned the walls, the heat of its reflected energy warming all after a journey looking into canyons. Anh gestured as the car stopped, "Sophie mentioned it in a letter months ago, that stone building dates to Roman times. The vineyard and family olive grove cover fifty hectares."

Anh's face beamed as they exited the limo. She stretched, grateful for a safe arrival, then put her hand in the fountain as it burbled a soothing welcome. Fadia stood by the car carrying Bai and held Michael's hand, while Munirah clutched a tired Mahomet.

Amir helped the driver with luggage as the door opened. Anh rushed to the door, rapping energetically with an old brass knocker that glistened smugly on the weathered door where a small black ribbon hung.

Tooley extended his arms expecting a hug as he moved to the journalist from beside Anh, "It's great to see you."

Stefano stepped slowly into the sunlight, followed by Sophia. His face blanched, tears flowing down ashen cheeks. His body shook as he hid his face in his hands. Tooley and the others gasped, caught off guard by the emotional response. "What is it? What's the matter?"

Frightened by Stefano's behavior, the new arrivals stopped in midstep. "Our daughter just engaged, then a car crash." He stuttered, "Marta is dead. She is gone, killed in accident, two days after her engagement. They were hit by a truck and went over a cliff a week ago."

Stefano paused, tears painting his cheeks, "In the night I see her before my eyes. Sophia and I completely collapsed. We prayed to understand ... how could God take the daughter before the father or mother?"

Stefano's body quivered, "I lost my belief in God. I had been under fire from artillery and lived in fear of IED, saw death, yet here in Italy such a thing!" He lingered ... without uttering a word. "I stay here with Sophia. We felt so bad we could not tell you, the words too hard to say – her funeral but days ago. Please forgive us."

Sophia hugged her husband. He uttered a broken string of unintelligible, emotion filled words consoled by every face. Words finally emerged, "I try not to think of ... of Marta's death."

Sophia squeezed his hand, the others unable to interrupt their anguish, "Our world fell to pieces. I was consumed by Marta's death ... until Marcus told us, 'You must go on. Marta is gone, and I miss her, but we cannot bring her back by tears. We must look forward.' Our Marcus kept us strong."

Anh clutched Bai more snugly. "Our kids do that also; they pull us together with words that burst out without thought or restraint. Bai tells me often about God."

Michael, Mahomet, and Bai, too young for the loss to register, went inside, where Fadia, alone of the young, felt Marcus' lonely pain, hugged him and they cried together.

Munirah moved to and hugged her distant cousin, "Sophie, I'm so very, very sorry."

Chapter - 9

The two families trickled back to the Kingdom, the Ubaidi's there first by three years. Tooley, Anh and the kids had celebrated the Millennial in Paris before returning. The year was 2000, but back in the 'sand box' it was the 13th century, 1420 *Anno Hegira* in the Muslim calendar.

Tooley adjusted his new bifocals, the stylish progressive design that magically changed color in sunlight. He squinted nevertheless as he hugged his friend. "Slam and Lickem, I had to come here. It's my final tour, how about you?"

Amir snickered at his friends' abuse of a familiar Arabic greeting, "I am fine indeed." Then he broke his big news. "I was recalled to active duty - to serve 'in a time of need ... with pay as a

Lieutenant General.'"

Tooley quipped, "Like you need that rank or more money. Certainly not more money."

"I couldn't refuse the orders. You understand."

"I do. I understand orders. I was given a similar deal to return. I was reluctant considering what happened to us the last time."

The general looked at his friend with a smirk, "I understand, all those bullets and blood at *As Sulayyil*. This time it'll be, how you say, a piece of cake. A question - if you were to speculate, what do you think my recall is about?"

A three star ... probably running a weapons or missile program. "Lieutenant General, eh. As a betting man I'd say your recall has something to do with some missile or other, like the ones that almost killed us."

"Could be," Amir hedged, averting a clear answer.

"That sounds like a challenge. I like challenges."

Tooley tried to read his friends' face and body for any indicators of plans, "Remember what happened the last time you posed that sort of dare."

"Things are harder to figure out these days, given the passage of time. Now what was it I was talking about?" Amir chuckled.

"What will you do to earn your pay?"

"I'll defend us against the guys in the neighborhood, rattling their sabers again. I pray not more than that." Amir's smirk came and went.

"At least we don't have to worry about security here, like we did in Morocco. We were there for three years, had fun in Morocco. It has such great beauty, and the people there, so open and welcoming." Suddenly he showed unease at saying he wanted to be anywhere else, he looked at Amir, "Oops, sorry."

"Not to worry. I know Morocco has churches, wines, even a synagogue or two, surprising in a Muslim country. I'm certain you loved it there," Amir said. "There are even Jews, a few too, in the Yemen. Those countries are very, very different."

Tooley told Amir he saw this assignment as a twilight tour. "I want a really quiet job, away from bullets, to watch my kids grow up. I told Anh as soon as I'm eligible to retire we're out of here."

"You can go. I must stay. I will ease my way out of the Saudi military after we all figure out if there will be more shooting. Pray for peace."

Tooley paused. *Was there a deeper meaning in that?* "Being here is hard, not being able to take a photograph, hold my wife's hand in public, or worry about my kids saying the wrong thing near a *Mutaawah*. I'll be glad ... to get home."

I understand what you mean. My two year tour in Pakistan was two years too long. Munirah hated it there. Despite her education and wealth she felt herself treated like a second class woman."

"At least you have homes abroad," *and can move.*

It was the boys first sleepover in the Kingdom, at the O'Tooles villa in the Diplomatic Quarter. The pre-teens were busy discussing spies and plotting intrigues. Their play acting displayed youthful bravado that contrasted with their awkward feelings and thoughts.

"Ubaidi, Mahomet Ubaidi – I like my camel's milk stirred ... not shaken." Mamo said that repeatedly, struggling to say it with Sean Connery's Agent 007 accent, a base tone he struggled to achieve at his age.

The boys laughed uncontrollably and repeated it until Bai threatened, "You boys are hopeless, only lacking enough body hair to be gorillas. Stop it."

Bai chimed in, "I've read some Clancy and James Bond books. Spies are not about swordfights and shootouts; they're about observation and analysis."

The boys ignored her, alternately posed as Jedi warriors, spies, or pirates, slinking along in sneakers with the 'swoosh' emblem, changing their minds and focus as fast as a NASCAR drivers' speed shifting. They huddled, whispered, and then swaggered off to bother their fathers in another room.

They strolled in, arms across their faces as though they were hiding from facial recognition scanners. The boys blurted out a question that caught the dads by surprise, "Are you secret agents?"

Tooley took the challenge, "No. We're not, but we can summon Voldemort and assign you extra chores, so stop fixating on being spies."

As the evening's movie sleepover started, Mick asked Mamo, "Can you swim?"

"Yes. You don't have a pool do you?"

"No, but there is one on the compound. We can swim tomorrow. And we have a prayer rug in case you need one – for after eating Mom's dinners." They laughed and Mamo swatted Mick's shoulder. "Mom always has soup warming in a crock pot In case you're hungry. It's really good, and it goes with popcorn and movies."

"Got any new movies?"

"You mean like *Indiana Jones*? Yes, and I'm dying to see the first Harry Potter movie. When it comes out I'll get a copy. We'll watch it over and over 'til we know all the lines."

"Right. And Mick, I get to be Holmes next time," Mamo said.

"Then I get Holmes' detective cap and pipe." Laughter and snickers emerged as Mick adjusted an imaginary deerstalker hat on his head. "Hey, let's toss the ole pigskin around" he offered.

Mamo gave him a puzzled look, "You're kidding? Do I need to retrain you?"

"No, I wanted to pull your chain. Hey, does your school have any cool chicks?"

"You're kidding now. There are no schools here where boys and girls go together. Even men and women can't take classes together. It's very different from the countries we've been in."

"What does Fadia think of that, coming back here to stay, with the veil and all," Bai asked.

"She's only here this week, on vacation. She's going to school in Paris," Mamo replied.

Munirah edged into the conversation. "Fadia responded differently to returning. She refused to come to stay. She's nineteen and decided to stay in Europe after college, but promised to meet us in Lebanon. She said there'd be few trips to the Kingdom. She said 'Mother, there's no freedom, women are slaves in all but name. Mahomet can drive there but I must be driven. I can't even walk by myself. I can do so much there, nothing here.'"

Amir was troubled by his daughter's decision, but acquiesced; Munirah exalted silently. "My daughter has become a woman. She told her father something different in same direction. I heard her say ... 'Father, there are good men in Europe, even in Lebanon, perhaps one or two good Muslim men."

Fadia, home on a week's vacation, listened. Her face now had a coy look, suggesting more fun and exploration than her father intended. "I'll find out the actual number. I'll count them at the taxi station near my apartment," she grinned, "next to a dance club."

"Tooley, I even asked Munirah to stay in Lebanon with her parents. But she said 'No I can't do that. I belong here with you. We'll be safe. No one will trouble me.' I think she's right about her own safety. But I'm not sure about Fadia. She is young, like our sons. She'll be here later."

At that moment Mick hit the Play button and an *Indiana Jones* adventure began. Harrison Ford's adventures were already in motion, reminding the youngsters of different places and people, some magical.

Chapter - 10

Commander Nahari had supervised the building's construction five years earlier, unaware it was the start of a covert project. Externally it looked like a plain industrial structure, in the open on a well travelled part of the Saudi Navy base in Jubail. Technically the ugly block was a Harpoon Missile Maintenance Facility or HMMF. Its acronym, HUMPH, was one letter longer but easier on the tongue of engineers of many nations as they constructed it. Technicians would later perform maintenance and updates on missiles there.

Few noticed that construction years before; fewer still knew that Nahari had built a larger replica underground in *Al Kharj*. Beneath that innocent looking building labs had been busy for three years rebuilding two damaged missiles. Used in the attack on a Saudi Medium Range Ballistic Missile base, those shattered Israeli missiles had been meticulously disassembled. Now a Captain in the Navy, Nahari had taken Harpoon missile specs and upgraded them, adding range, maneuverability, and new warheads.

Nahari told General Ubaidi, "prospects for achieving all project objectives are mostly on schedule. A resized fuel tank, frame, and flight controls are nearing test." After the briefing, he said, "I need some help to finish the software."

"I have someone who can help. Colonel Khalid will join the

missile program. When will be convenient for you to meet him?"

Three weeks after Nahari briefed LG Amir on the *Sadeek* land attack missile program, Khalid arrived. As the elevator descended Nahari he thought about the schedule. The captain knew that *Ramadan* meant no food, beverages, or cigarettes during daylight shifts, resulting in weakened, lethargic workers. *Three more prayer calls and religious restrictions will go away and production will improve.* The fasting applied to him as well, but he knew his moodiness would resolve itself.

Nahari told another officer "ahead are tests of guidance units, JATO boosters, and a promising fuel additive, all critical parts of the program. I think we can regain schedule. At least we have six months slack, and I'm about to get help from Colonel Khalid Al Hassai. Do you know him?"

"No. ... Isn't that a Shia name?" The officer knew that Shias were typically not given real authority within the Sunni dominated military.

"Yes, but the general trusts him." He stressed the close relationship of the general and colonel, "Amir has a very personal interest; those missiles we've been resurrecting almost killed him years ago. We'll be meeting Khalid today."

Colonel Khalid told his mentor, "I failed selection to Brigadier. I must go." There was resignation in his tone.

Amir grabbed his friends' shoulder, "I know someone on the selection board, an influential member. I'll speak with him. Stay to help me. I need your help." He then informed Khalid of ongoing missile tests, "You get a briefing from Nahari in thirty minutes. Trust him; he's a good engineer."

"Good morning General, Colonel. I have an update on our missile program. Let me go over it." Nahari described how fuel tests at *Al Kharj* had accelerated recently. "We upgraded the curved ramps built to redirect F-15 engine at full thrust. The deflectors should obscure our experiments. The injection systems lower and disguise the temperature, and underground exhausts blend with those of fighter engines. They appear colored, extend the life of the structures, and obscure satellite identification."

Satellites observed and down linked data of the subsequent plumes, some meant to be seen. Techreps working at the base were told the colors resulted from chemicals injected to create air show displays. Base workers saw the rainbow hues and shimmering heat rising above test cells and gave them no second thought. It seemed natural for showboat aviators, whether Saudi or western, to display their peacocks plumage.

On the other side of the globe, a CIA analyst noted the colored plumes in his report. "The blue, red, yellow and orange flames were in the visible spectrum. The data is not typical of that expected from jet engines, but nothing seems suspect," he told his supervisor as he handed him the document.

The report went up the chain, arousing scant interest. The senior analyst found the story provided a plausible explanation and let the questions lie, "There is nothing to suggest we need to worry. The colors are due to fuel contamination."

A copy of the analysis was routed to the Riyadh Chief of Station, one Padrick Marcus Michael O'Toole. As Tooley glanced over the words, he felt a twinge in his gut. *What's really up? Are they using additives to add colors, or to do something else? I'll ask Amir.*

Nahari read the test report and turned to Khalid, "It won't be a problem with our missiles. We thought the exhaust could destroy them in flight, which proved unfounded. We were worried because one engine scattered in flight. *Sadeek* exhausts don't reach that temperature."

"I'm just an old infantryman; tell me what that means," Khalid asked.

"One fighter on after burner crashed when dust plated on its compressor blades." That remark raised an eyebrow, but no response.

Nahari then described using gold as a missile fuel additive.

Those comments triggered Khalid's interest, confirmed as he tabbed a page, "I'll tell General Amir; he'll be pleased." The Colonel looked up as he closed the report, staring at Nahari, "Is the software operational, our flight tests begin next month?"

"Our software, most of it, is in the final stage of testing and will complete in two months ... if all goes well."

"Two months … but will the software tests hold up C-130 flights?"

"No. The tests now deal with launch controls and warhead fusing." Nahari turned, "Colonel, if it is agreeable with you, I'll take over the software, while you control fuel and flight tests. I need to focus on the software so we can complete on schedule."

"Your idea of dividing the work between us works for me. That approach will speed up the schedule. I know a pilot crazy enough to fly with a missile under his wing." Khalid's fingers traced across the report again, and the corners of his mouth arched upwards, "I'll take charge of the flights as you suggest. I'm fascinated by this gold in the fuel. It is a clever way to increase range."

Nahari extended his arm and they shook hands. Weak in software practices, he wanted to immerse himself in the testing. As a good engineer he used pressure on coders and testers to keep software on schedule. While his budget was essentially unrestricted, there was little test time left to do the right things.

Ubaidi knew the proper methods to develop software, and wanted confirmation of their use in his *Sadeek* program. Amir thought back to those classes, sitting next to Nahari, and expected today's brief at *Al Kharj* to cover each step.

Amir glanced at process diagrams on Nahari's office wall, ones he and the captain had seen years before. "We make a good team, me the operator and you the engineer." They had learned the actual nuanced processes of weapons development, knew the dangers inherent in getting systems fielded, to the men who pulled triggers or pushed FIRE buttons. That was what counted.

Amir pointed to the wall, "Are we complying with those flow charts?"

"We are. We're keeping our team small, focused … and modifying US and Israeli code only in minimal ways."

"So you're finding ways to reduce the chances of bad software, and Khalid has the fuel flight tests?"

"Yes. The colonel is to take full control of the C-130 missile tests, while I do the same for software."

Ubaidi looked at the graph of Trouble Reports or TRs in front of him. "Captain, tell me about these 'minimal ways.'"

"General and colonel, what it means is we're leaving most Harpoon software unchanged, only adjusting the program for new maneuvers, extended range, and new warheads. All software issues are ranked by priority, with Safety at the top. We've had just 58 TRs to date; only one was for Safety. We are busy making sure things are right."

Tooley, surrounded by techreps, overheard casual but tantalizing remarks at a weekend BBQ at the compound. A growing feeling in his gut and those comments tipped him to something which caused a stir. That Intel convinced him Amir was reworking the very same missiles which crashed right in his face and almost killed them years before.

A new concern of far greater import emerged. He'd confirmed in a test document that this missile required two man controls. O'Toole knew the US used similar controls for nuclear capable systems, and knew the Saudis had Medium Range Ballistic Missiles. He *felt* they possibly had dirty bomb kits.

What did the requirement mean? The Saudi military had complex electronics that needed constant tweaking, but two man controls raised another level of concern. Such software controls implied *at best* that the missiles required MODA level launch authorization; that made them strategic weapons even if they turned out to be non-nuclear. *At worst* it was an 'Oh Shit.' The report forming in Tooley's mind would lay out all the implications. It was certain to raise eyebrows at Langley. *This is definitely hot info. Better dig more.*

He called the general from his cell phone, "Amir, I'm curious what happened with those Israeli missiles, you know, the ones that almost killed us," Tooley asked. "Let's meet."

As they sat at a coffee shop he casually scanned Amir, anticipating some facial tell, movement of hands, foot or body shifts, or disclosing eye motions as his queries continued. His friend's displayed no such signals.

"I suggested to MODA that they make them into a monument, sticking artistically out of the face of a traffic roundabout. I didn't get a warm response ... or a smile. But I thought it was a hoot."

Ubaidi had confirmed the Kingdom still had the missiles, but cleverly deflected knowledge of their condition, location, or use.

Tooley smiled, glanced at his friend, “If you build one – a missile, not a monument, launch it at that SOB who shot us. Just don’t tell anyone I said that.”

“I will if I get a chance, and I *won’t* say you gave me that order.” The generals’ serious face indicated intention, not humor.

Khalid mused about remarks he’d heard before the *Al Kharj* brief. He knew Quality Assurance procedures ensured the software coders worked to the specs and tested for compliance. QA audits of critical processes and plans frequently provided suggestions for operational sanity, but QA was present only when a customer had deep pockets and insisted.

Amir’s program had the necessary funding, and he knew the captain was a competent engineer. That inspired confidence. He looked up, “Nahari, I recall that auditors are rarely welcome. If a project lost funding, the first workers to be cut were auditors, followed by Independent Verification and Validation testers. Ensure the right methods are used to modify code, test and proof it as operational.” Nahari nodded agreement.

Khalid closed his briefing booklet, “I grew up on a farm.”

The captain stared at him, a puzzled look on his face. … “And?”

“I learned not to plow a field twice,” the infantry colonel said. “Don’t IV&V testers just redo tests with the same code, write up Trouble Reports or TRS?”

Nahari’s face became pensive, his brow furrowed. “I never looked at it that way.”

“And you’re confident that critical tests were OK and the TRs are insignificant?”

“Yes, so I see your point, don’t retest. That could save us months. Thank you.” The captain’s face beamed. *The general’s friend has really helped.*

Nahari added, “Colonel, I recall that most software projects don’t appreciate QA members glancing over their shoulders, but they never, ever forgot the operator. In any case I’m doing things the right way with the software. You have to ensure nothing is missing with your tests. I’m sure your pilot takes the same approach.”

“Yes. He’s a great pilot … and flying demands absolute confidence in a plane’s systems.”

Colonel Khuman witnessed the missile test at night, the unit strapped down in a lab, covered with sensors like a hospital patient undergoing an EKG. Those midnight hours by the colonels and the general followed the brief on software status. Base techies merely saw golden yellow flames ascending into the cool night air.

The test results verified the missile processed inputs correctly and hit all simulated targets. Khalid's face was confident; Khuman's sought reassurance. "Khalid, my first flight is in a week. Only when I fly it can we verify the tethered missile responds to the terrain. All this lab stuff is fine, but I need to fly the damn thing."

The aviator shook his head, "It will be scarier than that flight to South Africa." He didn't explain that comment and Khalid made a mental note to ask the general about it later.

Nahari ignored the remark. He knew the *Sadeek* flight test program was in the final stage, and worried his altitude was low enough to bother farmers. Khuman's face reddened, "Colonel, your flights coincide with activities planned to focus satellites elsewhere."

"How are you doing that?" the response confirmed his attention but concern remained on his face.

"We've circulated a story that your C-130 flights will map *qanats* using infrared imaging. We hope the flights will be written off as research. When we can, the flights will be scheduled during periods US satellites look elsewhere."

"I like that cover story. What are *qanats* exactly?" Khuman asked.

"They are underground tunnels." Nahari described the water networks dug by farmers.

"Khalid, doing these flight runs will not be easy. I can do it, and I think mapping is a credible cover. Water runoff data could optimize construction of well located dams and cisterns." Apprehension lingered on the flier's face.

Khalid, noted the pilot wringing his hands, "How difficult will the flights be?"

"Well, I'll be flying lower than I ever have, and doing what the software tells me. Flying a plane is not a kid's game. He rubbed whitened knuckles, "my life will be very much at risk. And along the way, as the terrain changes, I'll be using a *new* altimeter to fly *low*, barely avoiding Mother Earth."

"Is low altitude the question?" Khalid asked.

"Damn right it is, and having new software control my plane ... and my life. I must follow preprogrammed routes, so low I'll frighten camels. I must be ready to grab control at very scary altitudes, praying every mile to get home to my family in one piece."

Khalid smiled, "I have an idea." He paused, noticing sweat beading on the aviator's brow, "to keep you from crashing."

"Aviators don't like to crash; that's for sure," Khuman said.

It occurred to Khalid that few land surveys would actually be flown at 50 feet; that altitude limited the area being surveyed, and undermined the credibility of the cover story. "We should lie to the missile," Khalid suggested, "we can play with the altimeter; tell the missile under your wing it's flying at 50 feet ... while you fly safely at 200 or even 500 feet." Khuman's face brightened. Once more things were on track.

The general thanked Nahari and Khalid, then asked them to leave. As the briefing room door closed, he turned to the pilot, "Now tell me about your flight to South Africa."

Chapter - 11

That flight, it was two years ago, actually twenty-six months. I'll never forget what happened," Khuman looked at Amir, uncertain if he should discuss a clandestine operation, even with a lieutenant general he knew, "It was the most terrifying day of my life."

Amir looked at his colleagues' face, "Colonel, just to be clear, the plan for that mission was mine. I authorized and funded that undertaking ... well, actually Force Ten funded that flight."

The aviator wrung his hands, "It was a long time ago; yet I'm talking about it for the first time. Everyone on the Op was sworn to secrecy. It started out as a normal flight, even if it was across several countries, at night and below radar coverage. An hour before we were to take off, we loaded and filled two fuel bladders, and two armed ATVs. Then heavily armed commandos marched on board, guarding four small strong boxes with painted out labeling."

"I read the report of the operation, but much more went on that was not documented. Fill me in."

"General, I was comfortable with the extra fuel, but I hated having those ATVs onboard. They could break loose and disrupt my plane's stability. And those armed commandos made me nervous. My pre-flight brief covered just the route and little on the assignment. I'd never flown black ops before ... and we were flying a long, long way loaded for trouble. Even my plane's insignia was painted over."

"I expect you figured out what we were doing by the time you got back?"

"Yes. We flew to a clandestine airfield to meet a black market arms dealer and get some old missiles."

"That didn't all show up in the TOP SECRET report."

"Far more than that happened. When we landed, three armed pickup trucks surrounded my plane, blocking takeoff. We positioned ATVs and guards to provide our own security. The situation was scary as hell," the aviator said. He squirmed, sweat rolling off his brow despite the passage of two plus years.

"I thought we'd been set up, my plane would be stormed, and we'd all be killed. C-130s are a premium item on the black market and we were in a precarious situation. I nervously kept two motors running." Khuman's forehead wrinkled with anxiety, "Our men were confronting theirs. Takeoff seemed impossible and we were outgunned ... and I didn't have a clue what was going to happen."

"Go on."

"I figured out from our guards' comments that those boxes held gold as payment for missiles, air to air I think. They're the kind fighter pilots fire at another plane in a dogfight. We were surrounded by armed mercenaries, blocked in and carrying a pile of gold. And we were there to buy missiles which were old, decades older even than our fighter pilots. I was terrified."

"Those were entirely different missiles, but go on."

"Soon two trucks pulled up, old smoking US Army deuce and a half's. They parked near our cargo ramp. The drivers got out and unlatched the WWII trucks' loading ramps. At the back of each vehicle were twelve containers. I prayed those were our missiles. I mean, if those were missiles, we probably weren't going to be assaulted, robbed and killed. My fears subsided."

The general smiled, "Continue."

"But we were out in the boonies, buying ancient missiles on the black market. That was against all kinds of international arms transfer laws ... and I wasn't certain we'd make it out alive."

"Yes. I understand the sensitive nature of the mission."

"My crew chief, two crewmembers, and our escorts started moving containers up the ramp into the cargo area and securing them. Each weighed nearly 600 pounds and took almost the width of the cargo bed. The first dozen took almost an hour to load. My anxiety level was down from when we were first surrounded. There was still a chance some government unit would discover us, forcing a hasty departure."

The aviator rubbed his hands together, "We had turned over the gold by this time and were moving the final four missiles. Then all hell broke loose. One of the damn things ignited in the back of a truck. Parts of the container and missile parts blew all over the place. Fragments hit two of my men and the plane. The guards on one of the pickups nearby started firing into the tree line, thinking we'd been mortared."

"But you all made it back. Were any of your men injured?"

"No, but things got tense until we all figured out no one was shooting at us. The problem was a weird missile. We told the arms dealer we wanted reimbursement for the bad missile."

"Did he have more?"

"No. Apparently these were the last ones anywhere. They were temperamental, especially the rocket motors – susceptible to stray electrical charges. No one else seemed to want these old birds."

"We did," the general said quietly. "Did they end up giving you more missiles?"

"Not exactly. The arms dealer and his men huddled and talked. I saw them from the cockpit, but couldn't hear anything. Soon they sent one of their vehicles away. Ten minutes later it returned with wooden crates in the back ... four of them. Those four turned out to be old Zuni rockets. Those are smaller and unguided, and just as temperamental in terms of stray voltages."

"What happened then?"

He paused, as though trying to remember all the details. This was a general asking, so he had to be thorough, "As I recall, we loaded the Zunis, lashed them down, and hooked up the ground straps. My crew chief had patched up our wounded by then. None of their injuries were serious, and we were able to repair five holes in my plane."

"Was there any more excitement?"

"The Force Ten mission commander, with an AK-47 over his shoulder, walked over to confer with the arms dealer. They talked for what seemed an eternity, shook hands, and then parted. The officer boarded my plane. I lit off my other engines as the pickups roared off. Back to being in charge, I had my crew chief secure for take-off. He told me to get us the hell outa there."

"And that was it?"

"It was a long, long flight home. I was more mentally exhausted than I had ever been before ... or since. And it was all for some damn out of date missiles that were too unstable for fighter pilots to use. I wouldn't use the damn things!"

"Colonel, thanks for being frank. I'm glad you told me these things. They weren't in the official report, even the one I received. And don't worry about our pilots, those weren't Sidewinder heat seekers, but missiles designed to take out radar sites. Thanks to your help in getting them; they are being reworked now."

"They are being reworked ... why?"

Ubaidi shook the aviators' hands, "Colonel, thanks again for success in that Op. I have good people working on them."

Those missiles had shortened his life; he deserved an answer. "Who?" Khuman asked.

"My best people," the general responded, "but that's another story."

Chapter - 12

The final sleepover at the end of school term, before Fadia flew off in three days to 'the world,' was 'on.' She and Bai were comparing notes on classes, students, teachers, but mostly about boys. The young girl was enthralled and followed Fadia like a puppy whenever they were together. "Do you have a boyfriend?"

"Not yet, just a cute friend," the college girl replied. Fadia described him at length. Bai envied her cool twenty year old friend, unaware that Fadia was only home for a week. She'd been away at University, a very different world, and hated this place.

Bai filled her in, "Since your last visit even the names we call each other have changed. I call my brother Mick now, and Mahomet is Mamo. Mick used to call me Bye Bye, but quickly shortened it to Chao, like the Vietnamese and Italian greetings."

As Fadia watched, the boys walked in. They shuffled their feet, as if to assault their parents' ears. She observed them carefully, baby sitting two thirteen year old candidates for Ritalin before heading back to college. Fadia dubbed them M and M, the candy gang. They acted that way in her mind, alternately sweet and sour, as hormones made their lives a challenge.

When the boys got back to the Kingdom they were gangly. They had hair on faces, armpits, chests, and probably elsewhere as she now understood. Michael had slight Asian features and dark hair; Mahomet slender with the same facial shape as his sister. Mamo dressed in stained, frayed pants which cost extra, but he wanted the look of someone who had worn them for years.

Their attempts at looking cool diverged. Tee shirts were Mick's exclusive choice, the most frequent image Stonehenge. Mick thought they were 'cool.' His dad said they made him look like a mannequin from a Goodwill Store, while mom said his favorite hoody came from a bedu souq. It had.

M&M weren't hip or cool to their parents, but approached it with Fadia. It was the age when boys asked innumerable, unanswerable questions - why, why, why Mick asked. Why these clothes, why are there no churches, no movie theaters? 'Because' was the most frequent, but not the best response. There were so many cant's, do's and don'ts here. All his wanna dos seemed too hard, life suddenly strange.

M&M were intrigued by the separation of girls in Saudi society, that custom particularly puzzling to Mamo. "All kids are apart here. It is weird." Fadia heard the two term girls 'yucky,' but had noticed they checked them out at every chance. Fadia knew girls would also be checking them out from behind see though veils, unseen, giggling. She'd done it herself before she was immersed in western culture and freedoms. Now the young woman refused to wear a veil, a gesture of emancipation.

Tooley explained it to him once, after part one of 'the talk' on birds and bees. Mick said, "It's weird." *I have to see what Mamo's father told him, then ask Fadia.*

"Yup; you got that right." He turned and ended that day's banter.

Something of a family tradition emerged at breakfast the next morning. Bai saw her brothers' Eggos weren't buttered or dripping yet with syrup. She grabbed them off his plate, "Dibs."

This had become part of a standard contest between the two, fighting for attention or more cookies, whatever. Turkey bacon, not the real stuff, was a concession for their cousins.

"Chao, I wanted a normal sibling," Mick blurted out, "how come I got stuck with you?"

"Cause you're lucky, and so I can give you grief every day of the week," his sister responded. Chao's face grimaced with contempt, "Remind me why mom had you."

"She and dad had too much wine ... then they made a mistake."

"I vote they send you back."

"I hate you, dweeb."

"Ditto back to you."

He smiled, as did Fadia. Mamo then asked, "Waffles? I thought only Belgians ate those?"

"Nope, we do too, with strawberries and whipped cream on top. Want some?"

Ten minutes later, breakfast done, mom heard the inevitable sibling jibes. She gawked, separating the two hellions.

"Mom, if I have to walk a mile in Bai's shoes, or be inside her brain ... I'll go nuts," Mick stated. "There would be a fire storm inside me, like a tornado, filled with heat, noise and confusion."

"She can be a zombie at times; and when she opens her mouth weirdness comes out. She's not like you; you at least think things through before you blurt something out," then Anh corrected herself, "some of the time."

Mick chimed in, "You don't help or do your chores ... and you started it." Mamo laughed, but Fadia wouldn't be around soon for him to spar with.

Fadia spoke at last, "You two boys are like Bert and Ernie, or maybe a pair of Muppet Gonzos, whatever that is."

Mom smiled at Fadia's insight, while Tooley announced a plan to regain order, "Today we're going on a road trip ... destination the Riyadh Zoo. He mimicked grabbing a karaoke microphone on stage ... "its home to lions, and tigers, and zebras ... Oh my. Ducks, and pigeons, and pigs that fly." He gave an embarrassed look at their guests. "Well, not here."

Courtesy laughs came from Fadia and Mamo, real ones from Chao and Mick. Consternation initially spread on Anh's face, then she chuckled. *I can't wait to see when the next awkward remark will emerge from the lips of one of my three* kids.

Dad beamed at the prospect of the field trip. Mamo and Fadia told him they hadn't been to the zoo and were looking forward to the excursion. "We're going to see other animals" he said as he looked at his two. "Kids, I have a quiz. How many different critters can you remember and name?"

Mick broke the silence, "Chao, do you know how to tell boy zebras from the girls?"

Mom and dad glanced anxiously at each other. Did the comment mean 'the talk' about birds and bees had finally sunk in? They'd raised their kids in free range style, with careful guidance and aloof observation, only limited hovering. It showed all the time.

Bai had no response, but she hit back with a jab, "So what's your answer, Doofus?"

"You scan the UPC codes of their stripes, booger breath." The parental units almost gagged, but Bai looked puzzled.

"OK Sis, Rock, paper, scissors – to decide."

"Decide ... what?"

"Who's the dork?" He quickly made a fist and started, "Go!"

Bai won the confrontation and yelled, "Dork, dork, dork. Crawl back under your rock, rock, rock!"

Mom's responded, "Both of you, calm down right now ... or I'll get dad to inflict some real punishment. Let's gather our stuff and get on the road."

Finally at home, after admonitions at the zoo about cleaning his room, picking up his mess, doing chores, vacuuming the rugs, clearing the table ... and being nice to his sister, he'd had it. As his sister Bai, Fadia and Mom listened, Michael 'Mick' O'Toole threatened to run away from home.

Mom found dad in the living room, and told him of the plot, then packed Mick a lunch. She turned to 'the son,' "Are you taking your Harry Potter books?"

Mick looked to his twelve year old sister, expecting a partner for his rebellion, or at least encouragement. Bai's face was non committal. Mick thought about his plans to flee. Dad was a pushover, a softie. Mom was a dragon, and dad's role was to maintain peace ... and discipline.

Mick hesitated and checked out his mom's face - expressionless. He was sinking, the sky falling on him? "No, only the last one. Chao wants the rest of the novels."

Mom interrupted the train of the upheaval, pointedly asking, "Want some soup?"

"Only if there are cookies, mom," Chao replied.

A change of mind seemed to be forming in Mick's mind, but it required capitulation. *Stay out of the Dark Forest unless ....* "Mamo can't go, why should I? I don't have a car or a camel to escape on."

Bai went over to her brother. He expected a jab but got a hug, "I don't want you to run away."

Mick stared. *I thought I knew what she'd do. Must be her hormones, whatever the hell that means. I'll ask Dad, he'll know.*

Mom interrupted and brought her son back to earth, "Michael Nu-Win O'Toole, you're grounded."

He knew when he heard his full name things had reached critical mass. Mick hesitated and put his hobo bag away, uncertain what grounding meant.

Anh looked at her daughter's expression of one-upmanship. "Bai, cleanup your room before you say goodbye to Fadia. And no arguments, young lady."

The door bell rang. Munirah arrived with her driver to pick up her kids. Fadia embraced all before heading away to University, while Mamo hugged their cousins.

Chapter - 13

The plant visit had not been publicized, but was not a secret – except to its manager. The facility built Unmanned Aerial Vehicles for the British army. Basil Rathbourne, BAE's PM, was scrambling to put a good foot forward as a foreign delegation walked from a chauffeured Rolls Royce to his plant's entrance.

"Welcome gentlemen. We're happy to have you with us at our production facilities." He paused with a particularly awkward expression and addressed an obstacle, "Your request came through diplomatic channels and was quite ... vague. It requested a plant tour and presentation. We weren't informed of your requirement, why you wish to buy our UAVs. If you can help me understand your requirements, I will try to make your visit a success." Rathbourne continued to look puzzled, but was certainly willing to earn a commission on any sales.

Mohammed whispered to his aide, "Don't arouse any suspicion. We must be careful not to mention other uses with these people. We need discuss only the locusts, they will want to believe that image of a customer with lots of money anxious only to save crops from dreaded locusts. That will do the rest."

Hamid nodded agreement.

Mohammed, dressed in a western suit except for his country's traditional red and white checkered ghoutra, thanked the plant manager as he and his aide walked to the building. "I'm Mohammed Zafir, from the Ministry of Agriculture in the Kingdom of Saudi Arabia. My delegation apologizes for any misunderstanding. I am certain our Embassy's request informed your Foreign and Commonwealth Office of our needs." He shivered, pulled his coat close, and rubbed his arms. "In any case, I will explain our wishes after we get inside, out of this chilly wind."

"Yes of course," Rathbourne said as they moved inside. "We have prepared a short presentation describing the drones available for purchase, and a demonstration flight which we will view remotely." The manager led his guests past a Security checkpoint to a large conference room with seating facing a stage with large screen displays. He pointed to the side of the room. "We have refreshments ... coffee, tea, local bakeries on the buffet table. Please help yourself at any time.

… And a lunch is planned in our Executive dining room."

He thanked his host, "Let me tell a story to explain my country's needs. As a young man I saw them come, a black cloud and deafening hum. Locusts drowned out the sun. In two hours they devoured every blade of grass, wheat, every corn stalk for miles – anything which could sustain life. If we have drones to find them, then we can use bigger planes to spray chemicals to kill them. We desire to keep locust far away. This program is seen as best way to locate locust swarms before they fly from Africa. I have witnessed locusts fly up to 60 miles per day, up to 6000 feet; they darkened the sky. It was horrific sight I tell you."

He looked for acknowledgement in his host's face. To his relief recognition of a valid and supportable requirement appeared on the plant manager's face. *I have just told a big lie, but Allah forgives.*

Zafir shook the plant managers' hand, and then saw the UAV. Rathbourne began a briefing which described the Merlin as slides appeared on the screen behind him. He rattled off the UAV's wingspan, reliable 26 HP motor, and great operational record. "As you will see, it is launched from a truck by a single operator, and is recovered by parachute. A service package with field support is available." He pointed to the replica suspended above his head in the conference room, "She's a dependable gal."

"Can maintenance be done by regular control team?" the aide asked.

"Yes, of course. The engine has history of many thousands of hours of operation – with nil failures in flight. We'll witness a demonstration flight here in the conference room using remote hookup to the big screen display. All data from onboard sensors covering the drone's operation will be recorded."

Rathbourne motioned to a technician nearby and the display transitioned to show the launch team at the plant's field, preparing to start the engine. "You're about to see a launch."

"Please record the demonstration flight to help me, how you say, sell the program as part of the Five Year Plan of the Ministry," Zafir asked. "I must convince my department to do this."

"We need detection package," the aide added, "to find these pests, find among birds, clouds. We have many *schmaal.*"

"Pardon," interjected Rathbourne, "what is a … *shmawl*?"

"It is what we call a sandstorm. It can block out the sun for hours ... like locust."

The manager responded to the thought of a bonus forming in his mind, "We have different sensors, radar, and infrared that will meet your needs."

As the large screen showed the launch, Zafir asked to no one in particular. "How high do they fly, your drones? I understand locusts can swarm up to ten thousand feet." He whispered to his aide, "The Israeli version flies up to fifteen thousand feet. Their engines are more quiet, but give off same heat image as ours will."

It was a singularly accurate business fact that the proposed UAV, designed to find locusts, would have the same engine, control system and heat signature as the Merlins used by British and Israeli militaries.

Chapter - 14

Fourteen months previously, weapons engineers gathered at the *Al Kharj* directorate to consider ideas about tank ammunition. The initiative which generated the March 2004 meeting had festered for months in the mind of Colonel Khalid, the meeting's coordinator. He recalled a casual remark by a fellow graduate student years before; it was a subterfuge which influenced a critical WWII battle.

American Rangers had parachuted into occupied France, rendezvoused, and then hoofed it to a German ammo dump. They weren't tasked with blowing it, but to pull a fast one on Fritz. The ammo they carried, captured German rounds had been disassembled, then reassembled. If Axis units fired these shells, their mortars, anti-aircraft and artillery pieces blew apart. The explosions were few. Enemy gunners Hans, Emil and Gottfried became reluctant to fire, a serious morale issue. The newly cautious krauts supported a front where an Allied offensive needed an edge.

Around the table experts discussed a similar scheme with a select group of Saudi combat veterans. "The central question," Khalid stated, "is this; if we remanufacture some 105mm tank rounds, would an enemy gunner use them?"

A colonel in the tank corps, known for a keen engineering mind, responded, “Possibly, depending on the tactical situation. If the rounds were anti-tank ones they will. Sabot rounds are the first to be expended. When you’re out of them and facing other tanks, you’d better be ready to retreat – or die.”

“A minute please for an old infantry man,” Khalid interjected, “What is a sabot?”

“A sabot is a plastic insert surrounding a high density, dart like projectile. In flight the insert comes apart, separates from the dart. We call the whole round, the powder case, projectile, and the plastic part a sabot. Is that understandable?”

“Yes. We’ll take anti-tank rounds, change them to give our tankers an edge,” the infantry officer suggested.

The armor officer’s face lightened up, “You could redesign the powders which propels the projectile when it’s fired. It’s a pretty standard mix, but if you change the mixture of components.” He explained another idea, altering the components.

“Wow. That could work. Any more ideas?” the meeting director asked as he looked around. Seeing no participants eager to offer a suggestion he turned to an aide, “Begin immediately.”

Ubaidi years before had marveled at Fourth of July fireworks in the US. Amir the business man saw the profit potential. He contacted Innocenti Displays from Florence, which provided those fireworks. His fax had been straightforward, all about potential business, “I wish you to design fireworks for the King’s visits to major events and ceremonies. I envision displays to launch and burst at between one hundred and one thousand feet. The colors must be brilliant. Can your firm do that?”

Isabella Innocenti looked over the fax dated June 2004. The request came to her desk the week before. She responded to the queries. Now she was in Bahrain meeting with the wealthy Saudi. “Certainly. I look forward to the challenge, and your business. We can make displays for your King’s visits, camel races and other events in the Gulf region.” Business was in the air and it meant euros.

Head design engineer of Innocenti Displays, she also marketed her family’s fireworks throughout Europe. She extended her hand and a business card with contact data in Firenze, “I can modify a display I did for Bahrain's Sheikh. It set off fireworks for the inauguration of the causeway from Arabia. I can design for how high the displays ignite, and how fast the car will be going."

Amir turned her business card in his fingers. He knew Italian manufacturers made lots of Euros selling such fireworks around the world. They discussed a deal, and over a handshake became partners in a joint venture. Rough requirements were drawn up to trigger displays from ground level up to a thousand feet. The business plan called for sales throughout the region.

"My name and business contacts will open doors in the Gulf States," Amir said. "Our first effort should be a sales pitch to the Bahraini Ceremonies Department. If you agree, my lawyer can draw up the required permits, controls of formulae, storage of components, and fax you a copy this week. I'll also set up a plant in *Al Kharj*."

"That would be fine," Innocenti chimed in, "*Bellissima*."

"Can you design displays using radio controls?"

"Yes, we can work out any controls needed." Isabella smiled, "What colors would you like?"

"Greens, blues, reds, yellows, and brilliant whites."

"We can do those. We have the full pallet of colors you require - greens, yellows, whites, reds. We can even do blues. Are they used in this region?" she queried.

Amir chafed at the inference to the color of Israel's flag, but this was business.

It was the start of another hot day and grounds keeper Kafir Bakroglu saw a stray bit of paper in the hedge. His work area was outside a building in Ashdod that he suspected housed some Israeli intelligence organization. But a job was a job, and such possibilities were *mafee mishkillah,* not a problem. He walked over, picked up the paper, and placed it in the refuse bag hanging from his shoulder.

His eyes glazed over with excitement. In the hedge he saw what might be a treasure to make his grandson happy. The faint glint of a tall wire antenna had caught his eye. It was from an RC car, the type his grandson would love, but older. It was green with mottled brown stripes and blended with the shrubbery.

He looked cautiously around to ensure no one was watching. If they saw him he wouldn't be able to put it away and retrieve it later.

He quickly bent down and put it in his collection bag. The RC car was far heavier than one he'd priced just weeks before. *Perhaps it has a bigger motor, or better batteries. Probably older in any case.*

He walked to the bin by the lake one hundred feet away and emptied his treasure into the container, his back to the building. Bakroglu called his grandson, knew the boy would be ecstatic. "I found a special toy for you. I'll come back later and retrieve it, bring it by in two weeks." *I hope I make others happy with my cleanliness.*

Chapter - 15

The Riyadh Chief of Station welcomed the Italian journalist to his embassy office. The sign on the door read Cultural Attaché. Both knew the job had a different function – gathering Intel. "Stefano, it's great to see you again. How are Sofia and Marcus? I haven't seen them since we visited your home in Tuscany."

"My family is fine. Marcus is studying sculpture, and Sofia is an 'artiste' now."

"And how are you?"

"I stay busy. I was depressed for months after Marta died." He stammered, "Sorry, I don't talk of it."

"How did you get over the depression and pain?" Tooley asked awkwardly.

"Marcus took me to our village, got me how you say ... plastered. He told me to get on with life, not forget I had a wife ... and a son. That cleared my head. He gave me the will to go on. How is your family?"

"Anh is full time at King Khalid Hospital, back where we met. The kids are doing well in the Diplomatic School, learning French, Spanish, discovering the opposite sex, and becoming smarter than their parents. It sounds like your Marcus is quite popular. Say, let's get some lunch."

The two walked to the cafeteria for lunch and ordered Reuben combo plates; both chose iced tea. They moved to a table away from the noise of the food counter and sat. Tooley moved the fries on his plate, stared at his sandwich.

Stefano looked at his Reuben, "It has been months since I've had American food. I love these."

"After this is over I want to go home, and run a news bureau office in Florence, be with family." Then Stefano thought about the other cousin's family, "How are the Ubaidi's?"

"Amir is off doing something, probably classified, and no doubt will make another couple of million in business deals. He is into many things. Fadia lives in Paris; Mamo spends a lot of weekends with my Mick."

A smile crept across Tooley's face. He gulped a swig of tea, washing down a bite bulging with sauerkraut, "I'm glad you're here. Your reporting might influence public opinion towards peace."

"The news agencies took a chance on me after I got sober. They shuffled me to hot spots everywhere, Chechnya, Kosovo, up in the hills with Kurds. I was very careful; I didn't want to appear as though I was gathering Intel. That revelation would have meant certain death. Now I go to find out what is happening in Iran-Iraq. Over the last year friends told me of many changes there."

"What did they say?" Tooley asked.

"Colleagues said protests started in both capitals over border disputes. Soon each navy and customs service impounded boats along the coast. There were bombings of houses and market places, but not connected to events at the border."

Tooley paused chewing on his sandwich half, sauce dripping out, and put it down, "I hadn't heard that before." *But read it in numerous reports.* "Go on."

Stefano squeezed a lemon slice into his tea, "Many Iraqi bases are very active. The big base at *Al Taqaddum* has new long runways; more hangars; reopened barracks; and enlarged ammo bunkers. Most worrisome, both militaries activated reserves last year. But at least no one has declared war."

"Why all these moves towards war? Is it because of nationalistic TV and radio?"

"Yes, to a degree. Iraq and Iran fought years ago and I've seen great changes during my news group stints. Iraq is still rebuilding; run by Shias now, kin to those that control Iran, yet also despised by them. The Iranians consider Arabs uncultured camel herders. There is much hatred from earlier. Peace is in place, but not trust."

"I heard much the same. I understand the people in those countries are war weary, yet want a war." O'Toole tapped nervously on the table, "I can't imagine that, or how the Romans went off to war for centuries on end?"

"It was an endless thing, like here. Could it ever change? We can only hope. It will be eye opening going back to that region. I've seen torture and death up close in many places. Some nights I can't sleep." The Italian fidgeted, stirred another sugar packet into his tea, "Now I'm back. I have just an overnight in Saudi, then I'm off to Iran. I'll get to see Iran and Iraq in quick time."

"Hopefully things will be different," the American predicted, "It may not be quiet though, as you will be with military ... embedded right?" O'Toole played with the salt shaker as though forming a question, concerned what the future held for Stefano.

"Things seem to be moving towards regional rearming and CNN wanted someone with background. All those horrors seem so long ago. I left, but now I'm digging in before another armed confrontation. My boss told me ... 'You do good work, are experienced, and can be trusted. We need you there, telling us what the hell is going on, to keep things from going sideways.'"

He looked curiously at O'Toole, "I didn't know what sideways meant, so I asked; but I didn't get an answer."

Tooley's brow furrowed as he twiddled his thumbs, leaving the question rhetorical.

Lacking a reply, Stefano continued, "They'll screen what I see, and censor every word I say - everything I'm sure. There will be military around my cameraman and me all the time. I hope they'll be less stringent than we expect, but we won't know until we are embedded."

"I recall in Vietnam that journalists could go anywhere, say anything. What they filmed we saw get to TV or the headlines in a day. The military had no control. Now governments want to control everything you see, every word you say. With military around at all times, that says something all by itself. It tells me that there will be war." *I hope like hell I'm wrong.*

"CNN told me embedded reporters will report without censorship. I doubt that openness exists. I'll let you know." He sounded like he wanted reassurance, "You know, I think this embedding thing, it's just a way to control the news." *Both militaries have cell phone jammers.*

"I think you're right there." Tooley said without conviction, "Remember, we're on the same team, but I'm not sure you'll get to tell the truth."

"Same team, but you're safe here." Stefano paused and raised his palms, open in apparent prayer, "and I'll be off in a potential war zone, a target."

Tooley tried to put a positive twist on the anxiety, "Look, despite being a foreigner infidel, I'm sure you'll stay out of crosshairs. You're good at your job. You have the skill to build rapport with a private or a general, and discover a military unit's movements or morale. Just don't get hooked on the graphic stories you capture so well." He trusted Stefano to find out what others sought to hide ... what the US wanted to know.

"I worry about dying, and if you'll be in the office when I need help. You can help. Give me a contact or two ... and a secure phone. If the balloon goes up, you're the only one who can summon the cavalry."

"Stefano, about the cavalry, they'd be hours, days away ... if at all. You're really on your own. Here's what I need to know -both Iran and Iraq have been procuring Scud missiles for a year. I have no Intel to confirm where the missiles are, and whether they're fixed or mobile. If you could confirm that and let me know where they are it would be extremely helpful."

"If I find out where they are I could phone you. I'll say 'Yada Yada' to confirm location and if I identify the rest I'll include 'Yada Yada Yada' in the sentence.' Would that work?"

"That's a nice touch. Here's a mobile; there's a microchip inside that will cause the thing to self destruct if you don't sign in correctly and scan your thumb. It's a single user device with serious encryption. Use it only to call me. ... And stay safe."

"Thanks." He turned the phone over in his hands, "Keep me in your prayers."

Chapter - 16

Colonel Khalid, squirmed in his chair and closed the Infiltration Susceptibility Report. "This is troubling."

Jubali nodded agreement. There was a knock on the door, and the two watched as the units' officers and NCOs straggled in. Force Ten's senior NCO entered, walked to the front of the room, and barked, "Attention on deck."

All rose as Lieutenant General Ubaidi strode to the podium. Colonel Khalid looked at his mentor, puzzled. Amir asked all to sit ... except for Khalid, whom he asked to 'step front and center.' "I am here to share welcome news. Congratulations, *General* Khalid."

Ubaidi walked to Khalid and presented his comrade a letter of promotion. He pinned on new rank insignia and the shoulder boards of a brigadier general, "You've deserved this for some time." Raucous applause rippled through the room.

Touching his old friends' right arm, he quietly shared the story of bribing the promotion board. "My recording of the bribe is leverage for future use." The room cleared quickly leaving two generals and Jubali to talk ... of spies.

"Spies will try to infiltrate Ashrah. They know of the missiles, our *Sadeeks*. They can do great damage, and we've become a threat. So, how can we detect infiltrators?" Jubali asked.

"The easiest way will be to screen new recruits, start with new ones, rather than seasoned veterans," Amir suggested. "Our vets have long service histories and can be ruled out. We can improve our interview process; pose uncomfortable questions which force open answers." Make them uncomfortable; create stress and observe their reaction.

Khalid directed Jubali to put on track another way to identify 'infiltrators,' "Let's implement screening of suspects using chairs fitted with sensors to detect changes in blood pressure, temperature, and heart rates."

"I'll assign my aide to do that. A few eventually might emerge. And eventually all recruits must be more thoroughly screened." Jubali nodded agreement.

"That approach looks good as a start," Jubali asserted. "One of our NCOs suggested we get someone from customs. He thinks their personnel, skilled in psychological profiling, can train our men to quickly assess recruits."

Ubaidi banged his right hand on the table, his tone implying urgency, "Try as many ways as you can, sort out what works."

Khalid closed a personnel file, "Colonel, that's a great idea. We can't afford a traitor in our midst. Maybe we can find software that does this."

"General Amir knows several companies coding such software," Jubali said. "He says if we buy the package we can start using that in four weeks, after some training."

"That's too long to wait," Khalid replied. "We started systematic screening to detect infiltrators two weeks ago. We checked recruits' speech patterns, inflection, and dialect for inconsistencies with identified homes, and to assess each individual's behavior against tribal norms. No suspects have emerged yet. Do we need to call on Major Hourani's special expertise; her experience training Israeli snipers gives her special insight."

"Yes, general," Jubali paused, hesitant.

"Thank you. I have another meeting, so I'll let you get on with this," Ubaidi rose to leave, then he added before checking his watch, sitting again. "Are there other behaviors of infiltrators we should anticipate, discover, and control?"

The colonel keyed the intercom and summoned Hourani.

She entered and sat. "Colonel, you asked me to identify any unusual recruits who may not be what they seem. As examples, some might excel or perform poorly in military drills. Those behaviors might imply something different, like prior experience, or deceit. I have two recruits in mind, but I must check further to be certain." Her statement hinted at progress despite uncertainty those individuals were traitors or merely klutzes.

Khalid glanced at Hourani, "We have another way to interrogate infiltrators. It's a cistern with sound, vibration, and body sensors to detect reactions to questions. We take a suspect, put him in, and analyze how he responds. Do you think it will work?"

"I don't like torture," Hourani noted, "it seems a poor choice compared to the biometric chair idea."

Jubali concluded, "The most certain method to verify if suspects are spies is to catch them communicating. If we detect them it will probably be as their satellite flies over. My bet is they use cell phones. The governor agreed last night to let us use the Province Signals Intercept Unit."

Khalid told the colonel, "Ensure our NCOs and officers don't discuss intercepts with recruits. We must find out how they communicate."

Ubaidi checked his digital watch, "I have another meeting." Suddenly his face transformed, "Could it be their watches?"

Jubali's face brightened, "Yes, it could. That technology requires messages to be uplinked when a satellite flies over. The van can intercept any signal and get a location when they transmit."

Chapter - 17

Three days later the intercept van confirmed use of microburst transmissions. "I was told the message was after taps," Jubali said. "The burst transmissions were in the ultra high frequency band. Their messages have weak encryption, but a pattern of signal times. We'll set a covert watch in the barracks to discover unusual late night behavior."

Khalid swore, *Yelann*, dammit, "The signal overlap suggests more than one infiltrator. We *need* to identify them."

One infiltrator, Ahmed Baladi, was identified that day. He misidentified which dates grew in his home town, and was rushed to the clinic. He'd become disoriented from eating a meal of dates with other recruits. His abnormally low blood sugar suggested he wasn't a Saudi, whose sugar levels were typically high enough to kill others. The doctor diagnosed the symptoms and treated Baladi, terming the abnormal response 'most curious.' When arrested, Baladi was wearing a distinctive digital watch.

The colonel examined the watch, then ordered analysis of its function. "If we discover more recruits with such watches we have proof of their status."

Of two other suspects, Kareemi al Khali and Barak al Hassab, the former seemed too skilled at tactics and weapons use; the latter was suspiciously weak in those areas. Hourani thought they were hiding skills, or lying. The suspicions focused her efforts. “I have a feeling about Al Khali. Ask him some questions while he’s in a biometric chair. How does it work exactly?’

“We ask a series of questions,” Jubali started off, “while observing the reactions. We compare heart beat, blood pressure, and other responses to expected norms. Abnormal responses may confirm, or at least give an idea of something unusual.”

“Interrogate Private al Hassab first,” Hourani suggested.

The subject reported to the training center’s conference room, was seated in a biometric chair. His demeanor didn’t suggest he suspected ulterior motives. His responses to questions were observed and recorded in the adjacent room, where Hourani watched.

Hourani froze the frame of the video of the interview. She then selected others, zooming in on al Hassab’s neck. He had been fiddling with his collar and something was now visible.

“Arrest him,” she whispered over a mouthpiece, then added, “I recall his tattoo from when I stood over him sighting in. He was a sniper trainee years ago.”

Jubali tapped his ear piece as he sat in the interview room to acknowledge her update.

Hourani lifted the phone, “Security, send two armed guards ASAP.”

Al Hassab sensed something unwelcome and fidgeted in his seat. His heart rate sky rocketed as did his blood pressure. His eyes scanned the entrances and the colonel.

Hourani whispered over her mouthpiece to Jubali. “Colonel, al Hassab is a former Mossad trainee. I’ve called guards. Have them restrain him until we decide how to proceed. I believe he is Daoud Tashoom. By now he’d be an officer or senior sergeant.”

Jubali gave a Thumbs Up as he looked at the mirrored glass. He turned to face al Hassab as two armed NCOs entered. The colonel motioned to the guards and spoke, “Daoud Tashoom, I believe that’s your name. You are under arrest. Do not resist.”

Al Hassab rose to his feet, clenched his hands as his face reddened. Both guards drew pistols and chambered rounds. Jubali addressed the prisoner, “If you force us, we *will* shoot you.”

Tashoom swore in Arabic, then muttered *Ben Zona*, sonofabitch in Hebrew. He was handcuffed as more guards arrived. The spy was led off to solitary.

Hourani joined Jubali in the conference room. The two officers gazed at the large digital watch which had been on Tashoom's wrist. Hourani questioned, "Where do we go from here? We're still scrambling to identify them before they cause big trouble. I suggest we hold a unit meeting early tomorrow to discuss the arrests" she recommended.

"Good idea, Major," Jubali said. "Arrange that, and good job remembering that tattoo."

"Thank you sir. Now we can screen for identical watches. Before the meeting we should interrogate those two in biometric chairs, watch their reactions. Maybe we can find a way to play one against the other?"

The information of a meeting spread quickly to all recruits. By taps all knew the next day's schedule had changed, with no explanation.

A coded targeting message was microburst after 22:30 that night. Decrypted at Mossad's signals room, it read: BREAK. URGENT TARGET 50 METERS EAST LAST GPS POSIT THIS XMTR. 03 SENDS. BREAK.

Khalid's brow furrowed as Jubali spoke. "General, the van intercepted another signal last night. Lieutenant Badr told me of it after midnight. We have another traitor, and he's probably aware we caught his comrades."

"Colonel, let's take care of this matter at the unit meeting," Khalid said.

"Yes, but we could make things worse," Jubali worried aloud. "We don't know what was transmitted."

Khalid grinned, "Perhaps it was a pizza order."

Jubali grinned, then shook his head, "I don't think so. How do we control the meeting, some simple change perhaps – in case?"

"How about moving our meeting's location?" Khalid proposed.

"No. We have no other place large enough ... and we need to see if others have the same watch. I have an idea." Jubali explained it.

"That sounds workable. Do it!" Khalid's smirk disappeared. *Will this work?*

Chapter - 18

Two weeks earlier Israeli Intel identified Samir Jabari as the new head of Hezbollah, days after his predecessor died mysteriously. Israel's satellite and Intel units' data mining finally located Jabari's phone in Army sector 28, of Lebanon. The Mossad watch officer turned to the technician, "Unlock his conversation."

The intercepts technician adjusted the decryption parameters and smiled, "Target Alfa just called his wife on his cell phone. He told her 'I'll be home in an hour for dinner.'" Jabari's location was plotted on a street map. The plans meant he'd cross *Shukan bin Shukan* Bridge at roughly 15:45. He'd just signed his death certificate.

"Confirm the intercept." The tech dialed Jabari's cell phone, spoke softly in Arabic. The number and order was believable enough, his voice on the phone polite. "I'd like to order baklava, *khubz,* and *hummus* for a party of twelve."

The reply was curt. "*Majj Noon*. You have called the wrong number."

The technician apologized, "A thousand pardons." He smiled and hung up, *Crazy one indeed. We gotcha you bastard!* He checked the car's predicted route, then phoned a description of Jabari's car and ordered road blocks to funnel it onto Such and Such Bridge. Two agents moved into place to ensure that car drove alone across the span.

Twenty minutes earlier a section of two Israeli F-16s had scrambled. They were now orbiting overhead at fifteen thousand feet, in anticipation of this very mission. Earlier the mission leader had checked in. "STORM SIX THREE TWO on station with ONE SEVEN at Angels ONE FIVE." The response acknowledged their location and mission.

"SIX THREE TWO, your target using signal freq One Two, enroute Such and Such Bridge. Advise when you hold target signal."

Two clicks on the radio confirmed the targeting order. SIX THREE TWO radioed his wingman, "Lock and Load."

"THREE TWO has a visual on target." Wingman ONE SEVEN powered up his laser designation system and a spot of intense light appeared on the car's roof. The dot remained there, stabilized despite the relative movements of the car and the aircraft illuminating it.

The section lead selected the target's returning laser signal and his missile's seeker synced with the reflected light. LOCK and SYNC buttons lit bright green. Beneath his right wing a Maverick missile packed with 130 pounds of explosive passed its pre-launch checks.

He keyed his radio and his head phones screeched. "SIX THREE TWO, seeker acquisition confirmed."

"SIX THREE TWO, you are WEAPONS FREE."

"SIX THREE TWO is RIFLE." The missile rocketed away and homed on the Mercedes.

The terrorist saw the flash of a missile launch above and yelled "Stop. Get out of the car." Doors open, with driver and Jabari struggling to exit, the car disintegrated as the missile detonated. A fireball spread out across the old bridge as bits of terrorists and a luxury automobile splashed across the structure and tumbled to the creek below. A burning tire rolled to a stop twenty feet away.

"This is SIX THREE TWO. Target terminated, returning to base."

The co-pilot keyed the plane's intercom, "Good shooting champ. That was easy. When we get back I'll have the crew chief paint a car on the side of the fuselage." The planes banked and headed to home plate.

"Well ... no one was shooting at us, and the bad guys bought the farm." The pilot's voice softened, a tone of apprehension mingled with bravado. "It might not happen so easily our next mission."

Chapter - 19

Al Khali and the other recruits listened as barracks speakers announced fallout outside for an urgent meeting. Then sergeants yelled to muster in company order. Mustering NCOs reported "All present or accounted for" to the Company Commander after all fell in, and dressed right.

As he formed up in the second platoon, Al Khali looked around cautiously. He didn't see his friends in their platoons, and NCOs from the weapons range surrounded the company, under arms. Al Khali's gut twinged. Something seemed wrong, very wrong.

"Attention to orders!" The Company Drill Sergeant barked out. He read the day's routine with schedule adjustments, which now included a unit meeting. The platoons marched off quick time, then double timed to the training center. As they returned to normal pace and halted, all were energized, sweaty, and breathing fast.

Officers and NCOs, hastily summoned, had gathered moments before the meeting. Jubali summed up their orders, conduct musters, search barracks, and placement of armed guards. All were to observe recruits for a digital watch. He held one up, "Like this, it'll be worn by a spy. Be careful!"

Above the units leaders was a scalloped ceiling hung with *bedu* rugs and tribal *ghoutras*, the male head covering. Saudi provincial seals adorned the walls, reminding recruits of duty to country and tradition. "Several biometric seats," he told them, "are in use to detect body temperatures, heart rates, and anxiety levels. They must not be mentioned to the recruits."

Jubali glanced around the room, thought of the security cameras concealed unobtrusively by *Bedouin* artifacts. He whispered to Hourani, "Our video system, have it recording before they enter." She nodded and walked to the control room.

Outside in the midday heat, the recruits stood at ease in ranks. These gatherings were examples of the Same Ole Shit, hurry up and wait, and they pondered the eternal question of every boot, What The Fuck, or WTF Over? The men overheard guards being directed not to let any recruits in the room yet. *More of the SOS!*

The Fucking New Guys' adrenaline was pumping, their situational awareness frenetic as they noticed more armed guards. First there had been the new schedule, then this hastily called meeting, then armed guards, and finally two men, reported as not present, but accounted for.

At last the FNGs were marched to the far entrance, told they'd enter there. Al Khali's eyes widened at this direction. He knew missile targeting was now way off. His message gave an aim point fifty meters east of the watch's last GPS position. He thought all would enter the western door. That entrance was at least 100 meters from where they actually lined up. *They changed where we'll go in.*

As ordered, each squad entered this furthest access, their names checked against muster lists. Al Khali bent down near a seat to retie his left boot. He quickly retrieved his digital watch out of a pocket and slid it under the end seat cushion. He calmly retied his boot and moved casually to his seat.

Armed guards entered the room and moved to flank each door, their expressions displaying uncertainty. Other NCOs began barking orders, telling the recruits by squads to stand for a visual check if a digital watch was on any wrist.

Al Khali's pulse and heart rates escalated. *The guards are looking for some type of watch.* His shirt dampened. Al Khali's eyes flitted around the room, attempting to find a way out, past the guards.

His concentration was interrupted as the Senior NCO on stage shouted, "Listen up ladies."

A figure strode to the podium, and paused. All eyes were on the older, unfamiliar officer. "Men, I'm Colonel Jubali, Deputy Commander. I'm sure you want to know why you're here." The colonel looked around, made eye contact with each guard, and directed them loudly, "You guards, stay alert. No one leaves."

The recruits singularly and collectively squirmed in their seats, looked nervously at each other, and then at the guards' assault rifles and side arms. Biometric chairs in the room recorded the accelerated heart and breathing rates of those sitting in the seats.

The colonel continued, spoke slowly, emphasizing each word. He described the capture of two infiltrators, now under guard and being questioned. His eyes glared intently as he scanned each row of recruits. "If one of you is an infiltrator, surrender. You'll be imprisoned, exchanged later. If you wish to be shot as a spy, do not." Jubali doubled his fists and slammed them on the podium, "This is clear, we *will* find you."

Jubali smiled at the men cowered before him, like he was a hungry shark about to make lunch of a single tuna in a school, and he knew the spy among them lacked shark repellent.

The watch's position signal had been interrupted when Al Khali entered the earth sheltered training center. The OFFEQ satellite tracking the GPS signal registered the interruption, and transmitted a pre-arranged signal to STORM ZERO ONE SEVEN, the assigned launch aircraft. There a missile warmed up, it's Built In Test or BIT checked all flight parameters, and reported readiness to the pilot.

With a Launch order in effect the pilot activated the missile beneath his wing. It dropped free, lit off, and streaked ahead and down to its pre-programmed target. ZERO ONE SEVEN radioed BRUISER, code for launch of that missile, then altered course to return to base.

The US satellite in geosynchronous orbit above the region witnessed the Israelis launch a missile towards Jordan. As technicians at the NORAD facility followed the missile entering Saudi airspace. An alarm flashed on the Cheyenne Mountain status board. The colonel on watch saw the flashing red Alert, pushed a red button on the speaker console, and was connected to the National Military Command Center.

"General," Colonel Jacobs said as he spoke to NMCC's Duty Flag, "We've got something hot you need to be aware of."

"What is it?" General Davies asked.

"The Israelis air launched a missile. It went through Jordan and is now in Saudi airspace," Jacobs said in a monotone.

"Do we know where it's headed?" Davies queried.

"No sir. Could even be Iran, but its projected track suggests somewhere in Arabia. Check it out." Jacobs held up three fingers, "on video screen three."

Davies looked up at the monitor as the track history flashed and updated. "Damn. The Head Shed needs to be aware of this. I'll get my ass reamed if they're blindsided." He selected the red button for the Situation Room in the White House, gave the military officer there a migraine with this status. *A hot time in the old town tonight. What's the target?*

Chapter – 20

Israeli satellite images had given precise targeting for the bases' bunkers, barracks, helo pad and control tower, mess hall, underground fuel tanks, and covered vehicle buildings. The missile now enroute sought none of those, just the structure where the units' entire leadership and one recruit company was at this very moment. The missile flying through *wadis* to the room was not a bunker buster. It was, however, designed to penetrate a buried command post, and explode within, killing a hypothetical unit commander and his entire staff. That was the plan.

Moments before the meeting was to end the missile struck. It penetrated ten feet of sand and exploded. The point of impact was roughly one hundred fifty feet from the eastern entrance.

The sound reverberated through the floor, ceiling and walls of the training center. The dull thud echoed briefly. Smoke and flames rose from the sands, mingled with the winds and were gone.

The senses of all present were imprinted by the low frequency sound and deep shudder that shook their seats. Guards braced themselves as the floor moved. Recruits gripped armrests, or the seat backs in front; a few bent over and covered their heads.

Every recruit reacted to the horror of being buried; most ran for the exits. The room cleared quickly.

The crush of bodies was not controlled even by veteran NCOs, some under arms. The guards outside were unsuccessful in preventing recruits from dispersing chaotically in every direction. One recruit tripped and clandestinely retrieved something from under a seat cushion.

In the underground room Colonel Jubali, Major Hourani and two guards quickly assessed structural damage. There was little. There were no dead, no wounded. The missile attack was a failure. But another spy was on the loose.

The officers quickly agreed a plan to regain control. "Let's muster them outside, quickly with guards."

Finally Jubali swung his arms as if embracing the area. "Have the NCOs gather them, from wherever they ran," then he coughed from the dust, "we must get past this mayhem."

Khalid, Hourani and Jubali met, brain stormed where that recruit went, scrambling for ideas to capture him, and analyzing the missile attack. "How were they so close?" Khalid asked. "The missile they fired, it used precise targeting. Do we know more?"

"It probably used GPS targeting," Jubali suggested.

Khalid's face became tentative and he quipped, "If it used GPS, why didn't it hit top dead center, and kill you all?"

Jubali spread a base map on the table, folded to show the training center. He tapped the plot several times, "Look at where the missile hit, about forty to fifty meters from the eastern entrance."

Major Hourani pointed to the impact point, "The missile burst underground. I think it was programmed to attack our meeting."

"But we changed the entrance for the unit meeting." Jubali raised his palms, as if in prayer, "Another infiltrator knew we'd all be there, and sent a message to target the room." He smiled, "but he didn't know we'd go in a different door."

"You all changed the access after announcing the meeting," Khalid interjected. "He must have been inside. But no one spotted the telltale digital watch." He glanced at the others, "How do we find him?"

Hourani frowned, "At least two recruits are locked away, secure. As for the final one, let me analyze video from the meeting. I'll see if anything unusual shows up. We might get lucky."

The message was shot gunned, or routed with absolute urgency, within Headquarters, Israeli Defense Forces. It was Unclassified but OP IMMEDIATE, the highest operational priority. That meant lives were on the line. As Lieutenant General Gersh Aviv, head of IDF, scanned his copy, he grimaced. He'd only read the attached mission summary and confirmed its distribution.

Among message destinations were the head of his Air Force and Mossad's Director of Ops. *They, along with aviators in sundry squadrons, are dealing with this matter. Guess all the right folks know about this.* Aviv looked at the message again; his frown deepened. *Damn!*

The Date Time Group (DTG) of the message indicated transmission a scant twelve minutes earlier. Aviv reread it, rapidly drumming fingers atop his copy. The message read:

BREAK. URGENT. FLEEING IN HUMMER TOWARDS BORDER. OTHERS ALIVE, CAPTURED. REQUEST HELO PICKUP WADI MUSA. 03 SENDS. BREAK.

This was *not* the sort of message Aviv wanted. It meant big trouble. Probably, no - certainly, a Cabinet level shit storm would descend on his head no later than high noon tomorrow. He asked his aide to ring the Defense Minister, and then scrolled a note to ask an expert about the Kill Probability (P_k) of a recent missile strike. The general knew he'd get a long answer, but needed a short accurate one.

The expert, Elon Rivlin, was summoned to explain the probability of success for that missile attack. Rivlin was very competent, but also an insufferable know-it-all. When asked the time, he began by stating that Sumerians measured time by a system based on the number sixty, and thus 'our hour has sixty minutes.' Twenty minutes later, unless you derailed the freight train of Rivlin's mind and mouth, you found out what time it was. A good guy to have on your staff, but best kept on a short leash.

Rivlin entered the general's office, walked straight to a chalkboard, and started scrawling math formulae. "The concept is simple. Let's say you're trying to kill someone with a 1000 pound bomb. If it hits 650 feet from your aim point, it has a low probability. But a grenade at close range gives a higher chance of success, or kill probability, in this case. P sub K is way better than eighty five percent, general."

An upraised open palm cut off his words and scribbling, "Wait one damn minute," Aviv ordered, "explain it in terms a ten year old can understand." *I have to explain this to politicians.*

A dumb look spread on the man's face, suggesting he'd never been ten, had started life as a thesis researcher. Aviv brought the civil servant back to reality, "I have to explain two men captured, and now"... as he scanned another message thrust at him by a messenger, "It seems our missile strike failed." *Damn!*

"Really ... one would think it had," Rivlin stammered, "succeeded."

"That is one nasty neighborhood down there. Prophets lived nearby, and called down God's wrath on folks they didn't like." *It's clear no prophets interceded on this Op.* Aviv grumbled aloud and dismissed Rivlin, "Thanks for your figures and insights."

Aviv then lifted his phone off the cradle, pushed the flashing button, and connected with the Defense Minister. "I have an update, Minister. I just ordered helos launched to rescue Sergeant Megoonar. Crews are suiting up, getting ready to launch as we speak. I expect they'll be airborne in fifteen minutes."

"Thanks. Good luck; keep me posted."

It took Major Hourani thirty seven minutes to review the meeting video. Her analysis spotted a recruit stooping to tie a boot. She rubbed her eyes, froze the frame, then scanned the images before and after. "He tied his boot on the way in. How could a boot come undone while seated? That means *he's the one* we're looking for, and that is the watch we couldn't find, hidden then retrieved in plain view," she said to no one in particular.

Jubali, asked to confirm the discovery, looked at the video as Hourani focused on the movements of one recruit. The video footage established Al Khali as the spy, with the digital timepiece everyone sought. With Khalid's approval, Jubali issued an arrest order.

The command muster finally ended. The report reflected two men unaccounted for. One of those missing was a recruit, the other a sergeant. A vehicle was dispatched to the Motor Pool, where the missing Sergeant, Ahmed bin Awazi, was in charge. Soon the radio barked search results, "Sergeant Awazi was found; the spy has not."

The sergeant was accounted for, but the search team report, confirmed by the clinic doctor, said Awazi's neck had been broken by someone with strength and training. His weapon and a vehicle, a Hummer equipped for rough desert use, were missing.

Pairs of armed NCOs were dispatched in Hummers to check other base buildings. They drove off excitedly, weapons charged, and radios on. First four, then all their reports came in. Al Khali was not found.

Provincial Police were requested to block all roads, be on the lookout for the murderer. The police and base patrols were given a description of Al Khali. He was to be approached with great caution; he was armed, and definitely dangerous. Where had he gone?

A recruit in ranks, who heard the radio mention the dead NCO, raised his hand. "I saw a Hummer leave the area by the Motor Pool."

When asked which way it went, he pointed. All eyes moved with his gesture. The location of recruit Kareemi Al Khali, a murderer, was uncertain.

On the base's ring road the Signals Van intercepted that message. The bearing was due north. The signal parameters matched those seen previously from the infiltrators watches. "Tell the colonel," Lieutenant Badr exclaimed to the sergeant manning the display.

Badr dialed the command's UHF frequency. "Colonel, your Al Khali is driving north. Can you cut him off?"

Chapter – 21

In a Ramat David Air Base Ready Room pilots and helo rescue personnel updated mission boards, completed gear checks. They geared up, grabbed helmets, and rushed to the flight line. There techs were topping off VIPERs TWO ONE ZERO and FIVE FIVE SIX.

The crews climbed in, buckled up, muttered prayers, and checked the helos' weapons. The pilots and crews lifted off, trigger fingers ready. Eight men headed off impetuously to rescue one sergeant.

The flight of two Israeli helicopters towards Jordan was detected by a US satellite. Search priorities in the region were at the highest level. An Israeli missile followed the same route two watches earlier. Technicians at the Cheyenne Mountain facility tracked the birds south. The supervisory tech noted an alarm flashing amber. With the duty colonel's approval, he pushed the red button on the speaker console and was connected to the National Military Command Center.

Al Khali stopped the Hummer after driving flat out for an hour. His butt was sore. His wrists and hand muscles felt taut. His senses had been jarred by driving over the terrain. He needed to stretch. Using his watch he transmitted his position, route, and requested helo pickup. Then he got back in the vehicle, knuckles white on the steering wheel. He continued north, fleeing for all he was worth. Dust swirled up from oversize tires as he prayed a Search and Rescue team would save him.

The vehicle bottomed out several times as he drove off *wadi* walls, dropping up to four feet. *I'm in the clear, no pursuers, and buddies are coming to get me*. He grinned, "I'm safe!"

Amir phoned O'Toole, "We captured two Israeli infiltrators. That country may win a war, but we've won this battle. And we may yet catch one more." The general imagined a heart stopping seizure or a gasp occurring at the other end of the phone line as he told his friend of the effort to find 'another spy' using an intercepts van.

"One more?" O'Toole asked in shocked disbelief, the blunt tone betraying his loss of composure. "What the hell is going on?"

Amir told him once more, "We caught two Israeli spies."

Tooley sensed Amir's' voiced dripping confidence. Aware their phone conversation was almost certainly being recorded, he asked, "Are you sure, really sure they're Israelis?"

"Absolutely. We have proof they're Israelis, here as spies. That gives us leverage. Israel will trade in earnest for them, so we don't execute them." Amir glanced at his phone, "I'd like you to visit the base, talk things over."

It was the gambler in him, hedging all bets. It was not a bluff, but was definitely a long shot. Tooley knew getting permission to see the 'spies' was a two edged proposition. Seeing them and reporting that certainly meant Intel of their capture would be shared. Israel would know they were alive, and it would be clear who told them. O'Toole's request would be made known within the highest levels of MODA. Amir wouldn't allow him to visit without getting approval. But such a visit would imply these 'spies' wouldn't be shot out of hand.

"I want to see them," O'Toole said calmly. *He trusts me, but he won't say yes unless I ask.*

"I'll check and let you know. You may have to watch through a mirrored window, during interrogation."

This is hot stuff. The Israelis know by now, may try to rescue them. And Amir's troops will be ready. War is not out of the realm of possible outcomes. Tooley decided to push his luck, shoved all his chips forward on the table, "How about tomorrow?"

An OP IMMEDIATE Situation Report or SITREP was faxed to Langley inside the hour. O'Toole's report noted source credibility and urgency. He described what he knew, what was surprising ... and what was not. Together the facts and suppositions made a lengthy list, few encouraging.

The report suggested the Israelis might try to rescue the captured spies. That idea was more than a hunch. Israel had from the first turned the world upside down to retrieve a single soldier, dead or alive. But they could walk into a trap, right? The capture of two spies might lead to dialogue between two enemies. Talk is always better than combat. The other side of the coin was that the Saudis had discovered and captured them. Spies there, in that unit, demonstrated a long term effort to infiltrate a Special Forces unit.

We may never know how the Israelis did this, the words continued, 'How the two were detected is not yet clear.' The report went on to say 'I'll find out.' It ended by saying, 'I have every reason to believe LG Ubaidi's statements. Something big is up. I hope to visit the base and see these two men. Seeing them would constitute proof of life and hopefully keep them from being executed.'

The phone trumpeted in the US Cultural Attaché's office. *Who can it be? Ah, blocked caller id. Odd for the Kingdom, eerie.* He lifted the receiver, but didn't get a chance to greet his caller. "Tooley, things are frantic at the moment. I must delay your visit to the base." Amir paused, "The base is in lock down."

"What's up?" O'Toole asked. *I wonder if those two men escaped.*

"Well, you remember we caught two infiltrators. The base identified another, and searched everywhere for him without luck. He killed a sergeant, stole a vehicle, and fled. Khalid sent a helo after him."

Amir paused, "Pardon, just a moment."

Tooley heard someone enter the room and whispering in the background. He discerned Khalid's voice, then Amir blurted, "*Mushkillah*!"

The excited use of that Arabic word confirmed there was a very serious problem, "I must go," Amir said, and the phone connection went dead.

O'Toole looked at the phone receiver and his brow furrowed. *What the hell is going on?*

Chapter - 22

The Saudi helo pilot phoned the weapons NCO, asked Force Ten ordnance techs to break out five hundred rounds for his mini-gun, along with six beehive anti-personnel rounds. He turned as 'Dude' Peters, his advisor, walked up. Major Najeed told Peters, "We're off to capture a murderer; he's heading north."

Retired US Army Warrant Peters hadn't been listening, and stammered, "What's that, Najeed?"

He was given an abbreviated two second briefing, "Dead NCO, a stolen Hummer, and a spy fleeing. We're going after him."

"What?" Dude questioned, disbelief on his face. "We, as in the two of us?"

"We, yes!" Najeed said provocatively, "unless you wimp out."

The two soon completed the pre-flight check off list. Both buckled up as techs slid the final rocket into the Huey's starboard launcher. "He's probably thirty to forty miles ahead, traveling through *wadis*," the pilot said. "We'll find him."

Peters plugged in his head set, muttered a quick prayer, and grumbled as the rotor blades started turning. His face tensed, "Do we stand a chance of catching him?"

The pilot fumbled as he clipped his mission board to his right knee. "Yes we do; hang on." Dust swirled in all directions from the rotor downdraft. As the bird lifted off he radioed Base Ops their readiness.

The tension in Najeed's reply increased the unease Peters felt.

My contract doesn't cover this, but I can't argue with capturing a murderer.

"GUNS EIGHT EIGHT, this is ASHRAH, WEAPONS FREE. Advise final disposition of the Hummer, over." Before he could respond, the command circuit again interrupted Najeed's concentration, "EIGHT EIGHT, show that bastard he can't get away with murder."

The pilot acknowledged the order. After liftoff he increased speed, eased the controls back and climbed to a thousand feet. He headed north, and radioed the Hummer ahead, "It would never have worked, you as a Saudi." There was no response.

Najeed grumbled, "Asshole, that won't get you out of this. It makes my job easier."

After thirty minutes flight the pilot advised Base Ops, "EIGHT EIGHT has a visual on the Hummer." As he finished his transmission, he pushed the controls forward, down and right and kicked rudder. He banked the helo, dove toward the Hummer, and fired a sweeping mini-gun burst ahead of it.

Al Khali swerved from what passed for a road avoiding the rounds, hit a patch of lava rock. He jammed into his seat belt as the vehicle careened off a sand mound. As he regained control the speaker on the dash erased any semblance of situational awareness.

"Surrender, return to base, or." The pilot did not explain what 'or' meant.

Al Khali pushed the vehicle's accelerator to the floor. *"Lech La Azazel."*

Peters understood the tone of the reply. He turned to the pilot, his face white, "That was Go to Hell, and he meant no fucking way, right?"

Najeed nodded agreement with the advisor. His concentration was interrupted by an order he expected, "Take him out."

Dude heard the order, glanced at Najeed, then tightened his harness another notch. *Hell of a time to be controlling the weapons. Here we go again.*

Najeed remotely triggered the Hummer's airbag. The safety device deployed and covered Al Khali's face, obscuring his path. The spy stomped on the brakes, locking them. The vehicle panic stopped with dust flying.

The pilot selected single fire and tapped the trigger twice. The Huey jerked as two rockets took flight trailing white smoke. They burst five hundred feet from the vehicle. Hundreds of dart-like flechettes hit the Hummer. They shredded the vehicle's top, sides, tires, seats, and fuel tank. Vaporized fuel ignited from sparks of shorted wires. The blast swept forward through the vehicle, which disintegrated in a massive orange and red fireball. Kareemi Al Khali incinerated as he slammed against seat restraints.

"ASHRAH this is EIGHT EIGHT. BEEHIVE, scratch one Hummer and driver, over."

Najeed banked left. He smiled at a job well done, a murderer punished. As his helo's nose swung he spotted two helos out of the corner of his eye. His pupils narrowed as two hostiles materialized. The Blackhawks were on the horizon and closing.

He pushed the rudder pedals right, cyclic right and down, diving to stay out of their field of vision. The pilot's voice cringed as he told the man in the adjacent seat, "It wouldn't be an even fight. We're outgunned and outnumbered!"

"Time to call the cavalry," Peters insisted, "while they're distracted by that burning Hummer."

The pilot warned, "Yeah, cause when they see us they'll really be pissed." He switched frequencies, radioed Tabuk Air Base about the Israeli helos.

His request for help seemed to be met with disbelief, "Say again, over."

The pilot swore, *"Yil'Anek,* damn you! This is not BS. They ... are ... Israelis *and I can see them."* he screamed. "Request Emergency Scramble of Ready Alert aircraft. We need help."

Knuckles white, wrist and forearm muscles tensed on the controls, Najeed prophesized. "It won't be long before those Israelis come looking, and shoot our ass down." He didn't expect the reaction he got.

Peters smacked the pilot on the leg, pointed to the horizon. A Blackhawk was closing in the distance just beyond the burning Hummer. "They've seen us!"

Najeed yanked the controls, "Hang on. We're going to test this birds' gee limits, pull a Cuban Eight."

Peters' voice cracked, "This beast can't do that maneuver; the rotors will come off."

The helo banked violently, forcing Peters into shoulder and seat straps. "We can't outmaneuver a Blackhawk, you crazy shit." He swore, prayed Najeed would just haul ass, somehow escape. "You're friggin nuts! We'll fall out of the damn sky."

"I can pull it off." Najeed smiled, but it wasn't convincing. "We only have to do it once, then MODA will buy me a replacement."

Concern dripped from Peters' brow and voice, "Can it *really* do it?"

"We'll find out in a couple of minutes, one way or the other. We can't wait for Tabuk to scramble fighters. Najeed's hands tightened on the controls, "Turn all armament switches to ARM. *Allahu Akbar*!"

Peters crossed himself and kissed the fingers of his right hand, "Jesus, Mary and Joseph ... protect us." He looked at Najeed, "OK, let's take him on."

Najeed maneuvered like a demon possessed; down, up and over; went upside down; then right side up. *Hold this flight attitude for just one second.* "Watch this! I'll show you what I can do with this beast." *Now - Aim, Set, and Shoot!* He fired four flechette rockets one after the other.

The first rockets' circuitry, corroded from decades of storage, refused to trigger enroute its target. The missile roared on. The Israeli pilot saw it pass, feet away, gasped, "What was that?" *Ben Zona! Incoming!*

The Blackhawk pilot twisted the controls hard, praying to gain altitude and evade whatever followed. His instincts told him more were inbound. The men in the helo struggled to reach defensive system controls as they strained against harnesses.

The pilot's tactical training, beaten in over years, prescribed the maneuver to escape incoming. The helos' momentum was now dominant. The Blackhawk's cutting edge technology activated. Flares deployed in all quadrants, conformal jammers pulsed, and decoys were launched.

The last three beehive rounds initiated, sending hundreds of mini darts towards the Blackhawk, now maneuvering and exposed. The flechettes impacted, shredding everything as though nails from a hundred nail guns hit at once. The Israeli helo evaporated in a spectacular fireball. Pilot, co-pilot, and two crewmen died instantly, unable to counter four decade old weapons.

Peters, flight suit soaked and face ashen, exclaimed, "Oh My

God!"

Najeed radioed the base, "ASHRAH, this is GUNS EIGHT EIGHT. BEEHIVE, one Blackhawk down, over." There was no acknowledgement.

Peters, relieved at being alive, cajoled the pilot, "That was scary. Now you can write a new chapter."

"To what?" Najeed asked.

"Helo Combat for Dummies, as told by one crazy ass pilot flying a forty year old piece of junk."

A muted sadness sounded from Najeed's lips, "I hear it is the case, the old, slow, and crafty win over the young, impatient, and inexperienced. But that wasn't the case. We were just the luckiest sonsabitches around," Najeed said, barely restraining his pounding heart from shaking the helo.

Peters brought back reality, "We're still outgunned and out of ammo. Let's haul ass before that other Blackhawk flies our way."

In Tabuk Ready Room Three, pilots sat in leather chairs drinking gawa, Arabic coffee spiked with cardamom. Four pilots were jarred from a boring video tape as bulkhead speakers blared. "LAUNCH ALERT FIVE, LAUNCH ALERT FIVE."

Four aviators sprinted to HMMVs outside, struggling to keep from dropping helmets. The drivers spun the tires as they accelerated towards F-15s on the flight line. Once parked, the pilots ran to their planes, scurried up ladders to cockpits, and strapped in. Ground crews struggled to detach power cables as the engines revved and check lists were mentally signed off. Then encouraging arms pointed to the runway. Each pilot gave a Thumbs Up.

The radio barked, "EIGHT FOUR, you are cleared to runway TWO NINER ZERO. Winds ONE TWO FIVE at five knots. Go get em!"

"Roger. EIGHT FOUR is rolling. Give us a vector."

"EIGHT FOUR, come to ZERO ONE FIVE. BUSTER," which was code to use afterburner. "You are WEAPONS FREE."

Both F-15 pilots got to 500 feet and 400 knots, jammed their engine controls to the stops, and poured fuel at max rate to their twin engines. "GUNS EIGHT EIGHT, this is TABUK EIGHT FOUR with wingman FOUR FOUR. Your cavalry will be there in twenty, over."

Chapter - 23

The surviving Blackhawk pilot heard the radio exchanges about the launch of Saudi fighter aircraft. He decided to Return To Base before he was shot out of the sky. VIPER FIVE FIVE SIX, tearful, reported the loss of TWO ONE ZERO.

It was a strange day" Tooley told Anh. "Amir called and told me the base was in lock down. Then he got a call on another phone, and hung up." His eyes arched as he looked at the family room.

Anh's face mimicked his look. She knew din din couldn't cure everything, but it might help. She pecked him on the cheek, "Love you." Then she ran her hand playfully through his hair, "I'll fix dinner. You better talk with Mick; he looks confused about something."

Tooley walked into the family room where Mick paced. Confusion, joy and pain were on his son's face.

Mick shuffled his feet nervously and stammered, "Dad, she kissed me. What do I do?"

O'Toole was glad his son wanted to confide in him. He knew they had a closer relationship than his with his own Daa. *Hope I can string together the right words.* "How did you react?"

"I was embarrassed at first. It happened in the hallway. I felt like I couldn't breathe. I closed my eyes and everything felt tingly. At least my buddies didn't see the kiss. That was cool." He looked at his father, "Then Judy walked away. Is there something wrong with me?"

"Judy?"

"Yeh, Judy Simpson."

"Tell me about her?"

"She's the most stunning girl at school, but she's older, in different classes." The ring of insurmountable challenge was in his tone.

"OK, it's not Valentine's," the father queried, "why did she kiss you? Was it because of something you did or said?"

"No. She's got tons of older friends. I can't remember even talking to her. Do I avoid her, or say something?" Mick paused,

"Maybe it was a dare, or some kind of joke. Do you think so?"

"She might like you, but I can't imagine why," a grin spread on Tooley's face, as if to say the kids' got some moves. "I don't think it was a dare, but I could ask."

"Please don't," Mick implored, "I don't want you to prove I'm a dork."

"Ok, then you check things out. See if she reacts if you smile or wave. But only do it when none of her friends are around. Don't be direct. Make any question a joke."

"I'll figure a way to talk with her alone."

"Don't overreact at her response, or lack of one. Think of it this way, you can't give her a Hogwarts potion and make her like you. And her family will rotate to a new duty station at some point. You might not even see her in another year."

"How do I tell if she likes me, seriously likes me?"

"Well, if her friends weren't watching, she probably didn't kiss you on a dare or to show off. I guess that's a good sign. Did she hug you when she kissed you?"

"No. She just walked up and kissed me on the lips, and her hand touched mine as she left."

"Did you say anything?"

"No. I just stood there. I couldn't think or breathe."

"Well if it helps, the same thing happened to me when I was your age. But she was playing a joke."

"Thanks for making me feel better. You're the best, dad."

"Don't forget to tell your mother." Tooley patted Mick on the back, "Next time."

Chapter - 24

Stefano opened his jeweler's tool kit, pulled out a small Philips screwdriver. He carefully removed a cover plate from his TV camera's body and extracted an encrypted cell phone. The journalist unhooked its power cable and selected the preset number. A squelch echoed as two phones synced.

"Tooley, how are things in your neck of the woods? How is life in the trenches? Did that grab your attention? I ought to use those words, right?"

O'Toole laughed at his remark, and then summed up the exciting weeks' events. "It was as you say, BREAKING NEWS! Spies were caught, a missile attacked the base, and a helo pursued a Hummer driven by a spy. The piece de resistance was an aerial battle in which an Israeli helo bought the farm. And I hope to see gun sight video of it soon. The King is at the base now, so I have to wait before getting to see anything in person. It was a week of A roll video, right?"

"Certainly sounds like it." The phone conversation went on and on, Tooley thought. *This all has to become part of still more reports. More tired fingers.*

"I read papers here in Tehran mentioning the Saudi events; even saw a Saudi TV channel segment. They said a unit identified a foreign infiltrator. Aware of being discovered and apprehended, he murdered a soldier, stole a vehicle, and fled towards Jordan. Saudi forces pursued the man and were engaged by an enemy helo. The reporter said the infiltrator died in his escape attempt," Stefano added. "It was far more exciting coverage than I'd ever seen from Saudi."

Tooley said, "Tell me more about your neck of the woods."

"One soldier told me that an Iranian-Iraqi front is developing, roughly appearing like a saw blade, with flat, buck tooth edges, rather than jagged triangles. It seems a strange alignment, but I have no way of determining if it means anything."

"I have no idea what it means, but maybe analysts back in Foggy Bottom will. How is troop morale?"

"I see vets telling combat stories to boots, changing the place, the time of year, the units, but rarely the outcomes. These stories are part and parcel of building esprit de corps in any army, but it seems almost like required training here. There's the standard BS, a lot of bluff and bluster. Many brigade size maneuvers turn out to be paperwork drills. I witnessed the movement of some heavily armed units. I wouldn't call them real armies, but certainly bigger, more coordinated units. The aviators naturally put on the real show. The Iranian and Iraqi Air Forces faced off every day, yet no planes were shot down. I wrote in a dispatch that they 'danced in mid-air like dervishes.' Is cute, eh?"

Tooley chuckled. His reports would note that Iranian forces

were operating at joint levels, with infantry, air, artillery, armor. Radio circuit discipline of units was weak, but improving. Special Forces officers and NCOs were coordinating many small unit maneuvers and discipline was improving. O'Toole suggested caution, "Recognize the danger you put them in. Get a quiet, private place to talk, unseen by informants and officers."

The journalist had thought of that, but it didn't seem an urgent concern. "I would have thought that, but I am out in the open. Interviews are unrestricted, authorized without question. I'm not sure why."

"Stefano, listen as they talk, remember what they might have seen, heard. I want to know how many hangars, tanks, where the foreign advisors work or sleep? I especially need to know where the SCUDs are. They can hit Israel or even Saudi, like before." He paused, "Be careful, shells are flying, very real ones that go boom."

"Forgot to mention the SCUDs. Both sides are buying them from anywhere they can, Afghanistan, Uzbekistan, all the Stans. I hear they're restarting courses to maintain, and launch the buggers." The journalist confirmed he'd find out the desired Intel about SCUDs. "Occasionally I get very open statements, but many don't make sense. A SCUD missile battery commander told me something puzzling. He said 'We cannot shoot at cities. We can beat their army in the field. We fear retaliation on our cities, so we move often, do not shoot at their cities.' It is certainly not how they fought previous wars. Back then, they tried to utterly destroy each other ... in every battle. It seems odd."

The day before conflicting After Action Reports arrived at MODA from Tabuk Air Base and Force Ten. The base and its fighter squadron reported the launch of Ready Alert fighters, while Ashrah reported destruction of a Hummer, the death of a spy, and downing an Israeli Blackhawk. It was the story of David and Goliath, with a mere helo pilot upstaging fighter pilots. The imbalance of results certainly wasn't expected, wasn't normal. The rotor head, Walid Najeed, now held top bragging rights in the Saudi Air Force. He told Peters as they ate, "TV stations want to interview me. I'm a star."

Peters listened. That comment about TV interviews emerged without any effort at boasting; not, as Peters observed, as a fighter jock would have shouted it. He personally thought the world of Najeed. The helo pilot hadn't looked around for a wingman to impress, didn't hesitate. Najeed had analyzed the situation and pulled an incredible maneuver. Best of all, they had lived through it. "I'd say you are one incredible aviator, even if you almost killed us," Peters rejoined with a chuckle.

Najeed smiled broadly, "Channel One and Arab News articles reported on two spies, and the explosion of a military vehicle while another fled. They glossed over our high jinks, but they aired edited gun sight video from the encounter. Their viewership has soared. One TV viewer in particular lives in a really big palace; his name is His Highness. And he's coming to see *us*.

Najeed looked at the advisor; Peters' mouth was open in shock, a piece of broccoli visible between front teeth. "Lay your best clothes out."

Chapter - 25

How is it going? Anything exciting to tell me?" O'Toole asked CWO Peters during lunch, where he was told about the helo encounter at an expensive Riyadh eatery.

"Najeed laughed, then told me not to tell anyone of our helo encounter. He confided that Colonel Jubali asked him if he thought I'd comply. Najeed said 'The colonel said human nature would take care of publicity.' I bet that's what they want, to make it public; wave it in Israel's face." He grinned, "But I'll tell you, cause parts of the story will be on TV again. Najeed will be center stage; our new light colonel is to be interviewed. I get to be there. Cool eh?"

"Definitely cool," O'Toole confessed. "I took some flight training and did that maneuver myself in a jet trainer. I didn't think helo could do it."

"I am one lucky SOB." Peters went over the details of the aerial engagement, "He flew it upside down, well past every gee limit I know for the Huey. I was praying the whole time that the rotors didn't come off. We damn sure torqued that bird beyond the specs, twisted several structural members. We were lucky as hell to make it back to the base." There was relief in his tone and a smirk on his face, like he had enjoyed the engagement immensely.

"I bet it was *the experience of a lifetime*, especially since you were an 'advisor.'"

"Yup. That helo is now scheduled for a complete factory rebuild. When it was over we were Winchester, flat out of anything to shoot back with, and there was another Blackhawk looking for us. Glad that kinda shit never happened in NAM." Peters halted with a strange look, "Gawd, that was forty years ago."

"I know what you mean," Tooley offered, "especially before it rains."

"I've got even better news, O'Toole. I'm getting an award for bravery from the King, and a years' bonus from his employer. On the other hand, company suits chewed my ass. They stressed some corporate mumbo jumbo about liability risks in combat. It pissed me off. I mean, I almost bought the farm and they pull that crap? I told 'em I didn't know about going into combat. We were just going to arrest a guy. I even took along cuffs. Well, actually nylon zip ties."

Tooley replied, "That's both sides of the situation here. The same scuttlebutt of higher insurance rates is making the rounds among contractors in Iran. The muckee mucks there are worried about their employees getting pulled into combat. Those guys worry about paying out indemnities to families of employees killed, and they don't even build or sell war material."

"It all goes to prove," Peters grumbled, "we have to watch out for wild people and places."

"And insurance pukes; don't forget them," O'Toole said with a smirk. "Congratulations on your bonus and award. Say hello to the King."

Amir looked at his friend. "His Majesty, the King, flew here yesterday. It caused quite a stir. There were wall to wall guards. His security wore *Bedouin* robes, carried AKs, pistols, and jambias. There was a simple ceremony; Major Najeed was awarded the *Nut al Shujaat*. It is our highest decoration for bravery. Then the King promoted Najeed and granted him a year's salary.

Amir didn't linger on the King's visit, "I believe you know Warrant Officer Peters, a US Army vet? He was there."

"Yes, I know him. He's a Vinnell employee, an advisor on helo ops."

"Yes. An advisor, as you are my advisor." There was a hint of suggestion to Amir's words. "I stayed away from the ceremony. Najeed and General Khalid deserved the recognition. It is a feather in Khalid's cap. He is sole Shia general in MODA."

"I've commissioned a plaque to be erected where that Israeli missile struck," Amir said with a smug look, like he had something in mind. "Come, jump in the Hummer, we have some things to see. First we'll stop and you can see two of our prisoners."

Ubaidi stopped at a heavily guarded building surrounded with multiple sets of fencing. The guards outside came to attention as they walked to the entrance. Inside a room, O'Toole saw two men in leg irons behind a one-way window. He recognized one as Sergeant Daoud Tashoom, alias Tariq al Hassab, from a photo in his embassy file. The man's neck tattoo had apparently branded him for scrutiny. The second was a Sergeant, Elon Mekhab, AKA Ahmed Baladi, whose abnormal blood sugar reaction proved his true identity.

"The last of three infiltrators, Kareemi Al Khali, killed Sergeant Awazi at the Motor Pool. He was killed during his escape attempt. His remains were burned beyond recognition. The crash site is still under investigation." Amir's statement closed off any questions about the helo crash site.

O'Toole knew Al Khali to be Sergeant Levi Megoonar. Israeli TV had even identified him, but O'Toole didn't have authorization to share that identity. "Thanks for letting me confirm those two are your guests." *I expect their hotel bill will be worthy of a royal ransom.*

"Have you seen what you need? I expect you'll tell the appropriate people we have these two and that they're well?" Ubaidi stated, expecting Israel to know within a day, if they didn't know already.

"Yes, thanks. I know this puts you in an odd spot, but I hope it generates some good."

"As do I. Maybe it will keep Israel from shooting at us again." The look on Amir's face told Tooley the general didn't believe that hope for one heart beat.

"That was some encounter," Tooley offered. "Najeed deserves recognition for his skills."

Amir added, "Najeed and Peters walked away. That

engagement was *Mojeza*, a miracle. Najeed is a national hero."

"Perhaps his town will put up a statue to him, or name a street Najeed to break the tradition of naming streets after royalty. That'd be nice. Say, can I get to see the 'watches', the ones with a satellite link?"

O'Toole postured about how much to prod, to get answers to questions he'd been told to ask. Tooley's visit was a delicate balance between seeing a friend and snooping. "Busy week. Anything else to see?" O'Toole prodded.

"Not much, no," Amir replied. "Now we eat a Bedu meal in the desert. I'm sure the Israelis are mad as hell about all this, but I like that."

"Why is that?" Tooley knew some of the answer, but was hoping for hints of more.

Amir stared at the small empty *chai* cup in his hand, rocked it side to side, swirling it to read imaginary tea leaves. "Cause they can't do anything about it."

Tooley felt a plan evolving before his eyes. The plans, and O'Toole knew there'd be some, were unreadable from Amir's expression. *Must be a contingency plan ... but for what? He's setting something up. The Israelis fired a missile, trying to take out a whole unit ... or perhaps a particular General. Then Ashrah captured two spies, and two helos invaded. Only one made it back. Why are they so interested in Ubaidi? It's like a Mafiosi vendetta.*

"My fingers are going to wear out typing reports of all this, Amir."

Amir grinned, "I hope so. Now, let's go eat. I'm hungry and we have a traditional *Mansaf* in store."

Chapter - 26

Munirah motioned to Anh; they moved away from their children's all-hearing ears, "Nice to see you." All were ensconced in the Ubaidi's earth sheltered home. The house represented safety beneath the madness that spread above. "He worries you know, as do I," Munirah confided, "But we shielded our family from such concerns, except when Amir and your husband got shot. The men joke they're off solving the problems of the world, but they're just being guys, having fun. You say that way, right?"

Anh knew both husbands were at a base where a missile struck recently, wanted not to talk about threats. She nodded, grabbed a knife from a wooden block on the counter. "Can I cut some fruit?"

"Yes ... of course, here," Munirah pushed two bowls of fruit toward her, "I worry. Threats were made to Amir while we were in Paris, and then Turkey. And he was run off road twice in England. In the tribe, Amir has enemies, anxious to take leadership of the Samar, to control its investments. I hear this from wives that confide."

Anh cut up several apples and began peeling a bowl of mandarin oranges, "I worry also, though my Michael never seems to. It's part of his charm."

Munirah paused, looked self consciously at her friend, tears forming in her eyes. "Amir has enemies in our military, others jealous of his wealth. I told him he'd be safer in Israel; he didn't like that idea. Israel may be trying to kill him. That missile attack was to take my husband. A crazy idea, I know. Please do not tell this."

"I won't confide your concerns with Michael," Anh agreed, then hugged her friend.

"Home helps me feel better. My children are big now, much less to manage each day. Mahomet is daily at school, Fadia mostly in college or Europe. My businesses run themselves." Her concern aired, Munirah felt relief. "How are your children?"

"They are fine, growing, learning of life." Anh hesitated, "They're watching a Harry Potter movie Mick brought."

M&M watched *The Prisoner of Azkaban*, the latest movie in the best selling series. The boys tried to explain Hogwarts and magical terms to Bai, while Fadia ignored their chatter as laughable noise, or residue from a stray curse.

The two teens traded swats with cushions, bickering about their fathers, over which could 'kick dementors' ass.'

"Dad is a big general," Mamo boasted, "but he doesn't lead soldiers anymore."

"Mine has a desk job. Mom is happy cause he can't get shot again," Mick replied, a puzzled expression revealing he didn't fully understand what he'd said.

Both teens knew being shot required a shoot-'em-up, unless a wizards' wand was involved. The magical moment ended abruptly as a

Call to Prayer reverberated from the speaker system. It interrupted everyone's thoughts. Mick paused the movie, "What was that?'

Mamo reached up and muted the speaker. He began explaining the prayer call until a siren suddenly pierced the air. All covered their ears and stared incredulously towards the alarm. Flashing strobe lights added further tension, magnetizing everyone's attention. The security panel near one light loudly announced a recorded warning:

INTRUDER AT STAIRS! INTRUDER AT STAIRS!

Munirah fluttered her right hand in a horizontal gathering motion, beckoned Anh and the youngsters. "Move ... quickly." She hurried ahead to a cabinet, took a key, and opened it. From a rack within came a handgun and several magazines. She inserted one magazine. The expressions of the teenagers and Fadia accelerated from curiosity to fear.

Munirah turned, alarm on her face, and pointed down the hallway, "Get in our safe room ... Now!"

Glassy with adrenaline, eyes cycled frenetically between horror, fear, and disbelief at the dual stimuli of the alarm and the pistol. As they assembled, Munirah pushed a button inset in the wall. A motor activated and a solid metal panel closed off the hallway.

Like a mother bear, the mothers' eyes swept up to a security monitor as their youngsters moved to the room at the end of the hall. Munirah believed no one would mess with her cubs with mother bear around. Those that did risked getting their faces eaten off.

Mamo, suddenly aware of the implications of an intruder, turned to his older sister, "Will they hurt us?"

Fadia pulled the boys and Bai closer, "No!" Her answer was not convincing. "I'll protect you, and the alarm summoned an Emergency Team from the base." Her tone was now calm, "They'll be here soon."

Fadia shouted, "Mother, shoot him, or let me slam him." She assumed a martial arts stance.

Munirah pointed, "No, Fadia. There are two Tasers in the cabinet. Get one!"

Fadia scurried to the cabinet, and grabbed a Taser, tentatively fingering its trigger, "How do I use it?"

"Don't worry; you've seen enough movies to know. I'll shoot him, *if* he gets in. You're our backup." She paused, looked around, mentally assessing if all preparations were in place. "A team is coming from the base," Munirah pronounced.

M&M, Bai, and Fadia had earlier each imagined some personal heroics. They uttered prayers in multiple languages ... "Save us, we pray, from the sword of the stranger."

"Anh, we'll be safe. They can't get through the barrier, but I'm ready." Munirah slid the barrel assembly back and chambered a round, "Amir trained me to shoot."

Fadia's expression paled as she watched her mother's finger rub the trigger guard.

Then all eyes shifted instantly to movement on the monitor. The pet *Salukhi* slunk behind the stairs beyond the fountain and yelped.

"Mom, don't let them hurt Allat," Bai pleaded, "Maybe she'll chase them away."

Soon the monitor exposed the intruder. A stray dog had snuck in; the monitor soon gave a close up of the *Salukhis* coupling. The on screen action generated chuckles from the mothers.

Fadia and the boys shared knowing grins. Mick tagged Mamo's shoulder with a soft punch, blurted, "They're humping, Mom!"

A puzzled look spread on Bai's face, quickly replaced by an uncomfortable blush, "Yukky!"

Munirah pushed the button again and the metal panel motored back. Everyone walked to the family room and sat. Allat walked over, lay down, and licked Fadia's foot.

Fadia whispered, "That stray was handsome for a *Salukhi*. I bet their puppies will be cute." She bent down, grinned, and hugged Allat, "You slut."

A split second of awkward silence followed. Then Bai turned, "Mom, can we get a puppy? If Fadia says it's OK?"

Anh looked at Bai, then Mick, and proclaimed, "I'm sure your dad won't object."

Munirah smiled at the release of tension, "We'll save you a puppy."

The boys snickered, pointed at Allat. Mick, the image of dogs coupling in his mind, asked, "Mom, what does 'getting lucky' mean?"

Anh's face tensed. She wanted desperately to deflect his intimate question. Anh looked at Munirah for support, but her face was blank, unaware of the awkward implications of what the teen had asked, "Why do you ask?"

"I overheard you whisper it to dad last weekend. One of my school friends said it means 'you're going to have sex.'" It was a pointed question, difficult for a mother to avoid.

"Well, it's something like that, but more. "Dad said he'd discuss it when you talked to him about your girl fan Judy." Anh shuffled her feet, and the evasive eye movement closed that question off, shifting the burden to dad to answer. "I take it your father hasn't talked to you about the birds and bees?"

Mick shook his head, "No."

Disappointed not to hear an awkward response, Fadia was jarred from that expectation by her mother, "Fadia, contact the base to recall the Emergency Team."

Munirah pulled Anh to her and they hugged, "I'm so relieved it was a false alarm. Let's phone our husbands so they won't worry."

I want to eliminate that camel humper," Major General Moshe Ben Bedoo vowed.

"Yes. But we mustn't piss America off; we need their planes, bombs, and missiles too," Lieutenant General Aviv, head of Israel's military cautioned. "Of the cell phones we're tracking, that Saudi's been a target for some time."

"So, how do I find him and kick his keister?" Moshe posed, playing coy.

"It's simple," Aviv replied. "Locate his cell, track it, then take him out!" It wasn't that easy, but flag officers only considered the forest, not trees. When trees got in the way, the Brass ordered them trimmed and shredded. As he left Aviv said, "Good luck."

Ben Bedoo turned to his aide, Colonel Gazi, seeking technical assurance about the mission. "Can we track such a target?"

"Yes. Remember that mission at Such and Such Bridge? It was a complete success; the bastard never saw it coming."

"I still worry. He's a fox that one, even if we're using more effective bombs."

"It *can* work, general," Gazi stated confidently. "Let's hope he doesn't know we can track his phone."

Moshe tapped his fingers on the desk, then asked, "Are the planes ready?"

"Yes, Sir. They're fueled, bombs checked, and the seekers

calibrated," Gazi boasted. "We know precisely where he is."

"Then get the SOB."

The colonel marched off, mentally drafting orders to the attack squadron at Ramat David Air Base. "Do your thing. Go drop some bombs."

Chapter – 27

A Hummer with multiple antennae skidded to a stop nearby. A tall major ran to Amir, saluted, and whispered in the general's ear. Amir turned to Tooley, his face tense, "Someone's broken into my home. An Emergency Team is enroute. They'll be there in two, maybe three minutes. Don't worry; Munirah will get them to our safe room. No intruder can get in; no intruder can get in."

He repeated the words, as though convincing himself, "There's a back way out, and my wife has a pistol."

Tooley pulled out his phone, dialed Anh. *Intruder, wife and kids, safe room, and a pistol. Not good.* His pulse quickened as she answered, "Are you OK?" he asked quickly, "and the kids?"

Anh snorted, "We're fine. The intruder was a stray dog. He snuck in and gave the kids quite a show." Laughter echoed in the background over the phone.

"A show? Of what?" Tooley asked cautiously.

"The dogs humping. You need to explain it to *your son*," Anh ordered. Then she shared the story of Allat and the stray getting it on on the big screen. She paused, wiping away tears of relief. "Mick asked what 'getting lucky' means. You can explain that too, or again."

O'Toole acknowledged his orders, "Glad you're safe. We're about to eat. I hope flies don't find us. Stay Safe."

"I love you. Stay safe." Anh clicked off.

The rugs were tribal, woven in patterns unchanged for centuries. Tooley sat, looked at the huge platter on the red, white, black and gray rug. It was heaped with rice, cardamom seeds, raisons, pieces of carrots, and chunks of lamb. *Must follow the rules; use only my right hand to touch the food. Don't eat too much, or Anh will kill me.*

Khalid, Jubali, and Lieutenant Colonel Najeed also sat around the rug. Several guards in tribal wear watched as he ate. O'Toole suspected they were checking his behavior. He turned to Amir, and whispered, "Goat grab, that's what we call these feasts." O'Toole rolled some morsels into a ball. "I love this stuff."

"I know," Amir acknowledged, "you westerners use humor as we do. We bedus *often make fun of city dwellers."*

O'Toole ate more rice and lamb, reached for his bottled water, "The food is excellent, tribal cooks?"

"Yes. A recipe unchanged forever," Amir smiled, "still satisfying."

Tooley ate another chunk of lamb, as his eyes scanned the dull green water truck nearby. He knew Amir had stock in Mercedes; their plant in the Kingdom built trucks for construction and hauling water. This vehicle had hydraulic outriggers. O'Toole mentally made a note. *No doubt to stabilize the weight in sand. Why were they necessary besides wide knobby tires?*

O'Toole's speculation was interrupted as a speaker report caught his attention, "ASHRAH, this is EAGLE FIVE. BOGEYs DELTA TWO FOUR and TWO FIVE inbound your location." The AWACS report meant that unidentified aircraft were approaching. They were identified as two BOGEYs, aircraft about which no identifying data was yet available.

Tooley thought of the radio report. It reminded him of the fears for his family with that intruder. They were all underground when an armed team responded. He had foreseen shooting near Anh and the kids. His heart rate and BP had soared. He grinned at the drama's final scene; it was just a horny dog.

He looked around. In the distance he could make out four or more armed ATVs and a Hummer with multiple antennae. Two men stood next to what resembled shoulder fired missile launcher stands. He chuckled. *Guess we don't need to worry about another tribe stealing the food.*

Amir reacted calmly to the mention of BOGEYs, "Tooley, we're fine, nothing to worry about."

Tooley swallowed more food, added an alternate assessment of the unidentified aircraft flying their way. "Probably some pilots hot dogging it."

Amir turned, a blank expression on his face, "Hot dogging, what is that?"

"It's what fighter pilots do. They crow like roosters; fluff their plumage," he wiggled his hands in plane like maneuvers, "fly the lowest, fastest; do dangerous stunts; show off to their fellow pilots ... hot dogging."

"Oh, showing off. Now I understand. Pilots showing off."

Amir's aide, the tall major ran again to Amir, saluted. "General, your daughter called the base. The response team has been recalled. The intruder," he smiled, "was a stray dog. Everyone is safe."

Amir turned, the lingering tension gone, "Let's get back to this feast." They laughed, and reached toward the food platter.

The next AWACS broadcast shattered the calm moments later, "All stations, this is EAGLE FIVE. BOGEYs DELTA TWO FOUR, TWO FIVE now confirmed as BANDITs. I say again, BANDITs."

Tooley put his water down, swallowed, then stammered, "Wait! Enemy aircraft ... coming ... here." He twisted to look at Ubaidi. "They must be tracking your phone!" His mouth remained open, but no more words emerged. *Do something, anything!*

Amir held his phone out at arm's length, and gasped, "*Kharaa* ... Shit!"

Tooley rose, seized Amir's cell phone, and sprinted from where they were eating. He slowed and chucked the device as hard as he could. The phone arched through the air, landing beyond a sand dune.

O'Toole ran back, pulled Amir down between the tires, under the truck's center. "Time to kiss our ass good bye."

Chapter - 28

The lead plane's electronics recognized its target moving. Two missile seekers shifted minutely to follow the signal. They registered the cell's new location as it pinged cell towers. Two Cluster Bomb Units dropped free of wing racks, and began guiding to the target.

The outer casings opened at 100 feet, scattering hundreds of bomblets. As they hit, a wave of deadly explosions rippled the air. They showered death beyond the water truck. Those cowering beneath the water truck suffered a ringing, and a deluge of water.

The CBUs spread destruction beyond, exploding two fuel trucks in enormous fireballs. A train of camels tethered together grazed as exploding bomblets enveloped them. All were killed except two babies huddling by their mothers.

Munirah heard a rippling wave of explosions in the background. Her phone went silent; there was not even a whisper. She dialed the base, but the Duty Officer offered no reassuring words. Trembling, she looked at Anh, then told her of the explosions.

Anh's face paled. Her hand shook, her phone call went to messaging. She had no one else to call. The walls of the home closed in.

Both wives visualized the worst. They hugged, and cried, trying to shield their children from what could be. Concern on their faces spread concern among the youngsters, who fell together around Fadia on the couch.

Tooley recognized shit. It happened; it stunk. When it covered you, you got pissed - royally pissed! "Amir," he yelled, "do we have TARGET written all over us, or is it just you?"

Amir staggered to his feet, "Just me." He brushed his clothes, mud from the leaking water, sand, and metallic fragments. He spat, swore angrily in several languages, and started to apologize.

O'Toole grabbed Amir's wrist, stared intensely into his eyes. Blood vessels pulsed on Tooley's neck, "What the fuck is going on?"

"Some sonofabitch tried to kill me! Those Israeli pricks tracked *my* cell phone, flew all the way here to *kill me*."

"Yeah, well I took it as personal," Tooley bellowed. "I don't like being collateral damage! Every time you invite me to a base this sorta shit happens."

Amir rolled over, and rose clenching his fists. He screamed angrily to uniformed figures nearby,

"**WEAPONS FREE!**"

Sergeant Bukharah waved acknowledgement to the general. He hefted, armed his shoulder launched missile, turned and elevated the launcher. The earpiece confirmed target acquisition and he squeezed the trigger. A missile launched, blowing sand everywhere as it leapt skyward toward the fighter.

Tooley coughed from the smoke as the missile took flight. He swore at the round, "Get that sonofabitch!"

The missile hit the lead aircraft. Its right wing fragmented and wing controls flapped helplessly. The plane became unstable, shook. Captain Ben Bedoo spoke into his mouthpiece, "Prepare to eject!" He swung his arm upwards to reduce glare from his visor.

The co-pilot, distracted by flapping pieces of the wing, pulled the ejection seat control between his legs. Both aviators blasted skyward in turn, jarred by the twelve gee impulse. Emerging surrounded by a coffin of smoke, Ben Bedoo looked at his right hand and arm, which had been in the path of the ejection assembly. Both refused to move.

Chutes deployed above 500 feet. A breeze pushed the men close enough to see smoke from the wreckage of their jet. They drifted down, the pilot in shock from ejection injuries. Ben Bedoo's wounds prevented control of his imminent impact with the ground. He couldn't turn into the breeze.

The flight suit transponders activated. The locator signals were picked up by Israeli and American satellites. Signal analysts would receive notification of the transponders in their respective countries and react differently.

The pilots observed the launch of a second missile as they descended. The shoulder launched missile rocketed into the air toward Ben Bedoo's wingman. The plane went to burner and banked hard, as jammers activated, decoys and flares filling the air. The Redeye missile's seeker lost its lock. The pilots dangling in the air breathed a sigh of relief; their friends were safely away.

The chutes flapped on the ground as the two landed. Ben Bedoo unbuckled his harness and awkwardly pulled his helmet off with his left hand. He grimaced as his co-pilot walked up. "I can't move my right arm, Lev. Cut me free."

Barzouk freed the pilot from his parachute. He jerked up from kneeling as motors broke the stillness. On the horizon three ATVs approached. The vehicles carried soldiers with AKs. The junior aviator swore, *"Ben Zona!"*

A burst of gunfire ruptured the calm, then speakers on an ATV announced, *"Astaslema*. Surrender, there is no escape." The sergeant on the center ATV smiled, "No one is coming to save you."

The two aviators looked at each other, the pilot clutching his arm. Their eyes zoomed to soldiers advancing from several directions. Captain Ben Bedoo saw they were armed, "We are so screwed."

With no chance of rescue Ben Bedoo made a command decision. "We have to surrender, Lev. There's no choice." He slowly withdrew a pistol from a right breast holster with his left hand. 1st LT Lev Barzouk, the co-pilot, removed his survival knife. Barzouk held the knife horizontally overhead, then dropped it to his feet, "How do we explain this?"

A tall Saudi sergeant barked at the two, "Kneel down; put hands behind head. If you try to escape, I will kill you. Do you understand?" The sergeant made his middle and index fingers flutter like running feet, aimed his AK at the two, said 'Bang.' The aviators put their hands in the air. They nodded understanding. Both had been through POW training, knew the routine, the words, and saw AKs pointed their way.

Two soldiers without weapons searched the prisoners. They confiscated and inactivated the locator transponders. No weapons were discovered and they motioned to the sergeant, *"Mafee Mushkillah*."

Nylon ties soon secured the co-pilot. The pilot complained of shoulder and arm injuries. The junior enlisted blindfolded the prisoners, wrapped ghoutras around their heads. The senior NCO took the transponders and walked to his ATV. He pulled a radio handset from its holder, "ASHRAH, this is Mobile SIX. I have two captives. They are disarmed; one is hurt. Request an ambulance, and instructions, over."

Amir radioed Khalid, "Make it known their pilots are here, one injured. State you'll send them to Riyadh for treatment later. Right now, keep tactical control."

Amir knew satellites would be listening to the radio chatter, paused on the phone, "Khalid, I have a few ideas."

"That's worries me," Khalid laughed as Ubaidi hung up. "When he says he has *a few ideas*, it usually means trouble."

Subsequent radio reports identified one prisoner as Captain Ben Bedoo, the other as First Lieutenant Barzouk. The clinic doctor, dispatched in a Hummer with medical equipment and a stretcher, applied bandages and a splint to an injured arm. Ben Bedoo cringed at becoming a prisoner, immobilized by injuries. *Camel herders .... Ben Zona.*

The doctor examined the prisoner's follow-up X-rays later at the clinic, "You have no permanent injuries, captain. A dislocated shoulder, elbow, and superficial injuries to your right hand only. How did they happen?"

There was no response, but the doctor knew the prisoner understood what he'd said. He turned to the prisoner, "You'll need lots of physical therapy, but I doubt you'll get it anywhere around here." Again there was silence.

Amir grumbled to himself and stared at Tooley. The general had seen dozens of dead, burned bodies at *As Sulayyil* Air Base. He'd faced danger before, been shot right through his friend. In his wildest dreams he hadn't expected a cluster bomb attack. His face reddened.

"So, who was it trying to kill you?" O'Toole asked. "Must have been someone in authority, or perhaps a loose cannon?" *I wonder if they knew I was here. Probably not ... just like at Sooley Base. The Press better not hear of this; it would complicate things. Certainly means more BS reports to write.*

"This is good. Now we can anticipate what they'll do next," Amir boasted, then he dropped a bombshell, "I *know* who did this. It was the guy who shot us. I'm going to attack his office."

Tooley blanched. *How can he possibly know? Can't be!* He stuttered, "Are you crazy? You're going to attack a building in Israel!"

"I am. That bastard tried to kill me."

"Hell, that prick pisses me off too." O'Tooles' palm turned red as he rubbed an itchy right arm. There was wet blood on his shirt sleeve. "Not again!" *Anh will demand I retire. Not a bad idea.*

Tooley looked up from the distraction of a bloody arm. He became apprehensive as Amir strode away to talk with two officers by the water truck. Amir spoke loudly in Arabic, but the intent was clear.

O'Toole understood just one word – launch.

A driver moved the truck to the side of a nearby *wadi*, where a breeze still wafted smoke up from the crashed jet. Amir touched his friends' arm. "Hang back. Stay *right here*!" He pointed to where they'd cowered as bomblets exploded nearby, "Some fuel leaked."

O'Toole strained to see what was happening at the water truck. He watched as the top, right side of the water truck elevated. Right above the cab the sides of a structure swung outward like window shutters. A rail extended from the top; its front end held a missile. He mumbled, without intending anyone to hear, "Sonofabitch. It's exactly like ASROC on a Navy destroyer. It's a damn missile launcher."

Two officers approached the vehicle. They opened a panel at the truck's side and each inserted something. Tooley focused as they put in and turned the something, then attached a hand grip. O'Toole's eyes widened. *Those are firing controls*.

"Your Target ALFA TEN," LG Ubaidi bellowed, glancing at O'Toole.

"Target confirmed," an officer replied, "Coordinate entry verified. *Sadeek* ready, general."

Amir turned to the officers, "Launch!"

First Lieutenant Mohammed turned, a puzzled look on his face, "Request confirmation of order to 'lunch.'" He glanced nervously at O'Toole, "Should *he* see this, general?"

Amir grimaced, "Yes, lunch!"

Lieutenant generals couldn't be ignored. Mohammed's finger squeezed the trigger.

A blast thundered as a booster sent the *Sadeek* missile into the sky. The flaming exhaust scorched the sand behind the truck. The missile leapt into the air and its winglets deployed. A cloud of foul smelling booster gases enveloped the area. The two launch officers bent double, coughing loudly.

Tooley, his eyes watering, briefly studied the trajectory. O'Toole's eyes tearing, he followed the wispy smoke trail of the missile. *North by the look of it, the missile the size of ... a Harpoon. Oh, that's what he's been up to. Probably a satellite is taking this all in. Wish I had a camera.*

Amir grinned.

Tooley watched anxiously. *Dammit. It's happening, and I'm watching it go down. Some will say I had a goddamn part in it.* He yelled to ensure his words were heard, "Sonofabitch! Amir, did MODA authorize this?"

"No. They don't know yet," Amir's smile intensified, "but they will soon."

O'Toole raised his arm near his nose, smelled his reddened shirt sleeve. "Crap! Some of the missile fuel leaked on me. He scratched. His skin burned, felt itchy and warm. *It's slick, has a golden hue. Better save these clothes for analysis. Can't let Anh wash them.* "Uh-oh... Anh."

Tooley listened as Anh answered her phone. He didn't wait for her to speak, "Anh, we're OK. Tell Munirah we're OK. I have a minor flesh wound, but nothing to write home about." O'Toole chuckled, half heartedly, "I will have a bitch of a time explaining this to the ambassador though." "Langley's not going to believe it. Maybe they'll retire me. I should put that in my report."

"Michael," Anh cried. "The kids and I were scared as hell. I want to hold you and never let you go. We love you, Michael. Come home."

"I love you. Give Mick and Bai a big hug." He envisioned her pulling Mick and Bai close, kissing them on their heads, he looked at his blood stained shirt, "Tell them I'm safe."

Chapter - 29

The *Sadeek* flew low through *wadis*, following the same route as the Israeli missile, helos, and F-16s took coming the other way. Its flight lasted just twenty-seven short minutes. The missile descended to 50 feet after entering Jordan, bypassing Amman and Madaba. Then it angled briefly south, skirting Bethlehem and Jerusalem.

After the *Sadeek* launch, the dust settled and the cloud of booster gases dissipated, Lieutenant General Ubaidi, Saudi Forces, sent a fax addressed to Major General Ben Bedoo. The fax was timed to be received at the Mossad communications center precisely two minutes before the *Sadeek* struck.

The fax read: **"Duck!"**

Near the end of its flight the *Sadeek* ascended to 500 feet. It banked to its final heading and a seeker activated in the nose. Within a second it received a response. Moved by a maintenance man weeks before, the beacon used minimal energy from the battery pack. The homing signal was amplified by the RC car's tall antenna from within a trash container near an office building.

The *Sadeek*'s flight path adjusted, descended to fifty feet above the ground. It paralleled a street leading to the target. Pedestrians pointed, but the missile ignored their exclamations. The seeker detected the end of the building and released highly explosive gas.

Major General Ben Bedoo was reading the OP IMMEDIATE fax thrust at him by a messenger. From the corner of his eye he saw a vapor cloud form outside the picture window. Its purpose evident, he screamed "Everyone get under your desk."

He dove behind a couch.

In less than a second the vapor outside detonated, creating an expanding pressure wave. Shrubs and plants below were flattened. Decorative fencing nearby was bent over at an angle. Denuded trees clawed at the sky. Fire alarms in the building activated, and the sirens, horns, and flashing lights of responding emergency vehicles added to the pandemonium.

The building's frame bent inward along the second floor, as if a gigantic wrecking ball impacted. The front of the building was left without a window. Desks were blown inward against the building core, fragmented after sprinklers made the floors slick. Expensive wooden furniture became moist colored toothpicks, mixed with bits of padding and fabric. The fax that had been in Ben Bedoo's hands ended in a crumpled trash can, flattened against the interior wall.

The geometry of the building and the explosive wave screened most on the first and second floors from major injuries. Fragments of every manner of office furnishings and glass peppered personnel in the affected side of the building. Many in the building lost their hearing for days, or weeks. Twenty employees were injured. Some never fully recovered. Five died.

Passersby were blown over. An elderly couple from the Bronx, sitting on a bench by the lake, was pitched into the water, eardrums and senses buzzing. They survived, told all. "Oy vey, so big the blast!"

Amir muttered at his desk top. *What had the events represented, the spies, the missile attack, two helos, and finally two fighter aircraft with CBUs? All used the same route. I should build a highway, charge tolls.* He looked to Khalid, "Israel can't be happy with these ops. Not much to celebrate; they struck out. I hate just watching, don't you?"

"You know I do," Khalid smirked, "if that *wadi* route were a minefield, they know the safe way through now."

Amir looked at Khalid and grinned, "Unless we install more mines, or a speed trap."

"I'll have Colonel Jubali come up with a place to hold the prisoners," Khalid suggested. "I don't want them sent to Riyadh; that would create many problems. They're not seriously injured, and we could use them as honey, rather than vinegar."

"I'll get MODA to let you keep them." Amir glanced at Khalid, "It will involve your best men." He paused, reconsidering his decision to launch the *Sadeek*. MODA appeared outwardly upset with him; he'd attacked a foreign country, but envisioned proud, widespread smiles whenever he'd see fellow officers.

Khalid drummed his fingers on the desk, then responded, “Jubali will make a list, all urgent, high priority. Correct?”

“Correct.”

Chapter - 30

Welcome, Admiral Kimmel. Can I get you some coffee?” Master Chief Petty Officer Ramsey paused, “Colonel Framenstan is running late.”

“Yes. Love some, thanks. Cream, and sweet and low please. Where is it?” Kimmel replied.

The Master Chief led Kimmel to the coffee at the back of the briefing room. The space was configured like actual Pentagon War Rooms, had the latest bells and whistles, and lacked only its own SCIF. Sensitive Compartmented Information Facilities were where specific, highly classified programs were briefed, to a very, very select group with an absolute need to know. This room served to bring newly assigned flag officers up to speed before standing watches.

“Admiral, before we get into your South West Asia briefs let me tell you a bit about the colonel, so you don’t freak out. Bagem, that’s his handle; he’s a character. The man’s got a photographic memory, pornographic, some would say, cause he knows every limerick, off color joke there is. He definitely originated a few himself, uses them in every brief, so don’t be surprised. Was in Force Recon, later in Fleet Intel posts. He can recite the Enemy Order of Battle, still name every North Vietnamese officer above major, by unit and location, from the EOOB back in the day.”

“So he knows his stuff?”

“Yes Sir. Tough guy too, been wounded so many times he had to lie to the Corps so’s he could stay in. An SOB; nothing scares him. His mind is still the sharpest I’ve seen, but unique. He’ll rub you the wrong way. He’s the best; that’s why he’s here.” Ramsey stared, waiting for a reaction, but got none.

Lieutenant Colonel ‘Bagem’ Framenstan, USMC, retired, came in and gestured. “Evening Admiral, how the hell are you, ready for a whirl wind brief?”

"Colonel, I was told you had an attitude. You seem to delight in pulling flag officers' chains ... heard that from friends. It's been my experience that light colonels don't stand up to flags often." *Or live to regret it.*

"You have that right, Admiral. You see, I'm at 100 percent retirement pay. There's no way anyone can ship my ass back to NAM; that ship sailed long ago. So, I can't make more, can retire any day I want. With my wife gone I don't have a social life. I just happen to love this fuckin job, and there ain't a soul who's better. I figure if I ensure you're on top of what's going on, fewer troops die. That's the truth. I say it like it is, and a few flags don't like that."

Kimmel drummed his fingers, "Attitude or not, I think I could like you. So, Bagem, tell me how we got here?"

"Admiral, this room is equipped like a regular War Room; you can get the latest images from satellites at any of these consoles." Bagem put his palm on a screen, and explained the controls, "The real time take will appear above. Please only play with it at breaks. We have a lot to cover, so let's get going. This will take several sessions."

"So, now I know what's happening in Arabia." the admiral noted four hours later at the end of the briefing watch. "These attacks, all apparently aimed at one Special Forces unit, strange! First the spies infiltrating, and caught; that's a surprise. Then a missile, maybe trying to take out the whole unit at a unit meeting. Finally another spy killed an NCO, heading for the hills for a helo pickup. The spy and a helo taken out, pretty impressive. Then this damn CBU attack?"

"They dropped two Rockeye cluster bombs near a bedu encampment," Bagem paused. "The place blew up like some crazy ass B-52 strike, like when we carpet bombed the NVA in NAM. A CBU is indiscriminate; the Israelis must have been serious about killing someone. The Saudis at the bedu camp fired a couple of shoulder launched missiles at the planes that dropped the Rockeyes. One plane was downed, an F-16. Let me call it up for you." He pointed out the controls to access the video, displayed the bomblets rippling across the sands. The video was stunning.

"Holy shit fish," Kimmel muttered, "and the results?"

"Didn't hit much actually," Bagem stated, "the CBUs killed some camels, holed a water truck, which turned out to be a missile launcher. That may be important; it's a new, mobile land attack system we knew nothing about."

"And...?"

"The Saudis captured two pilots from the F-16. The Israelis don't like that sorta thing, captured pilots, or losing planes. My bet is the Israelis might be planning a rescue."

"Why?"

"I know Major General Ben Bedoo; one of the captured pilots is his son. And Ubaidi tried taking him out; put a missile into his Mossad building."

Admiral Kimmel looked up, his eyes intense. "How would you know where Mossad Intel hangs his hat?"

"I've been there, met the head honcho, that major general. The missile took out half of the third floor. It was a fuel air explosive missile. That place is a mess now. I saw the results on Israeli TV."

Kimmel, recognizing such a decision could mean war, and pondered aloud, "Do you think MODA authorized that missile strike?"

"Don't think so. But the Saudis are paranoid now, what with the missile strike, catching those spies, the helo encounter ... then that CBU attack. MODA will circle the wagons, say it was authorized. Might take things up a notch."

Admiral Kimmel checked his watch, and nodded, "It will take things up a notch."

I think this Lieutenant General Ubaidi has the pulse of MODA, and the Saudis wanted to track the fighters' home," Bagem postured. It was the start of another shift; another full work day of briefings lay ahead.

"How do you know all this?" Admiral Kimmel asked, aware it was not easy to determine where the colonel's facts ended and a sea story started.

"I read everything," Bagem asserted, "and have contacts up the wazoo. Most tell me what I *need to know*."

"OK, well it's a new watch. Can you give me an overview of the rest of the region?" Kimmel looked around, eyes focusing on the large screen display above in the briefing room under the Pentagon. "Are we connected well enough; getting the data we need, to make good decisions?"

"Yes indeed. Our satellite just sits up there, and as long as the sensor weenies get the right tasking, you get to analyze pretty much everything. NORAD gave us real time launch alerts for the strike mission, the CBU attack, and the Saudi missile launch. Higher priorities have been set to detect anything that flies, or goes boom in the night. Israel's satellite, OFFEQ, however, loses coverage as it circles the globe. Ours tracked all those intrusions, admiral. The Saudis know that, probably pisses them off," Bagem opined.

"Anything else to be concerned about?"

"Yes indeed. Iran and Iraq, they're dancing around each other like scorpions about to copulate or do each other in. SCUDs from Afghanistan and Kazakhstan are being shipped to Iran for oil; the same with Iraq. The weapons aren't new, but they represent an increase in long range weaponry."

"How many missiles are we talking?" The three star swigged some coffee and clicked his pen repeatedly, "Are they mobile?"

"These are the NATO estimates for the region," Bagem pointed to a display with figures, "In the last three months ..." Bagem went on to describe columns B and C, "they show the increases and estimates of mobile missiles. Remember Iraq fired SCUDs at both the Saudis and the Israelis. Both countries have asked President Ellington to send them Patriot missile batteries. The decision to approve those requests is his alone. No doubt increased regional tensions will factor in his decision. The Saudis are wired, trigger happy." The colonel's eyes trolled for a question.

"Understandably," Kimmel said, tapping his notepad with his pen, "What will their neighbors do with all those SCUDS?"

"Not sure yet, but Israel appears to have had suspicions about the water truck. It turned out it was their worst fear, a mobile launcher for that missile. Remember that Israeli TV video we viewed of the damage?" Bagem frowned, "Sometimes the news feeds are ahead of the Intel agencies. It's quite a capable missile, like a scaled version of the Tomahawk. These incursions and responses to them have become a major issue at the White House."

Kimmel put his pen down, "The White House, eh?"

"Yes Sir. The President said much the same thing, so the network political heads say. You can expect to become tight with duty military officers at the White House Situation Room. I expect you'll be talking to them at least once a watch. And CRITIC requirements, I'm sure you're aware of those?" Bagem asked.

Kimmel acknowledged with a nod, "I know of the requirement

to notify POTUS within fifteen minutes. The President just got a Daily Intel Brief. He gets one each morning, summarizing what's up in the world. His reaction to Israel's actions has been anger. Word is he's pissed; he doesn't appreciate them thinking international borders are there for crossing and bombing runs."

"I heard he told the Secretary of State to demand a formal explanation from Israel. Her note called the recent attacks a violation of both Jordanian and Saudi airspace, and cited the body count." Bagem stared, assessing whether the flag was a hawk, a liberal, or somewhere in between.

"What's your best guess, colonel, as to how we deal with the Saudis?"

"Admiral, the White House is up on all of this of course, obsessed really. And Langley is working up a Special Intelligence Estimate on the region for President Ellington. Ellington directed SECSTATE DeVries to tell Arabia that the US didn't cooperate with, nor condone, those attacks. But also that we wouldn't warn them of any future incursions," Bagem added, "I guess it said something like 'We aren't international traffic cops.'"

"Well, we 'police' terrorists," Kimmel countered, "all the time with drones."

"Yes, but that is a horse of a different color. The Saudis launched that missile in response to an invasion of its sovereign territory, the third to be accurate. War between nations could be the result here."

"Any other sea stories?"

"Just one, an American was wounded in that Israeli CBU attack. We're trying to figure out why he was there. I'll let you know later. Think of the President, protect him, and the troops. Expect to be grilled by the Press."

"President and the Press; got it."

"Some more bad news," Framenstan added, "the Saudis just went to DEFCON ONE. They'll be out diddling in the desert, conducting live fire exercises shortly. Mainly those will be heavy in armor and artillery. Use of air to ground munitions may go way the hell up. They've already initiated higher ALERT status at all Air Bases. Big Bird, the AWACS, has had its Op tempo increased. Saudi and Jordanian pilots are apparently being briefed at the Squadron level on joint ops."

Kimmel hung his head, "What about Israel?"

Chapter - 31

O'Toole dialed Langley on the STU, waited for it to sync with its twin around the globe. "Boss, I can't classify a report in its own right, and as far as I know, Ambassador Gonzalez can't either. The point is I have a No shit request. The Intel report I'm sending your way; I want it Classified Not Releasable to Israel. It's personal. I don't want to be in Israeli cross hairs again."

His boss, CIA Deputy Director for Intelligence, DDI Cezar Trujillo looked at his aide, "Just a moment." He muted the STU's speaker, "What did O'Toole mean by that remark?"

The aide leaned over, "O'Toole was referring back to being wounded by Israeli fire before." He paused, "Just the other day he was almost killed by CBUs dropped by Israeli aircraft."

"Shit. I remember now, from my in-brief. We have to run this up the flag pole with a recommendation and an explanation," Trujillo said, drumming his fingers rapidly on his desk's blotter. "Set up a meeting with the Director."

Tooley, back on speaker, added a reminder. "Someone needs to ensure they don't rain on my parade again. Those CBUs, while indiscriminate, were intended for one target, and I was standing next to him. My next report, by the way, extrapolates Saudi capability with mobile *Sadeek* launchers. Their Navy had approximately sixty Harpoon missiles, all suitable for modification to land attack. My guess is they've done the retrofits."

A call to prayer echoed outside, breaking the silence of Riyadh. O'Toole looked out the window. *I hope they're praying for Peace. Out there's the home of twenty million Muslims, and ground zero of the world's oil.* "Cezar, nice talking to you. Let me know the decision on the report's classification."

Trujillo acknowledged the unusual request, "Will do, and Happy Fourth. Keep your head down."

Tooley put his STU back in the cradle, looked at his fingers. They were sore from typing, despite dictating major segments of numerous reports. *Is this report the last cookie in the jar? Will I become too 'hot' to be left in Riyadh? Shipped home? Oh well, Fourth of July coming up, almost forgot. The kids haven't seen fireworks in years. I wonder if there'll be some here to enjoy."*

Family recipes were used, a formulation of chemicals promising a variety of colored airbursts. Isabella flipped through invoices on her desk. She smiled, "Bella!" The billing statement on top was an order marked URGENT and stamped PAID boldly in red. The document specified sensor units, controls, quantities, colors, and desired burst heights. Isabella Innocenti's face became quizzical, "What's the rush, and what's with blue and white fireworks?"

Ubaidi hurriedly explained the fireworks were for a *Shamri* tribal event. "I'll have them picked up early in the morning." "The colors are between just the two of us," Amir stared intently, eyes set, "I mean that!"

Amir frowned, "Khalid, they'll come you know. Nothing will change that." The generals were finalizing plans to welcome Israeli helos, and Ubaidi was already hours into a work day.

"Yes, probably in two days, three at most." Khalid established, "We can surprise them. I think we'll be ready."

"General, get your deputy," Ubaidi directed. "I have some final changes to go over, along with tactical plans. My Italian partner has some devices which we can use; the fireworks will be here tomorrow. This video shows them."

Khalid welcomed Colonel Jubali as he entered the office and sat. Ubaidi inserted a DVD and soon the screen showed fireworks displays in NY harbor, Rome, and London. Patriotic music of those countries played as vibrant colors streaked skyward creating smoke and sound.

The colonel stared at the screen and squirmed, his face blank, evidently unaware of the plan. "Colorful, but how do these help?"

Amir explained as Khalid and Jubali listened. Both smiled at their plan, and Khalid gave his observation, "Different. It may work. The fireworks will be part of our diversions, as we distract visitors into a field of fire."

Ubaidi clarified a few points for Jubali, then added, "Colonel, we're setting up a Tactical Operating Center at Pilgrim III. Our prisoners will be in bio-metric chairs, and we'll wire the room for connection to the TV network."

"By Pilgrim III you mean the rest stop on the road to Jordan?" Khalid asked to verify the location.

"Yes, and we'll need a backup Tactical Operations Center or TOC here at Ashrah," Amir directed. "The hangar has open space to use."

Khalid turned to his deputy, "Assign two squads with body armor, automatic weapons, with lots of ammo to the TOC. Have the Armory Sergeant, Hamdoun, man the mini-gun."

"Why him, he's new?" Colonel Jubali voiced reservations, "He could freeze, endanger others."

"I think he'll respond heroically. And it would be best if Major Hourani accompanies you to Pilgrim III," Khalid suggested.

Jubali grimaced, "Why her?"

"She speaks Hebrew flawlessly," Khalid asserted, "and knows the tactics of those who'll come to rescue the pilots."

Ubaidi broke in, "Tomorrow morning we'll need a lot of power equipment to set up the site."

Khalid's eyes swept the ceiling as though in thought. "Like what?"

"Well boring equipment, a back hoe, and lots of fiber optic cable." Ubaidi then enumerated technicians and equipment operators required, "We need them all at day break to get ready."

Khalid's body indicated anxiety at accomplishing the tasks in two days, "Sounds like a lot to do in such a short time."

"It is. I'll remind my local Tiger Team manager his workers will get a month's bonus if they're at Pilgrim III in six hours. And I'll give him a personal bonus if all equipment is there by tomorrow morning." Ubaidi smiled, confident that work would get rolling with lots of money as the incentive.

"Khalid, here's the name and phone number for my Tiger Team. Have him get that well auger there ASAP." Amir paused, "I'll pay whatever it takes. Remind him of that. Here's what I have in mind."

Khalid fingered a special cell phone Amir had given him. "These display tactical maps, and an alert sounds when aircraft are inbound. I need this programmed," he said to Jubali, who wasn't listening.

The Ashrah hangar was now a backup TOC. Two mornings later Amir greeted O'Toole, and walked him through the space. Tooley's eyes scanned the facility. He noted a row of dIsplays, a full comm suite, and numbers of NCOs checking out media connections to the Saudi TV network. *This place looks like a CNN network studio. Another damn report.*

"You plan to broadcast the Israeli prisoners' voices?" Tooley's voice quivered, "that will piss the Israelis off big time. My bet is they'll come to rescue the pilots."

"Yes. Our TOC is wired up like this, with fewer displays. You may be able to see it on TV in Riyadh, or your embassy," Amir boasted. "You just won't be here to see what happens at Pilgrim III, where we're holding the prisoners. The hangar has feeds to TV stations in Dammam, Riyadh, Jeddah, and of course MODA. We want to show the world any encounter. But I don't want you here, in case things go haywire."

Tooley grimaced and put his hand on his hip sarcastically, "What could happen?"He was packing a Glock and a protective vest, part of newly required field gear. *No chance I'll be here, not again.*

Amir looked at his friend, and smiled, "We'll welcome them, if they come."

"I know you will, but I won't be around. In fact, I'm leaving in an hour. Admiral Anh has given me marching orders not to be in the field with you." He smiled briefly, knowing the odds were he'd end up in another shootout if he were here. "I don't want to be around any excitement; I'll leave that to Khalid's' men."

Sergeant Hamdoun, we're setting up a mini-gun near the TOC, to pull off their fire." Colonel Jubali said, "You'll be manning it."

The sergeant's face paled, "Why?"

Jubali explained the tactical plan to the sergeant. "Have your men rest while they can. Keep a quarter of the two squads on rotating duty. Major Hourani and I will be inside the building, with the prisoners. Any rescue attempt will come in darkness; be ready for action when you hear STATIONS."

Hourani walked up to the colonel. "Colonel, we're set. The launch sites have been installed, checked out, and activated. If a helo comes through the *wadis* leading here a red burst will trigger at a thousand feet. More airbursts of different colors will follow at lower altitudes as they get closer. The fireworks, innocuous diversions, will provide a warning of the rescuers approach." She laughed, "They'll probably just wake up some camels."

The pilots met in Ready Room 3 the next afternoon to brief the rescue Op. The presenter, Major Yeddim, was the Squadron Operations Officer. He marveled at the circus aviators called a 'ready room.' Here pilots grab assed about the biggest fish, strongest drinks, biggest boobs, best dart game, and hottest aircraft. It was testosterone central.

Yeddim looked around. Squadron plaques adorned the south wall, along with personal lockers with nicknames and crude caricatures, locations of emergency landing strips, and bar menus taped to a large cracked mirror with the comment 'Who broke me?' Administrative charts, maintenance check off lists, training schedules, and Safety Bulletins were posted, all ignored. Every pilot had seen buddies brought down by gunfire, SAMs, a freak collision, or poor maintenance.

Pilots were serious, and crazy. All pushed the allowable maneuvers and gees their helos could withstand without rotors falling off. They stressed every part to Return To Base. RTB meant survival, but was not a given. Pilots rolled the die on every flight, calculating odds they would come back in one piece. Their demeanor said they were the best, but perpetual tension came from their eyes and voices. Yeddim stared at those around him. *I hope these yahoos settle down.*

Yeddim cleared his voice, "Listen up. Your mission is to carry an assault team to recover two pilots. Handle, you'll fly Shotgun." First Lieutenant Peled nodded. "If you slow or turn, give a heads up! You other guys follow at standard tactical distance. Waypoints Alfa, Bravo and Charlie are here, here, and here," Yeddim pointed to a terrain map marked with the waypoints and comm assignments, "The route is programmed into your flight control systems. This canyon will screen you from AWACS and other radars."

He looked around; all the pilots were listening, a good omen.

Chapter - 32

Call STROBE if your gadgets detect any radar." Yeddim saw one pilot in the Ready Room wasn't listening and put him on the spot. "Handle, did you get that?"

First Lieutenant Peled, AKA Handle, responded, "Yup. Got it!"

"Showtime in twenty. THREE ZERO, as mission commander you fly tail end with the assault team. Make sure they SAFE all weapons in flight." Yeddim breathed deeply; his reminder was a lesson from an assault team which shot up a helo in flight. The major muttered a verse from Psalm 118 under his breath, "The Lord is with me. I will not be afraid. What can anybody do to me?" It was a prayer for safe return.

THREE ZERO grinned, rolled his eyes, "I hope all birds are ready to fly; I get tired flapping my wings." One of the commandos waved his arms up and down like he was flying; muted but universal snickering followed.

"Doubt it very much." Handle countered. *Some damn thing always comes up to spoil the ball.*

The Squadron Operations Officer shook his head. He motioned for the tech watching the antics to give a mission reminder. The senior ordnance specialist walked to the front of the room, his face somber. "Pull all safety arming pins before you lift off."

The three pilots slammed their helmets together, "Roger."

Yeddim added, "Bring back our pilots," as he motioned to the door.

The pilots grabbed helmets and headed to the door. Their exit was interrupted by a crew chief entering, breathing hard. He held up his hands. "Wait. One bird didn't check out. There was a glitch." The tech explained that the final pre-flight of a Blackhawk found a hydraulic pump failure.

"Captain Avigdor, hate to spoil your day, but I had to down your helo. We're prepping FIVE FOUR for you. There'll be a ten minute delay in liftoff. We need to fuel it. But there is news," the tech said.

Avigdor tensed, "What is it? It better be good."

"Your new bird has a retrofit armor package. The engine

cowlings are armored, stray bullets can't take out your turbines. You'll also have a Kevlar seat and underbody. Your jewels will be safe."

"Thanks," the captain grinned, "my wife will appreciate that."

"Your new bird will be a bit slower," the crew chief advised, "and your laser warning system didn't respond to our pre-flight test. Do we still launch with it?"

"Damn straight," First Lieutenant Eshel, Mission Commander barked, "As soon as all birds are gassed up." He looked around, glanced at other pilots, and nodded.

"Everyone take a pit stop. Recheck your weapons, ammo, and protective gear. You lift off in ten; any questions?" Yeddim asked. There were none, and he saw prayers being mouthed, buddies fingering checkered scarves with tassels.

Nine minutes later the pilots and rescue team walked in the dark to their helos. The walk arounds verified that all arming pins were pulled, the weapons armed and safe from stray voltages. Shotgun, THREE ZERO, and FIVE FOUR stepped up into their cockpits, and buckled up. The pilots spun up the turbines and applied power. The helos rose in the air, hovered, then moved off.

The mission's route had been analyzed, each nuance known to plus or minus five inches. GPS and altimeters inputs adjusted the course, and projected directions on Heads Up Displays. HUD data was right in front of the pilots. They just had to follow it, staying low to avoid radar and immovable objects.

Shotgun was flying point for the helos going to retrieve two captive Israeli aviators. The helo carried heavy armament to deal with any bad guys. First Lieutenant Peled's helo had seven tank emblems painted on his fuselage.

The helos passed waypoint Alfa and entered Jordanian airspace without incident. HUD showed a smooth road ahead. The easy part was behind them. THREE ZERO keyed his radio, "VIPER LEAD to herd, descend to CHERUB ONE. Maintain radio silence."

A Cobra led two Blackhawk helos towards Arabia, through darkness, towards certain danger. "Vipers, Shotgun passing Point Bravo." Peled tensed, "ARM all systems and descend for final leg." Clicks acknowledged the pilot's directions.

Captain Avigdor, following in FIVE FOUR, was senior officer on the Op, but not its commander. He grimaced, double clicked his radio. *These kids talk too much. A fool intercepting radio circuits will detect the recurring squelch on our freq.*

The head of the rescue team exuded confidence, talking to his men rhetorically. "What is the worst that can happen?" Captain Katz looked at faces camouflaged with brown, black, and off white, "Nothing, absolutely nothing!" Serious banter mimicked his feelings among those who thought themselves this world's toughest muthas.

Three helos flew through canyons enroute their objective. "Hard to imagine anyone would be out here in the desert. We're heading to pick up our men, and hell awaits anyone who blocks our path. Wish we could come out of the sun. If we had it at our backs, they couldn't see us coming. Light and shadows are weapons." Abraham, First Sergeant of the rescue team, prayed with his team, "Don't let them be awake. They won't be, right?"

The night was perceptibly dark, about to end; dust from yesterday's sandstorm hung in today's air. Light reflected back down to the ground. They moved in the night at fifty feet and 125 knots to their objective, pupils widened by the darkness. Were it up, the sun would be off to their left as the birds swept like brooms through a tunnel. Their dash gauges glowed an eerie green.

"Nope, arriving on flying carpets gives us surprise. Those rag heads don't know we're coming; it's going to be a piece of cake. These carpets are better than prayer rugs," the First Sergeant offered, but heard no response from the pilot.

Avigdor forced a smile, "Most of them aren't religious enough to own a prayer rug. Let's do a flyby."

The sergeant's brow furrowed, "I'd say a firing run, as we leave."

The first glowing object hit forward on Shotgun, jarring the altimeter tube. The flight control system lost altitude and speed inputs and reset to STANDBY. In responding to the thud of what he thought might be an RPG, Peled maneuvered right then left. Additional bright flashes burst above and around his helo.

Another small flash drew his attention to the right of his path as the HUD flashed a warning. "What's that?"

A critical ALERT flashed, its blood red color indicating an urgent need to change course and altitude. Then another red flash erupted on the ground, with a yellow tongue of flame reaching upward to lick his helo. Shotgun pulled back and up on the stick. Still another white flash pulsed Peled's vision. The helo jittered as another object impacted and fell brightly back to the ground.

"Were those RPGs?" Peled stammered.

The HUD's bright red flashing cursor told him to steer left. Human brains can react to at most four strong stimuli. Peled had more than six critical stimuli bombarding him. Around him was a brilliant cocoon spun of white, red, orange, and gold gossamer threads. Alarms flashed all across Shotgun's dashboard. His instincts told him he was in crosshairs. His pupils shrunken like a sphincter, he weighed each flash and reacted.

Peled radioed an order, "Take ANGELS TWO!"

He saw another flash on the ground ahead. Then yellow smoke rose to meet him. His bird shook, hit by something. Two more fireworks burst ahead as he pulled left on the stick. Banking left as the canyon deepened, he then brought the helo right and lost situational awareness. He violently pulled on the stick. Ahead of the other two helos Shotgun next jammed his stick left. "This is Shotgun, I'm taking fire! Coming up and left. *Ben zona*!"

His words ended there.

Shotgun's rotors grazed and shattered on an outcrop. The Cobra slammed into the rim, rotated from impact, plunging down, parts cascading. The two aviators within accelerated against seat restraints into the windscreen. The helo careened downward, plastic and metal pieces whizzing in every direction. The fuselage, weapons, and aviators surrendered to brilliant flames.

Bright segments lit the sands and shale as the Blackhawk pilots approached in shock. THREE ZERO and FIVE FOUR had their vision inundated by white, red, and orange walls of light. The pilots maneuvered violently, around Peled's crumpled helo, and radioed an SOS. "Ramat Tower, Shotgun is down. All believed dead on impact. THREE ZERO assuming lead. Proceeding to objective, out!"

The remaining helos were now engulfed in brilliant light as green and white fireworks burst higher still. No time to think, two irreplaceable aviators had just died. Four more flew to save others they didn't even know.

Avigdor swore, "Was that an RPG? Could a bedu with an RPG spoil the party? Shit!" *Put it aside. If we fly higher radar will see us, if lower another cheap shot with an RPG can down us.*

"Those goddamn rockets, fireworks, and the fireball from the crash woke up every *bedu* here. They'll be armed and ready. Alert the troops," Captain Katz directed. "Sarge, we've lost surprise."

Bright bursts suddenly went off overhead, silhouetting the two helos in blue and white fireworks. "No," muttered the First Sergeant, "we're still going to hold Field Day on them."

The rescue team's eyes reacted to the bursts thought to be RPGs, though the Blackhawks weren't hit. Luck hadn't been a part of mission planning, but all clearly thought it mattered. Katz set his jaw, "Now we square things."

Chapter - 33

Khalid grabbed his radio mike. He'd seen blue and white fireworks burst in the distance, heard the shouting. "Colonel Jubali, BANDITs inbound your location," he breathed in deeply. "I hope we're ready."

The colonel walked to the building, "Pilgrim Three, STATIONS!" Clicks on radios acknowledged Jubali's order.

In his firing hole Sergeant Hamdoun twitched, and pulled aside the canvas that concealed his firing hole. Two squads were concealed behind the building, but he was alone. He saw a trio of fireworks burst in the distance and his heart pounded.

Jubali pushed the TALK button on the radio handset inside Pilgrim III, "Sergeant Hamdoun, aim and fire once you confirm your targets."

Hamdoun shook with fear, put his prayer beads in a pocket, "I'm ready."

The Blackhawks arrived at the objective area in Arabia. Enroute they'd seen comrades incinerated. The pilots pulled back on their collectives, increasing pitch and lift. With their right fingers the pilots confirmed armament switches were armed. The helos flared prior to touchdown. Rescue squads Alfa and Bravo, weapons charged, had fingers by safeties.

FIVE FOUR was confident, armored engine intakes and exhausts reduced his vulnerability to a stray shot. All was deathly quiet within the helo, darkness without. Prayers were being offered, accompanied by adrenaline fueled curses.

They know we're coming. Captain Katz checked his Galil, looked at his First Sergeant, "Safeties Off."

Hamdoun's mini-gun rested on a chest high mount. "How do I deal with this beast, hidden from prying eyes?" The sergeant's muscles bulged as he swiveled it around. His field of fire covered where any intruders would land. The three barreled weapon had handles for manual control, and a noise cancelling headset. A huge box of rounds rested at his feet. He'd latched it in place, checked his firing wires.

A helo came into view, and the laser designator nearby began tracking it. The NCO saw the aircraft swing left towards him, then aim to his right at the decoy. *"Allah u Akbar*! Do not let me fail," he prayed, "let me live through this."

As commandos exited two Blackhawks, Hamdoun fired. He aimed near the building door as two squads sprinted there. Noise and flash bang grenades went off, but didn't distract him nor slow their assault. The Saudi swung his weapon, catching them in the open. A horrendously loud burst resounded from the mini-gun, deafening him despite ear covers.

The Israelis pitched forward, caught in the withering torrent. Seven died in seconds, their protective armor no match for a solid stream of rounds. One charged him and died feet away as both helos hovered.

Hamdoun swore, “Israeli crazy, *Majj Noon*.”

Hamdoun’s gun jammed and two commandos made it to the building. He gawked as the duo set breeching charges, blasted open its doors, and burst inside. He cleared the jam and saw the closest helo pivot towards him. The overcast sky silhouetted the hovering form.

The sergeant squeezed his trigger as the helo pilot fired. Only the Saudi had a clear target for the next two seconds. His bullets arched across to the aircraft, hitting its skin. Most ricocheted off armor, as THREE ZERO’s pilot moved controls to center his weapon’s sights.

Hamdoun knew he’d be dead if he did nothing; the aircraft’s chain gun would shred him. The darkened shape hovered in mid-air, its weapons almost aligned on him. Armament barrels moved to stare into his eyes. Hamdoun fired at the cockpit, but his burst hit the engine intake.

The rounds initially bounced off the plating, then entered the turbine cowlings. The bullets, deflected by armor before, now stayed within. The projectiles shredded each stage of the engines. Compressor blading, diverters, and fuel lines failed.

The pilot gawked as alarms for engine temperature, fuel state, altitude, lift, pitch, and fire flashed. He could do nothing. Without lift the helo crashed fifty feet to the sand. His final acts were to activate his fire suppression system and to shoot. Eshel sent a long burst at the man in the ground, but his aim was high. The rounds flew off into the sands.

Hamdoun prayed, his body frozen in fright. *Allah Il Allah … There is no God but God*. His heart rate soared as his eyes closed, urine soaking his combat trousers. He continued to fire until his weapon jammed.

They had watched on the remote closed circuit TV feed as Colonel Jubali and Major Hourani set up Pilgrim III to receive intruders. Amir and Tooley now observed remotely as the captured pilots sat restrained, their Israeli insignia and names prominent. The two uncooperative captives twisted against restraints, bio-sensors transmitting their vital signs to confirm life.

Tooley looked at the two as Jubali and Hourani checked the video feed, causing the screen to become temporarily fuzzy. This is something I never would expect to see. *What will happen? Another long report to submit, especially if any Israelis come to rescue these guys.*

O'Toole knew TV video and audio of the two was being streamed to a distant Saudi TV network control room, allowing visibility of any action at whatever level the Saudi government wanted.

As the Israeli commandos entered, their eyes cleared the space for others, then focused on two men sitting in Israeli uniforms. Two Saudi officers stood beyond the prisoners. A colonel and a female major, their hands in the air, were a few feet away in the line of fire. Fingers tensed on triggers, as the two intruders were shocked to see explosive like belts on the prisoners. Katz recognized the captives as Captain Ben Bedoo and First LT Barzouk.

"Don't shoot!"Hourani said in Hebrew as the armed Israelis paused.

A female Saudi officer speaking Hebrew startled Captain Katz, his finger twitching on the trigger guard, "Who are you?"

She replied, "I'm Major Hourani. If you shoot us, your pilots will die before our bodies hit the ground."

The colonel broke the silence next, "I'm Colonel Jubali. We have this building surrounded. Surrender and you won't be hurt. We engaged your helos, and many of your assault team ... dead. If you kill us your friends will be blown apart. That would preclude *Kaddish*, your prayer for the dead."

Captain Katz' eyes moved around the room, "We seem to be at a stalemate."

Jubali's face begged for calm. "Turn over your weapons and you will be repatriated in prisoner exchanges. If you resist and try to escape, you will be shot."

Katz and his First Sergeant eyed each other nervously. Weapons fire continued outside. Katz shuffled his feet, "What if we refuse?"

The colonel half turned to Hourani, his eyes glued to the Galils leveled in their direction, "Major, explain their situation again."

"Neither Colonel Jubali nor I are armed. But, *do not* misread this. Killing us gets you nowhere. Your government will be very unhappy if *your* actions cause the deaths of," Hourani pointed, "your compatriots."

The two commandos looked at each other, fingered triggers, and paused as gunfire continued outside. Katz saw that both prisoners were wired with command detonated explosives. If their pulses stopped, the detonators would trigger. The captain nervously drummed his left fingers on the forward stock of the *Galil*, "we can just kill you both."

"Two squads surround this building. We are being broadcast live; if you kill us the world will see our murder on the evening news." Hourani pointed to video monitors, cameras with record lights flashing in red.

Hourani took a deep breath, stared directly at Captain Katz, but couldn't discern if they'd kill her or surrender. She spoke in Hebrew, "It's your choice." *Hell of a choice, life changing.*

Katz' eyes scanned her name tag, "Hourani, that's Lebanese?" His finger stayed on the trigger.

"Yes, and Katz is Jewish. Does it matter?" She eyed his trigger finger and prayed talking would stop loss of life.

Chapter – 34

President Ellington was enjoying a rare state dinner with Tomas D'Oliveira, President of Brazil. He was sipping a fine California wine as the duty officer from the White House Situation Room, Commander Metcalfe, came in. Metcalfe bent over and whispered. "Mister President, I hate to disturb you. You need to be informed of CRITIC level incidents unfolding in Arabia." Metcalfe described three Israeli helos flying to Arabia, one bird downed, one disabled, most of an assault team dead, more prisoners taken.

POTUS asked for 'the picture,' his term for the Presidential laptop with TS level WHSR video of satellite capture. As the image coalesced, Ellington gasped, "Sonofabitch! Tell my Chief of Staff to cancel all meetings on my calendar for tomorrow morning. Have the

National Security team meet."

He looked at Metcalfe, "Get the team together, and ensure National Security Advisor Bengtsson is there. I want the team at the Situation Room no later than 23:00. We need to look at some options."

Metcalfe acknowledged the Commander In Chief's directions. He noticed the Presidents' hair seemed grayer than just months ago. Ellington's face seemed worn, troubled. *The Big picture must really drain him. Each day more depressing than the last, too many people trying to kill each other.*

The Commander hurried off, cell phone already speed dialing.

POTUS, his forehead now sweaty, apologized quietly to President D'Oliveira, "It's another incident in the Middle East, Mister President."

"If it is critical," D'Oliveira offered, "we can end the dinner now."

"No. It's serious, but not critical. My pastry chef has a special dessert, Baked Alaska. I understand it's your favorite. I wouldn't want to miss that, would you?" Ellington insisted.

Ellington kissed his wife good night after the dinner and walked to the Situation Room. Commander Metcalfe greeted him, "Mister President. The Saudi government has re-opened back channel discussions with Israel through the Swiss. They provided proof of life, implied prisoner exchanges might be possible, and gave assurances that the dead would be preserved for eventual repatriation. Oh, and there is still more news, Sir. The Saudis are now actually at DEFCON ONE, not just on paper ... for real."

POTUS scrunched his hands into fists, "Son of a bitch!"

First Lieutenant Eshel and his co-pilot scurried past the building to FIVE FOUR, praying their legs would get them to the rescue helo and escape.

Hamdoun ordered his squads to fire over their heads and the Blackhawk. He hoped that they would escape to spoil the image of Israeli military invincibility. That was the bigger plan.

The Israeli aviators scurried aboard the helo, strapped in, and returned to their air base. Their expressions suggested sorrow at the death of friends, and anger at whichever idiot hung them out to dry. Their situation did not reflect the optimism of the July 2005 mission brief.

The phone screeched as its encryption routine synced to connect the handsets. Tooley saw the ID and number illuminate on his embassy desktop receiver. "Hi Stefano, haven't heard in weeks. How's your family? Are you staying safe between the Iraqis and Iranians?"

"Me, I stay low, but it's been quiet where I've been. I move a lot. Sophia and Marcus are fine. She's an 'artiste' and has her own gallery in our town." Stefano paused, looked out of the makeshift tent near *Jebel Al Ali*. "How is your family?"

"Wonderful, safe. Bai is doing well in school, getting all A's. Anh is still school nurse, keeping those kids healthy. Mick is suffering from puppy love, a girl named Judy. She's older by a year. Her family was transferred stateside, so he doesn't even get to see her. Mini-O'Toole just mopes around, but that hasn't slowed his attempts to eat anything within arm's reach."

"That normal, given his age."

"It is Stefano. Say, no one's listening. Did you catch any of it on the nightly news - F-16s and cluster bombs, one plane downed and its pilots captured? The Israelis attempted a rescue just the other day, but it turned out very poorly. I hope you have good news," O'Toole suggested. "I have none."

"Not me. I saw a TV newscast about that cluster bomb attack. You were there?"

"I got a minor wound," Tooley grimaced. "Anh told me I couldn't go play with Amir any more. She gave me orders to watch anything exciting from a distance."

A chuckle resounded over the cell. "As you know, I was initially embedded with both militaries," Stefano declared. "They told me they would schedule any interviews. Back in your Vietnam War journalists ran around seeing what they wanted, asking anyone anything. Newsmen were not controlled. In the Gulf Wars media got tied around the military's middle finger. Now it's different. Strangest, most implausible thing one could imagine."

Playing dumb, Tooley asked, "In what way?"

"As I mentioned five weeks ago, I was relocating between both sides. I'm with the Iraqis now, for the last three plus weeks. Both Air Forces face off repeatedly, but no planes get shot down. They seem to dance in mid-air. And all the call-ups in Iraq mustered far out in Anbar Province. Why, I ask, so far from the border they had to defend?"

Tooley sounded unconvinced, despite the units, numbers of artillery tubes, and places Stefano had listed. They'd moved past the details in a blur. "Maybe they aren't prepared for war yet."

"The Iraqis are operating as unified forces. They can respond to any attacks from many places, in force. Their numbers are growing, and they have more air support and artillery each week."

"You mean what, they're preparing?" Tooley quizzed.

"I've wondered for weeks now if the consistently dire Iraqi situation indicated something deeper. They kept backing away, without serious battles. Opposing artillery units squared off in staggered alignments a month ago, behind their infantry units. I heard reports of casualties along the shifting front lines, but found little evidence to confirm them."

"Maybe both sides aren't ready. I have enough trouble trying to figure out what the Israelis and Saudis are doing. Your situation with Iran and Iraq is too confusing."

"Why aren't the Iranians advancing on Baghdad above the marshes? That region can only slow an army if it lets them. My Iraqi sources told me the Iranians wanted to 'avoid trap' there. Yet the marshes are the most direct route to Baghdad." Stefano drummed his fingers against the cell phone holder, "Winning a war still means holding ground, like in Roman times, right?"

"You're right. Their legions marched out, beat up the locals, took over. War was straight forward," Tooley asserted.

"Well, two increasingly armed forces hereabouts *are* on the move. They're moving to and fro, the front drifting to the west. I ask myself why there are so few wounded and dead. How can there be so many fighter intercepts and none shot down?" the journalist postured. "Now the Iraqis move three infantry divisions, 30,000 men, but they don't fight."

"Right again. It doesn't seem normal for war."

Stefano became silent, talked quietly away from his cell phone. "I must go. Our unit is moving. Talk to you later." The circuit went dead.

Chapter - 35

The Iraqi Artillery Battalion Commander offered him a cigarette, the horrible local variety, unfiltered. *Bad for my health, like this job.* Stefano held up a hand, "La, no." He looked across at the eight artillery pieces nearby, "I'll pass this time. How are things going today?" The two had the forced familiarity of an inquisitive relationship the reporter required to get the day's story.

"Your army is pulling back, again. I don't understand why; they could hold." Stefano looked at Abdullah, fingering worry beads in one hand, rolling a partially smoked cigarette in the other. He put the colonel on the spot, "Your troops are confident, yet they continue to give up ground."

"I do what I'm told. I tell my men, 'We must not lose cities. We don't want to lose people, but land is cheap.'"

"Except for the people who live on that land. I suspect that what I observed over the past two weeks between your artillery and the Iranians was a sham. It's a lie that can end my career." The Italian reporter felt the tension reflected by deep trenches for cover against counter battery fire, but he prodded, "I'd like the truth, so the story I report is credible."

Colonel Abdullah shifted his body, becoming evasive, and avoided the question. "We remain ready, move so enemy artillery and aircraft don't hit us. Our unit has many radios to coordinate, for protection with air forces to ensure no friendly fire hit us."

Stefano figured these troops were serious about preparing for war, just not fighting at the moment. Fighting meant coordination with others, the guys on one's side. "Coordinate with whom?"

"With other artillery and division, as part of bigger overall forces." The colonel crushed out his cigarette, cleared his throat, a signal he wanted to utter some approved PR statement. Stefano stared, "We give up land, not cities or peoples. We must keep enemy from Baghdad."

Sergeant Bashar, the senior NCO, was upset again with Captain Mustafa, commander of his Iranian Artillery Battery. Bashar thought of the crews of the eight dug in 105mm howitzers, men like him feet from pallets of highly explosive shells. *He talks down to us, even senior NCOs, like he is better. He is arrogant, does not consider his men. An officer must do that. I will give him a headache.*

Bashar knew attention to coordinates was paramount to accuracy in each fire mission, and gave the howitzer's traverse and elevation wheels extra turns. The artillery piece was now aimed at slightly different coordinates, and he didn't care where that place was. *I do this and make trouble for the captain.*

The tubes' crew loaded a projectile with its powder casing, raised the breech block, and inserted a firing cartridge. The loaders then clamped hands tightly over their ears and braced. The battery's sergeant pulled the firing lanyard and the howitzer recoiled, kicking up a minor cloud of dust. The round and others went on their way as the settings dictated.

Rounds fell 1000 yards to the east northeast of him by Stefano's estimate. He'd seen rounds impact over the past three weeks; self preservation required that he figure out directions and distances. The rest of the Iranian salvo began to move closer. Stefano felt uneasy with their increasing proximity, and wondered what or who the target was.

A Call For Fire reverberated from radio speakers. The CFF assigned a new target, perhaps to hit those firing at them. The whistle of additional rounds pierced the air as an Iranian shell burst in the air and fragments whistled in all directions.

The Battery Officer screamed, "Counter Battery." Several artillerymen continued to traverse their howitzer. Five tube crews were preparing to fire.

Stefano saw three men in the gun crew fall. He hit the deck, covered his ears, and yelled a profanity at the colonel. The journalist glanced at his right arm, rubbed it slowly. It felt warm and wet. His hand came away bloodied, his shirt sleeve in tatters. *Stronzo*!

Chapter - 36

Rushed to the *Abu Nasari* field hospital on a stretcher jammed in a pickup, Stefano received urgent treatment. He found it odd that most of the staff concentrated on him. *Why are there so few wounded here?* He saw a soldier he'd interviewed before. The man laid, in a tattered uniform, the stress of combat aging his young face. The soldier's boots, by the bed, were worn, there were holes in his sleeve, and his insignia was askew. *Was he a deserter, about to be discovered and shot? No; he was wounded, a hero. They should not just patch him up, and send him back. I must tell his story.*

Stefano was bandaged, given pain pills, and his arm wrapped in a sling. He ambled from the dressing tent to an adjacent one. There he met a wounded sergeant from the 105mm battery where the airburst had ended young lives. He stared at beds occupied by other wounded. *So few, yet too many. Yes, the wounded or dead, are a family's constant worry. Do they send the message to parents, family, telling of bravery, death, regret?*

He gripped his arm, struggled to ease the pain creeping to his brain, the reality of war tangible. Stefano smiled, "Should I publicize my wound and get extra points with the network?"

The next day, after an eight hour drive from *Jebel Al Badr*, Stefano met with the embassy's military attaché. "Carlo, I've had the funniest feeling, a suspicion, that this whole war is a scheme, a put on."

Stefano wiped perspiration from his brow with a black and white checkered scarf. "Something strange happened. I saw the same man twice, in two different hospital wards. And though hundreds of shells are fired, planes 'fight' each other in the skies, very few die. I feel I'm embedded in a lie."

Polani listened and watched a tape deck in his Baghdad office record each word. Stefano went on and on, identifying opposing divisions by number, commanders, and locations. "Stefano, that Intel would have been invaluable to the other side. If one side knew that a particular general was a parade field wimp, rather than a deadly opponent, that would give a very real battlefield advantage."

"I know which units are good, and which would surely suffer in combat. I knew all that an enemy needed to win ... but no one questioned me?"

"They never asked?" Polani stammered, not quite believing this lapse of military common sense, "Perhaps they already knew, and weren't concerned because they were just maneuvering." The colonel's voice trailed off.

Stefano looked at Polani, "I've seen it for weeks on end, the slow cautious dance across the sands, never striking, almost never killing, but aware of each others' moves." The journalist rubbed his arm and grimaced.

"What was going on then?" the attaché asked.

"There was a pattern to the movement of Iraqi troops, and a week later, Iranians. They were dancing about like in a waltz, using the same steps, same music."

"Can this whole thing be choreographed?" Polani's forehead then wrinkled, "That's farfetched."

"They mean business," Stefano said, but not convincingly, "They've gathered all these forces. They're practicing for something big. C-130 and 707 tankers are in use, refueling aircraft daily. These men know if they attack without control of the skies, thousands will die. It *must* mean war."

Every morning Tooley sat in his embassy office, coffee cup in hand, reading Open Press accounts of what was going on in the world. These mirrored what circulated each morning over the dedicated SECRET Intel circuit. He wondered, did the most up-to-date scoop on what was happening come from CNN or CIA's analyses? He had it both ways, because his source at the front gave him eyes on the ground. It made him smile, knowing of a war, yet staying at a distance. *Better that way.*

The phone screeched, synced, and caller ID told O'Toole his front line source was waiting to share. Even as the phone system recorded the conversation, Tooley hurriedly scribbled notes. It meant an update, a lengthy report to Langley, one that made sense. Another long night of typing, what he'd just heard made his gray hairs lighter still. *They're ready, poised for an historic bloodbath.*

Stefano broke into the American's thoughts, "You and I, we

now share being bloodied in war. I must not make another mistake and get Rodolfo killed."

Tooley ended the lengthy talk with a request, "Stay safe." The phone clicked as he set it down.

Two days later POTUS closed the CIA's regional analysis report, as National Security Advisor Bengtsson ended his 16 August 2005 morning brief. The President injected, "How does this O'Toole come up with such insights?" Assorted blank stares from the assembled honchos of Ellington's National Security Council greeted his query.

"If I may offer a view, Mister President," General Peckingham answered, "he has a solid gold source at the front, one with unrestricted access to both soldiers and generals. He only seems fuzzy on the diplomatic side."

"So general, he has a thorough grasp of the military picture? Fine, now where do I get an accurate world view? Am I missing something? What are the Iranians and Iraqis doing in that sphere?" POTUS glanced at Director of Central Intelligence Trujillo, then at SECSTATE DeVries.

DeVries answered, and Trujillo nodded agreement.

Ellington saw the looks the two exchanged, wondered if they were confidants, friends and advisors, using the same script. *I need better briefers.* He pointed to Iraq's Anbar Province, "The Iranians pushed them here?"

"Yes, without a lot of fighting. There were very low casualties compared to before, when the Iranians launched human wave assaults." Peckingham asserted.

"Why is that significant?" Ellington inquired of his JCS Chairman.

Peckingham responded, "Well, one would expect any breakthrough to come with fast, armored divisions, followed by infantry, not the other way around."

The President's face showed concern that others of his assembled experts weren't as knowledgeable of what was going on as expected. Ellington turned to DeVries, "Damn it all, does the State Department have a solid handle on what's going on? What's next Mel, waves of tanks, dropping CBUs on troops, massed artillery fire? Or will someone start sticking flowers down rifle barrels?"

DeVries smiled at the President's reference to flower power. "Correct, Mister President, and some of the recent moves defy expectations. Iran, Syria, Iraq, and Turkey are each making peace with their Kurdish minorities. It suggests a whole new level of regional diplomacy." DeVries, always looking for the best in man and mankind, uttered a prayer aloud, "God just let those people talk each other to death."

Ellington's fingers drummed the report on his desk, "So they're neutralizing domestic discontent?" He looked for more thorough answers in their faces. His frustration dawned on the group as he angrily drew an arrow from Iran's border through Anbar province. "Where do you folks suppose this all ends, the direction of all these armies, gathering and growing every week?" His disturbance at no one having considered the momentum of those forces reflected in his face.

"I want to get a transcript of the conversations between this O'Toole and Gaiuso, or I want to listen in. Is that possible? I mean, you guys built their damn phones." Ellington glared at Trujillo, putting a lot of pressure on the messenger.

"Yes," Trujillo squirmed, "Mister President, can do."

The CNN van's dish synced with ARABSAT and other satellite feeds. The data stream was being broadcast from western Iraq live to news agencies worldwide. Local feeds were routed to Al Jazeera, Saudi channels, and throughout the Gulf. Audiences around the world listened. A bold, bright red runner flashed as it ran across CNN screens worldwide – BREAKING NEWS.

"This is Stefano Gaiuso for CNN. I'm at an Iraqi army divisional headquarters in western Iraq. I look around the front, between two huge armies." He emphasized each word, "Iranian and Iraqi forces are positioned in overlapping areas along a front stretching thirty miles. Armed soldiers stretch to the horizon. By my count roughly 150,000 infantry, 500 main battle tanks, 'a sizable force' by any measure, faces each other. The forces are a reminder of Allied Forces in the first Gulf War."

Rodolfo Carazon, his camera man, slowly panned from Stefano to a tent, and zoomed in on two stately figures in combat uniforms.

Gaiuso resumed his commentary, "This reporter has witnessed truly momentous news. Generals Humdillah and Badir, of the Iranian and Iraqi forces, have just signed a 'peace.'" He paused as Rodolfo, focused on their faces.

"Their governments have simultaneously issued statements that they are 'poised for peace.' We anticipate further information on what this all means, so expect updates throughout the coming days. This peace coalition has forwarded a proposal to the UN. Their proposal calls for a nuclear-free region, an Open Jerusalem controlled by the UN, and the return of Palestinian lands." There was a tone of hope in his voice as Stefano Gaiuso signed off.

The video showed the two generals and their staffs embracing. In the background one heard and saw weapons being fired into the air. Iraqi and Iranian troops hustled to meet and celebrate their historic but fragile new friendship.

As politicians, elected leaders, and average citizens learned of this news, everyone prayed it meant peace. Breaths stopped around the globe as TV viewers heard of the promising cessation of hostilities.

Within seconds Intelligence agencies of world powers fired the starters' gun to the Cover Your Ass marathon. Synchronized avoidance of accurate statements, hemming and hawing, and free style CYA guesstimation began. Their question, in many languages and dialects, became ... *How did we miss this?*

Israeli Prime Minister Geblar turned off the news, and turned to Defense Minister Jabeel at his office, "Update all war contingencies, defensive options. And find out how long they've been planning this."

Chapter - 37

It was August, and another Wednesday morning brief for President Ellington. He sat, coffee at hand, surrounded by NSC members. A series of muted big screen TVs hung on the wall, but their story was in everyone's thoughts. "Guys, I was watching CNN and BBC's coverage of this latest twist in the Middle East. I was comparing what they said. Turkey and Syria almost simultaneously declared neutrality with respect to this peace coalition. A fascinating development wouldn't you say? Hard to stay *neutral*."

He looked around; few had picked up on his comparison of neutrality to countries declaring themselves neutral. Ellington's eyes met those of DeVries, in a momentary understanding of what had happened, not of accord for what was to be done. Their eyes acknowledged *that* remained TBD.

DeVries injected herself, filling a brief lapse by the rest of an uncharacteristically silent NSC, "How do they stay neutral exactly? They're surrounded by armed neighbors. And the elephant in the room, well, we need to ensure Israel plays nice with its neighbors."

"How do we frame our reaction, our words?" Ellington asked rhetorically, "We're on record supporting a Palestinian state, and a Free Jerusalem. Hell, our embassy is in Tel Aviv; it's there to show we are neutral in our dealings in the region. Those positions have been consistent through the past six administrations. And the settlements, we've been against Israel seizing Palestinian lands, no matter that they call it something different."

Mel DeVries jibed Peckingham, "General, how *should we respond* to a group calling itself the peace coalition? Should we bomb them until they call Uncle? Should we send in your Marines?" She hoped he'd see, and forgive, her sarcasm. "I hope we want to circumvent obstacles rather than trying to drive over them. Better to talk, let the creative ideas come out."

POTUS turned to Vice President Counselor, "Maureen, I want you to fly to Tel Aviv tomorrow, ask Prime Minister Geblar what it takes to keep his forces in barracks. We need to keep Israel from attacking this coalition, despite questions of its potential *intentions*."

Ellington next looked at his SECSTATE, "Mel, hit the road. Meet the Turkish Prime Minister, then the Syrian President. Get clarification of this neutrality, especially with respect to Jordan and Arabia. Turkey is in NATO; we can't have them stray from the fold."

There was a reluctant acknowledgement in the eyes of Peckingham and DCI Trujillo of the action being assigned to DeVries. She smiled and gave CJCS a sloppy salute, *Gotcha.*

The big screens in the WHSR caught everyone's attention. A new ticker was running across the bottoms of the screen – BREAKING NEWS. But it wasn't new news; Turkey and Syria declare 'Neutrality.'

The President turned to his advisors, "Gents, I can already hear the uproar from the Hill, Hawks yelling to send in the Marines. The Doves will demand negotiations with the peace coalition and Israel. Anyway we respond, react ... we get blasted. Come up with some positive ideas," he paused, "something neutral."

"Maureen, get Israel to sign the nuclear non-proliferization treaty and protocols. That will help defuse this coalition; work that angle."

Peckingham smiled; his eyes drifted to the SECSTATE. He knew Israel would never publically admit it had nukes.

Ellington continued, "We don't want to be clothes lined by any surprises tomorrow, or the day after. On Turkey, find out what do they mean by this neutrality BS. Turkey is the flank of NATO." Ellington looked around, his eyes probing for answers to hang his foreign policy legacy on.

DeVries chimed in with another observation, "Maybe those countries are trying to keep a lid on things? I thought that was our job."

The President became blunt, "Maybe – but we're a long way from that decision point, and the wolves are circling. Please no leaks until we get some clarifications; no press briefings." Ellington looked at each of his advisors. His face showed he meant it – no leaks. "Turkey and Syria aren't trying to impress anyone with these moves. I want your best advice on what's driving them, where it's all headed, and what our options are."

The Commander In Chief folded his hands on the table and pursed his lips, "Be back here tomorrow at 08:00, before the Vice President and SECSTATE fly off to the sand box. Bring your inputs on how to keep the friggin sky from falling."

SECSTATE and VPOTUS were already in the air, flying east to the center of the quagmire. Thursday mid-morning in the WHSR, and more BREAKING NEWS was in everyone's mind. Ellington smiled, felt like his team was enroute, about to *make a difference*. He moved his fingers on the remote; the TV's volume amped up.

The commentator's voice came on. "CNN has more for you our listening audience, a new Middle East update. Syria has just informed the UN and the US Embassy in Damascus that it would not permit military aircraft to transit its airspace enroute Israel. Listen later today for the latest world news on this CNN station."

POTUS muted the TV, looked around the Situation Room, "Guys, our Ambassador in Ankara just informed us that Turkey has invoked a 'no fly' region in accordance with some obscure UN resolution, yet Turkey stated it wished to remain part of NATO's collective security."

"The Turks and Syrians, maybe they just want to stay out of the line of fire," DeVries stated as she moved closer to the Vice President's chair, the two now video conferencing enroute the Middle East on Air Force Two. "No one wants other countries' armies massing next door. That could be the real concern here. I'll try to decipher it, take action to inquire about these developments." She looked as VPOTUS nodded concurrence.

Late that afternoon the NSC reconvened, its live secure link with Air Force Two re-enabled. Peckingham was briefing information newly received from Riyadh, "Mister President, Arabia, at DEFCON ONE as you recall, agreed on a framework to enter Jordan and train defensively. The declaration states that Jordan and Arabia neither support, nor will they act to oppose, the coalition. Additionally the intention was stated to prevent incursions into land, sea, or air spaces by Iran or Iraq."

Ellington suddenly looked worn, "Any new moves by either the Saudi or Jordanian militaries?"

"Yes, Mister President. Their AWACS are up 24/7 now; and they've got Combat Air Patrol or CAP assigned, two sections. That's four fighters armed with every missile they could hang on them. The AWACS are even controlling some Jordanian CAP. The planes seem to be mostly along their respective borders with Iraq, with orders to shoot if borders are crossed. This is a dangerous new twist."

"How do we ... can we, win?" Ellington inquired. He twisted around, "My moon stone was dark this morning, general; how about yours? Give me your best shot, your options for this mess."

Peckingham moved some brief notes around in front of him, "I suggest we offer the Israelis another Patriot missile battery. It's a defensive system, so it can be described as a neutral act. And we should privately let their Defense Minister know the pre-positioned War Reserve ammo stocks are to stay in place ... at current levels."

"Not bad, general, I like those options. Anything else?" POTUS smiled.

"Yes, Mister President. Satellite and radio intercepts confirm the Saudis are moving artillery and infantry to their border with Iraq. Those forces are linked in with the duty AWACS for fighter cover, and they've put up two aerostats with air controllers as backup."

"Aerostats?"

"Yes, Mister President, they're tethered blimps, with radar and other sensors, like stationary AWACS."

"I see," Ellington acknowledged. "Pray those moves keep the coalition away from Jordan and Arabia."

"I will. There's more Sir. The Missile Launch Center at Sooley Base is now manned 24/7 and mobile launchers are being moved randomly, all armed with MRBMs, ready to launch. Those suckers can take out a city block; do much, much more if they're equipped with dirty bomb warheads."

Ellington hung his head, then looked up, "Is that possible? Can the Saudis do that?"

Peckingham's face wrinkled, showing his anxiety, "It is ... and they can."

Chapter - 38

SECSTATE DeVries knew Turkey was overwhelmingly Islamic, but officially secular. Religion in that part of the world was taken very seriously. Sunni Arabia and Jordan justifiably worried about Shia Iran and Iraq. The gulfs between these branches of Islam were not taken lightly, not anything like Catholics criticizing Episcopalians, or Baptists blasting Mormons. *These folks have been practicing hate and enmity with knives and swords for centuries.* She had attended services at the embassy before leaving Ankara that morning, thankful for the chance.

"Good morning, Mel. Is the sky falling?" Ellington asked, "or did you patch it?"

"Not yet, Mister President, maybe tomorrow." DeVries hoped tomorrow wouldn't come in that particular way with the heavens descending. DeVries was aboard a State Department 707, equipped with enough accoutrements to satisfy any traveling dignitary. She had just finished her onboard breakfast, eggs over easy, toast buttered with far too much butter. Sipping from a huge mug of Turkish coffee, she looked up momentarily. The cabinet officer commented to one of her diplomatic guards, "Great stuff, probably enough caffeine here to last a week."

"Yes Mam, strong stuff. You can probably read the grounds when you finish."

Beside her dishes sat a huge illustrated book, *Guidebook to Istanbul*, presented by Prime Minister Al Khurdi as a personal gift. She thought back to their negotiations over the past two days. The two had hit it off and he'd confessed admiration. "America is a true friend of Turkey. We can work together. Please have a safe trip." He'd hugged her, an uncharacteristic, and decidedly un-Islamic gesture, just before she boarded the plane.

DeVries smiled as the red STU squawked, bringing her attention back to earth, "Good afternoon, Madame Secretary. You have good news, I trust," POTUS said, hoping his confidence would somehow influence the world situation. What is all this other new stuff about?" Ellington asked.

"Arabia's emissaries to the UN Security Council just proposed an open Jerusalem, and denuclearization of the region. The Saudis sound more and more like this peace coalition. No matter how we respond I worry that we'll piss someone off, especially Israel." DeVries shifted in the deeply comforting black leather seat as the STU screeched again, "Mister President, it appears countries in the region are moving to isolate Israel diplomatically, and gain the moral high ground in anticipation of conflict."

Ellington listened, along with Peckingham and his Chief of Staff. The rest of the NSC was at home, probably parked on a couch watching baseball and eating burgers. Sunday was the day even White House folks got to unwind. That was the idea, a distant gleam these days of increasingly tense world news.

Peckingham nodded, then injected an opinion. "The biggest

indicator of peaceful intentions, as I see it, is that coalition forces haven't been slaughtering each other. That's very hopeful, given the numbers of troops they have mixed together. It tells me they have very good discipline. I hope the Israelis appreciate that." He looked around; Ellington wasn't listening, again, following the big screen TV wrap-up of sports events.

Richard DeMeers, the President's Chief of Staff, knocked on POTUS' office door, entered, and interrupted Ellington. He moved to his side, bent over, and whispered a reminder of the days' schedule commitments. "I just wanted to quickly bring you back to earth. You've got local issues, supporters, bitter political enemies, and all the fun people of your life, Sir."

DeMeers smirked, handed Ellington three notes with times, locations, and links to drafts of his meeting's objectives. The first covered an urgent meeting with the Congressional Conservative Caucus 'on that troublesome legislation issue.' Then there was a TOP SECRET meeting with the Commander of Delta Force on 'a rescue mission.' "Your final meeting is a fundraiser with political supporters at four PM."

POTUS looked up, "Dick, let me get back to you on these after I talk with the Vice President and Mel DeVries. I want to see if more crises are on my plate."

The COS bowed and walked back out, hoping this Sunday would end, and he'd get to see a baseball game with his wife, Brandy. Ellington glanced up, and saw he'd lost his audience. He signed off with DeVries and put the red STU handset back on the holder. *Mel does great work.*

An hour later Ellington drummed his fingers, sipped a cup of Blue Mountain coffee, among the world's best. He considered it up there next to Hawaiian grown Kona in quality. Despite the great flavor, he always dumped in brown sugar and creamer.

He looked up as one of the Presidential Protection Unit guards entered. "Jake, did you see that error?" as he glanced at the latest baseball recaps on the big screen and a replay. "Damn, how could the right fielder drop that fly? It was in his friggin glove." He grimaced, "I lost fifty bucks to my brother on that game."

"Yes Sir, even I could have pulled that one in." He handed the President a ream of papers for signature, a bottle of aspirin, turned and exited.

More to do before these meetings. Better get to it. Ellington pulled the STU controls nearer, selected the speaker configuration as he muted the TV. VPOTUS Counselor was winging her way home on Air Force Two, and he needed to assess her report before heading to other urgent commitments.

Counselor glanced out a window as Tel Aviv's airport receded in the distance. She pushed her plate aside. The chef had accessorized her favorite away from home meal with bacon. Her husband tried to replace that delicacy at home with turkey look alike strips, once a month. Her muffins had butter and honey lathered on. She thought today's selections were the best part of being on the road. She moved the coffee and bottled water closer as the chef retrieved the dishes.

VPOTUS swallowed some water with an aspirin chaser. *Glad I had that Patriot missile deal in my back pocket when I got here, or I'd still be negotiating.* It had been a couple of days of intense negotiations with Israel nonetheless.

"Madam Vice President, can I get you anything else," the chef asked as he retrieved the dishes and crumbs.

"No. Well, peace and quiet. Got any of those in your pantry?"

"I'll look, Sir." He walked away, past the guards.

Counselor moved her coffee cup aside just as the STU buzzed. *Ah, the office.* She smiled and pressed the speaker button, "Good morning, Mister President."

"How did things go?" Ellington asked.

"It was fairly productive, Mister President. Israeli Prime Minister Geblar formed a tag team of sorts, ganging up on me. I acknowledged their concern about this coalition and the growing numbers of troops, tanks, artillery, and planes. I offered them another Patriot missile battery, and asked in return that they exercise restraint, play nice in the neighborhood."

"And?"

"They were strident with concerns about the coalition, especially its SCUD missiles. They said the only thing that'll take them out is the Patriot. I felt I was listening to the woe is me, the sky is falling chorus. While the coalition is not near Jordan yet, the Saudis and Jordanians are both very nervous, flying their AWACS round the clock. The bottom line is they want the Patriots, and Jabeel requested two squadrons of fighter aircraft." She paused, "I sensed anxiety about the AWACS and round the clock CAP."

Ellington looked up, "Why?"

Chapter - 39

Techs in the vans nearby tweaked the uplink to CNN's headquarters. The data stream included tags for GPS coordinates and GMT time. The Saudis didn't appreciate this nuance, but it wasn't a problem because the location was only accessible by administrators. As the knobs were adjusted, the dish transmitter moved slightly, until a locked alert appeared on their monitor. The frequency allowed use of small antennae, but made alignment critical for effective use. The lock ensured clear broadcasts to CNN audiences worldwide. While the link was unencrypted, that hadn't been a problem; it was news after all.

The techs turned to Gaiuso and gave the universal thumbs up.

The Italian journalist nodded, acknowledging readiness to broadcast. He looked into the camera, "This is Stefano Gaiuso, reporting for CNN with a BREAKING NEWS update. We are here in Arabia, at an air base which I'm not allowed to identify. I'm no longer embedded with peace coalition forces. Here a new set of restrictions apply, which we're still discovering. I anticipate we'll see places and peoples here, and tell you about this unfolding drama of our time." He pointed off screen.

The camera swung to focus on two Saudi Air Force F-15s moving from a revetment to the flight line. As they turned in sequence their exhaust gases impinged on a blast deflector and roared skyward. The planes moved purposely towards the end of a runway, holding for clearance to take off. Heat waves wafted upwards from the tarmac ...

making parts of the scene fuzzy. The noise was ear piercing, softening as the fighters lifted off. Two more could be seen moving to the end of the runway.

Stefano couldn't identify his location, but recognized squadron insignia on fighters from *Hafir Al Batin* Air Base. The insignia could be identified by analysts in any case. No doubt OFFEQ, the Israeli Intel satellite, would verify HAB as the source of CNN's broadcast.

"I wish to read part of a declaration from the peace coalition, 'As approved by our elected representatives and the President, all units of Iraq are directed to maximum effort. Units will respond to attacks with maximum force. No unit is to initiate hostilities, but must stand ready to support the coalition.' He continued, glaring at the TV unit for emphasis. "The peace coalition, it seems, has formally said it will not attack."

In the journalist's mind he knew the stats on coalition forces arrayed, their numbers, and where they were. He was now constrained to what the Saudis said he could say. He didn't know where it was all heading, except that he'd be right at the center of it all.

He pointed, "Look at this map. Over there somewhere is the peace coalition. The Saudis, as the Jordanians with whom they are now operating militarily, are Sunnis. The peace coalition is Shia. These two branches of Islam have fought for over a thousand years. Iran and Iraq, previously enemies, now work together, without fratricide. We should state, that this is true so far."

"Yet their coalition has as one of its objectives a Free Jerusalem, suggesting actions including war to achieve that goal. There is tangible fear, on this base and with Saudis with whom we have spoken, of the potential for war." He paused, cleared his throat, and wafted the jet exhaust fumes away.

"There are new developments by the hour, some I'm allowed to share. Four tank battalions have been sent to the border with Iraq. Two more are to move north by rail, to work with Jordanian armor. The first ingredients of war are moving, or falling into place, but one can only guess whether anyone knows the outcome, or would like it if they did. For now it is a phony war, a deadly serious staring contest. Each side is waiting, to see who'll blink or shoot first." Stefano motioned to his cameraman, giving the roll em signal for background footage.

"This is Stefano Gaiuso for CNN, signing off. Pray for peace."

Stefano whispered, "Father, let me be an instrument for

peace." He put his mike down on a nearby table and looked at his cameraman, "Rodolfo, did you get enough footage?"

Rodolfo grimaced, "More than we'll ever need, more than I care to be part of."

Stefano knew the importance of this news, "Make sure you backup all our video, after you've confirmed that Atlanta has it." The journalist walked over to a van. He removed his phone from the camera's body and attempted a phone call to his American cousin. He scanned his finger, and then entered his twenty-four character security code. The single stored number was accessed next. He heard the cell buzz, then buzz again. There was no answer on the secure cell. *He must be busy, will try again later, after I get back and take a shower at the base.*

Chapter - 40

O'Toole felt his leg twinge. It was the special cell he carried for talking with Stefano. He ignored the cell phone's vibrations. *No time right now, I'll get you later. I'm driving like a madman amidst crazy people.*

His ride was the standard issue, white Chevy Malibu. Like other embassy staffers cars, it held a 100 watt power amp for the illegal CB in the trunk. The CB and amp were required in all embassy staff vehicles, in case the bubble burst.

He'd been driving an hour and a half on the Riyadh-Dammam highway, at near 100 MPH. At that speed he barely kept up with most other sedans. The drive always left him tense, stressed at avoiding twelve year old Saudis driving powerful cars like demons possessed. In between the hot rodders were huge Mercedes trucks overloaded with materials. One had to be on the alert, or become the subject of a police fatality report.

O'Toole soon passed north of Dammam, now on back roads. He drove slowly past miles of scrub brush and windswept dunes. Finally he arrived at his destination. The vantage point, in *Al Fadli*, was a WWI Turkish fort. The mud ruins overlooked something mentioned by Craig Alsop, a Raytheon tech rep. This was where one of the Kingdom's aerostats was moored. He'd heard scuttlebutt the Saudis would use airships as a backup to AWACS. The blimps were to be repositioned along the Arabian Gulf to stations along the borders with Iraq and Jordan. O'Toole wanted to confirm that Intel.

Surprisingly Anh had given him her blessing for the outing, though she worried he'd be near shooting or bombs. "No," he quieted her concerns, "I'll be touristing." He was aware she knew better, but she had acquiesced. He parked before the ruins, walked slowly through it and up to what could be only comically be called a roof. From a vantage point behind a concealing acacia tree, he saw an aerostat tethered close by. *Looks like a barrage balloon from the beaches of Normandy in WWII.*

He scanned the area fast with his binoculars, which served as a digital camera and laser rangefinder. He glanced beyond the aerostat's woven steel tether lines. Near the airship were several vans and satellite dishes and lots of ground control people. The airborne arrays had new radar and IR receivers, and been 'tweaked' to search for the engine exhaust and control frequencies of drones. Intercepted signals sent down the fiber optic cables were processed, searching for UAVs.

O'Toole's block by block visual sweep revealed something puzzling. A drone launch site was off to the right. One of the Saudi drones was revving up, apparently ready for launch using a stretch of deserted paved road, surrounded by lots of personnel. *Probably Vinnell, but why would they be here?* He thought for a moment. The rumors were they were to be used over the Eastern Province. *They are worried about their Shia. That was scary.*

Off to one side was a familiar shape, a rather large water truck. O'Toole's eyes flared as he walked back to his car.

The plan was simple; meet Craig Alsop at the *Thalatha* souq. O'Toole parked nearby, zigzagged past rows of *bedu* women clothed in black *abayas*. The women offered used camel saddles, worn copper cooking vessels, colorful fabrics, and spices. Arrayed in bright woven baskets, the spice' aroma was overpowering. As he walked to rendezvous with Alsop he noted ornate silver ornaments on the women, next to hennaed hands and feet. *Perhaps a gift for Anh.*

The taller Raytheon rep and Tooley walked to a solitary tent at the souqs' edge. Tooley scratched his stubbly chin; he hadn't shaved that morning, to better blend in. It was their first face to face, and the two shook hands stiffly. The tent's open walls, hung with fabrics, subconsciously softened the oppressive mid-day humidity. Sitting on a rug, they accepted demitasse cups of cardamom flavored coffee.

They sipped the heady *gawa* and Tooley ordered Saudi pizza. He loved its wide flat crusts with an olive oil coating topped with spices. As they ate, their skin felt the air's oppressive clamminess, despite the tent's shade.

Alsop's eyes rolled skyward as he uttered apprehensions about *Mutaawah*. "They're continually by our quarters, trying to protect Saudi morals from we westerners. Those bearded oafs, with their high water trousers, use canes to harass any they think are not religious enough." Alsop looked nervously beyond the tent, to discover any watchers.

O'Toole's instincts kicked in at the man's anxiety. "Don't worry about religious police here; it is too far from compounds to concern them. Few infidels come here."

Craig had phoned days before, told him that Vinnell was training intercept controllers. "They're training lots of em for the AWACS, and aerostats to track drones." Alsop's face seemed puzzled, "I haven't heard why."

"Why would be my question?" Tooley didn't voice his suspicions that the Saudis were concerned with Shias in their Eastern Province. That coastal region was home to much of the oil shipped to world markets. "What else is up, besides the religious fruit cakes?"

"Scuttlebutt is they've new missile seekers, mated them with off the shelf rocket motors." Alsop, still scanning for suspicious Saudis everywhere, then whispered new Intel. "The helo pilots were told their targets would be low and slow, the missiles said to home on a drones' heat."

"Have they run any tests of the missiles?" Tooley inquired.

"Not here, but they engaged several drones successfully in the *Rub Al Khali*. The friend laughed when he told me; 'only camels witness anything there.' I pictured plodding creatures looking up as the small shape exploded above."

Tooley phished for more details, "I didn't know they were into drones."

"Yeah, the aerostats have special processing. The computers sort stationary from moving returns, from planes, helos, even units on the ground. The system can identify infantry on the move and share data with aircraft. That's why they have so many vans at each location," Alsop boasted. "Oh, they've two other airships that I know of. I've worked on both of them."

O'Toole looked up, his interest peaked. "Where?"

Tooley's encrypted cell phone buzzed as he adjusted his seat belt after saying goodbye to the Raytheon rep. Alsop was the most nervous source he'd seen in ages. He felt his gut twinge, something made his instincts uneasy. *I'd better figure out what's up, before it falls on his head.*

It was Stefano again, probably calling with serious Intel to share. Tooley held the STU at arm's length, as though the words coming from it held noxious, deadly bacteria. So far it had been a hot, informative day in the field, perhaps his last as things moved into dangerous waters. Oh well, better find out what's up with Stefano.

Stefano's phone synched in, "Cuz, I'm in Arabia now."

"Where?" Tooley asked.

"Near the air base at *Hafir Al Batin*. You know the area, right, by the oil pipeline road?" the journalist asked.

"Sure do. Actually I'm quite near. A bit south, watching an airship, but I'm heading back to Riyadh now. Are you OK?" Tooley solicited.

"Just great. I've been doing CNN broadcasts here, though I feel nervous with censors watching. The Saudis may be playing me, steering me down some road. I hope it's not a dead end."

"Me too," Tooley guffawed, "so, what's up?"

"When you get back to the office, watch a re-run of my latest CNN broadcast. Check out what I say about their tanks, and fighter aircraft. I read the script MODA provided, or recited what MODA gave me as fact. I wondered if it's true. They're at DEFCON ONE, with AWACS up round the clock and fighters assigned. That's not new, but I was told to say they're moving four battalions of M-60 tanks around." The cell squealed a bit due to static, interrupting the conversation. "You record our BREAKING NEWS, right?"

Tooley acknowledged taping CNN, "Yes we do. Perhaps they're holding some things back. You didn't mention their M1A1 Main Battle

Tanks. I met one of their M-60 tank commanders a while back, he's Amir's nephew."

Stefano laughed loudly over the cell, "So, another crazy cousin going off to war? You know, a real war could develop out of all these moves. It would alter the world as we know it."

"Yes, and you'll be in the crosshairs."

Stefano chuckled, told Tooley of his attempts to trick the TV censors at the air base. "I mentioned the squadrons at *Hafir Al Batin*, the base I couldn't identify. I joked on air about planes not having enough *Mutaawah* to ensure their pilots prayed." Stefano lingered, "Say, did you ever watch the movie *A Few Good Men*?"

"Yes. Loved it! Jack Nicholson is a great actor."

"I made a statement at the base about wanting the truth, and that some watching would not be able to handle it. In the film Tom Cruise the lawyer, tricked the colonel Nicholson portrayed into revealing his guilt for killing a Marine. I was making a reference to the religious police. The comparison escaped the censors."

Tooley grimaced at the comments about religious police. He knew oil markets would be disrupted by a war, the world economy upset by any real conflict. Vast swarms of Shias now faced off against Sunnis; that was the truth. O'Toole considered that, told his cousin, "the Saudis have hundreds of MBTs, and Jordan has hundreds of tanks too, just not the M1A1s. I can't understand why the Saudis don't want that on the evening news." *Israel knows the numbers. They damn sure knew where those tanks were.*

"Hey Cuz, I've got to head home. Give a call and let me know if you can come to Riyadh. Stay safe."

Chapter - 41

O'Toole was at the office before heading home, bedu jewelry in hand as a peace offering. The timing sucked, as it always did. Blame the sun god for the time zones screwing up every phone conversation. The STUs synced.

"Cezar, my conversations with two sources was a free for all. One source told of Saudi preparations for war." He recounted the day, Saudi

Sunnis watching what Shias were doing, where they were moving. And Saudi forces at home are ready to pounce. What the sources said was just part of the puzzle." O'Toole hesitated, "I'll put all my discoveries, and suppositions into the report."

Tooley scrambled to organize his mental notes. The gods of paperwork needed another offering, and his resume did say his job was to kneel at their altar. There was a lot to report. He'd promised a report in the morning. He summarized the key points to the DDI, an aerostat with trained intercept controllers in vans. They had two more of the puffy blimps, were flying drones over Arabia's Shias, plus a new anti-radiation missile. And then, that water truck.

"I'll look forward to your report," Trujillo said.

Tooley then changed the topic, stress from the long day and drive emerging, "The coalition won't attack the Saudis or Jordanians, or Israel, without control of the air, or overwhelming artillery and tank support. The Israelis could be planning it; I would."

"What would you be planning?" Trujillo said inquisitively, not wanting to be left hanging by O'Toole's open ended statement.

"An all out attack to take down an AWACS," O'Toole offered. "I'd expect the Israelis would come in two groups, a swarm to distract Saudi attention, and another unit hell bent for Big Bird. They'll be determined to take out that lumbering 707. The Saudis consider their AWACS national assets, the equivalent of our carriers. They're worried about armed Shias on the border, plus have issues with Shias along the Gulf Coast. These things make the rounds of their worry beads five times a day."

Trujillo sounded incredulous, "Why would Israel attack the AWACS?"

"The Saudi's AWACS can see into Israel, pin point aircraft and troops. It can identify strategic, even tactical dispositions. OFFEQ, the Israeli satellite, isn't geo-synchronous, so it loses coverage much of each day, unlike an AWACS. The Intel can be shared with the Saudis' Islamic brothers, though I'm not convinced they would. The Israelis understand that strategic choice puts them in an untenable position."

"Damn! Will the Israelis attack?" Trujillo blurted.

Tooley's eye zoomed to the ceiling, "They have contingency plans for sure. But we can't know if they intend to."

The DCI's tone heightened, "You're telling me things that I don't want to hear, about a possible war between our closest allies."

O'Toole hedged his observations, "Remember, it's just what my gut is saying; it's supposition, instinct. There's no formula leading from guess to certainty."

"How often has your gut been wrong?" queried Trujillo.

"It hasn't, not when it's about people shooting each other." Tooley paused, becoming defensive, "Hey, it's your job to figure this mess out. I'm just a grunt in the field."

"I'll pray they won't," the Intel Chief implored.

"So will I, Cezar, or all bets are off." Tooley bowed his head, and swung his right hand upward, making a cross on his forehead, his lips, then on his left chest. *Our Father, who art in heaven.*

Trujillo posed a final rhetorical challenge, interrupting Tooley's prayer, "How do we prepare?"

"I don't think we can," O'Toole reckoned. "The Saudis are unconvinced by the coalition's protestations of peace. The movement of their tanks and troops shows their concern. I just don't know what will happen. I'm without any vision, zilch, nada. So, we wait and see." *And I buy a really big life insurance policy.*

"We wait and see?" The DCI's retort begged an answer.

Tooley's shoulders slouched as he looked at the STU. He shook his head, "You know, the second dumbest thing I ever did was coming here."

"What was the dumbest?" Trujillo asked.

Tooley rubbed his chest, scarred where a bullet had gone straight through, "Coming here."

Melinda DeVries had had a bitch of a time getting to the Tuesday meeting. There'd been a wreck on the I-66 artery outside DC's Beltway. It always took time to get around those, despite getting up at God's own hours. Then she encountered new White House guards, full of desire to let you know they checked everything. It didn't bode well for the day, expected to be long by anyone's timepiece. DeVries was cleared by the guard force, and walked to the Oval Office.

The President knew his NSC worked like dogs from sunup to sundown, and then had to work on briefing notes and trying to keep their lives together. The job was a bitch, compounded by DC's heat and humidity in late August. *Was hell this humid?*

O'Toole's day old report reverberated at the very highest levels, the National Command Authority, NCA, meaning the President himself. Trujillo told O'Toole the day before he was "the only guy who bridges the disconnect keeping the right hand and the left hand from communicating."

Ellington looked at the NSC members around the room. His brightest and boldest, but not the glibbest, sat in century old leather or brocade chairs, scanning notes, and to do lists on laptops. The President never shot a messenger; he needed the truth. And better decisions meant re-election. Doing the smart things strengthened his party, made him a man with coat tails. That translated into wider congressional support, besides the concept of a mandate.

Ellington thought back to the excitement, the rush of his January inaugural. One of his NSC spoke. It was Mel DeVries, his person for world views, a voice of conciliation.

"Mister President, considering the news, current world developments, and this report, I recommend caution in our support of Arabia and Jordan. We don't want to appear to favor Sunnis over Shia," DeVries postured. "It's best to distance ourselves from any semblance of religious affiliation."

Peckingham's forehead furrowed, tension heightened, almost in tune with a reduction on DeVries' face. POTUS saw that, termed them Ying and Yang, but only with his protection detail. He laughed to himself. *I encourage them to disagree, but not get personal or strident. But, strident describes Mel and Peck.*

Peckingham interrupted, "Mister President, I recommend we move a carrier battle group near Diego Garcia. We can do that without fanfare, and explain it as training, rather than a move to counter the coalition."

"Do it," Ellington ordered, looking up from SECSTATE's briefing paper. "We're still stuck between a Shia coalition and important Sunnis, and possibly Israel." This Commander-in-Chief, like Lincoln before him, wanted a band of advisors with strong, divergent views. He tended to provoke their inputs if they sat silent too long. Ellington got better, though colorful counsel using this approach, just like the Civil War President. It worked much of the time, just not now.

"Yes, and the Syrians and Turks remain on the fence, watching," DeVries injected. She glanced at Peckingham, "Frustrating eh; really makes a mess of your contingency planning."

"Hmm, yes," acknowledged Peckingham, surprised at her realization of his confined maneuvering room. "Will those onlookers pick a side?"

DeVries' forehead wrinkled. Her face looked like she'd just lost her puppy, "We need more options, besides putting a carrier nearby. That doesn't increase our range of viable options very much." DeVries voice softened, dripping with desperation. "Chairman, before you ask, I'm doing every damn thing I can diplomatically to just keep the Turks and Syrians unaligned and neutral."

"I appreciate your efforts," Peckingham chimed in. Then he presented another option, "Perhaps we should send an Expeditionary Strike Group too. There are pre-positioned war reserve supplies at that island they can access."

DeVries grimaced, "Sounds appropriate. Keep forces ready, but if things go to shit, who do we fight? How do we respond if the coalition attacks Israel?"

Peckingham frowned, "Do you have indications that might happen?"

"No, we have no proof of, nor do I see moves in that direction," DeVries replied, "but we are in very uncharted waters."

Peckingham framed his response, "Well, we can't get caught blind again, like when Iran and Iraq suddenly agreed to this coalition."

DeVries recognized the comment targeted her, "The coalition hasn't disintegrated yet; they seem to be getting on," her voice hesitated, then she laughed, easing the tension. "Maybe they'll hug and bond in a love fest. I'm not holding my breath though. Diplomacy is, at best, the process that epitomizes dysfunction ... and this whole situation reeks of dysfunction."

Peckingham nodded.

Ellington heard no solution, so no smile ventured to his lips. *I wish there were answers, not suppositions. Maybe I should appoint an astrologer to the NSC.*

DeVries shook her head, echoing everyone's concern. "We're damned if we do, or don't. It's a conundrum. We can't pick sides; friends and allies are on opposing sides." She paused, and the framework of a plan emerged, "We need to continue to coerce, even bribe Israel and the others to negotiate. We're on record as supporting an open Jerusalem, a Palestinian state, and peace."

Peckingham challenged, "How do we accomplish that?"

"General, we do whatever it takes," There was frustration in her words, "I still believe in miracles. Maybe, just maybe, there won't be a war." She paused, rolling her eyes upward, "You're always ready to march into battle. If that happens, I want you on my side."

Chapter - 42

Aviv briefed the group on the operational sequence of *Hatkafa*; the code word in Hebrew meant 'begin.' The closed door Israeli cabinet meeting, held in an electronically secure room, approved the op. Those voting included the Prime, Defense, and Foreign ministers, and General Aviv himself, head of Israel's military.

Aviv had memorized the brief and adlibbed, "All flight crews and pilots will stand down for briefings. Training, safety checks, and armaments allocations will proceed according to plan." All eyes were following him, and assured support.

"Twenty aircraft from Hatzor Air Base will serve as a diversion. Those planes will fly past Jordanian and Saudi CAP. Other squadrons are assigned to jam and suppress Jordanian air defenses. If the Scorpion squadron gets through, they'll take out the AWACS."

Defense Minister Jabeel held up a hand. "General, you said 'if' they get through. We are assured of success are we not?"

Aviv squirmed, "Yes Sir, I did say 'if.' In all ops as complex as this, there is risk. I am certain we will take out the AWACS."

Hatkafa was given the green light. Before Execute Hour all units synced time. Four additional aircraft would speed in from a different direction. Those pilots, volunteers from Tel Nof's Spearhead squadron, knew they were on a *Kamikaze* mission. All caution aside, they would fill the converted Boeing 707 with holes if the others failed.

The order to launch *Hatkafa* was given a week later over encrypted circuits, to prevent anyone discovering something was up. As Israeli fighters idled before takeoff, their pilots prayed.

American sensors and technicians had been monitoring Israeli tactical air frequencies for months. Israel's Air Force would be the first to go in motion in any attack. Signals specialists noted that over the past two days those freqs had grown ominously silent. A FLASH, OP IMMEDIATE message was sent by NORAD signals analysts, rerouted via satellite link to NMCC along with voice reports.

NORAD signals analyst Royce's voice bounced from satellite to satellite, then to fiber optic lines in seconds and up the chain of command. "It may not mean anything, or it may mean the Israelis are about to go out and reek destruction," the satellite analyst told James, his NMCC counterpart.

The data and video were routed from NMCC War Room Five's duty flag officer via secure phone to the National Security Advisor, and a limited number of others within minutes. As the Intel was informational rather than operational in nature, and not of the highest level of certainty, COS DeMeers decided to set it aside for the following morning's brief to the President.

Early the next morning, while Washington slept, the attack began. Both Sunni nations, Jordan and Arabia, were caught flat footed, watching the Shia coalition. The operational defense in place was to keep CAP aloft round the clock. Royal Jordanian Air Force planes were orbiting low, but closer to Iraq; Saudi fighters were high. Both air forces staggered their launches to keep planes in the air.

Air contacts are classified as Unknowns; those not yet identified as Friends, or as Foes, BANDITs. The final designation is by count, SNGL, FEW, or MANY. Within moments the number of Israeli planes reported broached the BANDIT threshold necessary to activate Jordan's contingency plans. Alerts went out over primary and backup circuits and Jordanian defenses went to wartime status.

There was little time to muster or count noses. Sirens blared, and citizens scurried for home, then to shelters. Surface to Air Missiles were run out on launcher rails; tanks and artillery units raced to new positions. Borders were closed, infantry posts manned, weapons charged, and all fighters launched.

In Amman, the King was escorted below ground to a bomb proof command center. For only the second time in his reign he supervised Jordan's military forces. Reports to His Majesty reflected a state of active war. The Saudis were alerted, given scant warning as Jordanian aircraft engaged Israelis sweeping south and east.

Israel's attack aircraft were first contested near the Jordanian border. RJAF hangars cleared of aircraft, revetments emptied, and every plane launched. Planes, inanimate objects with crosshairs on them, began to fill the sky.

The ready room at *Jebel Ibraheem* was small, and rarely used. Reservists did touch and go landings at the airfield. Besides those infrequent events, the base's sole function was basic training of new pilots. That was why Captain Hassan was here, to train Second Lieutenant Badr. Hassan was the oldest officer in service, retained because he'd trained the King himself as a young man. The captain still flew that same plane, and His Majesty himself gave Hassan the call sign ROAR, since the young instructor couldn't pronounce the actual one.

The training today would continue with that F-4 Phantom II, its' airframe older than the students' father. Hassan gave a pep talk. "It's a good training platform, and still marginally capable of combat, but only barely compatible with current air to air missiles. The way the plane maneuvers makes it excellent for reconnaissance, or as a bomber, so we'll work with it for now. Ground attack tactics come in five or six weeks, depending on how fast you learn."

Hassan looked at his young student, unsure how the man would perform. The instructor hoped his student was picking up the tactics, and reviewed the maneuvers they'd practice that day. "We won't fire any weapons; this is basic training. Weapons use later." He studied Badr's face, "Remember the Snap Shot technique?" the instructor asked.

"Yes Sir." Badr described the tactic of quickly firing a heat seeking or anti-radiation missile when suddenly faced with an enemy. The tactic was a desperate act, with a slim chance of success. "We use Snap Shot when we don't have seeker acquisition, but the intercept geometry and closure will give us a shot in a second or two." His face exuded the confidence of youth.

"Good. We'll practice Snap Shot, and the revised Thach Weave we flew yesterday," Hassan reminded him. "Remember, we split, do the weave when one of us orders DANCE. As lead I'll start first; I'll break right, climb, and slow. You dive left, gain speed. Then you swing back around to take a shot as you line up behind him. Do you have any questions as to what we do when we're in the air?"

Badr asked no questions. He knew Snap Shot was a desperate, round house swing at an aerial adversary. Without seeker acquisition, the tactic was at best a wild ass chance to get him before he got you. The young man voiced surprise that the other maneuver, used in WWII to defeat faster Japanese Zeroes, still worked. Slowly swinging open hands, he moved them through the air demonstrating the Thach Weave.

Hassan smiled. *He understands.* Then the tactical air speaker blared, and everything changed.

The announcement declared Jordan was at DEFCON ONE, WAR. The voice coming from the speaker was desperate. It ordered immediate launch of fighters to engage inbound Israeli planes. A brief accounting of the bases attacked suggested the Israelis were sweeping south through Jordan. Hassan wondered why.

A siren sounded; its shriek piercing the air. The radio fell silent after it stated - WEAPONS FREE.

The two men had no choice of aircraft; the days' schedule assigned them the oldest Phantoms in the Royal Jordanian inventory. Hassan called the magazine and ordered, "Bring every missile." He was informed that "only Sidewinder or Sidearm missiles are available." Any weapons he and Badr couldn't use were to go to two F-5s scheduled to train with them as the aggressor force.

Hassan reminded Badr, "Our missiles require us to close from astern, or try our luck with a Snap Shot. If we engage that way, we surrender any chance to engage unless we close." Badr nodded, but now showed scant enthusiasm.

The pilots zipped up their flight suits as techs positioned armed missiles on their jets. Within minutes they were buckled in the Phantoms, engines warming for something new – combat. "Ibraheem this is ROAR SIX with ONE ZERO, taxiing."

The tower answered, prayerful that the F-4s and F-5s got aloft to engage the invaders. "ROAR SIX, this is *Ibraheem*. Heads Up! I hold MANY BANDITS west at ANGELS TEN. Acknowledge."

ROAR SIX clicked his radio, acknowledging the status as the fighters roared down the runway. As landing gear swung into their wheel wells, they went to burner and armed all weapons.

Badr's voice on the radio reflected anxiety. This was only his fourth flight in the powerful but prehistoric Phantom. And they were launching to take on the region's best air force. Today was the first for many things, most not promising for his health.

The jets climbed, maneuvered as though executing delicate ballet steps. Finally BANDIT contrails appeared ahead on their twelve o'clock and ROAR SIX whispered, "This is SIX, DANCE." initiating the Thach Weave.

Badr, his flight suit already soaked with sweat, hyper ventilated. It was *the* day, his first actual combat - before he was trained. He prayed with every fiber, every pulse of his heart. His gut felt a chance as they closed on the Israelis, the Phantoms' radars strangled or off. Hopefully they'd be undetected by the Israeli formation.

Badr triggered two radar homing SIDEARMs, "This is ONE ZERO, SNAP SHOT. FOX TWO."

Hassan gasped as Badrs' missiles streaked past his wing tip towards the enemy. He swung his head around as he maneuvered to take position on ONE ZERO's wing.

Badr tensed as he watched two smoke trails creep towards the Israelis. He fired his last two missiles; heat seekers this time, hoping the enemy would maneuver and expose hot engine exhausts. He called "SNAP SHOT, FOX TWO."

The weapons spiraled through the air towards enemy planes newer by decades. The young officer nervously repeated his report, "SIX this is ONE ZERO, FOX TWO."

The captain watched the closest enemy aircraft turn towards them, its pilot alerted by smoke trails in his peripheral vision.

These first two missiles homed on the closest F-16s' radar, which were in search mode. The radar's frequency was in the center of the SIDEARM's search and said Come Get Me. The Israeli plane deployed no flares, chaff, nor jamming. Without any radar signal from the Jordanians signaling a lock on, its pilot had only a visual alert, and exploded in a ball of flaming debris.

The two Jordanian pilots maneuvered violently around the smoke and fragments.

Hassan rolled back around towards the Israelis, called SNAP SHOT, and triggered all four missiles on his wings. He radioed Badr, "This is SIX, FOX TWO. Follow me, we're RTB."

Having fired every weapon without any confidence of a kill, the captain prayed his missiles would distract the pilots of the more capable Israeli F-16s. *Better to cut and run; we're out of bullets.*

Hassan and Badr dove, reversing course. They pushed the throttle controls forward, to maximum power setting, accelerating back towards *Jebel Ibraheem*. Their sensors noted no missiles closing. Both pilots closed their eyes and took deep calming breaths.

Badr's second two missiles ignored the debris of the closer F-16. The missiles exploded, catching the wingman unaware. All four of Hassan's homed on another F-16, detonating next to the plane and the wingman nearby.

Unseen by the Jordanian pilots, fragments from the Lieutenant's second salvo punctured the Israeli wingman's fuel cells. The plane shuddered as control became tenuous. A hole in the wing and a visible dashboard Alert advised of low fuel state. The pilot radioed Bingo fuel state and diverted for home plate. He struggled to retain control and landed on a desert highway as his engine flamed out. Climbing down from his cockpit, he saw two truckloads of *bedus* surrounding him. The Israeli raised his hands, and glanced at his plane, a prize of war like himself. *Hope they don't see the kills stenciled on the fuselage.*

After landing, Hassan and Badr walked briskly towards the ready room, sweat evaporating from flight suits. Badr grabbed his instructors' arm, pulled the captain around, and kissed his forehead.

"Why did you do that?" the older man queried.

"Out of respect. You brought us back," the lieutenant gushed, *"Shukran*, thank you,"

A speaker on a pole by the revetment broke their joy like a pin bursting a balloon. It blared news of the battle above. Both F-5s from the base had engaged the enemy, fired missiles in anger. No further reports came from, nor did those two pilots acknowledge the orders.

One set of chutes was reported over an Israeli circuit, along with an intercepted confirmation of a kill. RJAF helos were requested to search for UHF rescue transmissions, and to report the status of pilot and student of the bases' fighters. No serviceable aircraft weapons remained at *Jebel Ibraheem*. The base, by itself on the sands, lay exposed and helpless.

The situation struck Hassan all at once. They'd gone into battle against newer planes with no defensive pod, no flares, chaff, nor jamming capability. *They'd have been, that American term he'd heard, toast, if the Israelis had pursued ... or attacked the base. Why hadn't they?*

He and Badr had been lucky. Could it be that simple? Was that all it was, luck? And they'd lived through it, while the newer F-5s hadn't. They'd gone up with no defensive systems, yet his rookie student walked away with two kills. *Allahu Al Akbar*!

Hassan, flight suit stained with sweat, stopped by a trash can at the revetment. He swung his helmet aside, put one hand on the wall, bent over and threw up.

Badr rushed to comfort his instructor, noticed blood in the vomit. The lieutenant called for an ambulance. The captains' days of aerial combat were probably over.

The old pilot stood, his face etched with the look of seeing a *jinn*. He ran ahead into the ready room, keyed the intercom system, "This is Captain Hassan. The Israelis weren't after our base. They're flying past, south to attack the base at *Al Azraq.*" Then his face froze with recognition, "or to take out the AWACS. Give the Saudis a heads up."

He turned, suddenly happy with the days' results. Badr was across the room, thronged by well wishers. Badr was the day's hero, and Hassan felt the glow.

Pilots Hirsh and Levi of Spearhead squadron chatted. "I'd like to meet the *schmeckel* who planned this," Levi muttered. "This op has all the survivability of those dam buster ops the Brits flew in WWII. We got conned into volunteering for a mission 'of national importance' without knowing the risks."

"Well, we're all volunteers. How can you resist signing up when your squadron commander volunteers at the start of a Ready Room brief."

"Yeah, no one can resist that kind of pressure."

Planes engaged near *Al Azraq*, the last Jordanian air base where operation *Hatkafa* was contested. As the Israelis continued south, each aviator punctuated clouds with weapons. Pilots knew deadly conflict was 99 percent boredom, 1 percent barely suppressed terror. Awareness of that composition pushed those flying to flight suit wetting moments. Fighters built in, and pilots trained in America by Americans, mustered on opposing sides in a duel to the death.

Pilots pushed planes to gee limits, deployed flares and decoys to survive, squeezed triggers, and watched missiles reach out to the plane trying to end their lives. Aircraft swarmed like angry African bees, attacking, and performing violent maneuvers to break radar locks. From wing pylons projectiles leapt towards other aircraft. Missiles made in American factories homed, killing pilots without distinction. Smoke trails zipped in all directions like a demolition derby. Across Jordanian skies planes disappeared, went down trailing smoke and parts.

Pilots of both sides, their trigger fingers itching for a kill, strained to avoid SAMs from below. Officers on the ground fired indiscriminately, convinced that unless aircraft were hit, those looking up might become victims. The battle was fought and ended quickly. Dogfights, at a heartbeat's distance, ended in minutes.

As the firestorm fizzled out, some pilots ejected, hung from nylon harnesses, and watched the air battle above Jordan. Burning debris of multi-million dollar aircraft fell indiscriminately on desert sands and towns. The numbers of estimated friendly and enemy dead, wounded, or captured rose. No reports identified captured Jordanians. The list of Israelis detained grew; they were roughly treated, but their captors understood their value.

No Jordanian borders were breeched by infantry or armored units, and their air bases went undamaged. The tsunami of deaths largely dissipated, planes in ones and twos landed, many with holes in their wings. With fewer aircraft, Jordanian pilots suffered most from the battle over their country. Most of their aircraft made it back to bases.

Chapter - 43

Lieutenant Colonel Hirsh and Major Levi of the Spearhead squadron radioed status, their voices hopeful. "We're in the middle of Jordan, will cross into Saudi airspace in one five minutes." Status reports from pilot after pilot reverberated over the conference room speakers. Most initial reports, from bombers rolling back Jordanian air defenses, were encouraging.

The AWACS was now off station, 65 miles back from the border, and apparently heading to Tabuk. Saudi fighters were scrambling, and those pilots were advised of alerted SAM batteries.

The Prime Minister leaned in, his face stern and spoke to his Defense Minister, "Is this op sound, Mikah?"

Jabeel smiled, his years as a hotshot pilot, though years ago, told him this was a piece of cake. "We'll roll over them." He paused a moment, then added, "My nephew is one of the pilots."

Geblar pursed his lips. *He's looking for my job if this goes well.* "I hope it goes as well as you say." The PM walked over to the side of the classified briefing room; several senior military were gathered there kibitzing, "General Aviv, a moment please."

The two walked off to the side of the displays, Geblar trying to reduce anxiety. The op involved significant assets and enormous political risk. "General, is this a good op?"

The head of Israel's military, LG Aviv, paused for just a second, something the PM knew wasn't his style. "I give every order I'm given my support, Prime Minister."

Geblar put his arm on the generals' shoulder. "Every order you're given. I see. ... Your full support?"

Aviv sensed he was being put on the spot, and evasion was not his suite, "Yes, Sir."

Israeli fighters still flew onward to incinerate a sitting duck 707. The number of those aircraft shrank to less than a dozen, including three kamikaze fighters still unknown to those defending Arabia.

The status reports reverberated upwards through American commands, identifying the battles, deaths, captured pilots. These reports could be summarized as "Oh Shit!"

Saudi fighters defending BIG BIRD heard the reports of Israeli aircraft over Jordan at medium and high altitude. The intercept controllers saw the attack on Jordanian fighters. BANDITs spread south across the sky at the 707's altitude. The motion vectors extended beyond Jordan, arrows at the heart of the AWACS.

The AWACS flew slowly, a cosmic crosshair on its sides. Frantic reports went out over every circuit, to the command network and CAP nearby. "EAGLE ONE holds aircraft inbound; estimate many BANDITs."

At a CAP control station on the AWACS, Sergeant Mohammed frowned. *Majj Noon*. Four F-15s defended the huge plane, their task preserving its irreplaceable crew of thirty-five. The sergeant radioed MODA's command center, confirming everyone's' worst fears, "General, if our defenses don't hold, everyone here will be dead in minutes. Please Allah, send CAP!"

The Boeing's pilot began a max rate turn, and with the BANDITs still beyond the prescribed sixty miles, turned off its radar. Colonel Hajami squeezed the controls 'til his fingers whitened, and applied full throttle, trying to put distance between Israeli planes and his cockpit. He yelled to the co-pilot, "Let's get the hell outa here."

Radios squawked, and blood pressure soared. Hajami looked aft through the open cockpit door to his men. He prayed CAP would come soon, as he steered the AWACS to King Faisal Air Base. "All units, this is EAGLE ONE ... HELP!"

Few onboard BIG BIRD thought they had a chance. The AWACS fled, implementing a shift to advisory control for CAP and the fighters Hajami prayed were scrambling from Tabuk. Controllers' in the airliner frantically downloaded attack solutions to specialists at the aerostats, TETHERs ONE and TWO.

Fighter pilots under advisory control were told only where the bad guys were. Then pilots took personal charge of the intercepts, exactly what every fighter pilot wanted in any case. Air warfare became in every sense personal for those in the converted 707.

When the first Jordanian alerts arrived in MODA's Command Center, they caused wide eyed alarm. A torrent of reports and radio intercepts flooded MODA, desperate reports of engagements which confirmed the inconceivable.

General Nazan recognized an attack was beginning. He swore, then acted. His FLASH messages and radio orders executed contingency plan *Hujum.* The code word signified an attack on the ungainly national asset.

Hujum meant 'attack' ... and stressed being at war. Recognizing the adrenaline tinged topic, the general knew some receiving the orders would only read the first paragraph. The implementing orders after the first words might be ignored. Nazan sent several messages, assuring compliance.

The second directive ordered immediate launch of aircraft at every base. The SCRAMBLE orders buzzed across all Air Force circuits. Fighters were to engage at maximum missile range to protect the AWACS. Every plane that could engage was to be armed and launched. The orders were acknowledged and pilots briefed at every air base. Ready rooms emptied, missiles raised to pylons, and safety pins pulled.

Another message directed Medium Range Ballistic Missiles at *As Sulayyil* brought to Full Alert. Two of the Sand Dragon MRBMs were to be readied for launch. The orders permitted no hesitation, allowed no misinterpretation, no latitude. Arabia was at war. All ground, air, and naval forces were directed to prepare for attack.

Follow-up Israeli reports flowed to HQ**.** During a lunch break in the *Hatkafa* mission updates, Geblar told his COS, "I want you to get with the Jerusalem Times, your other Press and media contacts, leak a little about Jabeel's Operation."

"I suggest something to distance ourselves from any expectations of mission success, rather than his personal vision and responsibility for this mission. Is that what you wish?" the COS asked.

"Yes. Stress his years as a pilot, a hero really, but one whose wartime experiences were in a time when Jordanian, and Saudi air defenses were in their infancy."

"So I should stress that he was in over his head on this mission, a bridge too far analogy?"

"Exactly. Perhaps hint at a lack of rank and file aviator support. I was surprised to hear that tone in General Aviv's remarks. Perhaps we should hold that back and await the results of *Hatkafa*. Get on the phone right now."

The COS bowed and headed next door to work his contacts.

Chapter - 44

Above the most northerly aerostat, MISH MISH SIX and SEVEN FOUR orbited, checking weapons readiness. Trigger happy techs at a Hawk battery below misjudged who was above, fired a salvo skyward. The pilots spotted a flash of dark smoke below. It drew their attention, right and down on their four o'clock. An object, white smoke following it up from the ground, became clear. "Shit, a SAM."

"TETHER this is SIX, SAM at three o'clock low. Breaking right and down." His wingman's pupils widened, his pulse spiked. Captain Harbi pushed the F-15s stick forward, dove left to avoid friendly fire, the danger now from trigger happy countrymen below. Harbi became nauseous, his throat acidic at the thought of fellow Saudis ending his life.

"TETHER ONE, this is MISH MISH SIX, calling SAMs. I see two more coming up east my posit," Harbi's voice shrieked, terror in his tone advising them to warn other CAP of a missile threat, "Tell those bastards we're on their side!"

The rising smoke trail was a direct order to him, Dive, release decoys, jam. Pull as many gees as he could handle. If he didn't get it right he died. SIX prayed, "Allah, fool the SAM; let me outmaneuver it."

The missile blew up overhead and he took a deep breath. MISH MISH SIX radioed the aerostat, profanities demonstrating anger at friendly fire. The aerostat acknowledged the miscue, and then ordered, "SIX, this is TETHER ONE. Remain on station. We'll advise if we hold any BANDITs closing this location."

MISH MISH SIX prayed no more friendly SAMs came skyward as he orbited with his wingmate.

In Tabuk's Ready Room Four an F-15 squadron commander hurriedly zipped up his gee suit and grabbed his helmet. The head gear was designed to let him know when every weapon was ready. In the free for all overhead, 'Pops' Samarra, would be the oldest pilot. He ran to his plane, the only one with kills stenciled on its fuselage. Pops, Call Sign BEDU SIX, had three, two shy of ACE. "I remember that Iranian hanging from his chute," he mumbled. *Gotta get up there. Just don't like our chances of stopping them.*

Samarra and his herd armed all weapons. Their displays showed BANDITs to the north. He looked at the three sections of fighters, twelve F-15s in all, ahead of him and his wing mates on the tarmac. The other section leads in turn radioed "ready to roll." They got clearance, pushed the throttles forward, went to burner, and roared into the air.

"All units, this is Tabuk. Take 'em."

Three sections, lined up abreast, wiggled their wings to section leads to acknowledge readiness to execute the briefed tactic. Aircraft in the first three sections were to fire their missiles in one simultaneous moment. All F-15s would be at the same altitude. The tactic required them to line up, wait, then illuminate the targets and stay lined up until their missiles impacted.

The bad guys had the same missiles, but were unaware of the tactics awaiting them. Hopefully the alignment would stop the Israelis, the spacing calculated to preclude a single enemy missile from downing more than one plane. Hopefully another tactic would win the encounter.

The Saudi pilots were briefed to engage with Sparrow semi-active missiles. Each would fire six missiles at enemy F-16s ahead. Samarra and his three squadron mates would fly as backup, to clean up any Israeli planes which got through. His section carried Sparrows and Sidewinders, the Winders capable of rear attacks.

Pops knew Israeli planes were sweeping south like an unchecked pandemic. He thought of it all, his job might just be a suicide assignment, a last ditch take no prisoners tactic. He'd been assigned this task because he'd already looked into the face of death and survived. He prayed he'd survive another.

"TOWER, this is BEDU SIX and herd. Armed and ready."

Each F-15 carried six AIM -7 radar homers and the first four Saudi planes fired theirs. FOX ONE boomed from four excited voices over the tactical circuit. One second later an additional twenty four Sparrows rocketed towards the Israelis.

FOX ONE in sequence then resounded over more aircraft radios. There was no longer silence on any F-15 circuit.

The F-16s enroute BIG BIRD had no warning of incoming missiles and no acquisition tones for their Sparrows. The Israelis continued, unaware, towards Tabuk AB and their target. For almost three seconds the airborne invaders had death moving closer and closer, knocking at their door.

Seventy two missiles homed like supersonic birds of prey, giving the F-15s a huge tactical advantage. Seconds after firing their missiles twelve F-15 pilots switched their fire control radars to radiate. Acquisition tones appeared on the pilots' panels and in headsets. The pilots aimed their jets like fingers of death. Instantly their missiles locked on and began homing on the Israelis.

Still beyond firing range to the AWACS, the F-16s' defensive alarms suddenly blared. Wide eyed, the pilots recognized the numbers of incoming missiles was overwhelming.

Opposing fighters closed at over 2000 MPH; the closure rate and pucker factor was increased by MACH 4.0 missile speeds. Israeli threat receivers refused to stop, buzz, or flash. Desperate shrieking in Hebrew was accompanied by soaring heart rates, with intense orders to the aircraft to perform emergency maneuvers.

As the missiles closed, the Israeli pilots maneuvered violently to break lock from scores of weapons intent on their deaths. The radio reports of desperate maneuvers and defensive tactics were intercepted by listening satellites. "HAWK FOUR EIGHT has a visual, many BANDITs ... all launching. *Ben Zona*."

Israeli pilots unleashed their own salvos. Israeli circuits saturated as HAWKs SEVEN TWO and EIGHT ZERO simultaneously radioed in their Sparrow and Winder launches ... FOX ONE, FOX TWO. The sky was filling with more missiles.

Saudi missiles homed while their targets maneuvered to break lock and escape death. Within seconds seventy two angry Sparrow missiles swept through the Israeli formation. Most F-16s fell, their radars silenced, and the F-15s went into similar maneuvers to elude any homing heat seekers.

When *Hatkafa* launched, the reports echoing from speakers at the Ministry briefing room were encouraging. Defense Minister Jabeel's words had flowed like summer wine.

General Aviv, Jabeel and Geblar listened now as reports came in with updates, of fewer aircraft remaining and their movement to destroy an AWACS.

Reports on speakers documented plane damage, missing squadron mates, and the destruction inflicted on their neighbors. The Defense Minister resumed, "Our data from OFFEQ showed only two fighters protecting the AWACS as the Op started. The AWACS is now about here," Jabeel pointed at a spot 75 miles inside Arabia, the projected location moving toward Tabuk's air base.

The Spearhead squadron headed by Major Levi had not been detected. Moments before Geblar, Jabeel and Aviv heard his voice, very much alive, "Give me a vector and distance to our target." Levi's voice was optimistic, fuel and weapons OK. The vector to the target was provided and progress was deemed as good as expected.

Geblar asked, "Is the AWACS still on station?"

"No." A mission commander at a console absent mindedly answered the question, which he thought rhetorical, "It's running for the barn. Major Levi's group is deep in Saudi air space." His tone sounded at best cautious.

The specialist turned to the general, "Sir, distance to the AWACS is still beyond Sparrow engagement range."

Further reports came in, mission progress becoming tenuous. Swarms of Saudis were battling Levi's group. Aviv clenched his fists. Jabeel stared in disbelief, his op apparently spiraling into the ground.

Another skirmish commenced far from the concluding mêlée. "BEDU LEAD, this is TETHER, I hold BANDITs low and to the west, range four zero miles." Samarra acknowledged the situation and ordered his section to divert west for an attack. He released the other twelve F-15s to return to base.

Samarra had three kills and he prayed he'd get just one more. "BEDU, this is SIX, coming left and down." The four F-15s banked. As they leveled off Pops keyed his mike, "BEDU, I hold three bad guys on my nose, low and closing. Let's get 'em."

The four F-15s selected and armed all weapons. Pops got tone for a head on Sparrow shot and fired at max range, "FOX ONE." His missile reached out towards the closest of three targets. Squadron mates SIX EIGHT and ZERO FIVE engaged the F-16s next, firing both Winders and Sparrows.

The Israeli pilots recognized these F-15s as the final wall defending their target. There was no time for distractions. In an adrenaline rush, the F-16s salvoed half their missiles, reserving some to take out the AWACS miles ahead.

ZERO FIVE saw one, then another of the enemy impacted by Winders. Samarra fired two more, and realized he was down to just one heat seeker. "BEDU, this is SIX. Weapons Check ... and heads up for missile radars." He'd fired four Sparrows and four heat seeking Winders. He prayed he'd be able to walk to the ready room when *this* was all over.

Suddenly Pops' head set buzzed. Incoming!

He pushed the stick, pulled max gees, dove left to break lock as he activated defensive decoys and jammers. Smoke trails went right and left of his plane. Samarra yelled, *"Shukran Allah"* over the radio. He had only cannon ammo, but had scored two kills, becoming an ACE.

His fellow pilots radioed their weapons status. FOUR SEVEN alone had all his missiles left. He pickled off his full load at the single F-16 still aloft. His missiles scored despite maneuvers he knew pushed that enemy plane to structural limits. FOUR SEVEN chanted his weapons expenditure ... "FOX ONE, FOX TWO ... FOX ONE, FOX TWO" interspersed with "Got Em, Got Em."

Nearby, Samarra's wingman SIX EIGHT was hit by a heat seeker. His tail rudder, peppered with holes, started to shred in the turbulent airflow. The pilot lost flight control and punched out through a shaking canopy. A chute opened and Pops sighed as he heard confirmation that a beacon was giving a posit for his friend's rescue.

Geblar noted the general's reactions to the man at a mission console, "Can we verify any of this?" the PM asked, staring at Jabeel, "Defense Minister, did you really expect that whole squadron to be shot down."

"It was considered acceptable, if we take out their AWACS," Jabeel replied. “It was a strategic tradeoff.”

A speaker reverberated with status of units returning from suppressing Jordanian defenses. One plane from Nevatim Air Base had returned trailing flames and dark black smoke. Its pilot, half alive, the plane leaking fuel and shuddering in flight, radioed, his voice heavy with desperation, “This is HAWK SEVEN SEVEN, clear a runway for an Emergency landing.”

Overhead speakers forced the Cabinet members to listen as crash truck sirens screeched. SEVEN SEVEN was cleared, landed on one strut, then veered into a revetment and exploded in a fireball. Reports followed of fire trucks trying desperately to extinguish the flames and recover the pilots’ remains.

A hush fell over the listeners, then Geblar confronted the Defense Minister, “Jabeel, is this as bad as it looks?”

“It seems worse. We didn’t get the AWACS, and lost a lot of planes and pilots.” The DM’s face whitened, his eyes tearing. He appeared on the border of collapse, “I lost my nephew, my only nephew.”

Geblar hugged his DM. Then he pulled back from their embrace, looked at Jabeel, “I understand he was a super pilot, had a great career. Do we know his status?”

“No ... but if he’s alive the Saudis will be ecstatic parading my nephew before the Press.” Jabeels’ voice softened ... “I’ve become an embarrassment. I shall resign.”

The speaker cut in with Major Levi’s voice. “If I get back, I want to hug whoever planned this op. If I don’t ... tell him I’ll haunt him ‘til the end of times.”

Smoke trails of four or more missiles reached out at that very moment towards Levi’s plane. He reported the smoke trails and radioed, “I’m punching.”

Chapter - 45

MODA desperately alerted its northern units to keep launching every plane. General Nazan’s voice boomed across radio speakers at every air base, “There may be more. Get every plane aloft. Another AWACS is enroute to provide air control. It will be on station in one five minutes."

Orders went to the aerostats to search for low fliers, look for clutter and jamming, and use every radar and sensor capability to detect further attacks.

Saudi planes on the ground were told to get airborne. Order after order went out; some were contradictory. Airfield procedures were stressed, then changed – turn radios off or on; hot refueling mandatory, optional, or recommended. Use hand signals only for hot refuels, engines at idle, use ground straps to keep stray voltage from ruining the day. Planes moved solemnly to and onto runways, ordnance and fuel crews working frantically to rearm them. Helos were scrambled to search for pilot rescue transmissions, then rescue or capture downed aviators. Not all these were done correctly; in the heat of urgency coordinates of pilots were often wrong.

Fire trucks stood by at every base, runway teams chatting with rescue helo crews, all waiting for the inevitable worst case. Protecting the AWACS and friends fueled senses, though the air battle above Arabia was now over.

Another kind of war was about to begin.

General Nazan issued the order, *"Hujum ... Hujum ... Hujum."* The Arabic meant attack, a code word repeated over all circuits for emphasis. MODA's Riyadh headquarters quickly confirmed the order on encrypted phones with each *Sadeek* missile officer, and LG Ubaidi.

Amir looked at his cell phone, stomped his foot and yelled *Alshshadid***.** His joyous outburst cut the tension, and cleared his mind. *Finally, I get to do something*.

MODA authorities verified the targets for each missile battery and the launch order. To achieve maximum effect, the plan called for all missiles to impact at the same time. That required a precisely timed pace of launches. Like many things in war, the plan fractured the instant the radio blurted *Hujum*.

LG Amir acknowledged the orders, then scanned his checklist. He radioed each battery to verify receipt of the order. The *Sadeek* sites, just repositioned across northern Arabia, were far from air bases. "MODA authorization confirmed," First Lieutenant Harbi responded from Battery One. Eleven other officers replied in sequence.

On the missile circuit Amir ordered, “Prepare for launch.”

Speakers at the *Sadeek* batteries rumbled with his order, and twelve sequentially acknowledged it. Engagement officers inserted enable keys, and then verified site and target coordinates. The officer’s voices at each location tensed as they stepped through checklists, mouthing a stream of directions to technicians and guards.

Tests confirmed all missiles ready. Harbi responded first, “Target coordinates verified. Ready for launch.” Then one after another launch officer replied with the same status.

Amir mentally checked off the last checklist box. All batteries had radioed in ‘READY.’

He gave the order –

FIRE!

The general envisioned the precise rhythm of a pendulum as missile after missile roared into the sky. Harbi’s battery launched the first *Sadeek*. The team wrapped scarves and arms across faces as sand and smoke blew back from the launch vehicle.

Amir told himself *Dageega, Dageega.* Be patient, then listened to each report of ‘missile away.’ He waited as each site radioed ‘missile away.’ An eternity seemed to drag by before the twelfth *Sadeek* rose into the sky.

Empty launcher cells repositioned, and the next cell elevated as officers mumbled the next steps. The sequence restarted and he ordered ‘FIRE.’ His experience told him the teams were diligent in performing each step. As smoke from the booster motor swept back from the Mercedes he chuckled at the irony of using water trucks as launch platforms.

It took thirty minutes to launch the forty eight missiles, far more than in training. When the last missile left the launcher nearby, rose in the sky, and unfolded its winglets, Amir knew. Within fifty-five minutes some very unlucky souls would watch the *Sadeeks* impact. He looked around, grinned. It felt good to pull the trigger, not be shot at or cluster bombed.

Amir worried each second. Rising booster trails could call down Israeli planes to obliterate launch vehicles, missiles, and men. The cluster bomb attack he survived two months before emphasized the need for speed. Now all batteries had to move before retribution arrived.

Israeli fighters returning to home airfields looked aghast as two slim shapes, hugging *wadis* in the mid-day heat, sped by below. FOUR EIGHT exclaimed, "What the hell was that?" as one turned toward him and a distant runway.

His wingman radioed, "Tower, this is TWO SEVEN. There's a drone on approach."

FOUR EIGHT maneuvered to avoid impact, radioed, "Unknown, squawk your code, over." The small shape flew on without responding. He muttered "Oh Shit!"

"Hatzerim Tower, this is TWO SEVEN. Is that one of our drones? Where the hell is it going, over?" He got no answer and Captain Schmeel blurted, "Tower, this is TWO SEVEN, get someone to direct the damn traffic."

"This is Hatzerim, it's not squawking; designate it a VAMPIRE, over." The base's identification of the shape as an incoming missile acknowledged lack of a defense.

"This is Tower, EIGHT SIX and ONE FIVE just smoked one with twenty MIKE MIKE near Hatzor." Sirens blared a warning at Hatzerim as the radio barked, "WEAPONS TIGHT. I say again, WEAPONS TIGHT." Fighters were not to engage VAMPIREs.

Captain Schmeel's voice broke the silence, "This is TWO SEVEN; are they heading for our base? Sure hope not, I just spotted more." He keyed his radio; it squelched with static. "TWO SEVEN has one of those bastards in his cross hairs. He's lined up on our runway. Request WEAPONS FREE, over."

The order repeated, "This is Tower, WEAPONS TIGHT. Be advised, one downed VAMPIRE scattered sub-munitions on a village, killing many." Hatzerim and other airfields were unable to stop the missiles, and the operator knew the base radar was unlikely to even detect them.

Schmeel's adrenaline level cued his finger. He uncovered the cannon's trigger and squeezed. In under a second a stream of 20MM shells vaporized the missile ahead. Wingman FOUR EIGHT listened in disbelief as TWO SEVEN radioed his engagement – "FOX FOUR."

The report overlapped a frantic order, "This is Tower,

WEAPONS TIGHT." Schmeel's F-16 flew into a cloud of exploding sub-munitions as if entering a dark viral mist. He flamed out just as the runway appeared through the explosion's turbulence.

The captain stuttered, "This is TWO SEVEN, losing power. Request clearance for Emergency landing."

"TWO SEVEN, you're cleared to runway ONE SEVEN. Crash Team alerted and rolling. Call your status, over."

"This is TWO SEVEN, engine out, gear won't lock down, coming in on belly. Request foamed runway!"

Sirens blared as crash trucks raced to the runway's midpoint with crews madly suiting up. Alerted by tactical transmissions, the Squadron Commander ran to his vehicle and sped towards Schmeel's plane.

No crash truck was yet positioned to apply the foam as the fighter landed on its belly. FOUR EIGHT landed left of the runway centerline, barely missing TWO SEVEN's flaming wreck. The captain swore as sparks flew from his plane, its belly sliding along the fiery runway.

Crash trucks arrived and began spraying white foam over the fractured fuselage. The crash truck commander screamed, "Foam the damn cockpit!"

The trucks swung their spray nozzles in unison. Schmeel stumbled out of his cockpit, and was quickly covered in foam. Schmeel smiled and descended the ladder to the runway as his Squadron Commander screamed, "You dummy. Rule one is land with your wheels down." The colonel berated the pilot about obeying direct orders and destroying a perfectly good airplane. He smirked and glanced towards the blackened wreck blocking the main runway, "Glad you got that missile. I don't think we can defend the base if more attack. ... Good shooting."

Both pilots' heads wrenched up as a white shape passed overhead. They gasped in unison.

Chapter - 46

The cell phone rang in the embassy's Public Relations Office; it was the encrypted phone and its owner wasn't there. Tooley's aide ran down the hall to the rest room to get him, "Your cell, the special one, is ringing."

Tooley nodded and zipped his fly. "Thanks. Be there in a moment." He hustled to his desk and went through his phone's biometric checks, then punched the speaker button. "Howdy, Stefano, what's up?" O'Toole prayed nothing else was wrong. The Saudis had just declared war on Israel; what could top that?

"We were driving north along the TAP line and saw a missile launched. Rodolfo pulled over and in twenty some minutes three more arched into the air. We recorded the last three launches and are about to uplink the video to CNN in Atlanta. I wanted to let you know before I do a voice track describing it."

"Whoa! Do you have watchers around, or are you alone?" Tooley figured he wouldn't be taking that kind of footage or talking about missile launches if they were around, but he wanted assurance.

"No, we're on our own, heading to Jordan to rendezvous with Colonel Ubaidi, Amir's nephew ... and his tank unit. As you said, he's quite the character."

"He is fascinating. Glad you're without watchers. Those guys could generate a lot of trouble now that a war is on." O'Toole figured he better grill Stefano before the Saudis discovered he took that footage. "Tell me something about the launches."

"Well, they weren't meteorological rockets 'cause they didn't go high enough, and not ballistic, because the boost phase was too short. Couldn't have been SAMs either; there's nothing around here to protect." Gaiuso paused, "Say, when you got cluster bombed a month ago, wasn't there a launcher nearby?"

"Yeah. I was with Amir and he launched a missile at Israel." O'Toole took a swig of cold coffee, set the mug down slowly, "What did the launcher look like? Was it ... like a big water truck?"

"Yes it was, and there were about ten men by it. Parts of the truck elevated before each shot, then lowered. It's moving now, but I don't know where it's going."

"Listen ... a word of advice. Don't identify yourself in the broadcast, or where the launches were. That ought to leave enough doubt so they won't stop you at the border." Tooley knew the Agency scooped CNN broadcasts, and this one definitely would be of interest. He also knew CNN video had GPS and time tags, so Saudis Intel types would be able to quickly figure out who had taped the event. "I doubt they'll appreciate seeing those launches on nightly news. Get to Jordan."

"Can do, but why would the Saudis be launching missiles at Jordan? That's the direction they were heading." Stefano's brow furrowed. *If the Saudis had fired at Jordan, and he was headed there. Would the Welcome sign still be out?*

"Within the past couple of hours Israel sent several fighter squadrons through Jordan to take out a Saudi AWACS," Tooley confessed. "It doesn't look like they succeeded, but the Saudis declared war in earnest. Just about every plane in the sand box is armed and in the air. Those missiles might be the opening act."

"If that's the case, I better send the story in and hustle to the border before it's closed. There ought to be BREAKING NEWS there very soon. And I want to record every minute of it."

"You must have a death wish, rushing to be in combat. Me, I've had enough of people shooting at me." *More than enough.*

NORAD's satellite tracking facility in Colorado Springs detected the initial *Sadeek* missile launch at 0100 local time. The heat image from the boost phase received immediate attention from the midnight watch. Colonel Abrams, the duty officer, turned to his senior image specialist. "Burton, zoom in on that launch site."

He brought up the video, his tweaks repositioning a recon satellite in space. Burton slewed the video, adjusting the size and clarity. Several more launch alerts flashed. He turned, his voice rising an octave, "Can't do it, Sir. I've counted twelve launch sites spread all over the sand box. The sites are too dispersed to zoom in on at once. I'll send the missile data along to NMCC."

"Holy crap," Abrams exclaimed. His hand moved to the communications panel and he selected the line to the Pentagon's Duty Flag Officer. "Admiral, I assigned PINNACLE CRITIC precedence to this data. We gotta let the head shed know the Saudis are shooting a bunch of missiles, probably at Israel. Would you agree?"

"Damn straight. Good call, Sam." Kimmel's face turned white, "Those weren't Ballistic Missiles were they? My God, they can take out a city block!"

"No, not boomers, thank God. The boomer base is way to the south. These generated smaller, shorter duration images at lift off. The boost and flight signatures we've observed are in another part of the spectrum, very different fuel. Definitely missiles though," Master Chief Ramsey emphasized.

Abrams and Kimmel discussed the launches and watched more appear on their large screens. Burton interrupted, "Admiral, we're detecting more launches. Motion analysis confirms the missiles moving towards Israel."

Kimmel turned to Ramsey, "Any idea what the targets are, Master Chief?"

"Not based on their trajectories, not yet. We'll know in ten minutes. My first guess, Admiral," Ramsey added, "is they'll target air bases. These missiles fly low, evading radar detection. I watched it on a TS training video of the missile fired at Mossad. These look like that shot ... maybe things will get better when the sun rises. One can always pray."

The War Room fell silent. "Dammit! Israel's satellite won't be back over the boomer site for another hour. They might react, do something foolish." Kimmel sounded out the colonel on the big issue, out of both their realms, "Do we tell them?"

Abrams injected, "I'd say ask The Man, and I'd put it more strongly. We *better* pray."

Israeli citizens had observed large numbers of planes leave, a quantity which stirred viral speculation. Far fewer returned than left. One Israeli air base had none.

Phone calls quickly swamped military commanders, and base phone exchanges and cell towers blistered with calls from anxious families, many to the government.

"Prime Minister, my operation failed to destroy that AWACS. No planes returned. We can't rescue the downed pilots without jeopardizing more lives." Defense Minister Jabeel handed Geblar his resignation letter, citing the failure of *Hatkafa*.

Within the hour TV Jerusalem's 1:00 PM newscast captured the nation's attention. "Defense Minister Jabeel, long a maverick member of Prime Minister Geblar's cabinet, resigned today after an important operation. The effort failed with the loss of what the Defense Minister's office termed 'numerous losses.'"

The camera panned to a dour Jabeel as he announced on screen, "my only nephew, Major Jakob Levi, is missing in action." Jabeel indicated that he hoped the young aviator might be a prisoner in Saudi Arabia. Additional updates will be coming in BREAKING NEWS on your favorite station, TV/Radio Jerusalem. This is Avril Benyameen signing off."

Geblar grinned as he watched the broadcast with his Chief of Staff, "Now I can get a less confrontational Knesset member to fill in." He smirked, "Tell the Press we're sorry to see him go ... and praise his long service to our nation." *Good riddance.*

Opposition within the Knesset quickly demanded Defense Minister Jabeel's replacement. Eyal, Geblar's Chief of Staff, suggested a way forward, "We might get support from America if we can put a moderate in, or a woman."

"I didn't like the maneuvers Jabeel used to increase his influence and have suggested a few names for his replacement." Geblar smiled; he hoped to maneuver a party friend into the Cabinet position. If pressured, he'd accept an opposition party member, or at least get someone better to work with.

The DM's office transformed into a space filled with dejected staffers, updating resumes, and filling boxes with mementos. One was a picture of Jabeel's nephew, now MIA. The pilot had been shot down, reports sketchy whether he was alive.

At his office barely an hour later, Geblar's day descended into another vortex. His aide burst into the office, bent red faced over a chair, and gasped, "Prime Minister, we are under attack!"

"Take a deep breath, Eyal. Tell me more."

"The *Tsahal* OFFEQ control station called. The spy satellite detected a rash of recent Saudi radio intercepts and now a number of missile launches. The launch sites are in northern Arabia. I suggest we go to the Crisis Room now. Satellite video is being routed there."

As they walked down the hall, Eyal provided more details, "The launches observed are not ballistic missiles, but OFFEQ is out of range of that site. We have no way to know if they'll launch them."

Geblar spoke in a low voice, "I pray they don't; they have dirty bomb kits."

Eyal softened the impact of his words about the worst case crisis, "General Aviv just ordered all Patriot sites to full Alert status; they're manned and ready." He paused as they scanned their biometric data into the Crisis Room control system.

They were waved inside, Geblar adding anxiously, "I hope things are not as bad as you suggest." As they entered Geblar identified those present, General Aviv himself, and the new Defense Minister, Tam '*Kibbutzim*' Elev. Geblar had quickly accepted *Kibbutzim* as the compromise DM to move past the *Hatkafa* disaster.

Aviv's eyes focused on three large displays on a wall. The monitors portrayed what Israel faced. Satellite analysts had identified twelve launch sites. Alongside the sites were numbers which flashed and increased as Geblar watched. His jaw tensed like he was biting down to ignore a large pain elsewhere in his body. "What just happened? Why did those numbers increase?"

"The Saudis continue to launch missiles," Aviv explained. "Preliminary analysis suggests their profile is similar to the one which hit Mossad's office in Ashdod." He paused, looked at the new DM. "Remnants of that missile suggest it was derived from a Harpoon."

Without an input from *Kibbutzim*, Geblar jumped in, "General, we can't sit idly by." The PM's face reddened, "The troops need to do something. Give me some options!"

Aviv cleared his throat. "As of a minute ago *Tsahal* and OFFEQ were off the air. We're moving shoulder launched SAM units to all airfields and major headquarters. I'm surging aircraft aloft; they're the only defense that will work ... if they get a shot. I'll also move radar controlled AA gun batteries, but without satellite coverage we won't know the missiles' targets."

Geblar was about to continue when *Kibbutzim* broke in, "General, check the list of probable targets, and ensure we're ready to protect each. Get OFFEQ's control station repaired, and make damn sure you're taking every precaution." Kibbutzim paused, "Prime Minister, you and I need to get to the Bunker, right now! We have," he emphasized, "many generals, but only one Prime Minister."

Geblar's jaw dropped, pleased by the newbie's forceful assertion of control. *There's hope for him.*

Reports to military HQ were trickling in, from planes, air bases, and radio stations in major cities. "How many?" Kibbutzim asked as

Aviv tried to give an assessment of the loss of aircraft and damage to bases. Status boards updated as the reports continually changed.

When Hatzerim Air Base was queried for its status, there was an uncomfortable silence. A few minutes later that base's Deputy Commander called on his cell phone. Other base reports trickled in, none encouraging.

"Prime Minister, it was more than we expected. The greatest impact seems to be happening at our air bases. We never anticipated these missile attacks. Our bases haven't been hit in twenty plus years. We'll lose a lot of fighters, hard to replace. Hatzerim Air Base radios are temporarily off the air. You may recall it sent twenty jets to *Hatkafa*. Now we have a report it is strewn with burning fuel tanks and ruptured aircraft. The base tower and radar were wiped out by the first missiles. Luckily all its runways remain operational."

Aviv frowned, "We lost many experienced pilots."

"Can we compensate?" *Kibbutzim* asked.

"Only if we get replacement planes, right away. If not, we may lose control of the air," Aviv told them. "For now OFFEQ's ground control station at Palmachim is not functional. We won't know if the Saudis launch boomers."

"We can get new planes. I don't believe America will refuse our request. But the pilots - there is no replacement for them," Aviv grumbled, wanting to convince PM Geblar most. "If this keeps up, in another hour we'll have no Air Force to protect ourselves!"

Geblar looked at *Kibbutzim*, "Should we issue a nuclear alert?"

Chapter - 47

Rousted out of his cot by the wakeup call, DeMeers wolfed down his last slice of stale midnight pepperoni pizza. *Bad for the waistline, arteries, but full of flavor.* He followed it with a swig of stale, cold coffee. Looking at the desk monitor, he acknowledged the buzzer and flashing red button. It was the War Room with another crisis, or another addition to the current mess.

"Call the Man; there's a friggin war starting over there," Kimmel told the President's COS. DeMeers was in the Situation Room, despite the time of day. Kimmel spoke again, "We need to inform the President! The info is PINNACLE, CRITIC!" This meant the Boss had to be advised, within fifteen Oh My Gawd minutes, that the matter was of national interest.

"What's up, Admiral? Tell me why I need to wake the President up again. He's been through a week of all nighters and if he can't act on this, or influence some outcome," DeMeer's voice was tired, but insistent, "he ought to get one night's rest." *I need to get more aspirin, a better cot, and a softer pillow.*

The NSC lived in the Situation Room most of the time now; events were ulcer inducing in the Middle East. DeMeers told his aide to wake the team - SECSTATE DeVries, General Peckingham, and the Man's National Security Advisor or NSA. *Oh Shit! Bengtsson is at Walter Reed, recovering from a kidney stone. Lucky guy gets to relax at a distance from this mess.*

"Madame Secretary, Mister DeMeers, General," Kimmel reiterated moments later to the gathered bleary eyed NSC members, "we've detected a flurry of Saudi missile launches."

DeMeers started to ask the first of ten questions that came to mind, but he was interrupted. He looked up, saw a figure enter the room, and stuttered ... "Good morning, Mister President, couldn't sleep?"

Ellington rubbed his eyes, red from many midnight hours, "Nope. Put up the video. Let's see what's cooking." As the NSC members stood, Kimmel chimed in a greeting to the Commander-in-Chief. All eyes focused on his face.

Master Chief Ramsey patched the video through and it emerged on several displays. Ellington's face frowned as he watched sub-munitions exploding on what Kimmel identified as one after another Israeli airfield. "Those missiles are tearing up every single air force base, Mister President," Kimmel said. "No estimate yet, but this will put a real crimp in their ops. Over forty Saudi missiles are in the air or hitting."

"Put the base video, together with their SAM batteries, on the top screens." Ellington let everyone know he was up to speed, or would be. Jordanian air bases and SAM coverage also appeared, the display updating to include fighter strength at that country's bases.

"The Israelis had to get past all that to go after the AWACS? Dozens of missiles are now heading for Israel," Ellington queried

Kimmel with his eyes, "And the Israelis may go off the deep end ... again." Ellington recalled seeing the attack on the AWACS barely an hour before.

"Both *sides* are our friends and allies for God's sake!" The President slammed his fist on the table. "This damn world is going to hell, and I can't do anything about it. Whoever said I was the most powerful person in the world." He put his head in his hands and bent over slightly. "That didn't help - I can no more control this mess, or those people, than take a whiz without wetting myself in a hurricane."

DeVries acknowledged his remark, knew POTUS meant PM Geblar, "Got it, Mister President!" No glimmer of a smile escaped her face, "That's how we say it at State."

"Do we know who won, or lost, even have a rough count?" Ellington asked. The status reports continued to reflect the turmoil of war. There was no confusion as to who was doing what to whom, though the results remained unclear. "Now, missiles in the air, starting to impact."

"The score card is mixed, Mister President," Peckingham replied. "Israeli planes and pilots are scattered, wrecked on every corner. Satellite video confirms that three specific bases were hit first. They're related to ... the Nuclear Alert, NIKUD, rippling through their units at the moment. Intercepts confirm the messages to Israeli nuclear capable units."

The remarks' possibilities raised nerves to critical mass. Ellington sipped his coffee, then swore, and swore, and swore again. He looked from Peckingham to DeVries, "And we still have the coalition to worry about. If the Shias and Sunnis get together they could topple the whole deck of cards. Pray that doesn't happen."

"This has really hurt Israel. My guess is they've lost up to a sixth of their operational aircraft. Many planes got aloft; most of those will survive. If one believed their pilots' reports there are no Saudi planes left." *Wishful thinking.*

DeVries broke in, "Mister President; we have received assurance from the Kingdom, Prince Abdullah himself, that no ballistic missiles have been launched ... yet."

POTUS turned toward Peckingham, "Chairman, I need your inputs on actions to take ... and your views on telling the Israelis ... that the Saudis won't launch their MRBMs!"

"Do it, Mister President, right away," Peckingham insisted. "Don't mention that *yet* part." DeVries nodded agreement.

Ellington looked at his SECSTATE, "Tell Prime Minister Geblar the Saudis won't launch ballistic missiles; we have received their assurance! Let me know they've acknowledged that status." His hands transformed into a prayerful clasp, "There's the phone!"

Eyal provided a running summary to the Prime Minister and company, "Media reports give scant details of actual damage; they merely describe the missile attacks as 'wide spread, troubling.' I'll concentrate on the bases at Hatzerim, Nevatim, and Tel Nof, our nuclear capable airfields. Their communications are temporarily out, transmitter towers disabled. I'd estimate a day to get them back in operation. At the moment those bases are executing the nuclear alert."

"And until them, we get the base status from ... where?" Geblar queried.

Eyal answered, "We initially tried to clamp censorship on the results to preclude panic, but those efforts failed. Public reactions went viral over social media. CNN, then BBC, and soon every journalist on the planet will come up with more stories. We have separate civil defense feeds here, which tap into local media coverage. I'll put Hatzerim on display twelve."

Geblar looked up, "Yes, I see it." Display twelve showed two HAT TV channel personnel in a delayed telecast of local soccer playoffs in Hatzerim. The sports fields on screen were filled with athletic teams and cheering families. Suddenly their coverage was interrupted by explosions from the airfield nearby. The video telecast suddenly went off the air. The voice feed continued, with commentator Ephraim voicing surprise to camera-person Yasmeen.

The speakers for display twelve blared with sirens. Ephraim's head set told him the station had voiced over his words. Management had inserted a recurring announcement requiring reservists to report for duty. Following the deafening blast, Ephraim said Yasmeen was scrambling atop the van to realign its dish. He joined her there as they gawked at the destruction as coverage was re-established. A huge black cloud spread upward over the base as if to accent the noisy telecast.

Yasmeen zoomed in, panned past a flaming fuel tank. Those in the Bunker saw many base personnel react as explosive shock waves swept outward. Most covered their ears; some put hands over their eyes. *Could they believe it would help dispel the images of death?*

Sporadic radio calls interrupted a temporary silence. The radio reported a fighter, call sign NORTH TWO SIX, veered out of control towards the edge of a runway and its fuel storage. Pilot Raf Kovan ejected and his chute opened as pavement erupted in chunks upwards. His plane slammed through chain link fencing, slid over the protective berm and catapulted into a huge fuel tank. The resulting blast flattened everything nearby. The reporters were blown off their van and the screen went black.

Eyal continued, "Things are still turbulent. We seem to have had another blast at Hatzerim." All eyes shifted from the blackened display twelve.

Eyal pointed, "This is from Tel Nof, our nuclear base in the Negev. Its' media feed is on display eleven. A Big Orange 10 TV reporter spoke, "This is Avi Regev. My orders were to interview some of the response team. I will be interviewing Rebeka Hirscht from Crash Response Unit Four. Her unit is in the background directing foam on burning aircraft and vehicles."

The bunker occupants watched in disbelief as a row of fighter aircraft went up in flames. Reporter Regev cursed planes which "seem incapable of providing protection. I see two fighters on the runway waiting to take off." All watched as the planes went to burner, rotated at liftoff, and started retracting landing gear.

"Another section of fighters waited for them to clear the runway so they in turn could take off. The right wing of one plane was hit by bombs, and blew apart." Regev's voice suddenly faded. He angled the camera to show the crash truck, lights flashing, and then wreckage of planes in flames.

A red faced Hirscht walked towards him from off-screen, glass crunching beneath her boots. His eyes and camera drew to her. Her uniform was soaked with blood, her body stiff. "How do you deal with the destruction, the death?" Regev prodded.

"The bombs took out lots of ground equipment. We must deal with this," Hirscht pointed her camera towards the base, "We save what people we can. Six of my friends are ... gone." Her face tensed, "How do I deal with this? I breathe deeply; ignore the blood. I search to find survivors, and administer aid. I try to force the images from my mind." Her voice quivered, "When time permits I'm going to throw up."

Regev stared at Hirscht, and saw tears form as she walked away. He knew he needed to distance himself from the emotion and panned briefly away. "Thank you. This is Avi Regev signing off for Big Orange Radio." The final image showed her bent over.

A tall figure entered the bunker and moved quickly to Geblar, "Prime Minister," Foreign Minister Gershawitz broke in, "I've just talked with Secretary of State DeVries. She relayed Saudi Arabia's assurance they will not launch ballistic missiles." Smiles filled faces around the room.

The PM, DM *Kibbutzim*, and General Aviv heard more reports, the traumatic status heard from the final nuclear base, Nevatim. The speaker related that another missile dropped bomblets along its runway. The grenade size bombs exploded as they neared the ground, missing the revetments and more planes.

The video showed shockwaves wrench the airfield's control radar antenna off its pedestal, wiping out plane control. Fuel tanker trucks, the control tower, fire station, and radio and cell towers were in flames. One helo pin wheeled into another. Seven helos went up in flames, crash trucks struggling to control the disaster in acrid smoke. Two fighter-bomber squadrons were instantly rendered out of business. Numbers on status boards updated, conveying hideous new realities.

At Nevatim, First Lieutenant Wiseman was climbing into his F-16 as more bomblets descended. One impacted his plane. Wiseman was bent over checking his connections to his aircraft, his helmet still unstrapped. The explosion blew him through his unopened canopy, breaking his neck. His squadron mates gasped as more bomblets exploded along the runway. Those in the bunker wondered if more were coming.

"Prime Minister, we can stand down the alert, but must get replacement aircraft," *Kibbutzim* stipulated.

Chapter - 48

The Red phone rang in the WHSR. PM Geblar was on the line for President Ellington. Geblar's voice was insistent, desperate. He demanded replacement aircraft and additional Patriot missile batteries. "I can't allow the peace coalition to catch us unprepared like in 1967! I need your release of the War Reserve ammunition in Israel." Ellington knew Geblar meant the pre-positioned missiles, bombs, artillery and tank ammo.

On Ellington's desk sat an identical request from the Saudi Ambassador; it was the other side of the coin. AWACS flew closer to Jordan now, with lots more protection assigned. KOSA and MODA were also scrambling to get the US to release War Reserve ammo, twelve Harpoons, lots of Sparrows and Winders. The President groused, *Maybe I should give them both all the ammo they want, let them shoot it out.*

Ellington paused, told PM Geblar he'd get back to him, "We're very busy just now." Ellington hung up.

"Only air bases were hit?" Ellington asked CJCS with disbelief, "No more missiles in the air?"

"Yes Sir. Only bases," Peckingham acknowledged. "And all the missiles have hit. That chapter is ending."

Ellington responded, "General, the next chapter may be worse. Can we ferry replacement planes straight to Israel?'"

"No, the air fields we need to use, Haifa and Palmachim, are out of commission. And we don't have enough tanker aircraft as a work around." Peckingham looked at his aide, stress on his face.

"Those SOBs," Ellington cursed, clenched his fists, and glared at DeVries, "How do we deal with this, Mel? Can we work around this obstacle? Perhaps work a deal off the grid? The Turks ... they're in NATO for Christ sake!" Stress, frustration dripped from the words.

DeVries paused, then responded, "We need to keep the Syrians out of any discussions." She slapped one fist into the other open hand. "They still have WMDs from the last war, and I don't trust them. I'll work on the Turks." She drummed fingers on the table, "but we *must* worry about Israel; they have few choices, only really bad ones."

Ellington swore again. He clenched his right fist, glared at Peckingham, "Like what? Remind me of these 'really bad choices'."

As CJCS elaborated the President hung his head, "General, after this meeting ... you and me. I want *all* the options to constrain Israel's choices." Peckingham stood erect, saluted. "Yes, Mister President."

The phone buzzed. It was an unknown local caller; Tooley lifted the handset. The voice was pleasant, "Good morning Mister O'Toole. This is Doctor Bedawi. We met when you were at King Khalid Hospital."

Tooley paused. *I don't want to talk to a quack right now.* He thought to himself, unsure how open to be, with phones all tapped here, then O'Toole asked, "What do you do at the hospital?"

"I'm the DNA Program Director. I want to discuss a patient whose case may interest you. Soon after his capture, the pilot who dropped cluster bombs on you was brought here and doctors operated on him, Captain Ben Bedoo. We typed his blood to ensure compatibility before the surgery, and detected something puzzling."

Tooley stirred his coffee with a pencil, "Continue."

"DNA testing protocols were run and flagged an event. That event identifies the genomes of blood relatives. We repeated the protocols, ran each three times. The sequence that stood out was IDB, Identical by Descent. Each time it gave the same findings. We're certain!"

Intrigued, Tooley thought of distant blood relatives Stefano Gaiuso, Amir Ubaidi, and his wife. Those revelations had been enough of a surprise. *Were there more ghosts in the closet?* "Certain of what?" he asked.

"He's distantly related to you and General Ubaidi," Dr. Bedawi stated. "None of the other prisoners are. Just the one."

Tooley echoed what he'd heard, "He's related?" *If the pilot is a cousin, so is his father.*

"It's a fact," Bedawi offered.

Tooley nodded, desperately wanted to tell family. He pursed his lips, "I can't wait to see the look on their faces. But today, today I tell Amir. I'm going to have lunch with him, inform him *that* SOB, *the* SOB who bombed us, is related." *Damn! Sonofabitch genes run in the family.*

"Doctor, I suspect the Kingdom is negotiating to repatriate prisoners and the bodies of the dead." *They've got others, one the son of a former Defense Minister, high value ... secret negotiations worth millions.*

O'Toole was experiencing the onset of fatality anxiety, not being shot at or bombed, as by a well guarded cousin squzzed in a cell nearby. "Where is this cousin of mine being held?"

A long silence answered his query. He expected that; the prisoners had national value. *I'll ask Amir.*

Tooley phoned Ubaidi moments later. "Amir, are you free for lunch? I have something important to tell you."

"I'm free; any suggestions for a place to eat?"

"Yes, I'm thinking something Chinese. Do you remember the Gulf Royal restaurant in *Al-Malaz*? We've eaten there before."

"I remember it; let's meet at half twelve?"

"Great! See you there." Tooley drove there, losing his tail in traffic. Amir arrived in a MODA sedan with security driver, aide, and his tribal guard trailing in a Jeep. Soon, using the restaurant's pull apart chopsticks, Tooley ate some of his stirred fried chicken. He followed it with a sip of iced tea.

"Why do you use those?" Amir asked about the choice of utensils as he dug into sweet and sour chicken with a fork.

"They make food taste better, and I need the practice." Tooley smirked, "my chicken tastes a lot like the dog meat I ate in NAM. It's quite tasty."

Tooley had seen a copy of Amir's report on the launch of forty-eight *Sadeek* missiles. It hadn't reflected any estimate of results. He knows I know, and Amir wants to also. I want to know about those prisoners, and that one SOB. He lingered on the words which came out next, "You've been busy?"

Amir blurted, "I hope every poor schlep by the runways would be *faqid*, gone, *finito.* I wanted them all to have burst ear drums. Certainly they'll have stories to tell their grandchildren. I hope they lost hundreds of planes." The general seemed curious about what the missiles had blown up.

"So," Tooley prodded his cousin, "your missiles were targeting air bases?"

"Did I say that?" Amir hedged, he knew a report would document whatever he said.

"No, I read your mind," Tooley parried, "like a *jinn*."

"Well, we are at war. They presented easy targets."

Tooley reached into his coat pocket, then paused awkwardly. He slowly looked over at Amir's aide and bedu guard at their table. He didn't want to appear threatening in any way; they were both armed. He slowly withdrew papers from his coat pocket using his finger tips. He listed the articles in his hand. "You're looking for some sense of the Bomb Damage Assessment, the results, beyond what new services were saying on television. These discuss the BDA. Did you see the BBC commentary of TV Jerusalem's coverage, or that bit from Tel Nof?"

"What did they say?" Amir asked.

Tooley shared his recollection of what the open sources said about the damage. Both knew such reports were often as accurate as highly classified Intel, though they lacked detailed analysis. Ubaidi's eyes brightened.

"I've got more news. You ought to enjoy it." O'Toole told Amir of their newly discovered cousin, half of a father-son duo who had each tried to kill them. "Let's visit that pilot and thank him properly."

"*Majj Noon*, that's a great idea. I'll shoot the bastard!"

"Let's do it. I'll hold him and you shoot," O'Toole said with a smile. "Isn't that what cousins are supposed to do, help each other?"

"Yes, and help our allies. I'll find out where he is, arrange a visit."

"I understand your country asked for war reserve air to air missiles, and replacement Harpoons." Tooley whispered, "What did you shoot them at?"

"Subs," Amir said sarcastically, "Maybe the one that launched missiles at us years ago."

Chapter - 49

Ellington, looking relaxed after a few nights of sleep, frowned, "General, run through this mess again so we're all on the same page."

Ellington ordered the Air Force to stage replacement planes through Europe a day before as part of a quid pro quo with PM Geblar.

The deal was replacement planes for a nuclear alert stand down. Geblar had ordered the stand down even before the agreement. Ellington knew of that action, but didn't want to divulge the national technical sources that whispered in his ears before the deal was struck.

Peckingham was in the hot seat, didn't like 'this mess' any better than others. He handed two CRITIC messages to POTUS, "Mister President, the reports from our replacement advance teams at Incirlik and Cairo ... contain disturbing news. There was never any question by either Egypt or Turkey where the planes were going. Everyone understood. Now, well - we'd got as far as requesting apron areas to accommodate the aircraft." He frowned, "The advance teams never got the expected thumbs up!"

DeVries chimed in, providing a fuller background, "Both Turkey and Egypt may be stone walling, but they are walking a tight rope, trying to maintain distance from any conflict between the coalition and Israel. While this is frustrating, it would be far worse if they chose sides. We're unsure which side they'd join. Their governments said they are struggling to keep on the sidelines, away from the prospect of another war in the region."

Peckingham, frustration evident from crossed arms, added, "They won't let the planes through. One squadron landed in Egypt. They were surrounded after landing, impounded. Follow-on ferry planes were refueled, but had to be sent back. The planes will be on the ground in two hours at the NATO base at Udine, Italy."

Ellington wrung his hands, "Two nights sleep; hope that run gets better. Continue, general."

"Yes, Sir. We had eight other aircraft enroute to Incirlik. They tanked over the MED, would have landed three hours later." CJCS shifted like he was walking to the end of a jungle pier with piranha below, "Another section would follow them in two hours, flying the same route."

Ellington wanted solutions, to develop workarounds. "We've another problem. The Egyptian Prime Minister told me he is not at liberty to let replacement aircraft even fly through its airspace. Beyond preventing resupply of aircraft, this impounding of twelve aircraft creates a real problem." The President glanced at DeVries, "Mel, please negotiate release of our pilots and crews."

SECSTATE nodded acknowledgement of the task. DeVries glanced at CJCS, who had more on his plate. With no replacement planes to deliver, that situation put pressure on Israel in any military standoff. The forces were unbalanced, and that was not good for peace.

Ellington saw the looks being exchanged, and read their minds, "General, try flying replacement planes into other bases, direct."

"I'll work it, Mister President. Just realize they may stumble into air battles or land on bombed runways."

Ellington frowned, "Shit!'

A column of three vehicles arrived at the prison. Inside two cars were security guards with LG Ubaidi, another vehicle with a MODA escort for him, and Tooley in his Malibu. Approaching the outer perimeter, they passed through two twelve foot fences topped with razor wire. Around the building roamed pairs of guards. O'Tooles scanning eyes noted surveillance cameras and poles on rooftops, the latter likely to preclude helicopter landings. The facility appeared secure.

The occupants were screened, names verified against authorized entrants, and waved to a control point. After parking, they walked to a guarded entrance. General Ubaidi was dressed in crisp combat fatigues, Tooley in a business suit. His American flag lapel pin incorporated a recording micro chip.

As the generals' guards diverted to a waiting room, Amir and Tooley proceeded to the Security Office to arrange an interview. They signed in, left their cell phones, and identified the prisoner. O'Toole's eyes spotted and memorized twelve Israelis names listed on a status board.

The Sergeant of the Guard pushed a button and yelled, "Open cell 110!"

Down a hall the visitors heard mechanical latches unlock and the sound of a sliding cell door. Footsteps resounded as they walked to a room where thick plate glass separated their table and chairs from those for inmates.

The prisoner entered and sat. David Ben Bedoo, Captain Israeli Air Force, looked through the glass from one to the other, uncertainty on his face competing with a pilot's confidence. He spoke into the intercom, "So, an American and a Saudi General! Who are you and why are you here?"

"My name is Padrick O'Toole; this is Lieutenant General Amir Ubaidi, and you are Captain David Ben Bedoo. Your father is General Moshe of the Mossad."

Ben Bedoo clasped his hands together as if in prayer, trying to control nervous agitation, "How do you know of my father?"

Amir drummed his fingers on the table, "Years ago I looked in his eyes as he aimed his Glock at my chest."

Then Tooley injected, "Then he shot us!" Noting disbelief on Ben Bedoo's face, he added, "I stepped in the way. The bullet passed through me and lodged in Amir's body armor. I only survived because Amir donated blood in the field."

Amir and Tooley watched Ben Bedoo's reactions. The pilot clenched his fists, confusion evident on his face, "I've never heard that story before. Where did this alleged shooting take place?"

"We were at a missile base called *As Sulayyil* in my country," Amir answered. "Your submarine fired missiles at the base just before your father shot us."

Tooley, his tone ambivalent, continued, "DNA tests of our blood proved the general and I are distant cousins." He paused, "Identical tests prove you are also. We decided to meet you, despite your dropping CBUs on us."

Ben Bedoo stuttered, "*Ben Zona*! We're cousins?"

"Yes. But last month," Amir added, "we both got flesh wounds. You bombed us."

"You shot my plane down," Ben Bedoo countered, then tapped his fingers animatedly. "We all miss what we're shooting at."

Tooley smiled, "And t*hat* is a good thing."

Amir rose, "Until next time then, don't practice."

O'Toole stood, pointed a finger pistol at the pilot. *Click!*

Ben Bedoo rose, and thanked them. "I'll consider what you said, separate fact from fiction." He looked at Ubaidi, then O'Toole, "Will I see you again?"

Tooley smirked, "God I hope not. Every time we're near your part of the family it causes hearing and blood loss."

Chapter - 50

A day later Tooley said goodbye to Amir over the office phone. It rang as he set it on the cradle. He sipped his last coffee of the day and was washing down a dry but still tasty morning muffin. It was a needed sugar high. Caller ID told him it was Anh.

"Hey Babe, just finishing up. I'll be done in about an hour, and then I'll come home. Does that work?" There was yelling in the background. He hoped it wasn't the answer; there'd been enough drama when Anh heard about the newest deadly cousin.

"Michael, get over here ... now! We need to go home! Come pick us up, Bai and me. Right now!" Anh's tone was up an octave. He understood the words weren't a request.

"Is everything all right?"

"I'll tell you all about it when you get here. Things have reached critical mass. Get here ASAP. I mean it!" Her voice, an octave higher still and punctuated by very direct words, was not soothing.

He overheard more yelling. Mick exclaimed," If you touch me again, I'll punch you out."

Tooley pressed the phone closer to his ear. Then the phone went silent. *Anh never hangs up. What the hell is going on?*

O'Toole raced across Riyadh in the white Malibu. He varied his route, looking in the rear view mirror for a minder. Mostly *they* were discrete, but today the guy hung on his rear bumper. He accelerated through a red light, and lost him. He made it to the USMTM compound in record time, stopped at the guard shack, and showed his ID. He was waved through, parked, and walked to the MWR Office. He asked about his family, "My wife and daughter are waiting for me."

"Yes, Mister O'Toole. Please be seated. I'll call her." He paced instead, scanning the parking lot through the windows and smiled. *No minder could get in. That's something to smile about.*

After an anxious moment, Anh and Bai appeared, and then Mick. He looked at them without a word. *The whole O'Toole family is about to ditch a fun Morale, Welfare, and Recreation outing, what's up?*

Anh gave him a reassuring hug. Bai scowled as Mick covered an eye which to Tooley looked like it might soon turn black and blue.

Bai looked at her dad, then at her brother as though *he* was a leper. She scurried behind her mother where her tone softened, "Hi dad."

Mick frowned, hustled ahead to the car. It was apparent he was avoiding friends' eyes. Bai scrambled in the back seat with her mother, after shoving Mick.

Tooley started the car. As the engine idled, he wondered if warfare had struck home. He drove to the gate, knowing he'd hear the story; it promised to be a good one. He looked at Mick's bloody nose.

Bai opened then slammed her door, and started whimpering. Anh hugged her daughter, then leaned forward, "Get us out of here."

Once home father and son escaped to the kitchen; the gals huddled on the living room couch. Bai, hormones dripping from her voice, blurted, "Mom, can we trade Mick in?"

Anh tensed, looked at both her children.

Mick overheard Bai and swore, *Enfant Chien*. The phrase was French for sonofabitch and caught both parents' attention, but not Bai's. Tooley smiled at the remark. *At least one kid is learning French.*

"It's not the end of the world, Bai. That's what your grandmother told me." Anh hugged her daughter, "The first time for me was in a Hong Kong refugee camp. It was hard; a British nurse helped me. She talked me through the cramps, migraine, shakes."

Anh wrapped her arm around Bai's shoulder, "I'll get you an appointment to see a gynecologist. She'll answer questions, ones you might not ask me. This is something we share as women."

Anh stroked her daughters' back, looked into Bai's eyes, "Why did you punch Mick?"

Bai withdrew slightly, cried, "He called me a witch, so I smacked him. His friends were watching." She looked at her mom, wiping away tears, "I guess I embarrassed him."

Anh rubbed Bai's arm, "This is a normal thing. Well, not punching your brother, but the rest. You'll get used to dealing with the emotional and physical changes. It means you're a woman now."

Anh got up from the couch, reached for Bai's hand, "Let's get you some feminine things."

"Dad, what's going on?" Mick asked as he gently touched his bloodied nose. His snide expression said he was convinced his sister had gone bonkers. "Is Bai on drugs?"

"Remember when we talked about women and periods?" Tooley saw the thought hadn't registered. He put his hands on his son's shoulders, "Your sister is now a woman."

Mick's face paled, "Oh." Then his look changed to fear. "She doesn't get to beat on me, right?"

Tooley smiled and inched closer, "No." He touched Mick's nose, "Can you breathe OK?"

"Yes, but it hurts. Is it broken?"

Tooley gently moved the nose side to side but heard no yelp. "No. I think it's just some broken blood vessels. I'll bandage it." Tooley placed a flexible aluminum brace on it. Bandages soon spread across the teenager's face.

Mick put his hand to his nose, grimaced at what his friends would see and say, "Can mom bandage it again in the morning?" His face wrinkled, "Dad, if Bai does this again, do I fight or run?"

He smiled, "I'd duck *and* run."

Mick got up, went down the hallway, and knocked on Bai's door, "Sis, come out and talk. Don't be a dork."

"Leave me alone," came from inside.

He knocked again, "Sis?" Still no answer. "Bai, dad says you didn't break my nose, but that was quite a poke." Mick waited, "Are we OK?"

A mumbled profanity came from the room. Bai opened the door and moved near Mick. She inched closer 'til they were nose to nose before flinging her arms around him and kissing his cheek.

A startled Mick blurted, "Why did you just kiss me?"

Tears formed in her eyes, "Cause I love you. I'm really sorry Mick."

He paused as they separated, "You're still the worst sister I have. You've got one helluva right."

"Yeah, I'm still Mom's favorite."

"Dip wad!" he countered as they shook hands.

Bai gestured to the family room, "Go!"

Anh overhead what passed for family peacemaking and walked to the kitchen, "Michael, we have to add some things to our shopping list."

"Like what, nose guards and bandages?"

"No, feminine products. I'll get Bai an appointment to see a doctor."

Tooley squeezed Anh's hand, "Well it's quiet in the trenches ... for now."

Chapter - 51

Stefano and Rodolfo's eyes scanned the truck park as they walked to a tent designated for interviews. Racks for RPGs, rifles, and tow cables adorned many of the trucks and armored personnel carriers they passed. Tanks and artillery units were down the way, back from the front, evidence of serious intentions of death and destruction. They'd recently repositioned, a twice daily routine.

Stefano was upset. He'd just missed 'the story' recently. Enroute the front, he and Rodolfo had seen four missiles launched, watched them arch angrily into a sullen sky. But the big scoop, the story journalists prayed all their lives for, he'd missed. He hadn't seen airbases aflame, planes wrecked, nor missiles perforating Israeli invincibility. Stefano feared the last battle had ended without him. If it was over, things couldn't be worse.

The elements of the story surrounded him, the armed men, the ammo, and the weapons. As a junior CNN journalist Stefano had seen conflict up close. He didn't feel it right to be just a journalist, observing and depersonalizing all he saw and heard. The story differed now, but the tale was the same. The book had chapters with mangled corpses, others who'd been sent back to fight, hospital wards filled with those clinging to life, and doctors struggling to stay awake and deal with death. He'd seen others babble incoherently from stress; they were in another, darker chapter.

The CNN'ers walked around, enjoying the encampment near Jordan's border. They saw carpets spread across the sands, on which small groups of soldiers ate and drank, and talked. A few prayed. Others ate in mess tents where paper plates, plastic forks and spoons, and water bottles assisted those assigned KP duties. The smells of food wafted on an easterly breeze, tickling their noses.

His CNN pager buzzed. He grabbed his mike and gave the high sign to Rodolfo. As they lingered the cameraman hoisted the device onto his shoulder. "This is Stefano Gaiuso for CNN. We're here to interview some Jordanian soldiers; most now live in these tents."

With that cue, Rodolfo zoomed in on a row of tents as Gaiuso continued, "Along the front are hundreds and hundreds of tents. And beyond those are thousands more, filled with young men prepared for war," he spoke slowly with a frown, "but who desperately hope for peace."

Rodolfo gingerly amped up the background sounds. "We hear little music here. The constant clickety clack of tank and armored vehicle treads, the throaty rasps of diesels, and the occasional screeched garble from encrypted radio circuits became what for this camp is a concert. It is conducted alternately by sergeants and generals, a symphony of the hordes."

Stefano fingered his mike like a flute and smiled. The two men let the video roll undisturbed, then added voice-overs when they wanted to reveal the more human story they saw, and western audiences and the network demanded.

Stefano pulled a finger across his throat, the kill signal to Rodolfo. He meant to find footage, but watch for censors. "Look at those backhoes digging latrines; men wedge prefabricated inserts and matting into those trenches to allow instant setup. The latrines are to the west, but it reeks even here. Get some footage of the swarms of bugs as they gather." He snickered, "They're ancient bugs, regenerating since the times of Vespasian - small, dark, insistent and insatiable." *Nasty critters, also soldiers of a sort.*

Stefano started the broadcast recording, "I just interviewed a young Jordanian soldier. Let's call him Hamid." The censor translated as Rodolfo panned to a soldier, his head bowed. Software pixilated the man's face, disguising his features; more software would do the same to his voice. Stefano continued the narrative, "I call him the solitary soldier. He is lost, alone in a war he doesn't want. All the soldiers here pray five times a day, and each must bathe before praying. But here, doing that is a dream. Water is precious, worth a squadron of F-15s. Those that pray substitute sand for water to cleanse themselves before prostrating. It does nothing to the value of the prayers."

Rodolfo waved the fingers of his right hand in a circle. Keep it rolling. "After interviewing many soldiers we have seen that Hamid's words and his feelings ... reflect those of others. The combat fatigue is termed Post Traumatic Stress Disorder now, and given its own acronym, PTSD. Naming the malady doesn't lessen the stress, nor make it easier to deal with. One can feel the tension here, the suspense in every man. Soldiers fear war will come, without warning and no place to hide. We sense it, know any new sound might mean incoming. Stress comes not just from physical wounds, but from the increasing expectation of them."

He took a deep breath, continued, "There is hope for peace, poised beside a palpable fear of war. It resides in men, women, boys, girls, privates and generals. The cure is evident to this reporter. Pray, light one candle for peace! This is Stefano Gaiuso signing off." The journalist and cameraman finished the interview and commentary. Their censor scratched his head and walked away. The men wondered what his departure meant.

The journalists envisioned the comfort of their tent as they ambled in that direction. They stared beyond tents; there was paradise within the town, air conditioners humming in each hotel room. Here simple military cots kept them off the sand floor, while voracious critters waited to suck their blood in the hot September air. Their temporary lodging offered only a solar powered fan as its version of heaven.

They sat and ate a simple meal, drank bottled water, and finished with local dates. Stefano covered his mouth with his hand and coughed. "Rodolfo, I know what that private said, but it meant something very different. I worry about the coming war."

"I can't help you; you pull words out of the air," the cameraman said, "I just capture faces, scenes, show the emotions." The rumble of tank treads broke his attention.

"They move constantly to alternate locations, reducing likelihood of being targeted by artillery or aviators' bombs," Stefano thought aloud, "after being located by Israel's satellite, OFFEQ. It gives only limited surveillance, and we're in an area Israel must be really concerned with."

The reporters knew that far above, unseen but seeing, was a satellite. They talked via theirs with Atlanta, broadcasting from east of hopeless, a bit north of tragic each day. "Yes, but they have dozens of drones, for when OFFEQ isn't overhead." Stefano grimaced, "Either way Israel has all the Intel it needs for war."

"Don't you believe there'll be peace?" Rodolfo said. It was evident he didn't, not deep down. Both knew there were too many fingers on too many triggers.

"If war breaks out, every male will be called up. Israel cannot let the enemy get through the front door. They'll fight to the death; hundreds of thousands will die." Stefano wiped beads of sweat from his forehead, "Defeat could mean the end of Judaism itself."

Rodolfo muttered, "Yeah, and I don't want to be buried here, without a headstone."

"We're screwed if war breaks out, you and I," the journalist offered, "we'll be at Ground Zero, in the final cross hairs. But let's get more footage," Stefano grumbled, "If we're lucky there'll be footage of us."

"We'll be historic," the cameraman countered, "but *very* dead."

Beyond their tents a vehicle backfired and they both ducked.

An hour later a Jordanian Hummer slid to a stop outside their tent. Stefano and Rodolfo were introduced to General Abdullah, who proceeded to berate them. "You have insulted my men, who are brave. The officers, the sergeants, fight with Israel before. They do not lose. They do not run or have this PTSD. They are anxious, as any man before combat would be."

"We live *here,*" the general pointed to a map, "and the Israelis live *there*." He pointed again. "*They* must not come *here.*"

Stefano bowed, touched his chest with his right hand, "I am sorry. We meant no disrespect."

"You must tell audience that Jews from Crimea, from Africa, must not come to settle Palestinian land. Tell them that!" He paused and gestured to an aide, "Major, take these men and their cameras, and satellite radio elsewhere, put them with the Saudis."

Soon they were being escorted past artillery batteries and tank revetments further away from the front line. Stefano recognized flags at a command post they passed. These Saudis were National Guard troops, allied tribally with the Saudi royal family. They encompassed the best of Arabia's artillery, tanks and infantry. Now they were positioned behind the Jordanians, kept in reserve.

The escort vehicle with the major stopped ahead; he walked to confer with a Saudi NG officer." Stefano heard the officer say, "I don't want them here; put them with tank force."

Stefano grumbled, "Rodolfo, this distances us from the front, away from any action, further still from any story. It's another disappointment." There was a rumble in the distance, farther from the border front - live fire training. "No doubt the Israelis hear that," he gestured with a thumb, "they'll know these people are ramping up their preparations. Maybe things will get more exciting."

Chapter - 52

Months before several ideas were discussed, and most were discarded. One with merit was adopted at the Al Kharj Weapons Directorate. Many engineers, unfamiliar with the project's real objectives, marveled at the time and riyals that went into rounds which blew up tank barrels. They concluded the tests went poorly; that evaluation was incorrect.

Six weeks earlier testing finished. Captain Nahari, the Saudi Navy project manager, was elated at its success. He glowed as he briefed General Khalid. "General, the new propellant mixture is extremely fast burning. If things go as tested, the barrel's breech will be unusable and possibly fracture."

"The report states that test rounds ruptured several barrels. Using them could put a tank out of commission," Khalid assessed. "That could tip the balance of an engagement."

Nahari smiled, "That's the idea, general. My only concern is how we ensure our tankers don't use the rounds." He glanced at the analyst down the table.

The man sitting shrugged, "We have no idea, Sir. We just shipped the rounds to Battalion 814. They'll figure it out."

Nahari glanced at Khalid, "I hope that unit has a plan."

Two days earlier Saudi railway's new tracks through the Eastern Province took the M-60s north to load out. All Battalion 814's forty eight M-60A3 tanks were approaching. They rumbled down the road from deep storage, diesel fumes saturating the morning air. Dust rolled into the air, obscuring the rising sun while clanking drive gears pierced the silence. For only the second time in four decades the tanks were given a full ammo load out. The only portion of a deserted station north of Dammam which felt these tanks was its loading ramps.

Sixty transporter cars, each capable of carrying eighty tons, were parked at the station. The units entrained after the possibility of Israeli satellite detection was past. It took over eight hours to load the tanks. Just days before, all but twenty-five of the Kingdom's newer M-1 tanks rolled north on the same tracks, also with war loads.

The final railcars carried the men, along with their support vehicles and chow. Major Youssef, the colonel's aide, supervised muster and loading. "Colonel, their satellites will discover that we've moved."

"*Ush Poor*, have patience Youssef. I will meet with my Jordanian counterpart and the commander of the helo squadron. The helos can help tank tanks and infantry, possibly influence a battle." Youssef nodded, glanced down at his notepad, probably praying they wouldn't have to rely on them.

"The Israelis train with the same manual we use. So," Ubaidi looked at the major, "we have to adjust our tactics to stay alive after the first salvo." Neither smiled, and Youssef looked back to his list of action items.

"Youssef, when we get there, verify comms and the status of each tanks' air conditioning. We'll be at the left end of the front, the flank. Everything must work. Get the First Sergeant to scope out alternate locations to move between." Ubaidi's brow furrowed. *Did I miss anything?*

Battalion 814 offloaded hours later, at the end of a boring journey. First Sergeant Ahmed motioned to the crews. "Mount up. Get these beasts to your marshalling points. We'll bivouac near the tanks. Now, move!" Maps in hand, he watched as *his* tankers complied, tearing up tiles at the border station. The Colonel had told him, there would be days or weeks of boredom ahead.

Ubaidi wanted to know who would lead the Israeli armor. He hadn't identify the SOB despite a week of reading all the Intel he could get his hands on. They wouldn't be shooting at him, but at a 55 ton tank. Despite trying to de-personalize the battle, he knew that wasn't true.

Ubaidi looked at his tactical maps. *They'll come through that wadi. That's where I'd come. Do I fight it out, or back away? What's the plan? Better talk with that Jordanian tank commander for answers. This won't be like engaging Iraqis in Khafji.*

It was noon the next day at the Armored Division's HQ. Two hours before Ubaidi's uniform had been pressed, crisp. Now it looked like he had slept in it for a week. He looked at maps spread on every table in the Command Post. There'd be others, duplicates, in at least two alternate CPs. Radio circuits, their cabling buried in deep trenches running to remotely located antennae and satellite dishes, provided added security against Israeli strikes. The communication gear was dispersed. They'd trained to do it that way; it was SOP.

The general commanding this part of the front walked in and the colonels rose. "Colonel Wasfi, this is Colonel Ubaidi. Ubaidi, you'll be on Wasfi's flank." He summarized the two officers' records, highlighting their combat experience. "Consequently you must coordinate movements. I'm counting on you."

The colonels kissed each others' cheeks as the general left. Ubaidi looked at Wasfi, "Nice to meet you at last, your name was mentioned very positively in briefings. Tell me what to expect, any tactical suggestions, you're the expert."

"The Israelis mobilize reservists for the bulk of their force. Their tankers have homes right across from us." Wasfi moved his hand across a map showing Israeli towns. "Colonel Chanan is our opponent**.** I know the guy; I've engaged him twice. He'll try to drive through and roll up your flank, draw out our reserves for their Air Force."

Wasfi spent twenty minutes going over tactical details, pausing only to sip tea, "If you can take Chanan out, the rest will pause," Wasfi told Ubaidi. "If we create a situation they're not prepared for, then the whole battle is up for grabs."

"They expect us to react, turn tail and run?" Ubaidi nervously drummed his fingers on the table, "They expect us to do that. Can we count on that?" *All of Wasfi's words suggested he'd been assigned to battle Chanan.*

"Yes. I'm alive after fighting him twice. Not many get to say that," Wasfi thumbed a set of prayer beads. "Train your crews relentlessly. Teach them survival. Never let them think about being *safe*. They aren't *safe* unless they shoot and move *before* the other guy gets sighted in."

"Even when we move, we can't hide a loud 55 ton hunk of

steel. We'll have attack helos in support. Do you have any other suggestions?" Ubaidi asked.

"Use 'Platoon Fire.' Have your platoons concentrate on the lead *Magach*, that's their name for an M-60." Wasfi pointed his finger at the Saudi, "The Israeli officers will be there. Use your first shots to take them out. Then move all shots to the next target."

Ubaidi pulled out a pad from his back pocket. It had notes and a diagram. "Here's something I've prepared; tell me what you think of the idea." He explained for twenty minutes as the Jordanian listened.

As time passed Wasfi's face transformed, then he spoke, "It may work, please Allah."

Wasfi's expression stiffened, "You need reckless men to pull that off. Do you have some?"

Ubaidi grinned, "I do."

He shook Ubaidi's hand, then informed him of an assignment, "There are two journalists here. They were at the front with our infantry, but pissed off a general. He consigned them to your National Guard. And *they* have passed them along. Keep them out of the way; they're your problem now."

Chapter - 53

As they walked back to their unit Ubaidi turned to the major, "Youssef, tell our engineers to set up several defensive positions for every tank." As he glanced around he saw combat dozers with blades contouring the sands. *Those positions might prevent visual targeting of our tanks.*

"The OP Order says our helos will have anti-armor rounds, missiles, rockets, even an occasional CBU. If we catch them, we'll give them a bloody nose," the major slapped his leg.

Ubaidi thought of the ammo. Every *Magach* carried the same 105 mm shells for battle as the Saudis. The most frightening were four canister rounds designated to take out infantry. At close ranges a soldier could shoot an RPG into your treads. A hit there immobilized a tank, then only Allah could save you. Canister took care of that temptation.

Every tanker knew his best hope of survival was extra protection. Every tank had jury rigged armor around hatches and turrets, and treads. The new protection hung down outboard covering vulnerable drive sprockets and rollers. Ubaidi touched the skirt on one of his tanks as they walked back to their CP. "Good idea getting the extra armor, Youssef. It might save a few of our tanks."

The two stopped by his tank and Ubaidi held a platoon commanders meeting. "The Israelis will try to break through where we butt up against the Jordanians. Here's what we're going to do." He explained his new tactic. Heads nodded and smiles swept around the map.

US satellites saw the Saudi tanks moving north, and had recorded the newest series of missile attacks on airfields at Haifa and Palmachim. That would prevent replacement aircraft landing for another week; he'd read the message traffic. His gut told him a bigger war was becoming certain.

The journalists' encrypted phone rang. He entered his biometric data and he connected with Tooley. "Hey, how's the family?"

Tooley grinned, despite troubles at home lingering in his mind. "Bai is bitchy; Mick is gaga over some girl whose family got transferred stateside. He ran up a hundred fifty dollar phone bill before we took away his phone privileges. Anh's still at the school, getting ready for the flu season." Then Tooley told Stefano about the DNA tests he had learned of.

"What, an Israeli cousin?" Stefano stumbled with his words, "wasn't he the one who bombed you?"

"Yes. We visited him in a prison. His name is David Ben Bedoo. He seems an OK sorta guy, for a pilot." Tooley said sarcastically. "Amir had a bigger surprise. He identified the guy's father as the man who shot us at the missile base. Amir remembered the fathers' name from his uniform that day."

"I guess the Saudis will hold him for a huge ransom, along with their former Defense Ministers' nephew," Stefano speculated.

"Pretty much what I'd expect, if things ever settle down." Another phone buzzed in O'Toole's office. "I've got a conference call. Stay safe, and don't get near any airfield. BBC reports say they're busy."

Stefano signed off, "*Stronzo*!"

General Khalid read the second set of reports. They dealt with upgrades to a dozen drones and anti-radiation missiles. He smiled, "Every software objective has been met." Glancing up he asked, "Captain, are things on track with the missiles?"

"Yes," Nahari stated confidently. "We bought UAVs to test our helos fire control system. Then we shot the damn things down in the Empty Quarter. We've concealed our efforts so they wouldn't be observed."

Nahari summarized the operation, "General, the Israelis will try to re-establish control of the air, then use armor to push through on the ground. If they lose OFFEQ coverage and require surveillance of a battlefield, they'll deploy UAVs before any engagement. If we detect their drones, we'll activate Operation Sniffer to shoot them down."

Khalid smiled and closed the reports.

Chapter - 54

13:05 local time - Helo Ready Room near Jordan's border - "Listen up. Your mission is to intercept Israeli drones." Major Asiri, commander of the helo squadron looked around, "You trained for this; downing a slow target is not beneath you. If you shoot one down, the Israelis could lose vital battlefield Intel." *And it will be a lot safer to take out a UAV than a fighter or another helo.*

First Lieutenant Dahi asked, "How do we complete an intercept without a visual?"

Asiri continued, "Good point. You may not be able to detect them. You'll have to trust orders from the airships." Laughter followed his remark. Two pilots grumbled, one mumbling something snide about airship weenies. Asiri paused to ensure the pilots were listening, then shouted in frustration, "Hold it down you morons. We're on the same side. Any targets will be below fifteen thousand feet, flying at 100 knots. If you get a visual, approach from astern, like you trained. Engage at six miles."

The pilots grabbed their helmets, put down their coffees, and walked to the door, still complaining. On the flight line one pilot, Captain Dahi, continued bitching as he completed a pre-flight. He watched as the red shirts pulled missile arming pins, and then he patted a missile, "Hope this thing doesn't blow up in my face."

Dahi buckled up, watched his crew chief rub one of the SIDEARM missiles and flash a Thumbs Up. The man yelled, "Get one and I'll paint an emblem on the fuselage" then he ducked as the rotor wash pushed him backwards. Radios quickly resonated with orders.

Watches at the airship control stations were running back-to-back. Far above each a nondescript shape filled with helium and sensors tugged at its mooring cable, held aloft by the desert breezes. Console operators in the vans struggled to detect drones, watching bleary-eyed as dreary bits of data bombarded their senses.

TETHER TWO vans detected the Israeli UAV first. Using dedicated monitors, its' technicians verified the objects control signals and heat signature. A drone was aloft. Suddenly the radio speaker squelched.

"ONE FOUR, this is TETHER TWO. BANDIT ALFA ONE bearing ZERO TWO ZERO, ANGELS TEN, range ONE ZERO, course ONE SEVEN FIVER, speed ONE ONE ZERO, over."

Dahi spoke as the attack helos swung right, "ONE FOUR and SIX EIGHT are turning to acquire."

"This is TETHER TWO. Execute SNIFFER. You are WEAPONS FREE."

The pilot keyed his radio. The clicks crackled across the circuit. Dahi slowed, checked his sensor readouts, and reported, "TETHER, ONE FOUR and SIX EIGHT are closing BANDIT ALFA ONE." As his nose steadied the Lieutenant saw a small blur ahead.

Dahi's earphones registered missile acquisition, and the alert tone intensified. He squeezed the trigger. The SIDEARM jumped from a pylon, and homed. The missile trailed white smoke as it arched upwards. "This is ONE FOUR, FOX ONE!" The target disintegrated in a yellow ball of flame and smoke.

A dark mass fell to earth, etching the sky with a thin line of smoke. "This is ONE FOUR, scratch one BANDIT." Dahi grinned. *Miskatuk*!

"ONE FOUR, copy your kill. Return To Base, over."

"This is ONE FOUR. Roger." The pilots maneuvered and headed to Home Plate. As First Lieutenant Dahi landed and stepped from his helo, he was hugged by an ecstatic ground crew. He swung his helmet in the air. "Sergeant, paint a small symbol on the fuselage. Put *Miskatuk*, and Gotcha in English, next to it. Make the figure small," The pilot smiled, "we'll get more."

Black Snake UAV controllers were tracking one of their units when its signal stopped. SNAKE, based at Ramat David Air Base, was tasked to discover enemy forces. The drone disappeared from all sensors, and Israel's military lost real time battlefield surveillance. "CONTROL, this is BLACK SNAKE. SIX SEVEN control lost, over."

Across the circuit came an anxious reply, "This is CONTROL, re-sequence control commands, over."

"This is BLACK SNAKE. Standby, preparing to re-start onboard systems." The tech tapped console buttons and the readouts reflected transmission of commands. He scanned the sequence steps, and frowned. There was no response from the surveillance platform.

The commander of Israel's northern air defenses glared, "How long before we know?" General Baruch asked.

"In two more minutes reboot will complete and I'll either regain control, or it will transition to recovery," the sergeant replied.

The general's face reddened, matching the color of alerts flashing on the status boards. "What does that mean?"

"General, after five minutes from loss of control the UAV will Return To Launch Point. It will turn around and head back to Ramat David ... if it's still in the air. We'll know in about a minute."

The sergeant anxiously entered the final commands to save data and re-boot onboard programs. Each step was met by lack of any response. "Not sure yet; it may have crashed, or been shot down."

He switched to a different circuit. *Better stay one step ahead. Some asshole will tell me to do that in short order.*

"BLACK SNAKE, this is CONTROL. All signals with SIX SEVEN lost. Do you hold data or TM, over?"

The squadrons' lead tech confirmed transmission of required maneuver commands. Real-time readouts, however, confirmed no usable data. "CONTROL, this is BLACK SNAKE. No joy. Request launch replacement, over."

The NCO turned to the control officer, "Major, we've lost one."

"How soon can you launch another?" the officer asked.

"We can put up a replacement in thirty some minutes. Then it will take an hour to get it on station. OFFEQ is going off station. We need real time data."

"Launch the damn thing!" the major ordered.

He replied "Yes, Sir," as swear words filled the HQ control room. "This is CONTROL. Replacement will be up in one five, over."

EAGLE TWO, this is TETHER TWO. GUNS ONE FOUR reports he scratched a BANDIT. Anticipate they'll launch a replacement in three zero minutes. Request priority searches all probable launch areas."

AWACS controllers acknowledged the request with two clicks on the circuit. "TETHER, this is EAGLE TWO, roger. Pass on to HATCHET – Well Done, over." Expectations had been low onboard the converted 707 and in the airship vans, but they'd proved their home grown system could detect a drone, and make it bite the dust.

As team members listened, an AWACS tech asked, "Captain, can we paint a Kill on our fuselage?"

"No, but the airship crew can. Let them know."

Chapter - 55

N**MCC War Room 5, 06:30 local time –** "General, I think an Israeli surveillance asset was just downed," CPO McNally blurted. "Cheyenne doesn't hold TM or a data stream. I wonder how that happened."

"Only two ways, Chief. The Saudis or Jordanians shot it down. Or some smartass told it to land upside down or backwards" the duty flag guffawed. *Pretty awesome shooting.*

Playing dumb McNally asked, "Should we worry?"

"Yes. Israel has a limited number of the damn things and employs them only when they've lost satellite coverage. This loss gives enemy forces an opportunity to maneuver unseen."

"Then you run this up the flag pole, general?"

"Yes. We'll be able to see how critical the situation is by how soon they launch another. Re-launch will confirm they lost real time battlefield Intel and need it." Anxiety appeared on Smoot's face, "And *that* could mean the Israelis are about to attack. Hand me the Red Phone."

McNally grabbed the handset, punched the red button for the WHSR, and handed it to General Smoot.

As Smoot waited for an answer, the Chief bent over and whispered. "NSA cracked some red hot intercepts. Saudi circuits confirmed the drone kill, and Israel is readying to launch another. It's for real, Sir." The flag nodded.

"War Room calling, General Smoot here. Our satellite over the Middle East just detected a Saudi helo downing an Israeli drone. Inform the Chief of Staff we've lost track of an Israeli UAV over the front line. They had one up and transmitting, but we can't track them as yet. But one has definitely disappeared - Gone! Nada!"

COS DeMeers came on the line. He paused, his tone rising. He recounted that day's battles between Saudi, Jordanian, and Israeli fighters. "Before midnight the watch kept us up all night after missiles struck the airbases at Haifa and Palmachim. Replacement planes can't land for a damn week. Don't waste my time, or that of the President, unless it's a No Shit *E-mergency*. Your info, general, does not warrant that level of attention. Are we clear?"

"Yes, Sir." Smoot stared at the status boards. *I better update my duty preference card, before that SOB screws me over. How did the Prez pick such a shit bird? That DeMeers doesn't understand grunts or warfare. He must have missed muster on the day brains were passed out.*

"Chief, we need to figure out how to track these things. If the Saudis can, we need to understand how they're doing it. Shit, they must be using TM or intercepting the control signals. Our satellite folks can find and crack those GD signals; they just need to include us in the loop. Make it your highest priority."

Gaiuso glanced around their new tent. It was different, but the same, being banished to the edge of the sand box. Stefano reckoned Second Lieutenant Harbi, his new guard dog, deserved a tent in Dante's Inferno, which seemed nearby. After two days under Harbi's thumb, the journalist wanted to bury the man, preferably by a latrine. *Hell must be around here. It's certainly not far away, our solar fan is missing.*

The connection Ubaidi felt, Gaiuso was a friend of his uncle and they'd met, meant little here in a war zone. He walked into the journalists' tent, agitation on his face. Stefano looked up as the colonel spoke, "The prodigal newsman is back. Why are you here?"

"Your generals didn't want us giving a bad impression of troop morale. We were moved away from the infantry. We're now pariahs," Stefano groused, "and will miss real news." He wanted a headline, but being under scrutiny cauterized his chances. "My friend Rodolfo says the story will find us no matter where we are."

Ubaidi moved menacingly towards Stefano. His face wrinkled, "I assigned Harbi to stay with you two, told him that he must be diligent. 'Monitor them,' I said, 'keep them out of our way.' After I told him," Ubaidi smirked, "Harbi thumbed his prayer beads, and stormed off to find you." He twisted his head right and left, "You are both supposed to be with the Lieutenant. Where is your cameraman? "

"Rodolfo is with Harbi," Stefano bowed his head, "asking him about prayer."

"Well," Ubaidi grinned, "getting the answer to *that* could take hours. Harbi will preach until he converts your friend." The colonel touched his heart, "The lieutenant believes *we* are all infidels."

"Did you say 'we'?" Stefano asked incredulously. "You're a Muslim, aren't you?"

"I am, but Harbi believes those who pray less than he are infidels. He acts as if he is the prophet Mohammed himself, praise be unto him." Ubaidi paused, "I am concerned where you go, what you see. You must not interfere with future operations ... or report on them. Tank engagements are quickly over, and I won't shed any blood saving you. We can talk after things are over. If you endanger my men," Ubaidi glared, "you will disappear."

Stefano's expression remained calm. "I've discovered some of your operations. All soldiers talk, and I see and hear things. It is my job.

Very excited techs painted that kill on their helo, and the image was too small to be a helo or a plane. He pursed his lips, "I haven't disclosed tactical information in any broadcast. I will not reveal your actions." *Darwin would love this job; only survivors tell the tale.*

Ubaidi assessed the journalist. *I must keep them away from our tanks and ammo. I'll give orders to Harbi.*

Chapter - 56

Ubaidi glanced at the setting sun, some *jinn* painting the clouds wispy reds and yellows. He prayed to be calm in the face of fire, to be strong. *I must find words to inspire my men to stay and fight ... not run.* "Major, come here; assemble the officers and senior sergeants. We need to ensure veterans are in each platoon. And, send Harbi and his prayer rug away from the front." *He will be useless in battle, so it is better he pray for us.*

Moments later Ubaidi's men gathered by his M-60. His sightline briefly met theirs. The stares hesitated, shifted, uncertainty visible. "I do not ask you to do impossible. Think of ten years from now, as you sit with your families to talk. Consider now what you will say of this day. You will tell them" his focus left his notes and his face hardened, "of the battle," Ubaidi dragged out his last words, seconds between each word, "of ... our ... victory."

Now energized sergeants straggled to their MBTs. Ubaidi stared at his officers, still listening, "You're ready. Don't give a *Magach* an easy shot. When you engage ... stay mobile." As the three Lieutenants moved to their platoons, he turned, "Major, conduct radio checks, then observe radio silence ... unless." Both understood 'unless' meant fighting had broken out.

"Israeli will throw fifty *Magache*s our way. They're poised to strike at bridges, highways ... and suitable terrain. They will come," Ubaidi pointed to a map, "through *our wadi*." He paused, tapped his finger on the plot. "There is something to be done." He pulled Youssef closer and for five minutes they talked tactics.

Youssef looked up, "Is there anything else?"

"Yes," he smiled, "move our tanks to their initial positions, and

I'll confirm our helo support."

"I have talked with them; the helos are ready. They'll be up within five minutes of when you or I radio for them. When we do that the helos will lift off, approach at about fifty feet, blending in with the terrain ... prepared for action."

"Youssef, our artillery can stop them at bridges and roadways, but this *wadi*," ... Ubaidi's features stiffened, "We *must* hold this *wadi*!"

Flares, tripped aloft by persons or things unknown, ripped the darkness like the flourish of a drum line. A distant rumble echoed. The booming thunder of exploding bombs and artillery moved closer, increasing like the bass drum beat of a marching band.

Pupils shrank, safeties were clicked off. Ubaidi climbed in his MBT, yelled on the radio ... "This is KHAFJI SIX, STATIONS!" Ubaidi's tankers heard the order and engines belched clouds of dark, suffocating exhaust, while radios crackled. Battalion 814's tanks scurried to new positions. Adrenaline spiked as rounds slammed into breeches.

Area artillery fire missions computed with GPS accuracy exploded within the *wadi*. Israeli artillery units fired at pre-assigned coordinates; rounds arching from long ranges fell, to hit the thinner armor atop tanks.

Saudi fire finder radars tracked the incoming, calculated its origins, and prepared counter battery fire. Artillery tubes belched in reply, firing two salvos, then 105 and 155mm crews repositioned their tubes before the next salvos found them. Artillery flashes crackled like brief, deadly Roman candles.

"KHAFJI this is SIX. TARGET tank, BEARING THREE FOUR FIVE, RANGE two thousand. WEAPONS FREE!" Radios reverberated in Saudi M-60s, the messages different, intentions identical.

"PALLADIN SIX, this is KHAFJI SIX, CALL FOR FIRE. AREA TARGET, boxes ECHO SIX SEVEN and SIX EIGHT. Will Adjust, over." The tank commanders' call for artillery fire quickly resulted in salvos sundering the darkness. Blasts shook the ground, flashes extending across the horizon.

Smoke rose ominously from where 814's ALFA Company anchored the left flank. Radio reports paralleled the incoming flashes. "KHAFJI ALFA ONE THREE this is KHAFJI ALFA SIX. Provide progress reports if possible, out." On the flank, fire rained on ALFA's commander as he radioed his platoons.

"KHAFJI SIX this is KHAFJI ALFA NINER. The company's XO gave a frantic report of devastating artillery fire. As thunderous explosions echoed in the background his final words were heard ... "This is NINER, unit decimated ... ALFA SIX KIA, over."

In ALFA Company, screams from one still effective platoon pierced the air, "NINE, This is ALFA ONE THREE. The transmissions cut in and out. Crackles, squelches, and blurps broke up the words but not their intensity. The ground quivered, then yellow red columns of flame emerged from nine M-60 turrets, lighting the horizon like erupting volcanoes.

Ubaidi heard only parts of the reports. He'd trained his men to space the MBTs, doctrine said 25 yards, to keep one explosion from causing detonation of others. Had they been too close, or had Israeli artillery been lucky? He *needed* details to help assess his units. *Don't break their situational awareness. They'll let me know when it's over. ...*

Ubaidi's patience failed... "KHAFJI ALFA, this is SIX. You are breaking up. Say again, over." ALFA company, all three platoons, remained silent on its circuit. His face transfigured. *My flank ... is gone.*

Then more rumbling explosions reverberated. Yellow flashes lit the horizon to the north, west, and east. Overhead fighters engaged with missiles, skies filling with brilliant white smoke trails, explosions, and a few parachutes.

Thousands of feet below those engagements, helos sparred with their missiles – no parachutes emerged. In the *wadi* nearby, 814 treads squeaked, tanks repositioning between shots. Concussions from artillery salvos jostled the sands, but were unfelt by the 55 ton MBTs.

"KHAFJI ~~~, this is KHAFJI. The radio transmissions continued to be sporadic, broken. Garbled tactical reports, one after another, from units unknown, followed. "KHAFJI ~~~, this is ... units strafed. ... Request GUNS assist, ~~~ Over." Screaming crossed the net ... then just a final punctuation - "Allah!"

"PALLADIN SIX, this is KHAFJI SIX, Adjust Fire. North two hundred, East five hundred. Twenty rounds, Ranging Fire. Fire For Effect. WHEN READY, over." FFE was acknowledged and shell explosions fell as requested. A *Magache* tank column was hit; two MBTs exploded. The others advanced.

QUIVER SIX, commander of Israeli tank battalion 418, listened to the night's disturbed silence. The thunder would last until the attack was over. The stillness reminded Colonel Chanan what came next was not subject to control. Lady Luck held the cards.

He knew this night might be his last, thought of the iconic work, *All in the Valley of Death. Charge for the guns!* Chanan transmitted, "QUIVER, this is SIX. Execute breakthrough!" *Those artillery salvos will open a wedge.*

Theirs not to make reply,
Theirs not to reason why,
Theirs but to do and die:
Into the valley of Death
Alfred, Sir Lord Tennyson

Chanan's *Magache*s pressed forward as a sandstorm swept past, his tanks maneuvering right, left. Three tank companies advanced as platoons, two moving while the third fired. Then the third repositioned as the others readied. Saudi and Jordanian tanks pulled back initially; both sides called in support. Israeli and Saudi battalions were each blanketed with high explosive shells.

Circuits quickly jammed as tactical transmissions overflowed with emotion and confusion. "QUIVER," Chanan directed, "this is SIX, move to contact." *The 'book' said exploit and pursue. But those rag heads ahead have the same book.* "QUIVER, this is SIX. FIRE at WILL. Charge!"

ACK clicks were heard. Israeli tanks advanced, locked on other MBTs. Artillery barrages walked through tank and artillery units on both sides. Death entered new names in its registry of recruits.

The sergeant glanced at the ammo racks, then the radio resonated. "CHARLIE SIX has heat images. Hope there's no infantry with them; I've only got two canister rounds." The commander of the single Saudi company operational on the left flank, CHARLIE SIX, was up against the wall. Reserves had been requested, but hadn't reported in. He keyed the radio, "SIX, this is CHARLIE SIX. I hold many Israeli tanks closing. Request reinforcement ASAP."

Ubaidi rubbed his chin. *Worst situation possible, better call Youssef.* "KHAFJI NINER, move our reserves up. I'm moving to help CHARLIE Company."

His flank pulverized by artillery, with only seven of his tanks operational, First Sergeant Talaf radioed again, "Only seven units left."

Then friendly artillery radioed in; a welcome break for Ubaidi's units. The artillery commander barked, "PALLADIN SIX, targeting is confirmed." The transmission continued until coordinates of six targets were acknowledged.

Within seconds artillery officers adjusted coordinates to engage the advancing *Magaches*. "CHARLIE SIX, PALLADIN is firing now, out." The radio turned to silence. Twenty seconds later it barked encouraging news, the day's first for Battalion 814. "STANDBY, out."

This told Talaf that artillery rounds would impact in five seconds. Concussion after concussion blasted across the radio, the explosions vibrating fillings in teeth as artillery rippled foot by foot through Israeli formations, dozens of rounds falling in four minutes. He looked ahead, winced.

"Charge for the guns!" he said:
Into the Valley of Death

Overhead another struggle continued, fighters engaging to dominate the air. Helos at lower altitudes shot it out, ignoring the pleas of tanks they were called to support.

"PALLADIN, this is SIX, Repeat Fire For Effect."

Colonel Ubaidi listened to the radio as more rounds fell outside the MBT. Then another report jarred his nerves as his unit rushed forward. "SIX, this is CHARLIE SIX. We're still operational. No, two of our support vehicles just bottomed out. They need a retriever to pull them free, over."

"This is CHARLIE SIX, looks like the right tire of one is blown." Ubaidi knew the situation - two Saudi vehicles sat, marooned like tethered camels, waiting as other tanks regrouped, shot it out, tried to muster reserves forward to stop an Israeli breakthrough. It was the plan.

"SIX this is SUPPORT SIX. I can't move either. We're bailing." Crews abandoned the two vehicles to flee the area.

Ubaidi breathed deeply, then implemented plans to help

CHARLIE Company. He radioed Major Youssef, "Get the friggin reserves forward, and get us helo support. Our flank is gone, the radios report two vehicles stuck." On the tank's intercom he spoke, "Gunner, drive us forward. ... FAST!"

The tank lurched and Ubaidi smiled weakly. *Perhaps what we planned will work.*

The lead Israeli platoon crested a dune and discovered two abandoned Saudi vehicles. The commander of the first tank, Sergeant Benyamin, closed the two Hummers. He scanned the sands ahead for mines or trip wires. *Even if they blow it, it won't hurt me in this beast.* He yelled on the intercom and radio, breeching protocols. "Hey, they shot out the tires but didn't burn them. Let's see what we got." He looked again, "Damn, looks like ammo."

Not tho' the soldier knew
Someone had blunder'd.

Benyamin turned, radioed to Lieutenant Baruch in the platoon nearby. "Ell Tee, come see what we found. They left sabot rounds, a shitload. I counted damn near eight pallets. At twelve cases per pallet that's almost two hundred rounds. Let's divvy them up."

As Benyamin looked around something caught his attention. He raised a clenched fist and radioed. "Hold Ell Tee. Don't move! Look what those assholes did."

Baruch's eyes scanned the ground ahead of his *Magache*. He dismounted and advanced cautiously, expecting a booby trap. He looked at the pallets, alerted to discover what caught Benyamin's eyes. Each case had a Star of David stenciled on it, along with a black diagonal stripe and obscenities in Hebrew.

Baruch recognized a treasure whether it was in a bazaar or on the battlefield. "Sarge, we won't get resupplied for another day. Have each platoon swing by. Take the sabot rounds. Torch the vehicles!"

The Lieutenant grinned as he got in his MBT. "Sarge, ram those rounds up some rag heads' ass."

"Yes, Sir. Delighted." He yelled to his crew ... "Let's ride."

Into the mouth of Hell

Rode the six hundred.

The sound of firing tank shells were almost absent within the MBTs. Chanan knew every soldier, even his, had an incurable desire to check out each target being engaged with his eyes. He drove forward as his unit advanced. He radioed, "Keep your hatches buttoned up."

The ground trembled again as Saudi artillery salvos rent the air, falling among his tanks, rattling those within. More shudders followed. "QUIVER, this is SIX. STATIONS!" Instantly his tank crews tweaked lasers and IR systems, verified tank to tank and internal comms.

"QUIVER, this is SIX," Chanan calmly reported. "TARGET tanks. Bearing FOUR SIX FIVE, range ONE SIX Hundred." He keyed the radio, "LOAD. AT MY COMMAND," On the intercom the colonel screamed to his gunner ..."If its turret turns, blow it away."

A tanker could see about 7,000 yards, yet effective range was barely 2,000. The space between the gunner seeing a target and shooting left room to worry about what the other guy was doing.

Chanan's two tank platoons slammed rounds into forty year old breeches, and closed them. "QUIVER, this is SIX. COMPANY ..." Nine tanks confirmed firing solutions, their commanders keying mikes once. Chanan lingered ... *We're primed ... the toughest muthas in the valley.*

Cannon to right of them,
Cannon to left of them,
Cannon behind them

Chanan whispered to himself, *Mohammed you rug merchant, prepare to meet Allah.* Each Israeli tank had entered laser ranges, confirmed readiness. Chanan's voice echoed over unit radios.

"FIRE!"

Firing keys closed and individual Israeli tanks tracked rounds towards Saudi tanks. Dust swirled from 105mm muzzles back blasts. A handful of the tanks revved drive motors, began shifting to alternate firing positions." Treads ratcheted noisily as they spun through the talcum sand, churning it into the air. MBTs spun and repositioned despite eyes harassed by the acrid cordite fumes within.

Destructive artillery rounds fell among both Saudi and Israeli tank formations, adding to the jarring felt despite armored suspensions. Loaders frantically grabbed rounds, opened breeches, and slammed sabots in. Tank crews had just three seconds to reload if they wished to live in battle.

Sabot rounds, many with blue Stars of David, black bands, and obscenities were fired. Four Israeli turrets catapulted skyward. Flames belched upwards in volcanic testimony to death. The force confined within the armored hull incinerated all life.

Chanan's tanks reported to platoon commanders, then to company commanders, up the chain of command to him. "This is QUIVER SIX. Check in." He heard reports of Jordanian and Saudi reserves arriving, stiffening the defense his MBTs faced. The circuits went silent.

Sabring the gunners there,
Charging an army, while
All the world wonder'd

Chanan's MBTs searched aggressively for enemy tanks with radio antennae, knowing commanders of enemy units were there. The tumult of sounds assaulted his consciousness, battlefield fireballs heightened by adrenaline. The scar on his right cheek twitched. He felt invincible. *Nothing can hurt me.*

The breakthrough was an all or nothing mission; HQ did not want to intrude on the effort. Breaking concentration during combat could cause someone with his finger on the trigger to lose focus. After minutes of no radio transmissions, headquarters guessed shock from firing, the maneuvers under stress, and battle explained the silence on the circuit.

"Fire at whip antennae," those were his orders, "their leaders will be there." Chanan's gunner fired, saw and twice felt explosions from blackened hulks and shock waves. Sabots flew at 4800 fps, creating sonic waves as they passed. 105mm barrels of death swung to point at new targets. Pungent cordite smells filled MBTs as shot after shot whizzed at the enemy.

Not muzzle to muzzle, but within sabot range, each shot kicked up sand clouds, obscuring visual images. Sand and dust did not confound laser range finders or tracking systems, nor stabilized fire controls. Furious firing continued.

"We'll crush them," Chanan said to those in his tank. He tugged at his body armor.

Beyond his view, the barrels of one *Magache* company were splayed back like banana peels across their turrets. The stunned crews crawled from their defenseless MBTs. Their hands went into the air, tears filling their eyes. 55 ton chariots of war were now desert road markers, littering the battlefield. In testimony to the test of wills, birds of prey hovered, waiting for the final score.

Shatter'd and sunder'd.
They rode back, but not
Not the six hundred,

CBUs fell from fighters streaking above, landed among Chanan's tanks. One *Magache* was caught with its hatch open, the driver smoking a needed cig. A bomblet snuck inside and the turret flew into the air, along with parts of the man. The crew was immolated, becoming part of the tally.

The colonel watched speechless as it happened meters away. His friends' tanks smoldered nearby. He keyed his radio, "Support helos neutralized; artillery falling in buckets. Unit surrounded, out!" Chanan's' report was the last HQ heard from Battalion 418 for twenty minutes.

A lucky RPG shot, fired by a lone soldier, as a report would later state, flew towards Chanan's *Magache*. The shoulder launched rocket left a tell tale trail of white smoke, pointing a finger of death at the colonel. The round didn't penetrate the tanks' armor; it only jammed a drive sprocket. The colonel had cheated death again at the hands of some desperate Saudi soldier.

Chanan's tank could only crab walk in a circle as its crew prayed. The colonel opted to abandon his tank rather than be killed by the next barrage of CBUs, missiles, or sabots. "Damn it to hell ... *Ben Zona*!"

Half of his MBTs were smoldering across the shifting sands. The remaining Israeli tanks moved in uncoordinated fashion, as doubt metastasized when they saw friends' turrets erupt. Few tanks remained effective, many breeches bulged and useless. Battalion 418 was down to a weak company of *Magaches*.

Of those left, Sergeant Benyamin's unit cohesion at last vaporized with the night winds. He had joked before the shooting began with his platoon. He told them, "We'll have easy shots fighting the same basic tanks. They'll be like Syrians, turn tail. These are Saudis ahead. They can't be good ... just can't."

CBUs continued to fall, raining destruction along with tank and artillery shells. The Israeli tank breakout stalled before a stiffening opponent. The force faced an invigorated Saudi advance. Hunkered down, the immobilized Israelis sensed cross-hairs on their turrets as those tanks remaining pulled back.

They that had fought so well
Came thro' the jaws of Death
Back from the mouth of Hell,

Chapter - 57

Peckingham, his forehead furrowed with concern, spoke. "Mister President, the Israeli tank offensive failed. Pray those really scary options don't come into play."

Ellington glanced at SECSTATE DeVries, "Mel, would Geblar do that? Is he that desperate?"

DeVries fidgeted, uncomfortable with the thought, beyond the question itself. "Mister President, Geblar told me just twenty minutes ago, flat out lied to me." *Or he has a case of serious delusion.* "He told me 'they bloodied us, but we held.' He made that statement despite clear evidence their tank offensive lost most of its tanks. They failed to break through," she paused ... "and withdrew. He has few options left."

Ubaidi granted a quickie meeting. He made that very, very clear, "This interview is just between you and I. Don't quote me." He mumbled to no one in particular, strong Arabic words not heard before. The vehemence on his face and clenched fists indicated it was curses. The colonel rambled of the battle in *Wadi Harram*, forbidden *wadi*, the place named as a gesture to the certainty of death there.

The colonel wrung his hands, thumbed prayer beads, ran fingers through his hair, pulled out some strands. He threw them on the table. When questioned he said only 'it is an ancient bedu spell, very old. He'd been up for many stressful hours, seen men incinerated. He'd radioed for tank retrievers, to collect his burned out M-60s for burial of whatever recovered remains allowed.

"Thanks for keeping us alive. Were you successful?" Stefano asked. "Did your men win the battle?"

"It was a stalemate. I am happy; we stopped the Israelis. We captured a few prisoners. We knew the best response was to deflect their force, ambush it in some way. But everyone knew the SOP for an ambush, and adapted."

"How close was the battle?" Stefano queried.

"It was like a grenade, killing all within sight. I lost half my tanks and men." Ubaidi frowned, "An assault could come again. That's scary, it means other things might happen."

The colonel wouldn't elaborate and there was no sense in asking. The curtness of his response meant something far worse was possible. It made the journalist consider the alternatives.

Ubaidi continued, "Three rounds hit my tank in the battle. Some projectiles glanced off, some were duds. A few were stopped by armor." Sorrow in his tone, his jaw clenched, "Many friends died. With tanks it is death or life, seldom in between. It is as Allah decides."

"Did you control the battle from the rear?" the journalist inquired.

"No. They broke through, blasting my men after an artillery barrage. The Israelis probed our lines," Ubaidi rubbed his jaw and grimaced like he needed dental care, "like a dentist looking for gum disease. As we counter attacked to fill the hole in our line I went forward."

Ubaidi cleared his throat, causing his cousin to infer more uncomfortable news. He the journalists sent them off, further away from a story, to a safer place. "I'm transferring you to a nearby town, a tourist place. You'll love it."Ubaidi coughed, and then smiled, "You won't have Harbi around to pester you. That will be like heaven itself I think."

Stefano wanted a story, more meat to put on the air, "Will they attack again?"

"The clock of war is still running. We must be ready. There are friends to bury and I must prepare for another attack. It's not over for me, not yet. But you, we must send away. Harbi's prayers go with you, for us all." Ubaidi's face tightened, "And now ... you must leave."

Stefano shook hands and thanked Ubaidi. *I'll tell Tooley how unfriendly this guy has been. Not like his uncle Amir at all. All serious about death. Guess I'd be too if really pissed Israelis were after me.*

Hunkered down at a distance from the war, Tooley went over Intel transcripts of Israeli and Saudi battle reports. *Not much to be happy about.* The office cell phone rang, he entered his bio metrics and it synched with the journalist in the war zone. The cousins caught up quickly on the lack of battlefield exposure and Intel.

"Family, that's what this is about." Stefano said as he looked at his cell. "The men here, they seem prepared to die; I'm not. What do they care about? It has to be family. I, too, want to see my family again, Sophia and Marcus back in Italy. Tooley, my goal has always been to tell a story filled with emotion, lust, anger, life and death. I don't want a touristy tale that lingers as a family treasure or a last memory, a weak human interest sound bite. I want something of purpose, not pretty."

Tooley probed, "Will there be more fighting?"

"It's not over." Stefano's tone was serious. "Ubaidi, the colonel that is, said Israel has not prevailed in the air, or with its tanks. What is left, negotiations? Ubaidi told me more is yet to come."

"We were allowed one human interest interview, just one, with a Lieutenant Harbi. He knew nothing of value, only prayer. He told me, 'Only Muslim prayers count. Others' prayers go to some other, lesser god – not to Allah.' That's what the zealot believed; others be damned." Stefano paused, "His words are part of the problem here."

"We're a hit, even though the military are afraid of our interviews. We can find and sell the big story if it ends up in our lonely tent. Let's hope that story isn't the final one." Both knew it was a factor in everyone's mind. "If we catch a real story, with a real person, we'll find out. It feels like I've been here before. Stay well." *I hope the story is not part two of the Holocaust!*

"Stay safe." Tooley said.

"I will."

Chapter - 58

Stefano glanced at the man's face, looking for any deception. He'd uplinked CNN HQ, asked for a quickie background check and photo. The interviewee matched the response bio, photo, and back story. The story he was to share was the story of a lifetime.

He turned to Rodolfo. "Let's roll." They started taping. "This is Stefano Gaiuso for CNN. We are in Jordan with a man whose words have BREAKING NEWS status. He is Adam Yokel, the nuclear technician who decades ago fled Israel, after exposing its nuclear arms program. He was abducted, returned to Israel, tried in secret, and jailed for fourteen years to impose his silence. Freed from prison, he was directed to stay within its borders."

As Rodolfo zoomed in on Yokel's face, Gaiuso queried the man, "Why did you turn up here?"

"I fled, with forged papers, and wish to make the world safe, for people in every village. I have an important story to tell. It is the most important news here. An ultra hard line general has been assigned to command both Beersheba Air Base, and more ominously, an elite special weapons squadron." He continued rambling, 'that unit is charged with use of nuclear weapons.'"

Yokel's conviction scared the journalist, "Mister Yokel," Gaiuso solicited, "how did you learn of this development?"

"Several sources told me these things." He looked at the journalist with troubled eyes, "That is what I believe is happening, based on statements I was told by civic minded Israelis. I know their families, what they value. They value life, all human life ... without exception. I believe in peace. I recognize that if you air this story, my life is at great risk."

"Why is that?" Stefano asked, trying to identify any fabrication. *Could this story trigger a Mossad hit squad searching for the sources identities? Damn, I'm in the cross hairs again.*

"Mossad kidnapped me before. They brought me back for trial. They will find me again; I accept that." Yokel's eyes were scanning the tent. Gaiuso instinctively looked, felt someone was watching.

“So, what you’re saying is you want to confirm Israel’s possession of nuclear weapons, and that they are preparing to use them?” Stefano’s face exuded horror at the prospect of a nuclear cloud.

“Yes. Israel can’t threaten the coalition with tanks, and the air battle is now a stalemate. Using nukes could dramatically change the balance of forces. We must stop this insanity.”

Yokel looked at the lens and continued, “The real story starts with the premise Israel can’t win with conventional arms. If you put this interview on air, I will disappear again. Yet there is no way to give credibility to the story unless you name me as your source.”

“So, you think they could drop a bomb or two? It would end the war, and Israel would win. The Arabs would never dare confront her again.” Stefano looked around, “If the Israelis did that, no one could live here for years. Yet others have such missiles.” He paused, wiped his forehead, angling for some indication this was all a scam, some reaction to a spoiled date or a brain aneurism.

“What of Israel’s government? Will it authorize use of these weapons?”

Yokel avoided an answer, “None of us, the people of Israel included, want to find out the answer to that question.”

Stefano balanced the array of forces in his mind, thought about the coming war. The scales of power were askew. He imagined who would win in a normal war - Arabs because of numbers, and who would thus lose, Israelis. The journalist made a promise, “I’ll do some research to confirm your identity and story. If I’m satisfied we’ll break it tomorrow, live in a village at the border. Then we’ll see what falls on our heads.”

Stefano looked hesitantly at his cohort as he stopped taping, “Rodolfo, will the network gods let us air this? Do we want to confirm the nuclear devil is in its hole?”

“If we don’t, we are part of the problem,” Rodolfo said. “We can’t ignore people in atomic crosshairs. Like a ping pong ball careening into a room of loaded mouse traps, we can’t save ourselves. Not here.”

Gaiuso worried as Rodolfo continued, “The world could well descend into another Dark Age. It is the story we wanted and now must tell.”

Tooley placed his encrypted cell in the office charger unit. *It'll rest easier being turned off to the worlds spies tonight. I'll find out mañana if anything happens.*

He flipped the switch, told it. "Charge you sonofabitch." The next call to the phone, the callers' ID noted as Stefano Gaiuso, went to messaging.

The next day, 29 September 2005, the story told by Adam Yokel hit TVs and front pages everywhere. It was *the* BREAKING NEWS on TV. CNN's HQ shared with the journalists the broadcast's impact and a congratulatory note from the CEO. Viewer count climbed, the numbers outpacing all other news on planet earth. The interview raised heart rates and awareness worldwide.

The consequences of a nuclear exchange became *the news* as eyes opened that day. Stocks plummeted. Oil prices soared. Everyone took notice, tried to make sense of what it all meant. People became uncertain. Social media reflected falling confidence in world leaders. One distraught Japanese citizen committed *Hare Kari* on national TV.

Arabic responses to the nuclear threat were conveyed to Israel through the Swiss. These initiated a flurry of exchanges. One stated, "We have SCUDs, some with NBC warheads. Your cities are targeted, in case you use your weapons against our forces. We propose negotiations."

In the UN General Assembly, delegate after delegate rose and spoke on the threat to world peace. One delegate, quoted widely in papers around the globe, stated, "If Israeli uses nuclear weapons, it will have spoken for utter devastation. The world needs to live without the threat of a nuclear winter."

The UN Security Council met to discuss the situation in the Middle East. Its top negotiator, Tanh Nguyen, was sent to 'resolve tensions between Israel and its adversaries.' It was hoped his efforts would defuse major points of regional conflict, and keep the atomic tiger in its cage. Before departing, Nguyen told assembled reporters of the hope, "to save the world."

Bashir Tamuz, head of the International Atomic Energy Agency (IAEA), accompanied Nguyen. Tamuz told the press, "my goal is to meet Prime Minister Geblar, clarify statements as to nuclear capability, convince his government to sign Non-Proliferization protocols, and foreswear the use of such arms."

Nguyen and Tamuz flew for twelve hours to Ben Gurion Airport, and were met on arrival by the entire corps of ambassadors. Only a minor Israeli Foreign Ministry official welcomed them.

Chapter - 59

US Ambassador Ebelstein, offended at this slight to peace, voiced frustration during an ongoing NSC meeting, where he was on speaker. An infuriated Ebelstein told SECSTATE, "If this reception indicated the value of peace felt by Geblar's government, I fear for the worst. I request direction how to proceed. Do I formally object, or just tell him he's an asshole who is threatening all of humanity?" *I'm sure this conversation is being recorded. Years from now I want people to know I hate dealing with Darth Vader.*

Ellington and DeVries both glared at the speaker. DeVries spoke first, "Ambassador, forcefully assist IAEA and UN peace efforts. Provide maximum support to the search for peace. If you must, burn any and all bridges with Israel." She looked at POTUS for agreement, and got it.

Ellington grabbed the Red phone, punched number three. The room went silent, as the connection was made to Geblar, "Prime Minister, *do not* use nukes! You'll be persona non grata everywhere, permanently." He slammed the phone in its cradle.

As the President glanced around the room, all eyes were on him. He cleared his throat, "Let's hope the Prime Minister reacts positively to the world's growing fury, reverses course, and meets quickly with UN Envoy Nguyen."

DeVries' face did not convey belief in that outcome.

DeVries called the Prime Minister an hour later. The phone rang seven times before Geblar picked up.

The PM told SECSTATE he had contacted Nguyen and Tamuz, "I plan to meet the UN's Nguyen and discuss these matters fully and openly." His voice sounded conciliatory as the connection ended.

Moments after SECSTATEs' call, Geblar phoned his right-wing supporters. Intercepts of that call recorded him declaring, "I will not knuckle under to these intruders, or that American President."

Shared within the Intel community, Geblar's intercepted statement was assigned BROKEN ARROW status, and given within minutes to a visibly outraged President. A full court press, ordered by Peckingham through military back channels, quickly made clear to Israel's military the impending shutdown of assistance.

Public demonstrations in the streets of Europe spurred similar efforts by EU military, economic, and security bodies to re-evaluate or shut off support. The threat of a nuclear exchange forced re-consideration of any transfers of arms. Several Scandinavian countries withdrew ambassadors.

The CNN journalists had been shuffled once again, were dumped the next day on the military in a border town. The soldiers knew of Gaiuso's broadcast with Yokel, and the potential for mushroom clouds. Despite the peaceful locale, they wanted nothing to do with the infidels, who were almost certainly targets of Mossad.

There were no hotel rooms, and the two had to bivouac with wary law enforcement personnel liaising with troops nearby. The local police were quickly told to keep them out of the way.

Stefano hadn't slept the night before. Artillery rounds exploding in the distance made him assess what each sound was. He'd grown accustomed to the firing. A new turmoil kept his eyes from closing, questions echoing in his head. *That interview was a headline across the globe. My name will be there, along with Yokels. He's gone, in hiding, location unknown.*

Stefano looked around, cautiously took a breath. *Where do I hide?* In the town of *Ukmar bin Jinn*, they went live, beamed new words and images to CNN and AFP in a simulcast.

Now their assignment would become only interviews with

towns' inhabitants. He yearned for another BREAKING NEWS story, with faces and words which would capture the screen. "How will plain townspeople play to audiences? It's good human interest, but does anyone care?"

Rodolfo responded, challenging his friend, "Tell them, the viewers, 'If they care for humanity, pray for peace." He did, and across the globe, radio stations in hundreds of languages asked for prayers. In towns big and small, people of all religions prayed to their god, gods, and goddesses. Humanity prayed, wept, and begged those willing to die to step back from the abyss.

Prime Minister, the figures don't lie. We are in a tight spot." *Kibbutzim* continued, "The tyranny of these numbers is clear. Look at that status board." The boards showed the latest enemy numbers, positions. The numbers of enemy troops assembling along the front increased.

Aviv spoke, "Week by week the numbers have gone up, down, sideways, but mostly up. Our satellite confirms the buildup. Their numbers and effectiveness are comparable to ours in all categories. Their infantry units move to avoid being targeted by our forces. Even in the air, while we win most battles, we lose pilots and planes in a war of attrition. Even coalition forces, after months of maneuvers and coordinated exercises, pose a threat."

Kibbutzim moved to the status boards in the briefing room, "We are ready. Our reserves are on station. We could possibly break the stalemate here," he pointed with a laser stick. "This town is lightly defended, has neither tanks nor artillery to slow us. We can quickly concentrate mobile forces there, achieve a breakthrough."

Aviv flinched, "That contingency is possible, but is more likely a miracle, unless we control the air. As of this morning that wasn't the case. If they keep their infantry massed, we might be able to hold them. If they move into a more dispersed deployment the outcome is a toss up. The only miracle I see happening is replacement of lost aircraft and Patriot missiles."

Aviv bluntly asserted, "Unless we use special weapons I can't guarantee we can stop them." He paused, looked at Kibbutzim, then Geblar, "unless you have a miracle in your back pocket, or other options?"

"We can turn the sands to glass." *Kibbutzim* boasted, "Operation AHARIT, conceived years ago, can instantly change the balance of power. However, if we succeed on the ground with your tank offensive, that option is not necessary."

Aviv briefed the tank contingency plan. The general considered what might happen in the days ahead, for him and others. He prayed for the tank option. *I have no way out, no way to refuse my orders.*

He looked at Geblar, "Prime Minister, what are my orders?"

Enroute an early morning meeting with a source, Tooley heard an Arab radio station describe Stefano's interview of Adam Yokel. *Oh shit! Better call and see if he's safe.*

Reaching his office at noon, Tooley was briefed by an aide of the Intel channel copy of Yokel's revelations, annotated by Langley analysts. He called the journalist and waited as the synching burble went on for what seemed forever.

They exchanged pleasantries, and then Stefano summed up the situation, "Nothing new since that interview. Yokel told it all. Now we're stuck in a little town." Then he paused, "Hey, there's rumbling in the distance, probably artillery practice. So, now I spend time twiddling my thumbs, watching for anyone who looks like a Mossad operative. What do they look like, by the way?" Stefano cleared his throat.

Tooley chuckled, "They have horns and a Glock in their hand. And I've never been to that facility under the desert, so I can't swear to it. His description sounds credible." He rolled his eyes, "It's not something I want to speculate on. I pray the Israelis don't consider using such weapons." *The Saudis have lots of Sand Dragon missiles, a few with dirty warheads. Better touch base with Amir and see what he knows.*

Tooley called Amir, intending to defuse or mitigate any Saudi actions to respond with MRBMs. "Let's get together, right away."

"About this Yokel guy?"

"Yeah, I'm praying the Kingdom doesn't launch any of its missiles."

Moments later, at a café on SANG Road, Amir chuckled as Tooley sat, and began nursing a tall cappuccino. "I had a better idea than launching our ballistic missiles if they do what Yokel said they might. We've dispersed the prisoners among units near the front." He paused, rubbed his chest where he'd been shot. "They'd never nuke their own people."

"Not if they knew they were among opposing forces in the field."

Amir smiled, "I'll make sure they know."

Hours later the fax machine in Moshe's office clanged, noting an incoming message from an unknown source. The message read – "General Ben Bedoo, we have placed our Israeli prisoners among various units along our lines of confrontation. They are being moved randomly from location A to Z. Your son David is among them. I pray Mr. Yokel's predictions are inaccurate." The facsimile signature read: Lieutenant General Ubaidi, Royal Saudi Forces.

Chapter - 60

Below the Negev, hidden by layers of reinforced cement, technicians in pairs readied several weapons. Fuzes for the noses of two sleek bombs, their color banding denoting them as MK 12 MOD 1A weapons, were inserted. Each weapon had a thermo-nuclear core.

Adam Yokel had disclosed this very facility's location and function decades before, giving it the status of a plague. Now the facility was being discussed widely around the world with the same sense of foreboding. In that deep bunker, men removed shields surrounding two warheads. The lead shrouds were to prevent satellites from detecting fission weapons being moved, armed, or powered up. US satellites far above registered the change, and sent multiple OPERATIONAL IMMEDIATE alerts as the bombs were transported to the nearby airbase.

Two ordnance techs glanced nervously at each other as the bombs were offloaded to a hoist. "I am not willing." one said, "My family will never forgive me." The other nodded agreement. The two had confided their plans to selected family members, fearing they would be killed if revealed as Yokels' sources.

Twenty minutes later the first MK 12 MOD 1A weapon moved to the flight line, was hoisted into place below an F-15, and connected to weapons release brackets on the centerline.

At a Beersheba Air Base ready room, two of Squadron 666's pilots refused orders to drop the bombs. The two captains told the Squadron Commander, "Our consciences will not allow us to kill so many non-combatants." They were removed from flying status and escorted, under guard, to a remote air base. The new duty station was a graveyard for derelict airframes and washed up pilots with terminal careers.

The taller tech walked to the plane's centerline after cutting the arming lanyard. He removed the RED tag, but left the arming safety wire in place. The other man inserted, but only partially connected, the power supply. These actions effectively SAFED the bomb. The status of these procedures wasn't checked by the plane's onboard system.

Captain Avriel heard of the arrests, and volunteered to carry out Operation AHARIT, the word Hebrew for end of times. He stated, "I will drop the bomb. I am ready." The right wing officer suited up, grabbed a flight clipboard, and walked to the tarmac. He did a walk around of the F-15, verifying the planes' flight readiness before climbing up and strapping in. One MK 12 hung on the center line station.

The tall tech got a Thumbs Up and a wink from his friend, then walked in view of the pilot. He flashed a GO signal, lying about the plane's ability to drop an armed eighty kiloton bomb.

Avriel mouthed the code word AHARIT over the radio, signifying his readiness. "BEERSHEBA TOWER, this is LION TWO FOUR, ready, over." He pushed the throttles forward, sending dust blasting against revetment deflectors.

"TWO FOUR, this is TOWER. You are cleared to Runway ZERO ONE EIGHT"

Avriel maneuvered the plane to the end of the runway, "TOWER, this is TWO FOUR, at Runway ZERO ONE EIGHT, over."

The tower radioed, "TWO FOUR, your vector is ONE TWO ZERO. Good Luck." The pilot flew to his target, a Saudi divisional HQ. All systems indicated readiness, and after initiating the required bomb loft maneuver, he pickled the RELEASE button.

The MK 12 did not separate. The lack of expected aerodynamic changes told Avriel the bomb was still hanging below him.

"TOWER, this is TWO FOUR." Avriel stammered, terrified at the prospect of landing with this weapons. Negative bomb release; am returning to base. Weapon status unknown. Request EMERGENCY straight in approach and techs to SAFE the damn thing!"

He landed, then performed an angry inspection in the revetment. He found a SAFE weapon attached to his F-15. The bomb had neither been fully armed nor powered up. He slammed his fist against the MK 12. *I should have done a visual before takeoff.*

The check also discovered that two techs were AWOL. A security report identified two specially cleared ordnance NCOs, who had commandeered a vehicle and fled. The general commanding the base and squadron received orders to report immediately to military headquarters.

Chapter - 61

POTUS had talked with PM Geblar two hours previously, the conversation unsatisfactory. An emergency meeting of the NSC was now ongoing in the WHSR. Only selected members were aware of a frantic call to Ellington moments before. The President asked for evidence to confirm what he'd been told.

Peckingham warned, "Mister President, not everyone here is read in on all aspects of this capability."

Ellington swore as he summarized what had happened at the Beersheba Air Base flight line, plane armed, launched. He read the eyes around the table, hoped they felt as he did. Now he knew it – they did. He saw determination in their eyes, "Screw that, General. Tell everyone here the details, right now." Ellington's face returned to a mild tan color, while Peckingham's reddened.

CJCS described the sensors' capability to detect minute changes in nuclear radiation readings. "Analysts can associate specific readings, by location, to confirm certain actions occurring there."

"God help us." the President blurted out. He looked around the desk, the faces there equally furrowed. "We cannot let this happen.

Would they dare try this again?" He got no verbal answer, but universal looks of concern. The shadow of the powerful Israeli lobby lingered, but Ellington knew the matter was about a potential nuclear exchange, and the possibility of tipping humanity over the edge.

"What about their nukes?" Ellington continued, "Can we take out their capability? Didn't I order the *Lincoln (CVN 72)* to the eastern MED the previous week? It joined *Enterprise (CVN 65*) with Alert Five planes on deck 24/7, correct?" He had, and it did.

Ellington scribbled a note and gave it to Peckingham, "Will our deep penetrator bombs go all the way to the nuke storage in the Negev? Would they make it unusable?"

Peckingham winced, "Mister President, we can't be sure, but probably. I'll check."

Ellington drummed his fingers, his face rigid, "They can't be this stupid ... can they?" the President stared at VP Counselor.

"Well, Mister President, they were prepared to drag us into a war with Iran over that centrifuge bit weren't they? You recall that right, and that attack on *Liberty* (AGTR 5) when they not only told us to pound sand, but shoved it up our butt. They do what *they* feel they must."

Two corroborating reports sat in front of Ellington. Stamped CRITIC, BROKEN ARROW, they flagged national interest sensor readings for immediate review by Presidential eyes. The Commander-in-Chief tensed as he conversed once more with PM Geblar on the Red phone, "This is unacceptable. Our sensors detected your old nukes radiating at an air base. Explain your country's actions."

Defense Minister *Kibbutzim*'s statement on the subject to the Press flashed across the bottom of a WHSR TV screen. It provided the standard issue, governmental non-answer, totally contradictory. It neither confirmed nor denied that nukes were part of Israel's arsenal. Every person on the globe believed they were, and wished they weren't. The script was background to the words between POTUS and PM.

Ellington thought about this crazy mess, weighing it in his mind. It was fiction of the worst sort, a nexus of nightmares. He deliberated on the report, the truth - a bomb actually on a plane and airborne, enroute a target. Yet the action was denied. We, humanity, were at the edge of the end, in a region where civilizations emerged.

"Prime Minister, this is madness. I pray this was an unauthorized act of some right wing zealot. Get control! Punish the SOBs that orchestrated this. If something even remotely like this happens again, I swear you *will not like* our response!"

Geblar admitted no mistake, voiced no regret. He gave a terse retort, "We'll do whatever *we* need to do, and you can't tell us what to do." The connection was lost.

Ellington drummed his fingers, considering his options. He hoped that reason would resonate with those whose fingers were on the triggers, before the embers of this war flashed to nuclear ash. His complexion reddened and he turned to his COS, "Schedule some time with all the networks; make it prime time tomorrow night. I wish to tell our country about this situation, before the game."

The game was the playoff between the San Diego Chargers and New England's' Patriots. Ellington, a huge Chargers fan, had bets with most in the Situation Room. The outcome would decide whether he won or lost big bucks. Other bets, on outcome affecting all mankind, dwarfed those on the game.

Chapter - 62

Rodolfo spotted it first, zoomed in and gave Stefano the high sign – Story! As Israeli armor advanced on the Jordanian border town, teenagers began sitting on the King Hussein, Allenby Bridge, texting on phones.

Rodolfo captured the images along Sarafia Street, a new level of human interest for CNN. The new emphasis was not of battle, but of hope. "Stefano, those children's faces may well capture the world's attention." His camera moved left, to visages which emerged from the homes. "It is growing, reverberating, expanding without pause." He prayed aloud, "Light one candle for peace!"

Stefano moved the mike, asked the cameraman, "What if their parents had stopped them, told them to stay home? Will parents come here, demonstrate for peace?"

The growl of a tanks' diesel down the block interrupted his thoughts. There were children sitting there, down the way. He saw hope on their faces. Rodolfo zoomed in.

No two looked alike, except for the few that held hands - siblings. Dresses, pants, blouses, scarves adorned them as they intoned a mix of prayers reflecting teens typically at arm's length. Their hair glistened; long, braided and adorned minimally, Israeli teens sat alongside a mix of Jordanians and Palestinians.

The journalist spoke again, enticing viewers' minds and hearts. "They are sitting side by side, two holding a sign written on brown cardboard. They have seen us, and are holding the sign in plain view. It says in English, Arabic, and Hebrew –

COME TO ALLENBY BRIDGE. SIT. STOP THE WAR!

Others could be heard shouting 'Tiananmen' as the teens lay down in front of several tanks at a nearby corner. The message of these youth pulled at Gaiuso's heart, and he muttered to Rodolfo under his breath. "We must tell this story; its simplicity is urgent."

He keyed his mike, motioned he was going live, "These children face grave risks, from parents, friends, and from neighbors. They are willing, like that brave man in Tiananmen Square, to stop the madness. Must the world deal with a nuclear war in the Middle East? This is Stefano Gaiuso reporting for CNN. Pray you are able to see us tomorrow."

His face tightened as the cameraman focused there, "Remember this street, this bridge, these children ... and Light One Candle!" The correspondent ended his transmission, and saw the frenzied look on the children's faces. He prayed against the possibly of a mushroom cloud. Down the block he heard the rumble of tanks. He signaled, continue the uplink. Zoom out, get their expressions. The cameraman focused on the faces of several children. Within moments, parents from nearby homes arrived. Awed by what their children had done, they sat.

Every major news station and talk show featured the highlighted images. Radio stations in millions of cities, hundreds of languages, watched, prayed, wept, begged for peace. In hours a reaction ignited in cities across Europe and America, Asia, Africa. People joined demonstrations against war.

Calls for Peace echoed over the air waves, on every front page. Liberals, conservatives, right and left wing voices called for people to mobilize, prevent a nuclear war. 'Every Man, Woman, and Child must help!' read one headline.

Israelis, in ones, twos, families, and then neighborhoods voted with their hearts and their feet. Like the peasants of Imperial Russia who wanted peace, now they wanted to stop any use of nuclear weapons. They sat in streets leading to that and other towns, obstructing movement of tanks, troop movers, mobile artillery, and every sort of war material. Palestinian refugees from numerous resettlement camps joined, becoming volunteer human shields. Many simply stood, clutching candles in the path of tanks.

Soon many towns' roads were filled with immovable demonstrators. No *Magach* moved, no tanker had the stomach to drive over pacifists like in Tiananmen Square. The offensive stopped.

Chapter - 63

The Knesset's most vocal opposition member, Avritz Klein, demanded an investigation and courts martial of 'those in charge of this insanity.' He shouted so loud no amplifier was needed,

"We cannot ignore what these children mean; they are the future. I call for a Vote of No Confidence. We must not destroy Israel and the region."

Within hours, support for Geblar's unity government evaporated. The Press quickly interpreted this as a sign of shifting Israeli political allegiances, but serious news types reported it as a deeper sign of human concern for survival.

"We must not become universal outcasts," Klein continued. The PM was soundly defeated in a roll call vote for his political life. At the insistence of the Knesset, a Cabinet and Security Council meeting voted for immediate elections.

Geblar announced his resignation, addressing the nation, stated, "Defense Condition Two has been set. The DM will order a cease fire in place, and recall units to preclude further conflict. I have directed Foreign Minister Gershawitz to contact Jordan, Saudi Arabia, and the peace coalition to discuss ways to move towards peace." Before leaving the podium he suggested *Kibbutzim* as his successor.

Geblar whispered an aside to *Kibbutzim*, "Who will be the sacrificial lamb?"

"I suspect one particular renegade general," Kibbutzim hinted, "is at the heart of this crisis."

"Indeed he is. Arrest him before he talks with the Press or does something stupid," Geblar ordered, hoping his earlier orders would remain a secret.

"I have already ordered that," the Defense Minister replied. *I must find out if he did this on his own.*

The Press Secretary walked into the White House Press Briefing room and strode to the podium. He asked everyone to silence their cell phones, looked to the entrance, then cleared his throat, "Ladies and Gentlemen, the President of the United States."

Several cameras flashed as the President entered and moved briskly to the lectern, his pace without hesitation. Ellington's face reddened. Television cameras of every major news agency zoomed in. The typical press leaks hadn't given anyone a clue what the President was about to say.

"Good day, Ladies and Gentlemen. Evidence of international importance has come to our attention. Less than a day ago, the Israeli Air Force armed an aircraft with a nuclear device. That plane took off with every intention of releasing the weapon."

Ellington paused, his muscles tightening. He swore, loud enough that one could imagine demonstrators along Pennsylvania Avenue being jolted. "Intelligence suggests tens of thousands of innocent men, women, and children would have been collateral damage." He clenched the podium, and the breath of each correspondent hesitated. "Such madness is unacceptable by every standard of civilized behavior. Only the grace of God stopped the dropping of that bomb." The podium concealed his fingers as he curled them into a fist. *Steady now.*

Ellington scanned the faces of those in the room. "I have ordered the Secretary of State," he waited as every eye focused on him, “to demand an explanation from the Government of Israel. The explosion of a single nuclear device could not, according to the best scientific counsel, cause nuclear winter. The probable death of so many innocents, however, calls into question the ethics of that government. Until a satisfactory explanation is provided, and suitable corrective actions taken, I have halted all support to Israel. US defense readiness has been raised to DEFCON TWO.”

He surveyed the rooms’ occupants again. Many had open mouths. “I will take no questions at this time. Thank you.” He picked up crumpled notes and walked out. All reporters rose to their feet, looking at each other with uncertainty.

Moments later in the WHSR Ellington turned to Peckingham, “General, give satellite imagery of the Negev to the alphabets, all of them, and the CINCs.” These last were the top US military commanders around the globe. “They need the latest data to evaluate the situation on the ground. We may need to do something.”

Peckingham nodded, “Will do, Mister President.” He looked down at the latest Intel, “What is this?” he blurted out as he read. “It says the coalition has assigned correspondents to every artillery, tank, and infantry unit. News teams are sprouting everywhere as highly visible sets of human shields. There’ll be satellite dishes with every journalist, covering opposition to the use of nukes. The world will see any death within minutes.” The general grimaced, “I bet it still won’t stop Israel from attacking.”

Ellington frowned, and turned to his VP, “Maureen, I’m sending you to see Geblar.” He handed her a note.

The VP looked at the note. In bold, blunt letters it read “DO NOT START A NUCLEAR WAR! If you do, you will be tried as a war criminal.” The official White House stationery was signed Bill, and was serialized and dated.

There was no way to misinterpret the notes’ meaning. Ellington’s brow furrowed, “Tell him we are dead serious. The world cannot afford a nuclear scenario. Got it? Make that absolutely clear to him! They must not use nukes!”

“Yes, Mister President, I’ll make it crystal clear.” Counselors’ eyes narrowed, “My kids will remember me as a peacemaker, not the one who let nuclear war break out."

Marine Two helos took the VP to Andrews AFB just as news of the Knesset's historic vote of no confidence made the rounds at the WHSR. Counselor's marching orders remained in force, to sort out who was the actual Israeli PM, and deliver the message. *Was it real? The DM replacing the PM might be only a shift of faces, not of policy.* If she had to, Counselor resolved, she'd judo chop the new PM, like the rotors chopping the air above.

Guards at the Andrews AFB gates saluted her as the motorcade swept by. She sensed there were more than normal, there to wish her success on the mission. *They support our mission, praying for sanity to break out.*

Counselor turned, "Coffee, Gunny! The strongest you have, grounds and all." She sipped a cup as Air Force Two took off for the Middle East, squadrons of fighters escorting her all the way. America's toughest mother was flying to Tel Aviv and into the teeth of a maelstrom.

Chapter - 64

A dust storm swirled across Lebanon, leaving a talcum like film coating everything. Street lights glowed an eerie yellow, testifying to the fragility of life before the elements, especially U^{235}. Inside the Intercontinental Hotel's conference room, UN negotiator Nguyen stood at the podium, welcoming the diplomats. Representatives of the coalition, Arabia, and Jordan applauded politely. Tanh gave opening remarks then added, "I have no doubt the threat for nuclear warfare is being reduced. Being in the same room in Nablus together without fighting is a start."

His mission was to get them to change the world, talk and not fight. He surveyed the room, knew old men with ancient wounds were there. Tanh muttered an expletive under his breath, *Troi duc oi*! He crossed his fingers, praying the mission would succeed.

Tooley, walking to a separate dinner gathering at the Intercontinental Hotel in Nablus, saw a face whose features were etched in his memory. "I know you." He scratched his head, then clenched his fists as a memory coalesced. "I remember; you pointed a Glock at me, and fired!" O'Toole moved menacingly towards the man, stopped and extended his hand, "Gotcha. Will you join us for dinner?"

"Can I bring my son, he was just exchanged?" There was a nod of assent to General Moshe Ben Bedoo and his son, and they walked to the reserved room.

Tooley, Amir, and Stefano gathered with their Israeli cousins. The room was hung with Bedouin rugs. The food, lamb, rice, vegetables and spices, was spread on a giant tray. It sat on a weathered black, red, and gray rug, surrounded by pillows. The scent of cardamom and ginger filled the air by the food, while incense sweetened the room beyond. Guards watched as soothing music played in the background, ancient beats blending methodically from worn instruments which had survived many conflicts, like the cousins.

"I saw them try to put round pegs in square holes, as you say," Stefano muttered. "The proposals, as objects, were sanded, wedged, pried, lubricated, and shoved into the openings of resolutions. I felt both sad and amused to watch. On the third day things seemed to make remarkable progress. A realization emerged that all issues were not just black or white; there were grays. Only after they let out the venom did the talks move forward. Compromise seemed possible. That was why I called you, to witness the end of this tragic war."

"Tell us about it," Tooley said. "Why the change?"

"I credit Tanh Nguyen with formulating the framework for peace. The unrecognized efforts of others over months bore fruit in his hands. Tanh's calming voice, gestures, and infectious smile won the hearts of many and smoothed ruffled feathers. Along with Tanh, the new Israeli Prime Minister, Kibbutzim Elev, signaled compromise. Like a virus, acceptance finally swept the assembly."

Stefano smiled weakly, continued his story. "I observed days of stressful negotiations. For CNN, the story of peace talks offered a hopeful end to the threat of nuclear war. The history of old wounds, insults, and distrust remained. I know of an old Syrian proverb which says, 'You shoot him or you break his head.' A Hebrew adage also states this is how you dealt with enemies. But both groups on that day finally saw the light, or maybe it was the image of a mushroom cloud." He moved his hands to portray a large bomb burst.

"Were you happy, broadcasting it as it happened?" Moshe queried.

"At first I was thrilled witnessing the end of a war that might have gone to the atom. I saw many talking and yelling. At the end of the second day I was frustrated. Solutions that were evident and seemed practical to me were ignored. They postured for our camera. Both sides said the same sort of things, in different directions thinking they were on different paths, rather than the same one at the cliff's edge."

Tooley waved his hands, palms upwards in the air, "What did they agree to first?" he asked.

"The first protocol was a cease fire and an exchange of prisoners. It was the easiest to arrange. It was sponsored by Arabia's King and the new Israeli Prime Minister. Peace seemed uppermost in their minds, not a nuclear cloud. Troops promptly began withdrawing from lines of conflict, which was the happiest of news for families. Many opposing units met and shook hands. A few hugged. Moshe's son, David, the pilot who dropped CBUs on you, he was just exchanged, and now," Stefano gestured to the young man, "he's here with us."

Stefano smiled, "Next they settled on a return of remains of the dead. It brought closure to many families and built enormous good will. Tanh saw to that. The third protocol, linked to the fourth, satisfied the most vocal Arab demand. It was agreed to merge East and West Jerusalem and place it under UN protection. All signatories agreed to establish embassies in Jerusalem, and exchange diplomats. The fourth protocol subtly recognized Israel as a sovereign state."

"Wow!" exclaimed Amir as he looked around. "Well, I'm surprised, but it was a fact wasn't it? We've been dealing with them back channel for years on anti-terrorism issues," Amir revealed. "The signatures merely added the final flourish. Ink on paper made it real, true. Peace became tangible, a list of simple statements on paper."

"How did they come to terms with the nuclear issue?" Moshe asked. "One would think that was uppermost in everyone's agenda?"

"Bashir Tamuz, head of the IAEA, was the driving force for the final protocol. The final document agreed to nuclear non-proliferization. The Middle East was declared a nuclear free zone. All wanted to make the bomb a thing of the past. The participants joined the non-proliferization body. Now the region will be nuclear free. It is something to be celebrated."

Amir smiled, "I agree." He ordered champagne, as did Tooley.

O'Toole looked across at Moshe and lifted his glass, "You SOB, you shot me." He paused, "How did this war end so fast?"

"I found out our prisoners were dispersed among your troops," Moshe declared, "and told the Defense Minister. My instincts told me he had not issued the order to drop a bomb."

Surprise at his revelation lit the faces around the rug. Tooley's face went blank, "How did you find out?"

Moshe avoided the question, but divulged part of the story. "A few techs neutralized the atomic bomb, and two pilots even refused orders to drop it. The general who gave the order was a hard liner, on the fringe in politics. He is now deceased." He smiled, "He fell out of the helo returning him to Jerusalem."

Tooley grinned, as he acknowledged the news, "His death conveniently silenced questions he would have had to answer."

"His answers would have become public," Moshe continued, "had he made them. Let's toast that, and Tanh."

All glasses lifted. Tooley looked at Moshe, "I'm still not sure I want *you* in the family," he smirked, "You're one crazy cousin." The group laughed, relieved at stepping back from the brink, especially with family.

Then Moshe lifted his glass, "To peace, the young people who braved the tanks, and those who refused immoral orders. I see hope in the next generation."

Stefano nodded, "Cousins, let's pray there's no more war, until ... the next one!"

Made in the USA
Columbia, SC
09 September 2017